Hello there!

Thank you very much for choosing to read *The Girl with the Scarlet Ribbon*. I truly hope you enjoy the story.

All of my books are set in the northeast village of Ryhope, where I was born and bred. In 1919 it was very much a village of two halves with the coalmining community on the colliery bank and the more pastoral and quiet farming community a short walk away in the village.

The Girl with the Scarlet Ribbon, perhaps more so than any of my novels so far, is set squarely in the village this time. It centres around a couple of streets known historically as Church Ward. The house in the story, which I've called the Uplands, is based on a building which still exists in the village. In fact, if you ever go on a walk around Ryhope village, you'll find many old buildings, stone walls and even some narrow cobbled streets that remain from centuries ago. Who knows, perhaps you might even find the building that inspired the Uplands in this book, if you look in the right direction. It's still there, as pretty as ever these days with a beautiful garden too.

The book also features my favourite seaside town of Scarborough. It has plenty of drama, but I won't reveal any spoilers here! So settle back, put the kettle on and put your feet up and sink into the story of *The Girl with the Scarlet Ribbon*. I really hope you enjoy reading it as much as I've enjoyed writing it. Jess is another fictional heroine who I'm proud to have brought to life.

With all my best wishes,

Glenda Young

Praise for Glenda Young:

'Real sagas with female characters right at the heart'
Jane Garvey, *Woman's Hour*

'The feel of the story is totally authentic . . . Her heroine
in the grand Cookson tradition . . . Inspirationally delightful'
Peterborough Evening Telegraph

'In the world of historical saga writers, there's a brand new
voice – welcome, Glenda Young, who brings a freshness
to the genre' *My Weekly*

'Will resonate with saga readers everywhere . . .
a wonderful, uplifting story' Nancy Revell

'I really enjoyed . . . It's well researched and well written and
I found myself caring about her characters' Rosie Goodwin

'Glenda has an exceptionally keen eye for domestic detail
which brings this local community to vivid, colourful life and
Meg is a likeable, loving heroine for whom the reader roots
from start to finish' Jenny Holmes

'I found it difficult to believe that this was a debut novel, as
"brilliant" was the word in my mind when I reached the end.
I enjoyed it enormously, being totally absorbed from the first
page. I found it extremely well written, and having always loved
sagas, one of the best I've read' Margaret Kaine

'All the ingredients for a perfect saga' Emma Hornby

'Her descriptions of both character and setting are
wonderful . . . there is a warmth and humour in bucket loads'
Frost Magazine

By Glenda Young

Belle of the Back Streets
The Tuppenny Child
Pearl of Pit Lane
The Girl with the Scarlet Ribbon

GLENDA YOUNG

The Girl
with the
Scarlet
Ribbon

HEADLINE

First published in Great Britain in 2020 by
by HEADLINE PUBLISHING GROUP

First published in paperback in 2020 by
by HEADLINE PUBLISHING GROUP

5

Cataloguing in Publication Data is available from the British Library

ISBN 978 1 4722 6854 9

Typeset in Stempel Garamond by Avon DataSet Ltd,
Arden Court, Alcester, Warwickshire

Printed and bound in Great Britain by Clays Ltd, Elcograf S.p.A.

Headline's policy is to use papers that are natural, renewable and recyclable
products and made from wood grown in well-managed forests and other
controlled sources. The logging and manufacturing processes are expected
to conform to the environmental regulations of the country of origin.

HEADLINE PUBLISHING GROUP
An Hachette UK Company
Carmelite House
50 Victoria Embankment
London EC4Y 0DZ

www.headline.co.uk
www.hachette.co.uk

For Scarborough – my happy place

Acknowledgements

My thanks go to: Sunderland Local Studies Centre; Les Mann; Jennie Lambert of Sunderland Museum & Winter Gardens; Sunderland Antiquarian Society, especially Norman Kirtlan, Phil Curtis, Linda King, Denise Lovell, Ron Lawson and Chris Sharp; Sharon Vincent for her knowledge of women's social history in Sunderland; Ryhope Heritage Society, especially Brian Ibinson, Peter Hedley and Rob Shepherd; Tony Kerr and Martin Wallwork for their invaluable advice; my friend Paul Lanagan for helping organise the *Belle of the Back Streets* guided walk around Ryhope; Janet Robinson and Fiona Tobin of Tyne and Wear Heritage Open Days; John Wilson and staff at Fulwell Post Office; Allison Hicks and Angela Wilkinson of Fulwell Community Centre; Paula Hunt at Ryhope Community Centre; Katy Wheeler and Fiona Thompson of the *Sunderland Echo*; Lisa Shaw and the team at BBC Radio Newcastle; Simon and Lauren at Sun FM; Nick Simpson, researcher and archivist at Sunderland Maritime Heritage Society; Neil Sinclair, author of *Sunderland's Railways* (Oakwood Press, 2019); my brother-in-law Robin Smith for his railway knowledge; Richard Lacey and Ian Mitchell of the North Eastern

Railway Association and Ashlynn Welburn of York Railway Museum.

In Scarborough: Dorinda Cass of Scarborough Writers' Circle; Tim Tubbs, Scarborough historian; Martyn Hyde and Stephen Dinardo of Eat Me Café; Scarborough Maritime Heritage Centre; Scarborough Library; Grand Hotel, Scarborough; Scarborough History Society.

Kate Byrne, my editor at Headline, and my agent, Caroline Sheldon, two wonderful ladies who I continue to learn a lot from.

And my husband Barry, for his love and support and the endless cups of tea when I lock myself away to write.

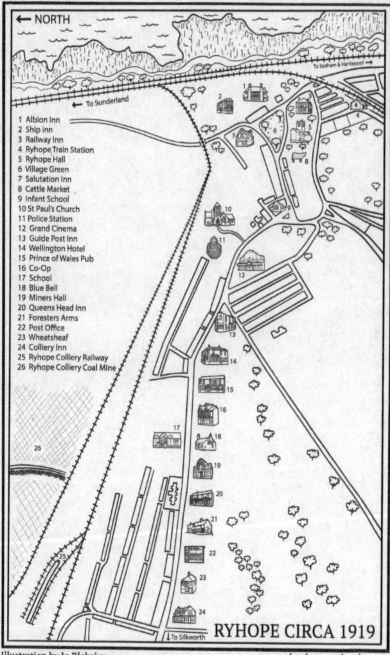

← NORTH

To Seaham & Hartlepool →

← To Sunderland

1 Albion Inn
2 Ship Inn
3 Railway Inn
4 Ryhope Train Station
5 Ryhope Hall
6 Village Green
7 Salutation Inn
8 Cattle Market
9 Infant School
10 St Paul's Church
11 Police Station
12 Grand Cinema
13 Guide Post Inn
14 Wellington Hotel
15 Prince of Wales Pub
16 Co-Op
17 School
18 Blue Bell
19 Miners Hall
20 Queens Head Inn
21 Foresters Arms
22 Post Office
23 Wheatsheaf
24 Colliery Inn
25 Ryhope Colliery Railway
26 Ryhope Colliery Coal Mine

↓ To Silkworth

RYHOPE CIRCA 1919

Illustration by Jo Blakeley

www.glendayoungbooks.com

Prologue

1919

At the back of the drawer Jess spotted a spiral of red. She pulled it towards her, curious to see what it was, and was shocked to find it was scarlet ribbon. And not just one length, but two. She sat on the floor with the ribbons in her hand, turning them over, wondering where they had come from. Both ribbons were about ten inches in length, almost an inch wide and both deep scarlet red. In all her life, Jess had never seen her wear a ribbon of any colour, and certainly not scarlet. She looked at the piles of clothes and underwear on the bed. The colours were practical whites, browns and greens. Set against them, the scarlet ribbons looked indecent, as if dropped by a harlot's hand. She was puzzled and confused. Scarlet was not a colour she associated with her. What on earth were the ribbons doing in her drawer? She wondered what their secret was.

Chapter One

26 September, 1903

Mary gripped the iron bedstead with both hands. She'd never felt pain like it before. She opened her mouth, tried to tell her mam not to pull so hard, tried to say something, anything, that would make her stop. But each time she tried to speak, her words were lost in a tortured cry. She clawed at the sodden bedsheet beneath her.

Mary's aunt Peg kneeled at her bedside, rinsing blood from a cloth. She bit her bottom lip.

'I told you we should've called the doctor,' she hissed at her sister Eva. 'How many times did I tell you? You're going to rip the girl apart!'

Mary was so wrapped in pain that she missed the look her mam gave Peg. But she heard every one of her words.

'It's a right little stubborn so-and-so. Doesn't want to come out,' Eva said, shaking her head.

Mary writhed in agony. Her breath came out of her thick and fast. She felt as though her insides were splitting open. Her dark hair was drenched with sweat, and long strands stuck to her face. The pain heaved in her stomach. Over and over it came; great waves of sickening agony.

Eva squared her shoulders and slid her hands back towards Mary.

'I'm going to try again, Mary. You hear me?' she said briskly.

'Push, Mary. Push!' Peg called.

Peg handed her sister another damp cloth. It was pink from Mary's blood, which was now swirling in the washstand bowl. Mary didn't feel the touch of the cloth at the top of her legs as her mam did her best to clear away mucus and blood. She couldn't feel anything other than pain ripping her in two as her baby fought its way out.

'Come on, Mary! Push!' Eva cried again.

The baby's head inched from Mary's body and into Eva's waiting hands. Mary roared with pain and relief. As the baby came away, there was more blood, too much for Peg's liking. She jumped to her feet.

'I'll get Dr Anderson!'

'Will you shut up about the flaming doctor!' Eva snarled. 'Do you think I'd be delivering this bairn myself if we had money to spend on him?'

Peg rinsed another cloth and laid it on Mary's brow as her niece lay sobbing on the bed. Eva lifted the bloodied baby and quickly appraised it. She was relieved to see that its tiny nose and mouth were clear.

'It's breathing,' she said.

She laid the baby on top of Mary's blood-soaked nightgown. Mary felt the weight land on her chest.

'It's a girl,' Eva said.

Mary's heart leapt at the words. A girl. She turned her head and saw Peg making the sign of the cross.

'May God keep her safe. May God keep her strong.' She spoke quietly, but both Mary and Eva caught her words.

'There's no point in asking God for favours for this bairn,' Eva said sternly. 'Mary knows what's to happen. It's all been arranged. Its future lies in someone else's hands now.'

At her mam's words, another, different pain hit Mary hard. Her mam was right: she knew exactly what was planned for her child. Or at least, what her mam had planned for it. But it wasn't what Mary wanted. She had ideas of her own, for herself and her bairn, but she hadn't dared breathe a word. She closed her arms protectively around the tiny life handed to her. Lying there bruised, torn and hurting, she was overwhelmed with a rush of feelings and emotions she'd never felt before. She was filled with a potent desire to protect the tiny baby, and for now, nothing else mattered.

Her daughter was crying at her breast, her tiny face ragged and red. Mary marvelled at the baby's hair. It was as dark and thick as her own. She kissed the top of the little head.

'It's sticky,' she said.

From under the bed Eva took the knife she'd kept ready. Peg saw the glint of steel and looked away. She couldn't bear to watch. Mary closed her eyes too. Eva didn't hesitate, and in seconds the cord was sliced through.

'Peg. The blanket,' she ordered. 'Wipe the blood off the bairn, as much as you can. Go gently now. And then wrap her tight.'

Peg did as she was told. Eva took one of Mary's hands, brought it to her lips and gently kissed her daughter's fingers. Then she shook her head as if to dismiss a sentimental notion that threatened to overtake her.

'Now, remember what we said. We'll keep the bairn three nights to make sure it's all right. That'll give you time to rest,' Eva said, businesslike. 'Tonight Peg will bring you food and help you get cleaned up. On the fourth day, as soon as it's light, you'll take the child as we've discussed.'

Mary cradled her crying baby closer. Peg shook her head and tutted at her sister.

'You're really going to make her sell it, aren't you? And for a pittance too.'

'What choice do we have?' Eva yelled. 'You know we can't keep it. I've got five mouths to feed and the bairns are starving as it is. We've been through it a million times, Peg. If I'd been able to get shot of it when we first found out she was pregnant . . .'

Mary felt an icy chill run through her.

'Mam, please,' she whispered. 'Not now. Let me have this time with my baby.'

Eva nodded. 'It's no wonder the bairn took some getting out of you. It's got a stubborn streak all right. And I know exactly who it gets that from.'

Mary closed her eyes to block out the sight of her mam's weary, lined face. Her aunt Peg was still bustling about the room, tidying and cleaning. Peg was a short woman, younger and thinner than Mary's mam. Her skirts rustled as she worked and the noise was as annoying as a wasp in Mary's ear. She wanted to be left alone with her baby. They only had a few days together and she wanted to make the most of each precious moment. She kissed her daughter's head again. The pain she'd suffered was suddenly replaced with great roaring waves of tiredness. Around her, she heard voices, her mam and

Aunt Peg. The bloodied cloths were taken and fresh water brought in. She lay still as her aunt cleaned her legs, her arms, her brow. When all was done to Peg's liking, Mary was finally left alone.

Outside the window, the grey light filtered down as dawn broke over the September day. Through the window, Mary saw the yard at the back of their tiny terraced home. She saw their tin bath hanging on the brick wall; she saw the door to the netty. The bedroom door slowly opened and her younger sisters Miriam and freckled little Gracie crept into her room.

'It's a girl,' she whispered.

'Can I stroke her?' asked Gracie.

Mary shook her head. 'She's not a puppy, love.'

'What are you going to call her?' Miriam asked, as inquisitive as ever.

Mary's heart dropped. The girls had no idea what lay ahead for Mary and her child. What she was going to do would break their little hearts. But she had no choice.

'Best not to think of it yet,' she said.

'Why?' Miriam wanted to know. 'Will she die like our Sal did when she was a baby?'

'She might,' Mary replied. Telling a lie to her sisters was easier than telling the truth. The less anyone knew what she was up to, the better.

'Leave me, girls, would you? I'm tired,' she said.

'We're sleeping in the kitchen for three nights,' Gracie said, excited. 'Mam says we can't sleep in here until you're better.'

Mary closed her eyes and felt two tiny kisses on the side of her face, one from each of her sisters as they said their goodbyes.

* * *

Mary lay a long time in silence cradling her newborn, her skin warming the baby. Stubborn, her mam had called the child. If that was the case, then it was a trait she had inherited from Mary, for there was none so determined as her. The gossip in the village was that she was too head-strong and wild. It was this, they said, that had led to her getting herself pregnant, and at such a young age, just sixteen. They called her the lass with no shame and that name followed Mary wherever she went.

It was true, there was something spirited and impulsive about Mary that was born from a restlessness in her. She knew what the gossips said and she didn't care. She just carried on in her hot-headed way, unconcerned about what others thought. But this time the gossip found its way back to Eva and the news had brought shame to their door. Eva knew they could never afford to keep Mary's child. They had neither the money nor the means to feed it. But she knew a woman who would take it off their hands and pay them for it too. And so she arranged the sale. What she hadn't banked on, however, was just how stubborn her daughter was, for Mary had a plan of her own.

The day passed slowly as Mary drifted in and out of sleep. In the bedroom, voices came and went, her mam's and Aunt Peg's, and she heard the door open and close. She felt the weight on her chest lighten as her daughter was lifted. She was aware of sounds in the room as the baby was cleaned. When she was replaced at her breast, Mary felt a cotton sheet about her child's body that was cool to her touch. And then there was silence, just Mary and her baby. She ran through her plan again. She thought of the route she would take, not the one her mam had told her to walk, but to somewhere else in Ryhope, somewhere her mam had never been.

Three days later, Mary was sitting up in bed cradling her baby. She was feeling stronger, less broken and torn, but still in pain when she needed the netty. The baby was growing too, feeding greedily from her breast. Mary was planning again, running through what she needed to do. Her aunt Peg came into her room carrying a tray. On it was a bowl of thin soup and a chunk of heavy bread, along with a mug of hot tea. Peg lifted the baby and cradled it in her arms as Mary began to eat.

'Your mam says you're to head out at first light tomorrow when the streets will be empty,' Peg said. 'And if anyone sees you and asks what you're doing out so early, you're to tell them nothing.'

Mary nodded; she had to keep up the pretence that she was following her mam's plan. She watched as Peg gazed at the sleeping child, wondering what thoughts lurked behind her aunt's affectionate smile. Eva had told Mary many times throughout her pregnancy not to let herself become attached to the child. Oh, Mary knew the reasons why; she understood only too well how poor her family was. Why else had she decided on her own plan? What use would it do her to do as her mam wanted and sell the baby for a small fee? The money would disappear in a heartbeat once her dad got his hands on it. He'd go straight to the Railway Inn to sink pint after pint while Miriam and Gracie shared clothes and shoes that didn't fit either of them and their stomachs rumbled with hunger. And there was already a baby to feed in the house: Mary's brother George, who was just six months old and in constant need of food.

Mary knew there wasn't enough money coming in to feed those who lived there, never mind another child. And then there was her dad, who'd threatened to throw her out on the streets when he'd been told she was pregnant. He'd demanded that she tell them who the father was, but Mary had kept quiet, even though he swore that he'd beat it out of her if he had to. Mary kept the identity of the child's dad a secret from everyone who asked. Mary lived with her dad's rage and her mam's tears for months, and it was all Eva could do to stop Harry from disowning his daughter.

All through the nine months of her pregnancy, on the days when Mary was heaving with sickness and dropping with tiredness, Eva had been firm, reminding her that her baby would be sold. Both Eva and Mary knew that to keep the child would be to ruin its chances in life. To keep it would mean subjecting it to a lifetime of poverty, hunger and thirst. To keep it would have been cruel too, for it would have meant Mary's child would always be known as a bastard; the child of the wayward girl who was stubborn and wild and caused gossip wherever she went. Worse still would be the malicious rumour carried on the breeze that Mary Liddle's bastard was the child of a married man. It was a rumour that would taint Mary for as long as she lived in Ryhope, made all the worse because it was true.

It was her dad's anger and her mam's shame that had forced Mary to plan her own future. She would run away, as far away from Ryhope as she could. She'd leave the gossips behind and the words that tainted her. She'd start again somewhere else, somewhere that would offer her excitement and possibilities of the kind a small village like Ryhope never could.

In the dead of night, Mary lay still in her bed. She knew she had to carry out her plan while she still had the bedroom to herself, while her sisters and brother were asleep in the kitchen. In her mind, she followed the route from her home to where she would take her child. She'd walked the pathways many times before, in all weathers too, day and night. It wasn't far and it wouldn't take long. But this time would be different. She would be carrying her daughter in her arms and a heaviness in her heart.

She slid one leg from under the sheet and touched her foot to the bare wooden floor. She tried to sit up, holding tight to her baby, but it took effort to steady herself. Working with just one hand, the other cradling her child, she dressed quickly, pulling a cloth dress on over her night-gown. There was a cotton belt at the waist to give the dress shape, but she let it fall. It didn't matter how she looked that night. She would need to tidy herself up in the morning, but tomorrow was another day. What mattered right now was taking the child to the place she had in mind.

She pulled a woollen jacket over her dress and slipped her feet into the pair of boots she shared with her mam. Eva would go barefoot the next day, and the next, when she discovered Mary missing. She ran a brush through her long hair then pulled on a black woollen hat and tugged it down low on her head. It was dark out, but there was still a chance she might be seen. She pushed her hair down inside her jacket and brought the collar up. She pushed her feet forward in her boots. Mary ached everywhere and was overwhelmed with exhaustion, but there could be no stopping her now.

She dipped a hand into the jacket pocket and was reassured when it rested on what she knew to be there. She ran the precious item lightly through her fingers before pushing it securely down. In another pocket she felt the piece of paper ripped from a page in the *Sunderland Echo*. It contained an advert for Mrs Guthrie's domestic agency offering a free overnight bus ticket to London. The ticket money would be taken from the first week's wages of work once in London, which Mary felt fair. When she was certain she had all she needed, and with her baby wrapped tight, she headed into the night.

She left the cottage by the back door, walked through the yard and into the lane. She kept close to the wall for fear that anyone who couldn't sleep and might be gazing from their window would see her. Her steps were silent, her breathing calm as she hurried. She had planned this so well, it was as if her body knew what her heart and head were asking. Ahead of her she saw the tower of Ryhope Hall, illuminated by misty moonlight, rising above the cattle market. She turned left on Station Road in the cold, airless night. Again she followed the high wall, using its protection to hide her features from anyone who might be about. She was still hurting inside and over-tired, but was driven to do what was right. On the other side of the wall, the windows of Ryhope Hall looked down to the road. She doubted very much if anyone there would know or care who she was, unless the staff had heard gossip too.

As she walked, she took care not to disturb her baby or cause her to wake and cry, for that would bring attention she didn't need. A dog barked in the distance and her heart jumped. She pulled the baby tight until the barking stopped, and only then did she continue on her way. Step by step along the dirt path she walked, with each step taking her closer to where she needed to be. To her right, trees and bushes hung over the wall, and a branch snagged on her jacket. It caught her arm, pulled the sleeve, and she cried out. Her eyes darted left and right, her heart pounded. Was there someone there? Was she being followed? She spun round but found only the blackness of an empty path.

She carried on walking until the village school came into view. Here, she knew she had to be careful. To reach the school she had to cross a wide expanse. There were no walls to walk alongside and no trees to hide under. Mary looked around and crossed the road, walking as quickly as her sore, tender body allowed. From the school she turned right on to Cliff Road. There were high walls again here, this time on both sides of the path. She was safe, out of sight. She was almost there. Just a few steps more.

Suddenly she stopped dead in her tracks. Her legs turned heavy, her feet seemed stuck to the path and her heart felt as if it would burst. Her baby squirmed in her arms. Was she hungry? Was she as frightened as Mary? Straight ahead of her was the Uplands, the house she'd worked in for years, the only job she'd ever had. She knew every inch of it, upstairs and down, for she'd cleaned and scrubbed it all.

The Uplands was one of Ryhope's oldest and grandest homes. It was three storeys high and its front windows looked out over Cliff Road. The side of the house with its rounded bay windows faced a lawn that sloped gently to a thicket of hazel trees. There were three sets of chimneys for the roaring fires that Mary had once stoked to keep the residents warm. She knew what lay behind every window, behind every curtain and door. She knew the layout of the gardens and what flowers grew where; knew what vegetables would be ready for pulling from the soil. She knew the Uplands like the back of her hand.

She knew all of its secrets too.

The moon's silvery light gave the house a mystic, icy air that Mary had never noticed before. A moment's hesitation caused her mind to spin again. Was she doing the right thing? She shook her head to dismiss the notion. There was no choice. She could not countenance taking a small fee for the sale of her child from the woman her mam knew. No, she would not barter her bairn when there was the chance of giving her a good life. It would be a better life, different to anything the Liddle family could afford.

She took a deep breath and laid her hand on her baby's head, taking comfort from the warmth of the child's skin. Then she forced her feet forwards, one in front of the other, step by step towards the black iron gate. As she lifted the latch, it rattled in the silence. She stood stock still, listening in case the noise had alerted anyone inside. Only when she was certain that no one was coming did she carefully push the gate open.

The imposing, solid, tall black door of the Uplands was directly in front of her, so close she could have reached out and touched it. She gazed down at the wide doorstep, weathered and worn by centuries of footsteps. This was the first time she had come to the front door. Her position as housemaid when she'd worked at the house had obliged her to use the side gate. She crouched down, wondering where best to place her precious child. She reached a hand to the step; it was cold to her touch. A rush of anger roared in her head. How stupid she was, how careless, not to have brought a basket with her. She was about to take off her woollen jacket to wrap the baby in, but thought better of it. She needed the jacket, even if it was shapeless and worn, more than her bairn ever would. It was the most respectable item of clothing she had. And she needed to look respectable when she met Mrs Guthrie's agent outside Sunderland Town Hall the next day.

Suddenly she remembered the woodshed in the grounds of the Uplands. As well as wood for the fires, it was where the gardener kept his supply of containers and crates. Holding the baby tight in her arms, she picked her way across the lawn, glancing nervously at the windows as she went. What if someone had woken at the noise of the gate? What if there was a party inside that was running on after midnight? But her worries were unfounded, for there was silence. Mary was relieved to see the Uplands in darkness. She ran to the woodshed under a spread of hazel trees. The door was unlocked, as she'd always known it to be. She opened it with her free hand, keeping her baby close to her. Inside it was pitch dark. She reached out to where she remembered the gardener's bench was, patting her fingers over what felt like boxes and tins. A rustling noise reached her and her heart jumped. Was it a rat? She calmed herself, and slid her hand back along the bench until it struck a wicker basket. She yanked it towards her and something from inside it spilled noisily to the floor. There was more rustling and this time a squeaking noise too. She forced herself not to be afraid. She wasn't thinking of herself now, only of her child, and it made her determined.

She carried the basket back to the door of the Uplands. In the moonlight she got a good look at it. It was a long, low kindling basket, the kind the gardener used to carry logs. The handle was strong and the basket robust enough to hold what she needed it to. There didn't appear to be any jagged edges. She laid it in the middle of the doorstep, then kneeled down and gently, slowly laid her sleeping child inside. She was determined not to cry, ready to do what she must. She had planned this for months. But before she knocked at the front door, there was one more thing she had to do.

From her jacket pocket she pulled a length of ribbon. In the dark of the night the colour was muted. But in daylight it was a vivid scarlet red. She bent low to the basket and tied the ribbon around the handle in a bow. All was done and she was ready.

She stood and knocked hard – four, five times – banging with her fist at the door of the Uplands, determined to wake those within. She heard a shout, a man's voice. James's voice. She would recognise it anywhere. Then another voice, this time a woman. She wondered if it was James's new mistress, of whom she had heard gossip. She banged again, and again. And then, without a backwards glance, she walked away as fast as she could.

With each step she took away from the Uplands, away from her child, Mary felt her heart break into pieces. It was as if she was leaving a part of herself behind. She forced herself forward, fighting the urge to turn and run back. And as she scurried away, her tears began to flow.

Chapter Two

The bells of St Paul's Church were chiming midnight as James McNally pulled his dressing gown tight and pushed his feet into charcoal-grey slippers. He'd been woken by an insistent banging at the front door and was determined to find out who was making the infernal noise. The housekeeper at the Uplands, Ada Davidson, had also been woken. She was already in the hallway wearing a long green nightdress that covered her short, stout frame. Light from an oil lamp in her hand spilled to the hallway floor.

'Who is it, Mrs Davidson?' James called from the landing.

Ada pushed strands of her wavy brown hair behind her ears. It didn't do at all to be woken in such a way, and she wasn't happy for her employer to see her in her nightwear. In all the years she'd worked at the Uplands, she'd never been caught in such a dishevelled state before. She knew it could only be bad news coming to their door at this hour. She set the oil lamp on the floor and, using both hands, slid the bolt on the front door. Then she lifted the lamp again and opened the door wide.

She'd expected to see a policeman standing there. Or if

not a policeman then the vicar, with word of a disaster at Ryhope coal mine. What else could warrant such a furious noise at midnight? But all she saw was the blackness of the night. She peered around the doorway, looking left and right.

'Who's there?' she called. 'Show yourself!'

A sound caught her ear, a tiny noise like a cat's cry from the garden. She swung her lamp low, seeking out the source of the noise, and that was when she saw the basket. She bent down and peered close, unable to believe her eyes. Behind her, she heard footsteps as James made his way across the hall.

'Who in God's name is banging on the door at this unearthly hour?' he demanded.

Ada straightened and handed him the lamp. 'You might want to see for yourself, sir,' she said.

James gave her a puzzled look, but nonetheless he took the lamp and swung it to where she indicated. 'Why, it's just a basket,' he said, confused.

Ada shook her head. 'No, sir. Look closer.'

He did as she advised. He stood a long time looking at the basket, taking in the truth of what had been brought to his door. Then Ada pushed past him, took hold of the handle and lifted it indoors.

'Put it there and let me take a proper look,' James demanded. He pointed to a table in the hallway.

Ada and James stood side by side staring at the basket, trying to take it all in. The baby began to cry, its face screwing up. And it was then that James saw the scarlet ribbon tied in a bow. Ada heard his sharp intake of breath. She wondered if he was more shocked at the sight of the ribbon than at the sight of the child. Ada herself had already noticed the ribbon but had kept her face as straight as she could. It wasn't easy, as her heart was going nineteen to the dozen. Because, oh, she knew what that red ribbon meant, and she knew exactly whose baby this was.

James looked from the ribbon to the baby, then turned his back on the basket.

'Get rid of it,' he barked.

'But sir—' Ada began.

'Now, Mrs Davidson! I want it out of my house this instant.'

Ada heard a noise on the landing and looked up to see a slim, bonny lass with light hair. She recognised her immediately as Emily Watson, who she'd seen about the place a lot recently. Emily was wearing what looked to be a silk gown, and if Ada knew anything about James McNally, she knew it would be real silk, for he liked to treat the women he brought to the Uplands. She had seen many such women come and go. She'd disapproved enough of James's behaviour when he was single, but now that he was married, she had no respect for his scandalous ways.

Emily made her way down the stairs, her eyes on the basket and what it held. Ada watched as she strode across the hallway. Her face was like thunder, and it was clear that there would be strong words between her and James.

'If you have a scrap of decency about you, James McNally, you'll leave that child where it is,' Emily said. She pulled the cord of her gown tight around her slim waist. 'I'd heard the gossip, James, but I chose not to believe it,' she continued in a low voice. 'I fooled myself into hoping you were honest, but now the truth has been brought to your door. How many more bastards have you got around Ryhope? How many more girls have you put in the family way?'

'Emily, listen—' James began, but she cut him short.

'I've been an idiot to think I could make a future with you. First you promised you'd leave your wife, and yet you're still to make good on your word. Then you said you'd move to Ryhope to live all year round, instead of just visiting from Scarborough. I think I've always known you could tell a good lie.'

Ada dropped her gaze. Emily's words weren't meant for her ears and she felt embarrassed to be caught up in them.

'And now this,' Emily said softly, pointing at the basket where the baby was moving inside. 'It's too much, James.'

'I'll get rid of it,' James said. He spun around to Ada, silently pleading for help. His dark eyes, stern face and black hair gave him a wicked look at the best of times, Ada always thought. But now, standing there talking about getting rid of a baby, he was giving her cause for concern. She turned away from his gaze. She had been asked to do some odd things over the years working for the McNally family, but she'd be damned if she would carry out an instruction to throw a tiny baby out into the night.

'Anyway, who says it's even mine?' James turned back to Emily. 'Any urchin could have left it on the doorstep. I'll fling it off Ryhope cliffs into the sea if I have to. I'll feed it to the pigs at High Farm!'

Ada lifted her gaze to see Emily recoil in horror.

'If anything happens to that child, I'll make sure word gets out about you, James McNally. The police will cart you off in a flash,' Emily hissed. 'And I've got your housekeeper as witness to your words.'

Ada locked eyes with her for a second, then, from behind James's back, gave her a brief nod. She watched as Emily composed herself and headed back up the stairs.

'I will be leaving in the morning,' she called back over her shoulder.

'Yes, miss,' Ada replied.

James ran his hand through his thick black hair.

'God damn it!' he cried. 'I will not be stuck with this!'

Ada lifted the basket from the table, then raised her eyes to the landing, where Emily had disappeared into her room. 'Seems to me, sir, that you have little choice if you wish to keep your reputation intact,' she said.

James walked into his study and slammed the door behind him. Ada knew from experience that he would go straight to the drinks tray. Rum was his favourite tipple and he always brought a bottle or two with him from Scarborough, packed in his travel bag. She carried the basket to the kitchen and set it on the large wooden table. Then she lit the coal fire and took a milk pan from a shelf.

Alone in his study, James McNally knocked back two glasses of rum without pausing. That damned girl, he thought. That beautiful, reckless damned girl. He thought he'd got away scot-free with their night of passion at Christmas, but now he rued the day he'd met her.

Mary Liddle was a beauty, with long wavy hair as dark as James's own. Her eyes were clear and bright, with a wildness to them, searching for excitement. There was a spirit to her, a rawness James liked. After first catching sight of her, the desire to spend time alone with his new housemaid became an itch James had to scratch. His opportunity came in the days after Christmas, when he escaped Scarborough on the pretence of doing business at Ryhope. In truth, it was to escape his newborn son crying at all hours. His wife Shirley, it turned out, was not a natural mother and was having problems adjusting to life with a child. It also turned out that James, to no one's surprise but his own, was not a natural husband and father.

James left Shirley in Scarborough when he came to Ryhope. He told his wife he was seeking advice on investing in the coal industry. Meanwhile, Shirley was as glad to see the back of James as he was of her. Her mother had always warned her about marrying a McNally man. It was advice she had chosen to ignore, blinded as she was by the family's fortune.

'They're in the fishing industry, dear,' her mother often said, with disdain. 'They're just a family of trade.' It was as if rotten fish guts lay under her nose each time she uttered those words.

Still, there were compensations to marrying James McNally, even if Shirley was to discover he was reckless with money, a shirker and, some would say, a scoundrel too. Gossip spread about him in Scarborough, travelling from pub to inn, from boarding house to herring boat. The word was that James was a feckless man, bad at business too.

'Not enough character,' people moaned.

'There's no backbone to the fella!' they cried.

'He's irresponsible, immature,' even his own father said.

Shirley was more than content to take James's money, even if that money did come from trade. Her mother never truly forgave her, and even insisted that Shirley keep her maiden name when she married James. It was an unusual request, but then Shirley's mother, Eleanor Banks, was an unusual woman. Elderly, with a stoop and a heavily lined face, she always wore black, as if she was constantly in mourning. She was strident in her views, opinionated, and would never countenance any man, or woman, telling her she was wrong.

Shirley and James were set up in a prestigious home on The Crescent, one of Scarborough's best addresses, overlooking parkland. It was a house that Shirley had to herself for a week or more each time James was in Ryhope. She enjoyed the luxury and peace of it and had no complaints that her husband spent so much time away from home.

The Uplands was the McNally family home in Ryhope, a place to escape the rigours of the fishing industry that the family were involved in on the Yorkshire coast. James's father, Angus McNally, had bought the house as a holiday retreat, and James had happy memories of spending time there with his father and brother. His mother, Florence, had died not long after he had been born, and his father had never remarried. Instead, Angus's energy and commitment went into the family business, running a fleet of herring boats in Scarborough.

James enjoyed the fishing season, he loved seeing the horizon clouded by the masts of McNally boats as they headed out to bring the fish home. In the past, once the season had ended and the family fortune was secured for another year, the McNallys would return to Ryhope en masse for a change of pace. Nowadays, it was only James who visited the Uplands. His father had no more use for the place; the five-hour train journey with multiple changes had become too tiring for him. James's older brother, Albert, stayed in Scarborough too. He was sniffy about Ryhope; he said it was made common by the coal mine at its heart. But there was another side to the village that Albert didn't appreciate. With its cliff-fringed beach and farming community, it provided a pastoral contrast to Scarborough's busy harbour, and it was one that James enjoyed. And once Mary Liddle came to work as a housemaid at the Uplands, he enjoyed it even more.

He cast his mind back to the summer fayre on the village green where he had first seen Mary. This was before she'd come to work at the Uplands, before James knew who she was. When he'd spotted her there, her beauty had turned him weak. She was standing beside a ribbon seller, running her fingers along the coloured strips. Two smaller girls had stood at her side, he remembered, both with long dark hair and one of them with a face full of freckles. He had watched Mary pick out a length of scarlet ribbon and hold it against her own hair. He remembered the ribbon seller trying his best to persuade her to buy his wares, but she kept shaking her head.

The next time he saw her was some months later, when he returned to Ryhope from Scarborough to find her working as his new housemaid. Ada had convinced him she needed help about the place. Her back played up badly, the pain shooting through her, and she wasn't getting any younger, as she often reminded him. He'd allowed her to choose and hire her own maid; he wanted nothing to do with the appointment. But when he saw who had been taken on, he couldn't believe his luck. He couldn't have picked better if he'd chosen himself.

The new girl lived out, somewhere in the village, though James didn't know, or care, where. He courted her discreetly. They flirted and chatted whenever Ada was out of the room. He thought Ada hadn't seen what was going on, but he should have known better, for it was rare that the housekeeper missed anything that went on at the Uplands. She soon put two and two together.

It was on one of James's visits to Ryhope in the days after Christmas of 1902 that he'd presented Mary Liddle with a scarlet ribbon as a festive gift. He'd wrapped it carefully and approached her one evening when he knew Ada was resting. Mary needed no encouragement to flirt with James as much as he flirted with her. He complimented her beauty and charm. She didn't blush and demur like the girls he'd known before. Instead she lapped up his compliments and gave them back in return. There was something about her, she was fun to tease and flirt with, though nothing more serious than that.

That night, he had offered her rum. When she refused and he helped himself to a glass, she came up behind him and flung her arms around him. Her hands found their way to his waistcoat buttons, and she popped them open one by one. James had stood still, eyes closed, savouring the sweet moment. Her hands fell lower, to his trousers.

'Wait, I'll lock the door,' he said.

'No need. Ada's snoring,' Mary replied. There was a flirtatious grin on her face as she pulled him to the sofa and ran her hands through his thick black hair. Then she licked his lips and planted hot, breathy kisses on his neck.

But now this! James banged his fist against the arm of his chair. There could be no denying whose child had been left on the doorstep. The scarlet ribbon said more than any note could. He threw another glass of rum down his throat. The baby in the basket was just a scrap of skin and bone, nothing more. How was he supposed to look after it? What would happen if Shirley found out, or worse, his father? Didn't he have enough trouble with his noisy son back in Scarborough? Who could have known such a tiny thing could make such a din? He came to Ryhope to escape all of that, to get away from his responsibilities. He came to Ryhope to enjoy himself – and now this. He would not have it! No!

There was a knock at the study door.

'Come in,' he yelled.

It was Ada. She opened the door but did not enter. She wanted to keep her distance from James; she didn't know what state he might be in from the shock of the night and the rum. She saw the empty glass in his hand.

'I shall feed the child, sir,' she said matter-of-factly. 'And I shall make it comfortable.'

James shook his head. 'Do as you wish. It is not my concern.'

Ada held her hand out. In it lay the scarlet ribbon. 'Will you require this, sir?' she asked. She knew fine well that he would not want the ribbon and neither would he want reminding of the girl he had given it to. But she could not resist making him squirm.

She thought of Mary Liddle, the wild and untamed girl she had taken under her wing at the Uplands. She had tried her best with her, had tried to instil discipline into her as they worked together in their domestic chores. But Mary had been a restless, unsettled soul. And with her beauty, it wasn't long before she caught the eye of James

McNally. Ada had seen it all unfold before her. And now it was time that James received his comeuppance.

Ada knew only too well what James got up to while he was at the Uplands. She knew about the women he brought there, a different one each time. And she knew about his wife and newborn son in Scarborough. She judged him harshly. He wasn't a gentleman like his father Angus and his older brother Albert. No, James was a cad of the worst kind, a womaniser and philanderer who cared nothing for his reputation or the family name.

'Get out,' he said.

'As you wish, sir,' Ada replied. She pulled the door closed and headed back to the kitchen with a satisfied smile on her face. She'd rattled James, just like he deserved.

James sighed deeply and turned to his bottle of rum. He tipped the remains into his glass and threw the spirit down his throat in one gulp. He remembered the February day when Mary had come to him to tell him she was pregnant. He'd been disbelieving at first, had thought it a prank she was playing. But when he saw the tears in her eyes and the grim expression on her face, he knew it was no joke. Once the shock of her news had settled, he had bargained with her. He'd offered to pay to get rid of the child before her pregnancy showed. But she denied him the easy way out. Her cousin Sarah Rickerby, her aunt Peg's only child, had died while having her baby ripped from her body. Mary had heard Peg whispering to her mam about the danger Sarah was in afterwards. She knew of the risks and wouldn't put herself through what her cousin had suffered. James had disappeared then, back to Scarborough, to his wife and his work in the herring trade.

In his absence, Mary continued to work at the Uplands under Ada's watchful eye. Ada saw the way she plumped out and didn't need telling what was going on. And then one day a letter arrived with a Scarborough postmark. On the envelope was the McNally family crest, a herring boat called a lugger with its red sails at full mast. Underneath the boat were the words *Silver Darlings of the Sea* – the phrase used by fishermen to describe their lucrative catch.

James remembered every word he'd written. He'd taken the coward's way out, of course, and had addressed the letter to Ada. In it he'd asked Ada to sack Mary, and he gave a tight purse as his reason. He lied, saying that finances in Scarborough were such that he couldn't keep on an extra member of staff. He knew Ada wouldn't like that, not with her bad back, but he didn't see what else he could do. He also said that he didn't know when he would return to the Uplands. And that, he'd hoped, was that.

He hadn't seen hide nor hair of Mary Liddle since the day she told him she was carrying his child, and nor did he wish to see her. He'd thought the coast was clear when he returned to the Uplands months later; he felt sure he was well shot of the girl. But he hadn't bargained on how determined Mary could be. And now here he was with a baby in the house that there could be no denying was his.

He staggered from the chair, woozy with rum, and reached out a hand to steady himself at the wall. He walked from the darkness of his study into the grand hallway, where an oil lamp was burning. From there he headed along a narrow corridor, past the drawing room and library, to the kitchen. He paused at the doorway and raised his hand to knock, for this was Ada's domain and he was not expected to enter. But tonight was no ordinary night. He put his hand to the door and found it unlocked. It swung open at his touch.

A coal fire roared in the hearth, sending light dancing around the room. Ada sat in front of the fire with her back to the door. James saw the back of Ada's head and her hair loose at her shoulders. He took a step into the kitchen and his breath caught in his throat. For in Ada's arms was the baby, his child. He took another step, taking care to be quiet. But he should have known Ada would find him out; she always did. She turned and looked into his face. He cleared his throat.

'You'll give it to the care of the hospital and leave it there,' he said abruptly. 'I'll arrange for transport first thing in the morning.'

Ada turned her back again. 'I'll do no such thing,' she said gently.

'Are you denying my request, Mrs Davidson?' James said.

Ada heard the slur in his voice, made heavy from rum. 'Are you denying the child its father?' she said. She paused, and then added, a sarcastic note to her voice, 'Mr McNally?'

'I will not keep it,' James said, as firmly as he could.

'And I will not give it away,' Ada replied, matching her tone to his. She gazed into the fire as she continued. 'Sir, I have worked for your family since I was a girl. The Uplands is my home—'

'That I can take from you at a moment's notice,' James interrupted.

Ada chose to ignore his comment. She knew that James wielded little power over her position as housekeeper. She answered to his father and no one else. Many times she had wondered how he had squared things with Angus after he'd sacked Mary. Oh, she wished she could have been a fly on the wall when that conversation had taken place! Once more she chastised herself for her cowardice in not writing to Angus to request help after losing Mary. For despite the girl's rebellious ways and the gossip that spread around Ryhope about her, she'd been a hard worker once she put her mind to the job in hand.

'The Uplands has been my home for many years,' she said. 'Your father hired me and I work for him. Until I hear otherwise from him, I will do what I think is right.'

At the mention of his father's name, James bristled. News of the baby must never reach Scarborough. It could be the final straw – he might be cut out of the family business completely. He was already afraid of losing his father's confidence in his abilities. His older brother was fast becoming a rising star in the herring trade. This was another reason why James spent so much time in Ryhope. He was jealous of Albert's success and felt unable to compete with him. He knew his father was judging him against Albert. He had always judged him that way. James feared that in his father's eyes, whatever he did, he would never match the skill and success of his brother.

'This . . .' He waved his hand towards the child in Ada's arms. 'No one outside the Uplands must ever know about it.'

Ada tutted. 'You think we can keep this quiet, in Ryhope of all places? You can't keep a baby quiet, sir.'

'Only you and I know,' James said.

'And your fancy piece upstairs, she knows too. And who can say how many other women around Ryhope will be only too happy to spread the news once it gets out.'

James felt a rush of blood to his face. He turned away from Ada in an attempt to disguise his anger.

'I will speak to Emily, see if she can be persuaded not to talk.'

'And me, sir? Can I be persuaded not to talk, too?'

James spun around. 'What do you mean?' he demanded.

Ada chose her words carefully. 'Seems to me that I'm the only one, apart from you, who knows exactly who this baby belongs to. You see, I know about the scarlet ribbon. Mary showed it to me the day after you gave it to her. That kind of knowledge has a currency, don't you think?'

James let her words sink in. He'd always known her to be wily and astute, always one step ahead. But even he was surprised at what she was suggesting.

'You're blackmailing me?' he laughed. 'You?'

Ada kept quiet, waiting for him to speak.

'How much for your silence?' he said at last, when he saw no other way out.

She allowed herself a little smile. She'd got him squirming again. 'It isn't your money I'm after,' she said. 'I want to keep the child as my own.'

James felt as if he'd been punched in the chest. He pulled a chair from the table and dragged it along the kitchen floor until he was sitting opposite Ada at the fireplace. The noise woke the baby and Ada shushed it gently. James leaned forward.

'This is your deal?' he asked her. 'That you keep the child? Nurse it and feed it, rear it as yours. And in return, I have your silence about it being mine and that of the maid who worked here?'

Ada locked eyes with him. 'Yes, sir,' she said.

Glenda Young

'I see.' James thought for a few moments, tapping a finger against his chin.

'An increase in my wages will be needed, of course,' she said calmly. 'To cover the costs for the child.'

'Of course,' James said. 'I'm sure I can square such an increase through the accounts.'

'And a lump sum for my silence. Fifty pounds.'

'Fifty pounds?' James cried. 'Ridiculous. I can offer ten and no more.'

'Twenty,' Ada said.

'Fifteen.'

Ada nodded. This was more than she'd expected. 'Fifteen it is.'

James looked at her with a quizzical expression on his face. 'You have no children of your own?' he asked.

Ada sighed. How little he knew of her after all she had given his family over the years.

'It was not to be, sir,' she said. 'And then Mr Davidson died, God rest his soul, and I never remarried.'

'I remember him. Michael. A good chap.'

'Martin,' Ada corrected. She glared at James but he didn't seem in the least embarrassed. How different the likes of James McNally were to the rest of Ryhope, she thought. He brought his airs and graces to the Uplands and took his secrets back to Scarborough.

He held out his hand, but Ada didn't take it. She stared at it for a few seconds before returning her gaze to meet his.

'I accept your proposal,' he said. 'I will increase your wages a little to cover costs you may incur. You will keep the child. And you must keep the secret. You must never breathe a word to the child about me being its father, nor

32

tell it anything you might know about . . .' He stopped himself from saying Mary's name. 'About its mother, the maid.'

'Yes, sir,' Ada said.

'But there is one condition,' James continued firmly.

Ada's eyes darted towards his face.

'When the child is old enough to walk and talk – when it can survive on its own, feed itself, clean itself, clothe itself; when it no longer needs a nurse in the night – there is something I demand you do.'

'And if I don't agree?' Ada asked.

'Then I will rip it from your arms this second and throw it from Ryhope cliffs into the sea.'

His words sent a chill to Ada's heart, not least because of the cold way he said them. She wondered if the threat was fuelled by the amount of rum that had passed his lips. No – she shook her head – she knew how cold and calculating he could be. She didn't doubt for a moment that he wouldn't be capable of making good on it. His dark eyes bored into hers, waiting for her to respond. She kept herself in check.

'What is this condition?' she said.

'When the child reaches the age I speak of, it must be removed from the Uplands. It will never again live in the main house.'

'Then where—' Ada began, but James cut her short.

'It will live in the grounds.'

'The grounds?' she cried. 'But there's nothing there, sir, as you know. Just the woodshed by the trees.'

'Then the woodshed will be the child's home.'

'Nonsense!' Ada erupted. In her arms, the baby squirmed.

'The woodshed,' James repeated. 'You will have three, perhaps four years with the child here in the house. Then you must arrange for the woodshed to be cleared, and that's where it will live.'

'But this is outrageous! A child can't live outdoors in a shed. You'll send it to an early grave!'

James held up his hands. 'No buts, Mrs Davidson. This is my demand. You either accept it, or I take the child to the cliffs right now.'

'I'll go to your father about this! I'll tell—'

'You'll do nothing of the sort. Not if you want to keep the child.'

Ada looked at the baby in her arms, its tiny face peeking from the cloth it was wrapped in. She knew how desperate Mary must have been to leave her child on the doorstep. What would become of Mary, Ada didn't know and had no control over. But what happened to the precious child in her arms, she knew she could determine and shape. She could save it and give it a life. Whatever happened, she would never let James take it and throw it in the sea. Never.

'Then we have a deal, sir,' she said. She shook James's hand, then he stood and walked from the kitchen.

Alone by the fire, Ada's mind raced. Worries and confusion mixed with anger at James and concern for Mary's state of mind.

'Don't you worry, little one,' she whispered. 'I'll look after you now.'

She looked around the kitchen, at the oak table standing in the middle of the room, at the shelves on the walls holding jars, saucepans and bowls.

'See all of this, little one?' she said. 'A part of the

Uplands should be yours. Forcing his own child to live in a shed in the grounds? I'll get him for this, I swear. And by God, even if it kills me, I'm going to see you get all you rightfully deserve.'

Just then there was a noise at the kitchen door. Ada looked up sharply, surprised to find James there. Her heart skipped a beat. Had he heard her words?

'I will be leaving for Scarborough first thing in the morning,' he said.

Ada wasn't surprised to hear this. It was just like him to run away at the first sign of trouble.

'Yes, sir,' she said.

He pointed to the baby. 'That thing. You never told me and nor did I ask, but I find myself compelled to know. Is it a boy or a girl?'

'A girl, sir.'

He sighed heavily. 'Just a lass,' he muttered, and then turned to leave.

Ada caught something of his words, and liked the sound of what she heard. She played the three words on her tongue, running them together, then beamed down at the sleeping baby.

'You'll be named Jess, little one. I'll register you as Jess Davidson, for appearances' sake. But I promise you this. When the time is right, you'll know of the McNally connection and of what it might bring.'

Chapter Three

The next morning, James's head was thick from lack of sleep and too much rum. He stumbled about his room, gathering up his belongings, throwing clothes and shoes into his suitcase. There was no sign of Emily in any of the bedrooms. He called her name but got no reply. She had left him, as she'd threatened to do. He felt nothing but a huge sense of relief at her absence; it was one less problem to deal with.

Usually, whenever James left the Uplands, he would say farewell to Ada and give instructions about anything he needed carried out before his next visit. Sometimes she was tasked with hiring a gardener to lay out the vegetable beds or a handyman to fix window frames. But this time James was leaving in unusual circumstances. He planned to walk out of the door without a second glance. He couldn't face seeing the child and didn't want anything to do with it now he'd made his pact with Ada. The child was hers now, her responsibility. She could take any gossip that came her way; he was paying her handsomely for it.

Through the dull pain of his hangover, a flash came to

him from the previous night, when he'd sat with Ada in the kitchen. Had he really offered to pay her fifteen pounds for her silence? Fifteen? Was he mad? He must have been more drunk than he'd thought. An increase in her wages he could square through his business account, although he knew he'd need to be careful, as his father kept a close watch on the family finances. But how on earth was he going to write off fifteen pounds through his books? Shirley kept a close eye on their family accounts for The Crescent; it would be difficult to get a large sum past her beady eye there. He decided to give the matter some thought on the train journey home. Perhaps he'd tell Shirley the money was needed to invest in the coal business at Ryhope, an amount that he wanted to keep secret from his father. She would never know, he thought. She had no inkling of what he did at the Uplands, and no desire to spend time there, away from her beloved Yorkshire coast.

James slammed the door of the Uplands and headed out to Cliff Road with his small suitcase in hand. He was dressed in his travelling suit of black trousers, jacket and a waistcoat under his overcoat. And with the late-September weather turning cold, there was a scarf around his neck. It was a green woollen scarf that his mother-in-law, Eleanor, had bought for him as a Christmas gift one year. The colour was not to his taste, but the scarf was warm and comfortable against the Ryhope sea air.

Eleanor was a woman he found difficult to get along with. James felt she was always looking down on him because of his business in the fishing trade, and he wasn't keen on the way she had brought up her daughter to have modern ideas. He detested the fact that Shirley took her mother's word above his, and it rankled with him that she had kept her family name and mixed it with his. She was known as Mrs Shirley Banks-McNally, and James didn't like it one bit. If he couldn't exert influence over his own wife, then how could he expect his colleagues in Scarborough to respect him?

He pulled the scarf up to his collar and tugged his hat low to hide his eyes made dark by the rum as he walked the short distance to Ryhope East station. There was no easy, direct way to travel from Ryhope to Scarborough; it was a journey of five hours, involving four trains, and he was not looking forward to it, especially with his hangover. But it would give him time to think and plan, to compose himself before he returned home to Shirley. It would give him time to get the damned baby from his mind, and set his memories of Mary Liddle free.

The first leg of the journey, on the North Eastern Railway from Ryhope East, terminated in Sunderland town centre. There James had a short wait until the next train arrived. This one transported him from Sunderland to Cox Green at Durham. As he travelled, he battled a growing sense of impatience. All he wanted to do was get away from the north-east. More than ever, he longed to be back in Scarborough, as far away from Ryhope as he could. At last the train arrived at Cox Green, and he began to relax. The next one, his third of the day, would take him all the way to York. He breathed a sigh of relief when he boarded, for there was a comfortable first-class compartment, much needed as the journey was long. Once in York, there would be a fifty-minute wait before the Scarborough train arrived, and he was looking forward to drinking a couple of pints of Samuel Smith's malt ale in the gentlemen's lounge there. After Sunderland's Vaux beer served in the Ryhope pubs, he was looking forward to Yorkshire beer again. Sunderland ales were not to his taste, although Sunderland women most definitely were.

He settled into his seat, removed his top coat and hat, and laid both on an empty seat. He was sharing the compartment with an older man, who sat opposite, next to a young couple holding hands, whispering and seeming very much in love. James ignored them and turned away from their display of affection, gazing out of the window as the train gathered speed. He thought of Scarborough and his heart began to race. He saw smoking chimneys and squat buildings. Above the chimneys, clouds of smoke filled the sky. He saw horses in fields and a notion passed through his mind that he might invest in livestock. The thought left him quickly; it was too much responsibility to care for another living thing, whether animal or human. He would not be bound by such things. He knew where he was with a catch of fish, they were caught to be killed and sold. However, he couldn't deny that it might impress his father if he went into business in the country, buying his own machines. He entertained another thought as the train steamed past manors and halls set in their own grounds. What if he moved from the Yorkshire coast to live the life of a country squire? He shook his head. No, he couldn't do that; it would be too quiet in the countryside. James was a man who needed grit in his life. He'd be lost without the salty tang of Scarborough.

'It's a pleasant view,' the older man said. He had noticed James staring through the window.

'Yes,' James replied. He glanced at the young woman

opposite, admired the outline of her shapely legs beneath the dark green of her skirt, then turned his gaze back to the window. 'A most attractive view,' he said.

He thought of Shirley. When they'd first met, she was youthful and slim and wore her brown hair loose and long. But since their son had been born, she had a tired look about her. Her slim frame had become thin and gaunt, and she scraped her hair into a knot at the back of her head. This new look brought a hardness to her features that James no longer found attractive. He knew that when he went home to his wife, she would greet him with a perfunctory kiss and a handful of bills to be paid. He thought of his son, who would no doubt be squalling and in need of food. No, he would not return home to The Crescent immediately he arrived back in Scarborough. He would head to the seafront to take in the air.

He always knew where he was with the sea. The changing of the tides was as regular and comforting as a heartbeat. He'd go to the harbour, and if anyone asked, he'd pretend he was there on business. But really it was excitement he craved, in his favourite tavern off Sandside. It was vulgar there, raucous and heavy with laughter. It was a place where he could enjoy men's company and women's kisses.

He thought about the herring girls at the harbour. It was late September and there was a chance the girls hadn't yet moved on. They travelled down from Scotland to work, following the herring fleet around the coast from spring through to winter as the fish made their way south. It was summer when the herring, and the girls, landed on the Yorkshire coast, spending the months of August and September in Scarborough. The sight of the girls on the harbour was impressive, all of them together, singing, gutting and packing fish into barrels of salt and ice. James marvelled at their speed and dexterity as they worked. Their knives flew over the silver fish, slicing, cutting and throwing the herring into barrels.

But there was more reason for him to enjoy watching the herring girls other than knowing they were making his family their fortune. When they worked, they rolled up their sleeves and pulled up their skirts, tucking them into their drawers. This was to keep fish guts off their clothes and the stench off themselves. But it also meant that as they sliced the flesh of the herring, they were putting their own flesh on show. Men flocked to the harbour to see the bare arms and legs on display. When James thought of the sight of it, a delicious thought filled his mind and he discreetly licked his lips. He thought of Jeanie, his favourite of all the herring girls, and hoped she might still be about. He'd take her to a cheap hotel, the one they'd used before, where he knew the landlady would keep his visit secret, for a price. He felt sure word of it would never get back to his father, in his house above Scarborough's South Bay, or to Shirley at home in The Crescent.

Over the coming weeks, James attended as best he could to business, his new son and his wife. He hoped it might take his mind off the unpleasant goings-on in Ryhope with Ada and the child. As the months turned in those first precious years, he visited the Uplands less frequently. On the rare occasions he was there, he instructed Ada never to bring the child into his presence. On this he was firm. He didn't want to see it or hear it. Ada knew his strength of feeling on the subject, and was more than happy to keep Jess out of his sight.

The years passed uneasily for James, although he did his utmost to pretend to Shirley and his family that nothing had changed. Knowing that his child was at the Uplands each time he visited brought an anger that was almost too much to bear. There were times when he thought of speaking to his father about selling the place, moving on and away, leaving Ada and the child behind. He toyed with the idea of never visiting Ryhope again. But what then? If he lost his bolthole, his one place to escape Shirley and his commitments in Scarborough, where would he go? And so he kept quiet while his secret burned in his gut.

Meanwhile, at the Uplands, the abandoned baby staked her claim to Ada's heart, quickly becoming the child Ada had desperately longed for but had always been denied. It was Ada who sang to Jess and read stories to her. It was Ada who sat up all night when Jess was teething, or crying, frightened by shadows cast by the hazel trees. However, the sleepless nights took their toll. A melancholy often threatened to overwhelm Ada as she struggled with the rigours of looking after a demanding baby. There was also the problem of taking Jess outside of the Uplands. For as soon as Ada was seen with the perambulator in the street, questions would be asked. She prepared herself for the gossip and rumours by inventing a story about a niece who was too ill to look after her child. For good measure, she also invented a wayward husband for her imaginary niece. It was a husband of the worst kind, one who had done a runner after the birth of his daughter.

'It's a terrible situation,' she would say, shaking her head when telling the tale. 'It was the least I could do to offer to take the baby in.'

Folk would nod their heads in sympathy and marvel at the saintliness of Ada Davidson, calling her an angel with a heart as big as Ryhope itself.

'How's your niece doing?' they'd ask when they passed her in the street pushing the perambulator with baby Jess inside.

'She's still not well,' Ada would reply. 'In fact, she's getting worse.'

'Oh, now that's a shame,' Ryhope folk would say as they peered into the child's round, pink face. 'And this one's such a gorgeous little girl, too.'

When Ada was out walking with Jess, as well as complimenting what they took to be her niece's baby, her neighbours would also pass comment on how generous James McNally was to allow the child to stay at the Uplands. Ada had to bite her tongue and smile through gritted teeth each time she heard praise heaped on the man who had threatened to throw the child in the sea.

Those who peered into the perambulator when they passed Ada in the street and made conversation with her might have noticed a blanket inside. It was a knitted white square with a pattern Ada had designed herself. In one corner she had knitted a lace effect different to the rest of the square, with holes in the pattern large enough to pass a ribbon through. It was a scarlet ribbon, the ribbon that had been attached to the handle of the basket left on the doorstep. It wasn't sewn into the blanket; Ada didn't want it that way. It was threaded through the lace edge, ready to be removed at a moment's notice whenever

James was at the Uplands, just in case he should stumble across it.

But despite the love that flowed from Ada, she knew she was too old, without the energy needed to be a more engaging mother. The aches and pains in her back niggled, and with no one to help her with the child, no one to advise her, she struggled. Occasionally she had regrets about taking Jess on. She was a widow woman, alone in the world with no family in Ryhope. But those regrets melted to nothing when she held the child in her arms, and her heart would sing. It was just her and Jess, the little girl wholly dependent on her for all her wants and needs.

After Martin had died, Ada had closed her heart down. She was too scared to love another man for fear that she'd be put through unbearable grief a second time. Besides, Martin had been her world. It wouldn't have felt right to try to replace him in her heart with someone else. All the love that had built inside her since he had passed away, all the love that had nowhere to go, was now lavished on Jess. Ada often wondered what Martin would have made of her and Jess living alone at the Uplands, enjoying the grandest house in Ryhope. But the arrangement suited her perfectly. She had her own room, with a bed for sleeping and a chair for sitting. Best of all, she enjoyed the splendour of an indoor bathroom. It was a luxury that few in Ryhope could afford with most having an outdoor netty in their yard. Jess slept in Ada's room in a cot Ada fashioned from a box from Watson's grocer shop.

However, it was no easy feat to maintain the Uplands in good order while looking after a baby. Ada worked hard to keep the place free of dust and dirt. On good days, when the weather was fine, she would carry her chair to the garden and watch as Jess crawled about on the lawn. And on the days when rain and wind lashed the bay windows, she would sing to the child by the fire in her cosy room. Jess would respond, always, to Ada's singing voice and Ada would smile. Her heart danced with joy when Jess made tiny noises, clapped her hands and tried to join in with the song.

As Jess grew, Ada dressed her in clothes she had made from material bought at the Co-operative store. The outfits might not have passed muster with fancy-minded folk, but as long as the little girl was clean and fed, that was all that mattered to Ada.

Ada had started in service at just twelve years old. Her schooling had finished on a Friday lunchtime, and by teatime she was learning the ways of the Uplands from Mrs Strickland, the former housekeeper. Mrs Strickland had taught her everything there was to know about working at the house. Well, almost everything. What Ada had to learn for herself was the ways of the McNally men. She'd got along with James's parents, Angus and Florence, and respected them dearly; they treated her well and with friendship. But when Florence passed away, it was as heavy a blow to Ada as if she'd lost one of her own. Since then, Angus had visited the Uplands less often, until he finally stopped some years ago. As for James's brother Albert, Ada couldn't recall the exact year she'd last seen him. She'd just about forgotten what he looked like. Now it was only James who visited Ryhope, and the Uplands was kept on for his convenience. The place was his bolt-hole, a retreat from the rigours of his working life in Scarborough. Ada soon learned to turn a blind eye to the women he brought as his companions.

James never let her know in advance when he might arrive, or once there, how long he might stay. Some of his visits lasted as long as three months, others just a week or ten days. This meant it was difficult for Ada to know how best to stock the larder. She played safe, buying ingredients from the Co-op in order to have at her fingertips all that was needed to bake bread and hot-water pastry for his unplanned arrivals.

The Co-op was one of the buildings that kept Ryhope's heart beating. Its fancy, full title was the Ryhope and Silksworth Industrial and Providential Society Limited, but everyone in Ryhope called it 'the store'. As well as offering all kinds of provisions, there was an abattoir attached. Freshly slaughtered meat could be bought, packaged neatly in white paper, and was sold from marble counters by men with oiled moustaches. It also had a bakery, and the sweet smell of freshly baked bread drifted around the colliery, filling noses and throats and making bellies ache with hunger. Upstairs there was a concert room, large enough for talks and dances. The vicar of St Paul's, Reverend Daye, was especially grateful for such a space, as it meant he could offer evening talks of a more general nature than those he gave from his pulpit in church. But the store offered even more than a community space along with groceries for sale. It also gave work to the men and women of Ryhope, feeding the families of those who worked at the coal mine.

Ryhope mine took boys straight from school to work at the surface of the pit before they were old enough to work in the hell underground. Many men and boys died in the coal mine. Deaths from accidents were sadly too common.

It was often said that Ryhope was a village of two halves. In the village itself, was the calm village green with farms around it, a cattle market and a path that led to the cliffs and the beach. Up at the colliery, towards Silksworth, was the Ryhope Coal Company with its mine belching smoke and grime. Down the bank from the store, on the corner of the Guide Post Inn and the police station, stood Ryhope's Grand Electric Cinema. It was another of the buildings that brought the community together, although Ada had no spare time, or money, for films. Across the road from the cinema, on the road to the village green, stood the imposing St Paul's Church, which acted as a magnet for both sides of Ryhope, miners and farmers alike. However, Reverend Daye knew he had more work to do in order to convince those who worked at the pit to regularly attend Sunday services. Their time above ground was too precious, he was told, for them to spend it in church.

Ada wasn't a religious woman and didn't attend St Paul's other than when necessary. She went to weddings, when she was invited, and funerals too. She didn't take Jess to be christened. Well, it wouldn't have felt right, she thought, with the girl not being her own. But she did register the birth, just as she'd promised herself on the night the baby arrived.

The registrar wasn't happy about registering Jess without her mother or father present. However, Ada was persuasive and gave the registrar her most becoming smile. When he complained about how unusual the situation was, Ada forgot about her dignity and begged.

'Mrs Davidson,' the registrar sighed. He took off his glasses and wiped the lenses with a cotton handkerchief he pulled from his waistcoat pocket. 'I'm a very busy man and I don't like my time being wasted. You're asking me to register the birth of a child that isn't yours?'

Ada puffed out her chest. 'I'm the child's great-aunt,' she said. 'What more do you need?'

The registrar glared at her. 'Paperwork,' he said.

Ada stood her ground. The only proof of her Davidson name was on her wedding certificate. She handed it to the registrar. She had no choice but to lie through her teeth and try to be as convincing as she could.

'Sir, I beg you. My niece is poorly. The doctor says she may not have long to live. Please let me give her child the name she deserves before the Lord takes her mother away. That's all I ask.'

The registrar glanced at the clock on his office wall. He wanted to leave before half past the hour as he'd promised his wife and daughters he'd take them to dinner that evening. He knew he should send the woman in front of him away because she didn't have the correct paperwork and she wasn't the child's mother. However, if he did this, there was every chance she might cause a scene. And a scene was the last thing he wanted after the busy day he'd had. He glanced again at the clock. No, he did not have time for a scene. Alternatively, he could register the child and be done with it. Then he could slip on his jacket and hat, lock up the office and go to meet his wife as planned. He sighed heavily and pulled two sheets of paper from a pile in front of him.

'Name of child?' he said, defeated. He didn't look up.

'Davidson,' Ada replied. She tried to keep the joy from her voice. Her heart was singing. 'Jess Davidson.'

The registrar scribbled on the first sheet. 'Address?' he

asked.

'The Uplands. It's in Cliff Road, Ryhope,' Ada said.

She saw the registrar's hand pause for a second as he took in the address. He glanced up at Ada, taking in her brown velvet hat. It was her best hat, but it was frayed around the edge, and her coat had seen better days too.

'I know where the Uplands is, there is no need to advise. Your niece lives there?'

Quick as a flash Ada answered, 'She does now, sir. But how long she has left, heaven only knows.'

'Date of birth?' he demanded.

Ada could remember the date of the night she'd found Jess on the doorstep and had to assume from how tiny she was that she'd been born just a few days before.

'Twenty-sixth of September 1903,' she guessed. She said it as authoritatively as she could.

'Occupation of father?'

Scoundrel, Ada wanted to say. 'Unknown,' she replied. 'He did a runner when he found out my niece was pregnant.'

'Occupation of mother?'

'Dressmaker,' she said without a pause.

'Mother's maiden name?'

Ada gave her own maiden name. 'Lewis.'

She watched as the registrar filled in the false details on the sheets, in duplicate. He handed one of them to Ada. She folded it neatly and slid it under the white blanket with the red ribbon in the baby's pram. Then she said a polite farewell and left the office with a smile on her face.

Ada's walk back to the Uplands left her in some pain. Her back had been acting up badly and she knew she should visit the doctor. But a doctor's appointment would cost money she didn't have. Although James had promised her fifteen pounds and the increase in her wages, she'd seen neither hide nor hair of him since he disappeared to Scarborough on the night the baby arrived.

Ada struggled on. Every step shot pain up her spine.

By the time James finally visited the Uplands and Ada received the money from him that she was due, Dr Anderson could do little to help. She had a growth so large that to remove it in an operation would not only be costly but could leave her in a perilous state. The doctor prescribed her painkillers to take when she could bear to suffer no longer, and advised her to rest when she could. Ada laughed at his words.

'Rest? Me?' she said. 'I'm the housekeeper at the Uplands, Dr Anderson, at the beck and call of Mr McNally when he's about. And when he's away, there's the upkeep of the house and grounds to oversee.'

'And a child to take care of, I hear,' Dr Anderson said.

Ada held his gaze. 'It is my niece's child,' she said sternly.

The doctor looked away, his face impassive, as he wrote out the note for the dispensary to help ease Ada's pain.

It was a pain Ada lived with and tolerated as the seasons turned into years, but it wasn't easy. She took to resting more often, her energy sapped and her tiredness overwhelming. Jess grew from a smiling, happy baby into a loving toddler, and Ada taught her to walk and say her first words. However, always in the back of her mind was James McNally's threat to put Jess out of the house as soon as she was old enough. The only outbuilding that stood in the grounds at the Uplands was the woodshed and it wasn't fit for a dog to live in, never mind a child.

But Ada's hand was forced. In August 1907, when Jess was almost four years old, a letter arrived at the Uplands.

She knew immediately who it was from. The envelope carried the McNally crest of the herring lugger. It was unheard of for James to write in advance of any of his visits, and Ada knew that what was in the letter would therefore carry a different message. She was right. In coded language, obvious only to Ada, James mentioned his son Alfie in Scarborough, who was almost a year older than Jess. In one paragraph, tucked away in the middle of the note from James, who had written to let Ada know of a forthcoming visit, he wrote of his pride in Alfie's ability to dress himself, cut up his own food and sleep alone at night. His words echoed those he had spoken on the night the baby had been left on the doorstep, and they sent a chill down Ada's spine. She knew they were her cue to ensure that Jess would no longer be living in the house by the time of James's next visit.

Her stomach turned as she read on. When she reached the end of the page, she laid the letter to one side and gazed out of the window. A pain in her back gripped her and she let out a cry. Jess was playing at her feet, and she looked up sharply with an anxious expression.

'Ada?' she called.

Ada turned away so that the child would not be worried by the look on her face as the pain coursed through her. She reached for her painkillers; the bottle was almost empty and she knew she would need to make another visit to the doctor very soon. She smiled bravely.

'It's all right, Jess,' she said. 'I'm fine.'

She looked into Jess's eyes. How could she banish this child, this pure, sweet child, to live in the cold, damp woodshed? It was inhuman. It was too soon. She was not ready to part with Jess, to make her live on her own. And what of the winters that would surely freeze her to death when the snow and ice came? No, she wouldn't do it! She couldn't. She would hide the child in her room and James would never find her. She'd make sure of it. He was away so often that he wouldn't know any different. But she had to make the woodshed look as if it was being lived in, that much she knew, for she was certain he would check that his instructions had been carried out.

Before James's next visit, Ada took Jess by the hand and walked with her to Richardson Terrace, a row of two-storey cottages behind Ryhope Hall. She planned to call on Arthur Atkinson to offer him the work on the woodshed. Arthur had worked at the Uplands before as a gardener and groundsman, trimming the hedges, tending the vegetable patch and cutting the lawns. Ada trusted him and liked him.

When the Atkinsons' door opened, a small boy with a dirty face stared up at her.

'Is your father home?' she asked.

The boy carried on staring, and Ada saw that it wasn't just his face that was mucky; it was the rest of him too. She noticed long scratches along his arms and legs and saw his bare feet were black with dirt. Without turning, the boy yelled out, 'Dad!'

But it was a woman who made her way along the corridor to the front door. Arthur's wife, Estelle, had a gentle way about her, always kind but fair. She was a good-looking woman, not beautiful or pretty, but handsome, with a firm jaw and good skin. She wore a green blouse with its sleeves rolled up and a brown pinny over her skirts.

'Ada! You're looking well,' she said, then she caught sight of Jess at Ada's side. 'And who's this lovely young lady with you today?'

'Tell Mrs Atkinson your name,' Ada said.

'Jess,' said Jess in a quiet little voice.

'Your niece's child?' Estelle asked. 'My, how she's grown.' A confused look passed over her face. 'And your niece?'

'She never recovered, God bless her soul,' Ada said. Oh, how she hated lying.

'I'm sorry to hear that, Ada,' Estelle said. 'It's nice to meet you, Jess. This is my son, Mal. Say hello, Mal.'

Mal disappeared behind his mam's skirt.

'He's a bit shy,' Estelle said. 'And you've seen the state of him today. He's been out working with Arthur, clearing brambles. I can't keep him out of the gardens; he loves it, won't hear of his dad going out without him.'

'It's a bit of garden work at the Uplands I've come to speak to your husband about, Mrs Atkinson,' Ada said.

Estelle laid her hand on Ada's arm. 'It's Estelle, please. No need for formality with me.'

Ada nodded.

'Come in,' Estelle continued, opening the door wide.

Holding Jess's hand tight, Ada followed the woman inside.

'I'm baking bread,' Estelle explained as they walked into the kitchen. Sure enough, the tabletop was dusted with flour.

Estelle tapped at the kitchen window. Out in the back yard, Arthur was tending to a climbing plant Ada didn't know the name of. All around the walls of the yard, plants were clambering up frames and shrubs were growing in pots.

'He's always pottering about out there,' Estelle said, catching Ada looking at her husband's work. 'Any old pots and pans I have don't get chucked away, not when Arthur can use them for growing things in.'

At that moment, Arthur looked up and saw Ada at the window. As she raised her hand in greeting, a spasm ran through her back and she let out a gasp.

'You all right, dear?' Estelle asked.

'It's just my bad back-itis,' Ada said, trying to make light of the pain that was running through her. She didn't want Jess to see her like that, or for Estelle and Arthur to know how much she was suffering. She didn't want anyone to know. She was terrified it could lead to Jess being taken from her if she proved unable to cope.

Estelle pulled out a chair and Ada sank into it just as Arthur appeared at the back door. He was a wiry man, all muscle and sinew from time spent working outdoors. He had a weathered face, soft wisps of brown hair and a slight stoop about his shoulders. Just like his wife, he wore his shirt with his sleeves rolled up. The Atkinsons were full of industry, all three of them, it seemed to Ada. Over his shirt, he wore a black tie and waistcoat.

'I'll not come inside, Mrs Davidson, if you don't mind,' he said. 'My boots are still mucky from this morning's work and the missus won't be happy if I get her clean floor dirty.'

'Too right,' Estelle laughed.

Mal ran to his father's side and held tight to his hand.

'Now then, Mrs Davidson, what can I do for you?' Arthur asked.

Ada outlined her plan for the woodshed. She asked for it to be made watertight, with an extra layer added to the roof. She explained she needed it as secure as possible. She avoided using words such as *safe* or *comfortable*, and certainly not *habitable*, in case her request raised questions. This was no one's business but hers. Arthur accepted her offer and between them they agreed a fair price.

While the adults were talking, Mal and Jess exchanged a shy smile. Just as Ada was leaving, Mal beckoned his dad and whispered in his ear.

'Ah, the bairn's just asked me something, Mrs Davidson. He says can he help when I come to do the woodshed?'

Estelle gave an encouraging smile to Ada.

'I promise I'll keep my eye on him,' Arthur added.

'Perhaps our Mal and your niece's daughter might become friends?' Estelle said hopefully.

Ada looked around the kitchen, taking in the flour-covered table, the utensils ready for making bread. It was a clean kitchen in a happy home; a family home. She felt another pain shoot through her back and laid her hand against the wall to steady herself. The pains were coming more often now and they were growing worse. She was not getting any younger. She couldn't run around the lawns at the Uplands playing catch with Jess, as much as she wanted to.

'Good idea,' she said. 'It's about time Jess had a friend.'

Chapter Four

When Arthur Atkinson came to the Uplands to start work on the woodshed, he brought his son Mal with him, as Ada had agreed. Mal was shy at first, holding his dad's hand and staying close to his side. But while Ada chatted to Arthur about her plans for the shed, Mal became more confident and went off exploring the trees and shrubs. Jess was curious to see another child about the place and, encouraged by Ada, she pointed out to him where spiders crawled in the grass. Mal was intrigued. She showed him the vegetable patch his father tended, and he stuck his hands into the soil, letting dirt fall through his fingers.

When the children were playing and safely out of earshot, Ada outlined her plan to Arthur.

'There's more I need you to do than I let on when I visited your home,' she said.

'To the woodshed?' he asked.

Ada nodded and took a deep breath. 'I need a chimney putting in, and a grate for a fire.'

Arthur looked at her as if she was mad. 'A fire? In a woodshed? Why, the whole place will go up in flames!'

'Not if you build a stone chimney and fireplace,' Ada said. 'Just for a small fire to keep the chill off.' She paused, aware that she had to be careful what she said. She didn't want anyone knowing that Jess would be living in the woodshed. She was determined to keep the child, whatever lengths she had to go to. 'It's for when I'm working in there over the winter.'

Arthur scratched his head. 'It's an unusual request, Mrs Davidson, but I'll do my best.'

'And I need a window putting in too,' she said.

He walked around the woodshed, surveying it from all angles. 'I'll take a good look inside after I clear the wood out today. Then I'll make a start on taking down a wall and rebuilding in stone. Should be able to get a chimney built for you by the end of the week,' he offered.

'Thank you,' Ada said.

The woodshed was slowly but surely made fit for Jess to live in. After much agonising, Ada realised her original plan to keep the child in her room when James was away might be too risky. She didn't want to do anything that would cause Jess to be thrown out of the Uplands and out of her life. That didn't bear thinking about. Ada had welcomed Jess into her heart. She knew she had to carry out her part of the bargain she had made with James. It was the only way to ensure she and Jess stayed together. She did everything in her power to make the woodshed as comfortable as possible. She even contemplated moving in there herself, although space would be tight. However, the pain in her back caused her to rethink. She knew she needed her own bed to help her cope.

It was just before Jess's fourth birthday when Ada took her by the hand and led her to the threshold of the woodshed. Jess pushed the door with her free hand and it swung open.

'Look, it's your new home,' Ada said, trying to keep the catch from her voice. She blinked back her tears. The last thing she wanted was for Jess to pick up on how upset she was. She knew she had to make it sound as if it was an adventure for the girl.

Inside the shed, she had made up a small bed of wooden slats for Jess to sleep on. There was a chair from her own room. Two of Jess's favourite picture books lay on the floor by the bed. A jar filled with sweet peas stood on the sill Arthur had built under the window. The sweet, peppery scent filled the small space. The stone chimney breast gave the shed an air of solidity, built with honey-coloured stones from the beach. At its base was the fireplace, with the fire ready to be lit when Jess went to bed. Ada couldn't bear to think of the bairn, *her* bairn, being cold in the night. An iron guard ran around the grate to keep Jess safe from the flames.

'My home?' Jess said.

She took one step inside, and then another. She walked straight into the middle of the woodshed, lifted a foot and spun around on one leg. Ada had to force a smile to her face as she watched her. She didn't want Jess to know how upset she really was.

'All mine?' Jess said.

'All yours,' Ada replied.

'And yours too?'

'No, love. I'm staying in the Uplands.'

Jess ran to Ada's side and threw herself at her. 'I want to stay with you,' she cried.

Ada sank into the chair, helpless against her tears now.

'Listen, Jess,' she said. She swallowed hard and wiped her eyes on her sleeve. 'This is your new home. You sleep here from now on.'

'No more Uplands?' Jess asked, confused.

'No more Uplands,' Ada said. 'But I can see you from my window; I'll watch over you and keep you from harm. And if you stand on this chair and look out of *your* window, you can see me too.'

'And I'll keep *you* safe,' Jess said with a serious expression on her face.

As Ada wrapped her arms around the little girl, she thought her heart would break. Outside, the wind began to whip and the hazel trees bent on the breeze.

'I think we should give your new home a name,' she said as brightly as she could. 'How about Hazel Cottage, how does that sound?'

'Hazel Cottage,' Jess repeated, trying the words out for size. 'Will you visit me, Ada? Will you come to my new house, my Hazel Cottage?'

Ada hugged her again. 'Every day, Jess. Just try keeping me away.'

As Jess settled into her new home, Ada gave her the love, care and attention she needed. When Jess fell over in the garden, Ada tended to her scratches and bruises. Each morning when she woke, her first thought was of Jess, and each night before sleep, Jess was on her mind. When she visited the doctor for her prescription of painkillers she desperately needed for the ache in her back, she would take the child with her. The two of them walked together, hand in hand, comfortable with each other and happy. Each evening, by the light of an oil lamp, Ada would read Jess a story from one of her books. Not until the girl was sleeping would she leave to head back across the lawn.

The short walk between Hazel Cottage and the Uplands seemed like a mile. Ada's heart hung heavy, but she knew it was the only way to ensure she and Jess stayed together. She didn't doubt for one minute that James wouldn't make good on his word to throw the child out on the streets if he found her living inside his home. She thought back to the night when Jess first arrived, a tiny baby in a basket on the doorstep. And James's cruel words came back to her again, when he'd threatened to throw the child from the cliffs to the sea. Ada was in no doubt about how evil James could be.

On the nights immediately after James had left Ryhope to return to Scarborough, Ada would let Jess stay with her overnight in her room at the Uplands. There was little chance that James would return within a matter of days to Ryhope. Ada felt safe letting Jess into her room on those nights. But when James's visits became more frequent, Ada took the heart-breaking decision for Jess to spend her nights in Hazel Cottage all year long.

It was only when Jess joined the village school that she started to question the arrangement at the Uplands. She began to think it odd that she lived apart from Ada. She was the only one of her school friends who didn't live with their families in the same house. And none of her friends lived in such a grand house as the Uplands. She became aware that living at Hazel Cottage marked her as different to her classmates, and for weeks she fought with Ada, refusing to return to the woodshed at night. Many tearful nights were spent with Ada pleading with Jess to go back to her bed. Jess would become angry then, frustrated by Ada's less than full disclosure about why they couldn't live together. Ada knew it was too early to tell Jess the truth. Jess was too young to understand. Jess then began to ask why she didn't have a mam and dad like most of her friends did. At these times, Ada simply hugged Jess close and told her she loved her. However, her secret pact with James ate away at her every single day.

One day, when the sun was shining and the air was still, Ada offered to take Jess to the beach. She sat on the stones as Jess paddled in the water in her bare feet. The tide was on the turn, and out at sea, powerful waves were beginning to form, growing loud and angry as they roared in.

'Don't go out too far,' Ada called.

Jess turned her head to reply, and as she did so, lost her balance and fell face down in the water. Ada panicked. She tried to stand, tried to call out to Jess, but the pain in her back meant she could only move slowly. Ahead of her, Jess was crying, soaked through with seawater and struggling to lift herself up. A strong wave caught her, then another, and Ada saw her thrown around like a rag doll in the sea.

'Jess!' she called. 'Jess!'

Other children were playing in the water nearby, but the roar of the ocean blocked out the sounds of Jess's distress.

Ada walked as fast as she could to get to Jess quickly but she wasn't quick enough. A man had heard Ada's cry and was running towards the little girl. He scooped her up in his arms, giving no thought to the fact that he was getting soaked through, and brought her to shore, where he laid her on the warm, dry sand at Ada's feet.

Ada sank to her knees, offering grateful thanks to the stranger who had saved Jess from the sea. Jess coughed up seawater and Ada tended to her. Beside them, the man watched and waited until he knew for sure that the girl was out of danger.

'Your granddaughter, she'll be all right?' he asked, concerned.

Ada felt a dagger to her heart. 'Oh. She's not my granddaughter,' she replied quickly.

'I beg your pardon,' the man said. 'Please accept my apology. Your daughter, then? I hope she'll be well. She seems not to have suffered too much.'

Ada didn't have the heart to tell the man that Jess wasn't her daughter either. Let him think what he wanted, she thought. Jess was as good as a daughter to her, in everything but name.

Ada rarely let Jess out of her sight after that day on the beach. However, there was one other person she trusted with the child, and that was Estelle and Arthur's boy, Mal. He was in the same class as Jess at school, and the two of them had become firm friends. With Ada's devotion and Mal's friendship, Jess grew into an outgoing, friendly child, with a confidence about her and a stubborn streak too. She could be dreamy at times, lost in her own thoughts – and she was always singing. She made up songs about the birds that flew around Hazel Cottage and about the trees that grew outside her door. Ada often heard her sweet voice drifting on the breeze across the lawn. She worried that James might hear it too when he visited, and she warned Jess to sing softly and low.

On the occasions when James did come to stay at

Ryhope, he often brought with him a briefcase of paperwork and a girl on his arm. Ada tended to his needs as she had always done, but there was a tension between them that hadn't been there before Jess arrived. Ada wondered if she was being too sensitive, but she noticed that James was terse with her, demanding and bad-tempered. She wondered if it was the effects of too much rum, for his face had taken on a haggard, wretched look.

One day when Jess was at school, Ada looked out of the kitchen window and spotted something moving by the woodshed. Her blood ran cold. It was James. She saw him open the door of the shed and step inside, coming out a moment later. Neither of them spoke of his visit, but Ada was satisfied that James knew she'd kept her side of their arrangement.

As Jess grew, her long hair fell in thick waves, just as Mary Liddle's had done. Ada brushed it each morning, making it bounce and shine. It had darkened to almost black, and she was not surprised to see it. It was definitely McNally hair. There were subtleties to Jess's features, too, that reminded her of James, and she worried in case others in Ryhope might notice the similarities.

One day in 1913, when Jess was ten years old, a girl from her class called Betty Thraxter took her to one side in the playground. Betty was followed by two more girls, intent on hearing what their friend had to say.

'My mam says you're rich,' Betty began slyly.

'I'm not rich,' Jess replied.

'You must be, you live at the Uplands,' another of the girls, Clara Pitfield, teased.

The three of them surrounded Jess, taunting her,

calling her Little Miss Stuck-Up because she lived in the grandest house in Ryhope. Jess stood her ground and waited for the taunting to stop. Her mind was dizzy; she was angry and had to stop herself from lashing out.

'I'm not rich! I'm the same as all of you!' she yelled.

Her cry caught Mal's attention and he walked across the playground to the group of girls.

'Are you all right, Jess?' he asked.

Jess nodded. 'I'm going to prove something to these idiots,' she hissed. 'Come on, all of you, follow me.' She stormed to the schoolyard gate, but the other girls and Mal stayed where they were.

'It's not home time yet,' Betty Thraxter said. 'I'm not going anywhere.'

Jess walked back to Betty and grabbed her arm. 'You're coming with me whether you want to or not. Want to see where I live, do you? Want to know how rich I really am?'

The girls stood in silence, staring at her.

'We'll all be for it from the headmaster if he finds out we've left school in the middle of the day,' Mal warned.

'Don't care,' Jess said. 'If this lot want to see how rich I really am, they'll come with me now.'

She glared at each of the girls in turn. Mal kept an eye on the school door, ready to alert Jess if he saw the headmaster coming. Betty Thraxter stepped forward.

'I want to see,' she said.

'Me too,' said Clara.

All three girls followed Jess as she left the schoolyard, with Mal bringing up the rear. It was a short walk to the Uplands. Jess knew better than to use the front gate; Ada had always told her to go around the side and use the housekeeper's entrance. But it was Ada's shopping day, and Jess knew she wouldn't be caught. She never gave a thought as to whether James McNally might be there. She was so incensed by the taunting that she barged in through the gate Ada had told her never to use, then ran to Hazel Cottage in the corner of the grounds and pulled the door open.

'Call this rich, do you?' she said.

It was dark inside the woodshed even with the door flung wide open and light coming in through the tiny window. What the girls and Mal saw in front of them shocked them into silence, and their joking and teasing stopped. The floor was rough-hewn, covered with an old mat to keep Jess's feet safe from splinters. Spiders crawled along the wooden walls and roof. The stench of damp seeping up from the ground made Betty Thraxter put her hand to her nose.

'Is that your bed?' she breathed, unable to believe her eyes. She pointed to a heap of blankets in the corner of the shed.

Jess nodded.

Betty turned to her. 'But where do your mam and dad live?'

Jess shrugged. 'I don't have a mam and dad. Ada looks after me. She lives in the house.'

At the back of the group, Mal tried to take it all in. He'd had no idea the shed his dad had worked on all those years ago was where Jess now lived. It looked like a kennel for a dog. He couldn't speak.

Jess slammed the door shut. 'Happy now?' she spat.

The girls looked at one another. Then Betty Thraxter stepped forward and slipped her arm through Jess's. On

Jess's other side, Clara Pitfield took her hand. They all returned to school in silence.

Despite the hardship of life in Hazel Cottage, Jess became an independent and confident child. And now that Mal knew the truth of where and how she lived, he helped her as much as he could. He offered her food that he took from his mam's kitchen, but it wasn't food that Jess needed. Ada fed her and looked after her well. Neither was it the toys and books Mal brought. It was answers she needed. Answers to her questions about her parents, about where she came from, about why she had to live in the woodshed, even about Ada herself. But Ada remained tight-lipped. And while Jess respected Ada's wishes to keep away from the Uplands when James was about, she could never understand why. Ada kept saying she would know when she was old enough, which infuriated Jess no end.

Ada struggled to cope more than ever, the pain in her back making it impossible for her to carry out her duties as well as she would have liked. She had to ask Jess for help with the dusting and cleaning and general upkeep, following the girl from room to room, keeping one eye on Jess's work and the other on the pathway to the Uplands front door. She lived in fear that James would return to find Jess inside.

Jess remained unaware of Ada's dilemma and of her secret pact with James. She was more than happy to help Ada inside the Uplands. After everything that Ada had done for her it was the least she could do for the woman she loved more than anyone else in the world.

* * *

In 1914, Jess turned eleven years old and the threat of war that had loomed large became a dreaded reality. The men of Ryhope were sent off to fight. Jess and Ada watched from the village green as they marched to the railway station in their uniforms and hats. Mal's dad Arthur Atkinson was among them.

'It'll be over by Christmas, you'll see,' Estelle told Ada as they watched the men go by. 'That's what the newspaper headlines say.'

Ada wondered whether James and Albert McNally would be joining up and heading overseas from Scarborough. She wondered if she should write to Angus asking what he wanted to do with the Uplands during this unsettled time. Of course, what she really wanted to know was whether James had been called up. If he had, it would be safe to allow Jess back indoors, secure in the knowledge that he would not be visiting for some time.

When all of the soldiers had marched by, Ada took Jess's hand for the walk back to the Uplands. When they turned the corner of Cliff Road, something caught her eye, and she stopped dead in her tracks.

'What is it?' Jess asked.

'Go on ahead of me,' Ada instructed. 'I'll be back in a while.'

Jess did as Ada asked and headed to the side gate of the Uplands. Once she was out of sight, Ada continued to the front gate. Sure enough, her eyes weren't deceiving her, although she wished to high heaven they were. Attached to the handle of the black iron gate was a scarlet ribbon tied in a bow.

Chapter Five

Ada looked from left to right, then spun around to see if anyone was watching. Cliff Road was empty; there was not a soul about. Her breath caught in her throat, her heart hammered and her legs turned to stone. She forced herself forward to the gate and ran her fingers across the ribbon. It was tied neatly, as if the gate was being offered as an exquisite gift. She pulled at one end and it slid easily into her hand. She stuffed it quickly into her pocket.

Her mind turned with questions. Who had put it there? What did it mean? She struggled to comprehend what was going on. She knew James was not sentimental enough to have left the ribbon, even if he had been in Ryhope. Had he played a cruel trick? Had he paid someone to place the ribbon there, sent instruction from Scarborough? No, Ada decided, that wasn't his style. When he'd said he wanted nothing to do with the baby that night years ago, he'd meant it. A chill ran through her. It could only have been Mary Liddle.

She pushed her hand into her pocket and ran her fingers along the ribbon. Mary hadn't been seen in years, Ada knew that for a fact. She'd asked around, done some digging, made enquiries after the night the baby had been found. And now? If she was back in Ryhope, did that mean she was hoping to reunite with her daughter? Ada tried to make sense of the feelings flooding through her. The woman had a right to see her own child, of that there was no doubt. But what if she and Jess bonded? What if Ada was left alone again? What if . . . ?

The list of worries went on and Ada's head was in a spin. She'd never explained to Jess the truth about her parents. She had always planned to tell her when she came of age and was able to understand what carrying the McNally name might mean. But not yet. She had made her pact with James, she'd taken his money and given her word. Her part of the bargain was that she got to keep the beautiful abandoned baby. She'd nurtured Jess, fed her, bathed her and loved her. From the night the baby had turned up on the doorstep, she'd given her life to Jess. She couldn't – *wouldn't* – let Mary Liddle take her away. But hadn't the scarlet bow on the gate said that Mary was in Ryhope and that she had never forgotten her baby? Ada felt herself going dizzy and pressed her back against the stone wall until the moment passed.

'Ada! Ada!' a voice cried.

Ada looked up and saw Jess. There was a concerned expression on the girl's face.

'Are you coming in?' she said.

Ada couldn't move. Her back was in spasm, the pain shooting up her spine and down her legs. Choking back tears from the shock of what she'd found, she closed her eyes. Then she felt Jess at her side, lifting her arm, holding her, supporting her as they walked.

* * *

In the coming weeks, Ada kept the secret of the scarlet ribbon in her heart. She didn't breathe a word of it to Jess, for what good would it do either of them to worry and fuss? Many times she puzzled over what she'd found. She asked her friend Lil Mahone if she'd heard news of Mary, for Lil was well known for keeping her ear to the ground, and she knew everyone's business in Ryhope. But Lil hadn't heard anything, and a sense of unease settled in Ada. She wondered what might happen next.

As autumn drew on, the leaves on trees at the Uplands fell to the grass. The air turned cold, and mornings were white with frost. Inside the woodshed, the fire burned each night to keep Jess safe and warm. Meanwhile, Ada's pain grew worse, sometimes confining her to bed. When Jess finished school each day, she brought her a copy of the *Sunderland Echo* from the store. Ada was eager for news of the war. But far from it being over by Christmas, as everyone had predicted, the newspaper was full of stories far worse than she wanted to read.

She had not heard from James in Scarborough for some months, although she had written to his father as she'd promised herself she would. In all the years she had worked for the McNally family, it was the first letter she had ever written to them. Well, it was an unusual time, and Ada was as unsettled as anyone. There had been no reply. She wondered if her letter had even reached its destination, or if it had been lost in the post.

Ada had always assumed that James and his brother would have signed up with the Yorkshire Regiment. But she was wrong. And it was with no small amount of shock that she found James McNally at the Uplands some months after war began.

It was early in 1915 when James arrived unannounced. Ada never asked, and James never offered any explanation as to why he hadn't enlisted. She doubted he would have been a conscientious objector. She knew his father would never have allowed him to shirk his obligation to the King. She wondered if he suffered from an ailment, either real or imagined, that had excused him from service. Whatever the reason, he never gave any clue.

He looked tired and worn, Ada thought, when he arrived that year. He explained that he had travelled to Sunderland by steamship rather than train. The journey, he said, had not been without its difficulties.

'It was a damn rough voyage, Mrs Davidson. But the railway is otherwise engaged moving troops and equipment and its trains are acting as ambulances,' he explained. Little did he know that Ada was already aware of this, her extensive knowledge of the war gleaned from the local newspaper. 'But there's a steamer that runs from London to Sunderland South Dock once a week, the SS *Percheron Blue*. It calls on the east coast at Scarborough to pick up passengers and cargo.'

'The harbour's deep enough for such a ship?' Ada asked. She was interested to know, always keen to hear about life outside of Ryhope.

James shook his head. 'An iron paddle boat, the *Comet*, takes passengers from the dock to the ship.'

Ada marvelled at the thought of travelling by steamer. She'd read of such things in the newspaper. She'd seen the advertisements from the shipping agent in John Street offering passage on the screw steamer that was lit through by electricity. She doubted very much that she'd see the miracle of it herself.

'Do we have more rum?' James asked.

'Yes, sir,' she said. She was about to head to the pantry when a thought came to her. 'Is everyone well in Scarborough, sir? Your family?' she asked. From reading the *Sunderland Echo*, she knew of the devastation caused by the bombardment of the east coast the previous year. Hartlepool, further down the coast from Sunderland, had been badly hit, along with the fishing town of Whitby. On the same day, Scarborough had been bombarded. Five hundred shells had rained down, killing townsfolk and destroying whole streets.

'Well enough,' James replied. Then he paused, holding her gaze for a few moments. 'And here? Is everyone well here?'

Ada searched his face. Why was he asking this when he had never asked before? She knew only too well who he meant. But then it was an exceptional time for everyone, even for James McNally.

'Quite well,' she responded coolly.

She waited for James to say more, but he dismissed her with a wave of his hand.

One day in the spring of 1915, Ada was sitting in the garden in a chair Jess had brought outdoors so that she could enjoy the weak sunshine. Jess sat at her feet on a blanket and sang to her. Ada marvelled at the girl's voice. It was clear and pure, every note perfect and true. Her talent hadn't gone unnoticed at school, and she was often called to the front of the hall to take the lead in morning hymns. When she came to the end of her song, Ada gave her a round of applause.

'You should be on the stage,' she joked.

The two of them sat in silence. Around them the leaves on the hazel trees fluttered in the breeze.

'I love this garden,' Ada said. 'I don't think I could be any happier than I am sitting here today. I've got the sun on my face and you by my side.'

Jess took her hand. 'Is that all you need, Ada?'

'What do you mean?' Ada asked.

Jess bit her lip. 'I mean . . . we've got each other, but don't you wish sometimes that you had a family, a proper one, I mean? A husband and lots of your own children living at the Uplands?'

Ada stroked her hair. 'You're everything I need, Jess. You always have been. I could never want for anything more. I loved my husband more than life itself. When he died, I swore I'd never love again. And now I have you, it's as if I've been given a second chance.'

'What was he like?' Jess asked.

Ada smiled. 'Martin? A good man. One of the best.' She raised her handkerchief to her eyes and dabbed away tears that threatened to fall.

'I didn't mean to upset you,' Jess said.

'I'm not upset,' Ada said. 'It's just memories, you know. Sometimes they catch you unawares. Anyway, listen to me going on. Martin would have loved this garden.' She took hold of Jess's hand. 'And he would have loved you too.'

Jess stood and hugged Ada tight, then sat back down on the blanket.

Ada gazed out across the lawns. 'The only thing I would wish for is more flowers,' she said, dabbing at her eyes again. 'Just a little patch of flowers, that's all I'd have. Snowdrops and crocuses in spring, daffodils and tulips to take me through to summer, then lavender and geraniums. Martin always liked lavender. But it's all we can do to keep the bushes and trees in order while Arthur's away at war. Mal's doing his best, but he hasn't got his dad's experience. And he hasn't got the strength. I expect Estelle needs the money, that's why she sends the lad out to work.'

Jess thought about Mal. She enjoyed his company when he worked at the Uplands and was grateful for his friendship. 'Will the war last much longer?' she asked.

Ada gazed at the hazel trees at the bottom of the garden that sheltered Jess's home. A sadness came over her. She was thinking of the news that the *Sunderland Echo* brought daily. She read it all, devoured every word about the numbers of lives lost and the names of those dead. 'I hope not, my love.'

Just then there was a commotion at the side gate. Despite the pain Ada was in, and her limited mobility, there was nothing wrong with her hearing. 'What the . . . ? Who is it?' she called. She made to push herself up out of her chair. But then a dark thought ran through her. What if it was James, returned already? Had he forgotten something? But no, he would never use the side gate, just as she would never use the front.

Jess stood, brushed the grass from her skirt and walked towards the gate to see what the fuss was. Mal was standing there. His round face was as mucky as always, and there was excitement in his deep brown eyes.

'I've got something for you,' he called.

She opened the gate and something shot straight past her legs. It was a small honey-coloured dog. It looked comical, with big ears flapping at each side of its head.

'For me?' she said. She felt flattered.

The dog ran in circles on the lawn, chasing its tail, and Jess heard a couple of swear words leave Ada's lips. She and Mal walked towards Ada and the dog bounded over with its tongue hanging out. It cocked its head, then lay down on the ground, panting, with its head on its paws.

'It's called Pebble,' Mal said. 'And it's yours if you want it.'

'We can't afford to keep it,' Ada said sharply.

Mal bit his lip. 'I brought it for Jess. I thought it might help, you know, with you living in the woodshed.'

'It's called Hazel Cottage,' Jess said firmly.

'It can protect you, like, in . . . Hazel Cottage,' Mal continued. 'It'll see off robbers and pirates.'

Despite her misgivings about having another mouth to feed, Ada laughed at Mal's words. She eyed the dog carefully.

'Where did you get it, lad?'

'Found it on the beach,' he said. 'There were two of them tied in a sack. I saw the sack moving, opened it and two dogs tumbled out. I couldn't get rid of them; they followed me home. They're both boy dogs. I called them Pebble and Stone, because of where I found them. But Mam says I can only keep one. I'm keeping Stone, he's my favourite. I thought Jess might like the other one.'

Jess stroked Pebble behind his floppy ears. She looked at Ada. 'Can I keep him?' she begged. 'Can I?'

Ada didn't much like dogs. But she knew the creature would be a good companion for Jess living out in the grounds.

'Do you promise to look after it and keep it in Hazel

Cottage?' she asked. 'It must never be allowed in the Uplands, you know that, don't you?'

Jess nodded eagerly. 'I promise.'

Ada sighed heavily. 'I must be going soft in my old age. Go on then, you can keep him.'

From that moment on, Pebble and Jess became inseparable, despite Ada's misgivings. Her main concern was that Pebble might make a nuisance of itself when James was about and draw further attention to Jess, which was the last thing she wanted.

In November 1918, when Jess was fifteen, came a day Ryhope thought it would never see. After four years of fighting, destruction and death, war was over and the Armistice signed. Around Ryhope, great celebrations took place as the men came home. However, not all families were lucky, and many a broken-hearted mother shed tears knowing she'd never see her son again. At the Uplands, Ada and Jess's hearts were made light when Mal gave them the news that his dad had returned safely.

The year turned and celebrations were planned. Each town and city organised a peace parade, and Ryhope threw its own. A village committee was formed by Estelle, and money was raised to buy bunting and flags. As much as Ada wanted to, she couldn't join in with the parade preparations, for now she could barely walk from the pain in her back. As the agony coursed through her, she took to sleeping longer in the morning, and Jess took on her duties. Not only did she feel it her responsibility to help Ada as much as she could; she did it because she loved her and wanted to help ease her suffering. But Ada would only take her help when James was not in Ryhope.

Jess knew by now that this was the way life worked at the Uplands. She no longer thought it unusual. She no longer begged Ada to tell her why she needed to keep out of James's sight. She accepted it because she had known no other way.

When Ada was too unwell to work, Jess filled Ada's metal bucket with water. She took a tablet of soap and a feather duster, as she'd seen Ada do many times. As she worked in James's study, in the drawing room or the bedrooms, Ada sat in a chair and kept a trained eye on the garden path, ready to alert her in case she caught sight of the master of the house. The grandeur of the Uplands seemed wasteful to Jess. But even dressing tables that were barely touched needed dusting, and braided curtains that were drawn only a few times each year needed cleaning. She took her tasks seriously. Ada had always taken pride in her work, and Jess did her best to carry out the housework to as high a standard as she could.

By the summer of 1919, Ryhope men had begun to settle back into mining and farming, although the toll of the war was never far from everyone's minds. Arthur took up his work in the grounds of the Uplands again, only this time with instruction from Jess.

In September, on the day before Jess's sixteenth birthday, she was working in the garden, picking courgettes and raspberries from the fruit and vegetable patch at the bottom of the lawn. Pebble lazed in the autumn sunshine, watching her as she worked. A flutter of blue caught Jess's eye, and she looked up to see Ada in her blue pinny making her way slowly towards her. She noticed that Ada looked agitated, and she was waving something in her hand. Jess walked towards her and held out her arm to support her. She saw that the object in Ada's hand was an envelope with the McNally crest on the front.

'Ooh, my bad back-itis,' Ada moaned when she reached Jess.

'Come and sit down,' she said. 'I'll fetch the chair from Hazel Cottage.'

When Ada was settled, she took the letter from the envelope. The contents had surprised and disturbed her when she'd read it earlier. Now she read it aloud to Jess, word for word, leaving out no detail. Jess was as startled as Ada by the strange request.

'A dinner, tomorrow night?' she said. 'But he never has dinners here, does he? At least, he's never had one that you've told me about.'

'It's unusual,' Ada agreed. 'But it's all there in his own hand. He wants to host a dinner for eight of the Ryhope Coal Company men at seven o'clock.'

'I'll help you,' said Jess.

Ada laid her hand on Jess's arm. 'No, lass,' she said firmly.

'But—'

'You know fine well you can't go in there when they're about.' Ada nodded towards the Uplands. 'It's not that I'm not grateful for your offer, but I've got to do this myself. Though how I'm going to manage to cook a dinner and tend to a party of eight, I'll never know. I'm jiggered just walking from the house to the lawn these days.'

'Let me help you, Ada, please,' Jess begged. 'Or if not me, then what about Estelle? She'd lend a hand, I'm sure. Or we can hire someone from the village, one of the girls I used to go to school with. You need help, Ada, and if

I'm still not allowed inside when he's there—'

'You know you're not,' Ada said sternly.

Jess felt an anger rise inside her. 'You're ill, Ada. Mr McNally can't expect you to run around after him and bend to his whim.'

'Oh can't he?' Ada said. There was a cryptic note to her voice that puzzled Jess.

'What do you mean?'

'Listen to me,' she said. Her breathing was shallow. Every word that left her lips was an effort. Jess knew that speech didn't come easy to Ada when she was suffering the worst of her pain.

'You're sixteen tomorrow. It's about time you knew the truth. The Uplands . . .'

'What about it?' Jess asked.

'The Uplands,' Ada repeated. 'James . . . he's . . .'

Jess looked into Ada's ashen face. She waited for more, wondering what she was trying to tell her. Ada's breathing had become laboured and heavy. Jess knew how agonising this was for her, and she felt as if her heart would break.

'You deserve more than you know, Jess,' Ada whispered. 'You deserve to know the truth about the McNallys.' Her body slumped forward and her eyes closed.

'Ada, please,' Jess cried.

Ada took a few moments to pull herself together. At last she opened her eyes and smiled. 'Take me indoors,' she said.

'You were telling me about the Uplands,' Jess said. 'What was it you wanted me to know?'

Ada patted her hand. 'Tomorrow. I'll tell you tomorrow when you turn sixteen. Today I have a dinner to prepare.'

* * *

The next morning, Mal arrived early at the Uplands, bringing his little dog, Stone. He was due to tend the lawns ready for Mr McNally's arrival that afternoon. He also brought a birthday gift for Jess, a pot of flowering pansies.

'Happy birthday,' he said as he walked towards Hazel Cottage. He held out the terracotta plant pot. 'These are for you.'

Jess was on her knees, washing clothes in her tin bath. Behind her a line of washing fluttered in the breeze. The door to Hazel Cottage was open and Pebble was snoozing indoors. But as soon as he heard Mal's voice, he came bounding out. Pebble and Stone ran around in circles, panting, sniffing, chasing each other. As the dogs played on the lawn, Jess stood and took the pot from Mal's hands. It was heavier than it looked and she gripped it tightly.

'Thank you,' she said.

'They don't look much right now,' Mal explained, 'but they'll bloom in a few weeks and keep going into the new year. They'll be purple and white. Might have some yellow in there if you're lucky.' He rummaged in his coat pocket and brought out a small envelope. 'Almost forgot. Mam and Dad sent you this.'

Jess placed the pot of pansies on the ground by the door of Hazel Cottage and took the envelope from Mal, opening it to reveal a birthday card. On it was a picture of a woman in a soft pastel pink hat, sitting on a garden swing. She smiled and looked up to thank him, and saw that he appeared to be looking at something behind her. She spun round to see a stranger, a young man, taller than her but, she guessed, about the same age. She didn't know what to do. She knew it wasn't James McNally, for she had spotted him many times when he was at the Uplands, although she'd been clever enough to hide herself from him. The man had hair as dark as Mr McNally's, but was less broad about the shoulders. Just who was he and what did he want? Jess watched as he walked towards her and Mal.

'Good morning,' he said politely. But what he did next made Jess see red. He turned and glanced inside the open door of Hazel Cottage.

Without thinking, Jess rushed towards him. Everything that Ada had told her about keeping a low profile, everything that she had had drummed into her over the years, was lost in a flash of anger. She was furious! How dare this stranger enter her home? It was the only thing in her life that was hers.

'Hey! What do you think you're doing in my home?' she demanded. She stood with her hands on her hips and a determined look on her face.

The young man swung around and stared hard at her.

'Your home?' he asked. 'Who are you?'

Jess pushed her feet forward in her boots. 'Jess Davidson. I belong to Ada, the housekeeper.'

The man gave this a moment's thought and then held out his hand. 'I'm Alfie McNally, James's son.'

Jess took his hand but didn't quite know what to do. She wasn't sure whether she should run and hide or if she should curtsey. She shook it. Alfie was tall and skinny, but there was something pleasant about his features that made her unafraid.

'Is this really your home?' he asked, peering inside the

woodshed again. Jess noticed his accent; it wasn't the warm Wearside accent of Ryhope folk. Then she noticed the horrified expression that flickered across his face as he took in the basic arrangements and her meagre possessions.

'It's called Hazel Cottage,' she said. She took a step inside, claiming her space.

Alfie stepped back and they skirted around each other until Jess had politely but firmly ushered him outside. They glared at each other for a long time. There was something about the girl that Alfie felt reflected in himself. It was a feeling that twisted in his stomach.

Mal was watching them. He was ready to help Jess the minute she looked as if she might need him, but she seemed able to handle Alfie. Still, he kept a careful eye on them, just in case.

'My father is arriving later today. I travelled on the earlier trains,' Alfie explained. 'It's my first time at the Uplands and I was curious when I saw this shed.'

'Does Ada – Mrs Davidson – know you've arrived, sir?' Jess asked. There was anger in her voice that she tried to quell. She still felt affronted that he'd had the nerve to enter her home without an invitation.

Alfie shook his head. 'Where might I find her?'

Jess closed the door of Hazel Cottage firmly behind her. 'I'll take you to her, sir. Follow me.'

Alfie's arrival had surprised her, for nothing had been said about him in the letter that Ada had received. She was further surprised by the discovery that James McNally had a son. But then, she realised, she knew nothing about the McNally family at all.

'I'm sorry, Mr McNally,' she said. 'I didn't mean to sound rude.'

'Please, call me Alfie,' he said.

Jess looked into his dark eyes and her anger melted away. A peculiar sense took her over, and right there, at that moment, she felt safe. There was a warmth inside her heart, a contentment, a comfort that Alfie brought.

'No, sir,' she said firmly. 'You're Mr McNally to me.' She knew it was the right thing to say. It was what Ada would expect of her.

'As you wish,' Alfie said. There was a shyness to his voice that hinted at a lack of confidence, one that Jess recognised in herself at times.

'If you'll wait in the drawing room, sir,' she said, 'I'll fetch the housekeeper for you.'

Mal watched the exchange between Jess and Alfie with jealousy building in his heart. He had heard Alfie's words, enough to know that the stranger was a McNally, a son of the master of the house. He brought the spade down heavily to the soil. He remembered things his dad had told him, gossip about James McNally from Ryhope's pubs. They were things that neither he nor his dad would dare repeat in front of his mam.

'Alfie McNally? He's just like his bloody dad,' he muttered under his breath now. 'Thinks he can have any woman he wants.'

Jess was unaware of the emotions rushing through Mal's heart and mind. She had no idea he was developing feelings for her. And she certainly didn't know how upset he was over her encounter with Alfie McNally. She headed to Ada's room to give her the news that Alfie had arrived. She never looked back at Alfie or Mal. If she had done so, she would have seen the look of concern on Alfie's face and the look of jealousy on Mal's.

* * *

That night, when the bells of St Paul's chimed eight, Jess was inside Hazel Cottage lying on her bed. She hadn't seen much of Ada that day; the housekeeper had been kept so busy that she'd only just had time to wish Jess a happy birthday. There was a lot Jess wanted to talk to her about, for Ada had promised to explain her cryptic words about the McNallys. But it would have to wait until this evening was over.

Pebble lay by Jess's side on her bed and the door was tight shut so the dog couldn't run on the lawns. Jess thought of Ada again, working hard inside the Uplands. Ada had refused to bring in a girl from the village, too proud to admit she needed help. Jess worried about her, could picture her walking slowly from the dining room to the kitchen with plates and bowls. She would be in agony, pain shooting up her back with every step. Jess felt helpless, but what could she do? It wasn't right that she couldn't help Ada. It wasn't fair. But she had sworn she wouldn't leave Hazel Cottage that night, or any other while James was at the Uplands. She had to keep out of his way.

She sighed, and closed her eyes. The peace and quiet didn't last long, however. She was disturbed by men's voices, arguing outside on the lawn. She kept as still as she could and prayed that Pebble wouldn't bark. Ada had told her to keep the dog quiet. She listened and tried to make out who the voices belonged to as they continued to bicker.

'Be polite to him, boy! He's important!' a voice roared. Jess recognised it immediately as it drifted across the lawn. It was James McNally, of that she had no doubt. But who was the other man?

'I never wanted to come. I'm only here because Mother forced you to bring me.'

Jess recognised the voice from earlier that day. It was James's son Alfie.

'And I still don't understand why we had to travel separately.'

'I had business to attend to before I left Scarborough,' James said.

He turned his head from his son. It had been a tasty bit of business indeed. It was his last chance to meet up with Jeanie before the herring girls left for the season. There was silence before Alfie spoke again.

'You didn't tell me about the girl.'

'What girl?'

'The one who lives in the shed.'

'Keep away from her,' James said. Jess heard an urgency to his words and his voice rose in anger. 'Keep away from that shed. If I find out you've been talking to that girl, I'll—'

'What?' Alfie taunted. 'What'll you do, Dad? She seemed perfectly nice to me. And yet . . .'

'What?' James growled. 'Out with it.'

'Yet you allow her to live in a shed, little more than a hovel? It's not fit for a dog, never mind a girl. And where does she work, this girl? Is she a maid in the house? Then why not let her live in the housekeeper's room?'

James's stomach turned with nausea. He had drunk too much port with his dinner. He'd have much preferred rum, but the men from the Ryhope Coal Company had no taste for it. However, he knew the sick feeling came less from the effects of alcohol than from hearing his son's words. He looked at Alfie's face. He recognised concern in the boy's eyes, but was there more to it? Was it desire Alfie felt? There could be no denying that if the girl had her mother's looks, she would turn any man's head.

'Don't you dare speak to her again!' he cried. 'Do you hear me?'

'Oh, I hear you, Father. But there's a lot I don't understand.'

James felt his stomach twist with a feeling he had to dismiss as quickly as he could.

'Get back inside,' he hissed. 'And remember, treat the fellas in there with the respect they deserve. We're going to need them on our side if we want to invest.'

Jess lay still, hardly breathing. Had she heard right? Was Alfie defending her? And why had it made James so angry to hear his son's words?

James stood alone. He couldn't bear to think that Alfie's feelings for Jess might be more than just friendly concern. Perhaps he'd had too much port and had imagined the look in his son's eyes when he spoke of Jess just now. Please, God, he thought, let it just be my imagination running away with me. How remiss he had been, letting Alfie travel alone to the Uplands. But he hadn't been able to resist an hour with Jeanie at the Sandside Inn. He knew he could never tell Alfie who the girl in the woodshed was. It was unthinkable. He could not – *would* not – risk news of his daughter reaching Scarborough. He would be ostracised by them all. He'd be cut out of his father's will, and Shirley would sue for divorce. James took a breath of night air and headed back indoors. He needed to ensure that Alfie and Jess never met again, but how would he keep them apart?

When he returned to the dining room, the men were in high spirits. He shot a look towards Alfie, who ignored him.

'Are we having pudding, James?' pit manager Joe Marshall called.

'Yes, where's pudding?' echoed deputy manager Benjamin Pascoe.

James looked around the table. The men were drunk, acting like spoiled children, but he had no choice other than to humour them. He not only desired their patronage, he was desperate for it.

Where was Mrs Davidson? She should have been in the room an hour since, serving coffee and cake. With no coffee to help sober them, the guests had taken to drinking more port; James saw that they had opened a third bottle.

'Where's your damn woman?' demanded Joe Marshall from his position at the head of the table.

'I'll go and find her,' James said.

He was glad to escape the room and the childish behaviour of the men. He much preferred the company of women; they were never so raucous and loud. He knew he'd be facing a dry spell as far as the ladies were concerned during this stay at the Uplands. A part of him wondered if Shirley had deliberately sent Alfie to Ryhope to keep an eye on him. Alfie was old enough now to understand the ways of men. All the more reason, James thought, for him to ensure his son never saw the girl in the woodshed again. He pushed her to the back of his mind. He would deal with that problem in the morning. For now, he needed to find the blasted housekeeper. Where on earth could she be?

As he reached the kitchen, he called out, 'Mrs Davidson. We're waiting for dessert.'

There was no reply, and so he strode into the room. 'Mrs Davidson, I said we're—'

He stopped, his heart in his mouth. There in front of him, lying on the kitchen floor, was the housekeeper. He flew to her side. 'Mrs Davidson. Wake up! Wake up!' He shook her shoulder, willing her to open her eyes. The men in the dining room were calling for him, yelling for more port, screaming for coffee. He'd be a laughing stock in the morning when news of this got out. There was no response. No breath from her lips or pulse at her wrist. 'God damn it!' he cursed.

He stood and looked down at the body lying at his feet. He knew that the doctor should be called and the coroner informed. Then another thought crossed his mind, and a mischievous smile played across his lips. His problems in life were many, but Ada's death had solved two of them in one fell swoop. For sixteen years she'd been the only other person who had known the truth about the girl who lived in the Uplands' grounds. Now it was over. She had taken his secret to her grave. And with Ada gone, there was no need for the girl in the woodshed to stay. Relief flooded through him. With the girl banished from the Uplands, Alfie would never meet her again. The second problem had been solved. James laid a hand on the kitchen table.

'Father?'

He spun round to find Alfie at the kitchen door. He gave a little cough, affecting concern.

'It's Mrs Davidson, son. She's gone, must have fallen. Run and fetch the doctor, Anderson's his name. He lives on Stockton Road. Ask anyone on the way, they'll tell you where to find him.'

Alfie ran from the kitchen. James stood alone. He looked down at Ada's dead body. He'd tell his guests first, apologise to them and send them away. Then, when the body had been taken, he had business to attend to with the girl in the shed.

Chapter Six

Jess felt a rush of cold air on her face and looked up to see a shadow at her door. Pebble jumped from the bed and barked.

'Ada?' she called. But when Pebble growled, Jess knew it wasn't Ada. She leapt out of bed and picked up the fire poker. 'Who are you?' she called. She raised the poker, ready to strike. 'Show yourself!'

'Who am I? Now there's a question.'

Jess recognised James McNally's voice. 'Get away from me!' she yelled. 'Get away or I'll use this. I'll set my dog on you. Go!'

James didn't move.

Jess gripped the poker tight and took a step forward. What was he doing inside her home? Nothing made sense. Where was Ada?

'There's no need for alarm,' James said calmly. 'I'm James McNally.'

'Pebble, quiet,' Jess ordered. 'What do you want?'

'There are two things you should know. The first is that you can no longer live here,' James said coldly.

Jess wondered if this was a nightmare from which

she'd not yet woken. What on earth was going on?

'And the second is that the housekeeper is dead.'

The ground seemed to shift under Jess's feet. 'No!' she screamed. 'I don't believe you! Get out!' She gripped the poker tight and took another step towards James.

James lunged and grabbed Jess's arm. He twisted it, and the poker fell to the floor. Jess yanked her arm from his painful grip.

'Listen to me,' he said. 'The old woman has gone. Believe it, because it's true.'

For a few moments Jess was too stunned to speak. When she finally found her voice, it left her with force. 'No!' she roared. 'No!' She stepped towards James, her features illuminated by the moonlight that streamed in through the shed window.

It was then that James McNally came face to face with his daughter for the very first time. He watched, intrigued, as the girl in the shed became flesh and blood in front of his eyes.

Jess was screaming now, denying the truth of what he had just told her. 'She can't be dead! No!'

James did nothing to help her. He simply watched as Jess's shock settled into something else, something raw and painful and hard. And as he watched, the sight of her disturbed him. There could be no denying who she was, with her long dark hair and that look about her. Oh, that look. Memories of Mary Liddle came to him unbidden. The lass standing in front of him had her mother's beauty all right. And what would she be now . . . sixteen? The same age Mary was on the night they lay together . . .

He shook his head to dismiss the past. He was here to get rid of the secret that had darkened his life.

'I must go to Ada,' Jess cried. She ran at James, expecting him to move away from the door. But he stood his ground. Pebble barked furiously and James kicked out. The dog fell like a rag.

'I need to see Ada. I demand to see her!' Jess shouted. She was confused, angry, trying desperately to make sense of what was going on.

'You're not in a position to demand anything,' James said.

Jess ran at him again, this time with all the force she had in her. James blocked her at every turn. She started screaming at him, yelling at him to get out of the way. Pebble struggled to his feet and growled as she hit out blindly.

'What have you done to Ada? Where is she?'

'Get off me, girl,' James shouted.

Jess was no match for him. He caught her wrist again and pinned her against the door. She couldn't move.

'Now listen to me,' he said. 'Mrs Davidson is dead. The doctor has taken her body. And as of now, you do not deserve to live here.'

An icy chill filled Jess's heart. It was that word again. *Deserve*. Ada had used it when she'd tried to tell her something the day before. Now she would never know.

'I'm not leaving. It's my home,' she said. She was too shocked by what had happened to take it all in.

'I want you gone before daybreak,' James hissed. He kicked at Pebble again. This time the dog moved more quickly, leaping up at him and growling through bared teeth. James let go of Jess.

'Daybreak,' he said. 'And take that bloody dog with you.' He turned and left the woodshed.

Jess slumped on to her bed and Pebble sat at her feet. She wanted to run to the house to find Ada, to see if James's words were true. But hadn't James just told her that Ada's body had been taken away? What would be the point of going inside the Uplands? Oh, what would she do without Ada? Ada had been all she had known. She'd been her mother and father rolled into one; had acted as her sister and best friend. Jess wasn't prepared for this. She wasn't ready to let Ada go. Her heart felt sawn in two. She was raw with the pain of losing the one person in the world she loved.

She closed her eyes and let darkness take her over. She wanted to cry, scream, let tears fall down her face, and yet no tears came. Her legs began to shake as the shock took hold of her, and only then did her tears begin to flow.

How long she sat crying, she didn't know. But by the time she had no more tears left, the sun was beginning to rise. Jess's heart was heavy. Where was she to go? She wondered if she should plead with James McNally to let her stay. And then she thought of Alfie. There'd been a friendliness to him when she'd met him the day before. Maybe he would help.

She pulled her skirt and blouse over her nightdress and stuffed her bare feet into her boots. With Pebble at her heels she ran across the lawn, determined to find out what had happened. But there was no one at the Uplands to ask. She peered through windows and knocked on doors. Nothing. No sounds from within, no movement in the grounds. She ran to the window of the kitchen, Ada's domain, hoping for a clue, but all she saw were pots and pans waiting to be scrubbed. Ada's metal bucket was filled with water, ready to mop the floor. Had she fallen?

Jess wondered. There was a mark on the floor, a dark reddish-brown stain. Was that Ada's blood?

Jess felt as if she'd been punched in the chest. The emotion hit her as hard and painful as any strike. She tore herself from the window and headed back to Hazel Cottage. She gathered her clothes together. She picked up the birthday card from Estelle and Arthur and slipped it into her skirt pocket. With the pile of clothes in her arms, she left the cottage. Pebble walked at her side, stopping only to lift his leg against a hazel tree. Jess headed for the side gate, and when she reached it, she paused. She turned to look back at Hazel Cottage, saw the pot of pansies that Mal had given her for her birthday. But it was too heavy to carry and she knew she must leave it behind. She stepped through the gate and closed it behind her. She heard the familiar sound of the latch. Would she ever hear it again?

Standing outside the gate, she forced herself forward, one foot in front of the other. She had no idea where to go. Should she find Dr Anderson, ask him what had happened to Ada? She walked as if in a dream, barely aware of her surroundings, just a girl and her dog taking a stroll along Cliff Road. She headed along Church Ward and saw the village green ahead. She would sit there a while, she decided. It would give her time to think. She was still in shock over Ada and in distress at James McNally's harshness. She wondered what Ada had been trying to tell her the day before. Was all of this connected somehow? Did James know what Ada had been planning to say? Her mind was playing tricks on her. She heard Ada's voice in her head, warning her not to let her imagination run away with her. Oh Ada. Jess felt as if the older woman was walking alongside her, and the thought gave her an uneasy comfort as her heart broke in two.

Jess sat on a wooden bench, Pebble at her feet. She heard the bells of St Paul's chime the hours. She had no desire to walk on, for where could she go? Who could she turn to? All she had ever known was Ada, and without her, she was lost. She stared ahead. She didn't move; she couldn't. It was all she could do to remember to breathe. Her home had been taken. How would she carry on?

Lost in her thoughts, she was unaware of people walking past and looking at her. She didn't see the village farm lads eyeing her curiously as they went about their business. She didn't notice Hetty Burdon from the Albion Inn open up her pub for the afternoon trade. And she didn't spot a small, thin woman bustling towards her. The woman wore a dark green coat with a black scarf tucked tidily into the collar. An old green hat sat askew on her head. Jess only became aware of her when she felt a movement at her side. She was shocked to see that someone had joined her on the bench.

'Penny for them?' the woman said. She didn't wait for a reply before carrying straight on. 'Although I can guess what'll be going through your mind. It's the same as what's going through mine. I'll miss her terribly and I'm sure you will too.'

'Do you mean Ada?' Jess asked. She turned to the woman and saw a thin face and pursed lips. There was a hardness to the woman's features and a clipped tone as she spoke. Jess couldn't recall Ada having mentioned any friends to her, but then perhaps there was a lot about Ada she didn't know.

'It's a sad state of affairs and no mistake,' the woman

continued. 'I've been to see Dr Anderson this morning. Seems she had a fall; working too hard, of course. That was her trouble. The funeral is set for Thursday at two. You'll be attending, I'm sure. It's at St Paul's, although she wasn't a religious sort of woman.'

'No, she wasn't,' Jess said. 'But who . . . ?'

'Who am I? I'm Lil Mahone. Mrs. I grew up with Ada. Lived next door to her on Tunstall Street before her husband died. That's when she moved to the Uplands, you know. I've known her all my life. I'd heard she'd taken her niece's child under her wing. You've turned out a bonny lass. Anyway, I was walking home after I'd finished work at the Albion Inn and I thought to myself, that looks like Ada's girl, the one from the Uplands. I took one look at your face and I knew you must have heard the sad news. And here I am.'

'I don't know what I'll do without her,' Jess said.

Lil patted her hand. 'Now, now. There's no need for more tears.' She looked at the pile of clothes that sat between her and Jess on the bench. 'Going somewhere?'

Jess opened her mouth to speak, but no words left her lips. She remembered something Ada used to tell her about keeping her cards close to her chest.

'Just moving some things,' she said. She had no reason to distrust Lil Mahone, but on the other hand, she'd only just met the woman and knew nothing about her.

But Lil hadn't lived in Ryhope all her life without learning a thing or two. She knew a young girl in trouble when she saw one, and she reckoned the lass sitting on the bench next to her was clearly in need of her years of wisdom.

'There's always widow women looking for a lodger in

Ryhope. If you're after somewhere to stay, that is. But if you're not, then you won't need my advice.'

Jess remained silent. Lil stood and gathered her handbag.

'Well, I've said my piece. Like I say, her funeral's on Thursday at two. I expect I'll see you then. Is there a wake planned afterwards at the Uplands?'

Jess shook her head. Lil sniffed.

'Ada gave her life to that place and they go and snub her like that. I don't know what the world's coming to. A funeral's not a funeral without a nice bit of ham afterwards.'

And with that, she walked away.

The short chat with Lil Mahone had pulled Jess from her reverie, and with the day turning colder, she knew she had to get indoors before she froze. She stood and took her jacket from the pile, pushing her arms into it. Pebble looked up, waiting to be given an order. But Jess didn't know which way to turn.

'You choose,' she told the dog.

Pebble cocked his head to one side.

'Whichever direction you walk, I'll follow,' she said.

He sat down and whined.

'Come on then,' she sighed.

She decided to steer clear of the Uplands. Returning was not an option. Whatever happened now, she would not beg to be taken back. She might not have much to show for her life, but Ada had always told her to take pride. She headed away from the green, towards the Railway Inn. From there she turned right and walked up Station Road. All the time she kept looking, wondering, daring herself to end up at the one place she hoped she might be welcome. She walked past Arthur Street and Scotland Street. And at the end of Richardson Terrace, Pebble ambled ahead.

Jess smiled for the first time that day. It was as if the little dog knew where they were heading. She followed him as he trotted ahead. His nose sniffed the air and his head turned at each doorway. When they reached the Atkinsons' house, he bounded up the garden path and jumped up at the front door, barking over and over. Jess followed warily, unsure of the reception she would receive. On either side of the path she saw vegetable patches where green tops of potatoes were shooting through soil. She didn't need to knock. Pebble had made sure their arrival had been heard. The door swung open and Mal stood there. Pebble rushed past him, straight into the hallway, seeking out his brother, Stone.

'Jess?' Mal said. He was shocked and confused to see her. And why was there a pile of clothes in her arms? He thought perhaps it was something to do with laundry, something for his mam.

'Is your mam in?' Jess asked.

'Mam? Yes, she is. Do you want to see her? Are you all right?'

Jess faltered on the doorstep.

'Sorry,' Mal said. He stood aside. 'Where's my manners? Come in. I'll fetch her.'

Jess stepped into the hallway. It was dark inside. She heard Pebble barking, and another dog too. She followed Mal into a small room. At one end was a sofa with three brown seat cushions, and an armchair covered with the same brown cloth. Opposite was the coal fire with pots and pans hanging from the mantelpiece above. There was a smell she couldn't place. It was pleasant and homely, as if bread had recently been baked, and it made her feel welcome. But it also made her stomach growl with hunger. Doubts spiralled in her mind. Had she a right to be there? Mal had welcomed her, but there were unasked questions in the look he'd given her. She heard a noise: heavy footsteps coming down the stairs.

'Jess? Is everything all right, love?'

It was Estelle. She reached for the clothes in Jess's arms.

'Here, let me take those,' she said. 'Mal? Put the kettle on the fire. I dare say Jess has got time for a cuppa while she's here. Now, what's this all about? Is Ada all right?'

At the mention of Ada's name, Jess felt her body fold in on itself. Her whole world had gone. She sank on to the sofa, lost in her grief. Estelle sat beside her and wrapped an arm around her shoulders. Mal hovered. He hated to see his friend upset, but he had no idea how to help. Estelle caught his gaze and shook her head. It was his signal to leave the room.

Through gulps of breath and many tears, Jess told Estelle everything. She told her about the blood on Ada's kitchen floor and Lil Mahone's words. She told her about James McNally throwing her out of her home.

'I had nowhere else to go,' she sobbed. 'I didn't know what to do.'

Estelle squared her shoulders. 'I'm going to have words with McNally,' she said.

Jess was horrified. 'No, you mustn't! He's gone now, the Uplands is empty. I checked all the windows and doors. And I refuse to ever go back. I won't live under him at the Uplands, not now I know what he's like.'

Estelle's voice was gentle but firm. 'You can stay here tonight, Jess. I'd like to offer more, and if I could, I would. But it's a small house, love, too small at times for just the three of us. What with two men about the place, bathing in front of the fire when they come in from gardening, well, you can see how we're fixed. There's not much room and not a pinch of privacy. And we can't afford another mouth to feed. I wish I could tell you otherwise. I take in as much dressmaking as I can, but it pays a pittance and we only just about keep the wolf from the door. But you're welcome to stay the night. There's an armchair you can sleep in, and I've a spare blanket.'

Jess sniffed back her tears and hugged Estelle gratefully.

The next morning after Arthur left for work, Estelle brewed a pot of tea and sat down with Jess and Mal at the kitchen table.

'Where will you go, love?' she asked.

Jess shook her head. 'I don't know.'

'Is there anyone who knew Ada, perhaps, who might be able to offer a room?' Estelle suggested.

Jess thought hard. The only person who came to mind was the odd little woman who'd talked to her on the bench on the village green the previous day.

'There's a woman, Lil Mahone. I spoke to her yesterday.'

Estelle raised her eyebrows. 'Hope you didn't tell her any secrets. She's Ryhope's worst gossip, that one.'

'She said there's always widow women in Ryhope looking for lodgers. I might find one if I only knew where to start looking.'

Estelle bit her lip. 'Can't say I've heard of any,' she

said. 'But there used to be a woman . . . Gilbert, I think her name was.' She shook her head. 'No. Gilbey. Miss Gilbey. She runs a . . .' She paused. She'd been about to call it a cheap rooming house, but that was the most unkind way of describing the home Miss Gilbey ran. Miss Gilbey took in girls from the streets who had nowhere else to go. 'There's no harm in trying there first. It's on St Paul's Terrace, by the Grand Cinema. Ask anyone, they'll tell you where to find it. She's a bit stern, but she's got a good heart. I heard she even took on guardianship for some of the girls who've lodged with her. That's something you might want to think about now that Ada's gone. You'll need a legal guardian to mind your affairs till you're twenty-one.'

Jess's head was swimming. 'Affairs?'

'Finances, schooling, that sort of thing.'

'But I haven't got any finances. I haven't got anything, and I'm not about to go back to school,' Jess said. She searched Estelle's worried face. 'Do I really need a guardian?'

'What about your mam's family?'

'My mam?' Jess said, confused. 'I only ever had Ada.'

Mal took a sip of his tea. 'Ada told everyone you were her niece's child. Didn't she ever mention your family?'

Jess shook her head. 'Never. I asked her many times, but she would never tell me anything. She said she was waiting till I was old enough, when I turned sixteen. But it was the night of my sixteenth birthday when she died.'

Estelle placed her hand on Jess's arm. 'You know, I always thought there was more to Ada than she ever let on. If there is no family, you might want to think about where you really came from.'

101

Jess dropped her gaze to the floor. 'Go and see Miss Gilbey,' Estelle said. 'See what she's got to say.'

'What about Pebble?' Jess asked.

At the mention of his name, the dog padded across the floor and laid his head on Jess's lap.

'Leave him with me,' Mal said. 'I'll look after him for you.'

'Mal's right, pet,' Estelle said. 'It'll be harder to get a room if you've got a dog in tow.'

Later that morning, following directions from a helpful, chatty woman who worked at Ryhope's Grand Electric Cinema, Jess found Miss Gilbey's house. She stood on the pavement looking up at it. It was a solid building, two storeys tall, with a square bay window downstairs at the front. Upstairs were two sash windows looking down to the street. The whole terrace was made of brick, not the limewash that covered the cottages in many Ryhope streets. Steps led up from the pavement to the neat and tidy front door. The door and window frames were painted black and the colour gave Jess a sense of foreboding. Other houses in the street had their paintwork in green or red.

She walked up the steps with her bundle of clothes and knocked at the door with her free hand. As she waited, she squared her shoulders, took a deep breath and fixed a smile on her face. The door opened to reveal a tall, thin woman with dark cropped hair. She wore a long black coat that hung on her skinny frame, and on her feet she wore black boots. Her face was neither kind nor too stern, and her eyes were piercing blue. She looked older than Estelle but not as old as Ada.

Jess gulped. 'Miss Gilbey?'

Miss Gilbey was direct and to the point. 'In need of a room?'

'Yes, I—'

'Then you'd better come in.'

She stood to one side and Jess entered. It took a few moments for her eyes to adjust fully to her surroundings. The hallway was painted dark green, with a dark tiled floor. Several doors led off it, and all of them were painted the same colour. There was a scent in the air, a sweet, fruity scent that Jess guessed might be polish. It smelled similar to the one that Ada used to use.

'Are you working?' Miss Gilbey asked.

Jess shook her head. 'No.'

Miss Gilbey rubbed her chin thoughtfully and looked her up and down. 'Where have you come from?'

'The Uplands,' Jess said. 'I lived with the housekeeper, Ada Davidson. She died.'

'So I heard. News travels fast in Ryhope. Done some housekeeping, have you? Cooking, cleaning?'

Jess kept her back straight and fixed her gaze on Miss Gilbey. She knew that what she said and the way she presented herself could mean the difference between being allowed to stay and being thrown out on the streets.

'Yes. I can cook and clean and do gardening.'

'I've not much call for the latter, but I can use a girl who can cook. There'll be cleaning to do too, and my standards are high. Think you can manage it?'

'I know I can, Miss Gilbey.'

Miss Gilbey pointed at the pile of clothes in Jess's arms. 'That all you've got?'

Jess nodded.

'I've a small room, upstairs at the back. We'll give it a week's trial in exchange for you working here. You'll keep the place spotless and cook two meals a day. And don't pick fights with the other girls.'

Jess felt her heart beating wildly in her chest. Was she really being allowed to stay? 'Yes, Miss Gilbey.'

'Got nits, girl?'

'No, Miss Gilbey.'

'Disease? Jaundice? Illness of any kind?'

'No.'

'Are you pregnant?'

Jess gasped. 'No!'

'Got any bairns?'

'No.'

'Boyfriend? Husband?'

Mal's face flashed through Jess's mind. 'No.'

'Any family in Ryhope?'

Jess dropped her gaze to the floor. 'No.'

'Do you have a guardian?'

'Do I need one?'

'If you don't have one, I could apply to the town hall to take on guardianship for you. I do it for most of the girls without family. Would you like me to make enquiries once I know if you'll fit in here?'

'Yes, please,' Jess whispered.

'Right then,' Miss Gilbey said. She headed towards the stairs. 'Follow me. I'll show you your room and you can start in the kitchen immediately.'

Jess didn't move. 'There's just one thing, Miss Gilbey,' she said shyly.

Miss Gilbey glared at her.

Jess pushed her feet forward in her boots before she

carried on. 'Thursday at two p.m., I've a funeral to attend.'

Miss Gilbey looked as if she'd been punched. 'You're asking for time off already?' she said.

'It's Mrs Davidson's funeral,' Jess said, trying to keep her voice even. 'I can't miss it. I won't.'

A smile played across Miss Gilbey's lips. 'Oh! You're laying down your own terms already?' She had to hand it to this one; she didn't often get girls demanding time off the minute they walked through the door. She liked the fire in Jess but knew she'd need to keep an eye on her. 'I'll excuse you for the funeral, but you're to come straight back here after it ends. Got it?'

'Thank you, Miss Gilbey.'

Jess's room was small but clean. As with the rest of the house, the walls and woodwork were all a dark shade of green. The linoleum floor was patterned with geometric shapes, but what Jess noticed first was that there were two single beds in the room.

'I'll be sharing?' she asked Miss Gilbey. She was surprised. She hadn't expected this and wasn't sure she liked it. She'd never shared with anyone other than Ada. And all the years she'd lived in the woodshed, she'd grown used to her own company. But what choice did she have other than to accept the way her life had now turned?

'Not straight away,' Miss Gilbey said. She didn't offer any more explanation. 'Pick the bed you want. Put your clothes in the chest and come down to the kitchen. I'll be waiting.'

There were two other girls living in Miss Gilbey's house, Jess was to discover. Miss Gilbey's rooms were on the ground floor where she had a living room of her own and a large bedroom too. Upstairs, Jess's room was at the back where the empty bed next to hers unsettled her greatly. Who would be joining her in the room, and when? There was a second, much larger bedroom at the front, currently occupied by two older girls, Amelia and Jane. Amelia was stocky, with chunky legs and hefty arms. She had red hair and her face was dotted with freckles. Next to her, Jane looked almost comical in that she was wiry and thin with stringy dark hair and a pale, washed-out complexion. The two girls could not have appeared more different, yet they got on well together.

They left the house each morning to work at the store, but when they returned in the evening, they were distant and aloof towards Jess. Not once did they thank her for the food she cooked them or the way she neatly turned down the sheets on their beds. Jess also had to clean the netty in the yard, her least favourite of all her harsh chores. She soon learned that Miss Gilbey did indeed have high standards as far as cleanliness went, and she made sure she was thorough and gave no cause for complaint. She settled in quickly, put to work by Miss Gilbey, who was often away from the house leaving Jess alone. But although her hands were kept busy, she missed Ada constantly. Her tears came often, mingling with the washing-up water while she sang to keep her spirits from sinking.

Ada's funeral was a small ceremony, with no fuss. It was what she would have wanted. Jess was there, of course, along with the Atkinsons. Lil Mahone was sitting in the front pew, her favourite seat. Each time a mourner arrived, she turned her head to see if she recognised them.

A few women from the village who had known Ada as a girl came to pay their respects, as did a couple of men who remembered Ada's husband Martin.

Reverend Daye opened his Bible and read the Twenty-Third Psalm. Then he began to pay tribute to Ada, calling her a hard-working woman who, he believed, would be grateful to be reunited with her beloved husband at last. After the prayers, he called Jess to the front as she'd asked him to do. She wanted to pay tribute to Ada in her own way. But it was not with a prayer or words of remembrance; it was by singing Ada's favourite hymn. For although Ada had sworn she wasn't a religious soul, Jess had often heard her singing heartfelt songs of praise. Sometimes, while Ada worked in the kitchen at the Uplands and Jess was in Hazel Cottage, the two of them would sing together, their voices mingling across the lawn.

Jess took a deep breath and looked out into the small group of mourners.

'I'd like to sing this for Ada. For Mrs Davidson. It was her favourite hymn,' she said.

And then she tilted her chin, opened her mouth and began to sing.

'All things bright and beautiful, all creatures great and small . . .'

Her voice took everyone by surprise with its clarity and power, every note sweet and true.

'All things wise and wonderful, the Lord God made them all. Each little flower that opens, each little bird that sings . . .'

In the pews, Estelle reached for Arthur's hand.

'He made their glowing colours, He made their tiny wings.'

The glorious sound from the girl with the long dark hair rose all the way up to the rafters.

Lil Mahone rose from her seat in the front pew and joined in with Jess word for word. No hymnbook or song sheet was needed. The words were etched on everyone's hearts. More of Ada's friends stood to sing, and Jess looked out at them all. Estelle too rose, followed by Arthur and Mal.

All the mourners were on their feet now, their voices rising in a homage that did Ada proud.

'All things bright and beautiful, all creatures great and small. All things wise and wonderful, the Lord God made them all.'

After the funeral, Jess excused herself from Estelle and Arthur's company, saying she needed a breath of fresh air. Mal offered to walk with her, and she accepted his support.

'Would you like to stroll down to the beach?' he asked once they were out on the street. 'We could take the dogs for a run on the sands. Or I could escort you back to Miss Gilbey's, if that's what you'd prefer.'

Jess shook her head. 'I want to go to the Uplands. There's something I need to do.'

Mal looked hard at her. 'Dad says there's been no one there since Ada died. He's not sure if we should continue keeping up the grounds. We don't know if we'll get paid.'

'I'm hoping to find it empty,' Jess said. 'Will you keep watch for me, Mal?'

'But it's locked up, Dad said.'

'I think I might know a way in.'

Mal was unsure, but he wanted to help. He knew how

important it was for Jess, otherwise she wouldn't have asked. He followed her round to the Uplands' side gate.

How familiar it all was, Jess thought. Just a few short days ago she was living here and Ada was alive. Hazel Cottage stood exactly where it always had. But it wasn't Hazel Cottage she had come to see this time.

'You can't go in there, Jess!' Mal warned.

'I've got to,' Jess said.

'What if the police come?' he said. 'Let me go instead.'

'No.' Jess was firm. 'I've got to do this myself. Keep watch for me, Mal. Help me up.'

Mal locked his hands together and bent low. Jess stepped up, balancing her other foot on the narrow ledge on the wall. Mal held tight, carrying her weight in his hands until Jess found her footing in the uneven stones.

'You all right up there?' he asked.

Jess didn't reply. She was concentrating hard on opening the window. It had never shut properly, and had always let in the rain. She knew the way it twisted at the frame and slid her fingers in to pull it open.

'Got it!' she called.

She pulled the window outwards, then heaved herself up to the wide stone ledge. Mal watched nervously from below.

Once inside the room, Jess jumped from the window down to the stone floor. Aside from the bed, there was a small chest of drawers, a dark wardrobe, a chair and a mat on the floor. That was it, the remains of Ada's life in the grandest home in Ryhope. Nothing had been touched since the day she died. It felt as if she might bustle in through the door at any moment with a duster in her hand, moaning about her bad back.

Jess walked towards the wardrobe and pulled open the heavy door. Inside were Ada's dresses and coats. She removed them and laid them on the bed. Clearing Ada's belongings was going to be one of the hardest things she'd ever done.

Next she went to the chest of drawers. In the top drawer were Ada's slips and drawers, neatly folded. Jess took them out carefully. She found Ada's blue pinny and her favourite brown velvet hat and piled everything on to the bed. She would keep anything that fitted her, for she needed clothes that weren't worn through, and she felt sure Ada wouldn't mind. When the top and middle drawers were empty, she kneeled on the linoleum floor and pulled open the bottom drawer. Here were letters and papers tied with string.

At the back of the drawer she spotted a spiral of red. She pulled it towards her, curious to see what it was, and was shocked to find it was scarlet ribbon. And not just one length, but two, both about ten inches long and an inch wide. She sat on the floor with the ribbons in her hand, turning them over, wondering where they had come from. In all her life, Jess had never seen Ada wear a ribbon of any colour, and certainly not scarlet. She looked at the piles of clothes and underwear on the bed. The colours were practical whites, browns and greens. Set against them, the scarlet ribbons looked indecent, as if dropped by a harlot's hand. She was puzzled and confused. Scarlet was not a colour she associated with Ada. What on earth were the ribbons doing in her drawer?

There was a noise from outside, a sound of footsteps and a dog barking.

'Jess!' Mal shouted. 'Jess! Someone's coming!'

Jess felt her heart pounding. She mustn't be caught in Ada's room. She stuffed the ribbons into her pocket, grabbed the pile of clothes, then climbed up on to the windowsill and jumped down to the grass below. Mal grabbed her arm as soon as her boots hit the ground.

'Run, come on, quick!' he whispered.

They didn't stop till they reached the village green, where they stood by the cattle market, panting, out of breath.

Mal leaned against the wall.

'You all right?' he asked.

Jess couldn't speak; her heart was still going like the clappers. She slipped her hand into her pocket, relieved to feel the ribbons safe inside, and wondered what their secret was.

Chapter Seven

At her home in The Crescent, Shirley Banks-McNally paced the drawing-room floor. In an armchair by the bay window sat her husband, James. Shirley was confused, trying to make sense of James and Alfie's sudden return from Ryhope.

'You said you'd be gone at least a week,' she said. 'I don't understand what's happened. Alfie won't speak a word about it and has locked himself in his room. And I know you're being less than truthful in the little you've told me. I can always tell when you're lying, you know.'

'I'm not lying!' James cried. 'The housekeeper died in the middle of the damn dinner party! I'm a laughing stock. I had to get away. Do you know how long I've been trying to get those men from the Ryhope Coal Company together for such a night? Do you?'

He and Shirley glared at each other.

'There's more to it than that,' Shirley said. 'Why won't Alfie speak? Mother always said I shouldn't have married you. I can't trust you. I never know what you're up to these days. You disappear off to that godforsaken place, leaving me here on my own—'

'Oh, bring your mother into this, go on!' James yelled. 'I thought you liked the peace and quiet of this fancy house when I was away. I might not be good enough for your mother, but by God, my money is!'

Shirley turned away, unable to face his anger.

'It's the truth and you know it!' he hissed. 'You live here in the best address in town, and all because of me. All four storeys of it. All six bay windows. All the balconies where the honeysuckle grows. It's all mine, Shirley. *Mine*. Those French windows on the first floor? *Mine*. The panelled doors, the fanlights, the Doric porch? *Mine!*'

Shirley raised her gaze and locked eyes with him. 'And who keeps it tended and clean?' she yelled back. 'Who sees to it that every inch of your precious palace is maintained to high standards? Who hires the staff to cook your meals and shine your shoes? Who pays the household bills and does the accounts for you? Who knows all your secrets, especially the ones you hide from your father? If he knew half of what you get up to, you'd be cast out of the family.'

James stormed towards the door. 'I've had enough. Get away with you, woman!'

'Give my regards to everyone at the Sandside Inn,' Shirley said calmly.

Her words stopped James in his tracks, and a chill made its way down his back.

'That *is* where you're going, isn't it?' she said. 'I hear you're a regular there. If you hurry, you might find the last of the herring girls, stinking of fish eyes and guts.'

He had been found out. He should have known Shirley was too clever not to know what he was up to.

'What are you waiting for, James? Hurry off to your

stinking whores, before they slither back to the sea.'

Without looking back, James left the room and slammed the door.

Left alone in the drawing room, Shirley fumed with anger. She needed to know what had gone on in Ryhope. Something had happened there, of that she was sure. Something more than the housekeeper passing away. She knew James too well. The death of a servant would never leave an emotional scar. And there was Alfie to consider. Since he'd returned from Ryhope with his father, he had said little and withdrawn to his room. No, something else must have happened for them to up and leave Ryhope so soon. Well, if James wasn't going to tell her the truth, she would get it from someone else. And she knew just the person to ask.

Upstairs in his room, Alfie heard the door slam below. His parents' anger with each other had drifted up the stairs. He'd heard every word of their row. The only time his mother seemed at peace was when his father was away from home. He thought back to the dinner party in Ryhope. It had ended in embarrassment, his father was right about that. The men from the coal company had been too drunk to discuss business or care about his offer of investment. His father might well be a laughing stock in Ryhope, but those men had not shown themselves in a good light either. And the truth of it was that everything that night had been overshadowed by the housekeeper's death.

It had been a tragic event, and yet his father had expressed no sadness about it. In fact, if Alfie was being honest, he would have said that the housekeeper's death had animated his father in a way Alfie felt was inappropriate, unseemly. Alfie didn't understand why they had left early the next morning, leaving the Uplands untouched after the drunken night. It was as if his father couldn't wait to get away. And there was more that he couldn't grasp. Why hadn't his father told his mother about the girl who lived in the grounds? And why had he acted so angrily when Alfie had asked him who she was?

He gazed out of his bedroom window. Ahead lay Scarborough's South Bay, where the sea sparkled under the blue autumn sky. Alfie saw the ornate iron bridge leading from St Nicholas Cliff to the Spa. Directly in front of his window were The Crescent Gardens, a small park with iron railings around.

A tapping at his bedroom door pulled him from his thoughts.

'Alfie, it's me.'

It was his mother. Alfie braced himself. Would he find her crying and upset after the argument he'd just overheard?

'Alfie?' she called again. 'Let me in, son. You and I need to talk.'

As Alfie slowly and hesitantly told his mother all he knew about the girl in the woodshed, James was out walking off his bad mood. He marched from The Crescent along Falconer Road and past the grandeur of the Palm Court Hotel. He needed a drink, but he wasn't foolish enough to head to the Sandside Inn this time. Shirley must have had him followed there one evening. The entrance to the Palm Court looked inviting, but he didn't stop. He was too well known in there and the hotel was too close to home. He needed somewhere to be alone with his thoughts.

He walked on, down St Nicholas Cliff. In front of him was the ornate Grand Hotel. It was a huge place, the largest hotel in Europe, designed to represent the theme of time. It had twelve floors, one for each month of the year, fifty-two chimneys for the weeks and four towers representing the seasons. It was said that there were three hundred and sixty-five rooms, one for each day of the year. The hotel had been built to attract the more affluent visitors who came to Scarborough to take the spa waters. It was a tourist destination through and through, and James thought it the perfect place for a drink. It would give him the anonymity he craved.

He walked up the impressive flight of stone steps to the hotel's main entrance. Inside, well-dressed couples lounged in the reception area, reading and drinking. A decorative staircase led from the lounge, and James took a minute to appreciate its beauty before heading to the bar beyond the main lobby. The tinkle of piano music drifted towards him from somewhere unseen. He sat at a table by a window overlooking the South Bay beach. A waiter appeared at his side and he ordered a beer, but then thought better of it and added a large rum to his order.

For an hour he sat watching from the window, his back turned to those in the bar. He had much on his mind and he needed to think. Watching the sea helped calm his mind, and by the time he'd finished his beer and polished off the rum, he knew exactly what he would do.

He walked quickly back to The Crescent, glancing at his watch. If he was quick, he'd catch the afternoon train to York and could be back in Ryhope by evening. He'd need to speak to his father about appointing a new housekeeper – that was the first thing he should do. But then he had another thought. No, the first thing he would do would be to hire someone to destroy the blasted woodshed. Then, when the grounds had been tended to and his dirty secret had gone, he would make amends with Mr Marshall and his men of the Ryhope Coal Company.

Arriving back at The Crescent, he flung some clothes into his travelling bag and left, ignoring Shirley's demands to know where he was going.

Shirley knew exactly where her husband was headed. After her talk with Alfie, she knew everything she needed to know about life at the Uplands. She had learned about the girl who lived in the woodshed and she thought it very odd. She had seen the way James's mood had turned after the housekeeper's death. None of it made sense to her. If running away to Ryhope was the way James wanted to handle things, then let him. But she'd be damned if she wasn't going to find out the truth for herself.

She went to the kitchen and gave instructions to her staff. Then she told Alfie of her plan to head to Ryhope in the coming days.

'Let me come with you, Mother,' he said. He was thinking of Jess, the girl in the woodshed. He was concerned about her. Something inside him made him feel protective towards her. It wasn't a feeling of lust, he knew. He'd had those feelings towards Beth, a serving girl who worked at the maritime college his father made him attend. What he felt for Jess was something else, different and pure. It was a safe, certain feeling, as if he wanted to help her, take her under his wing.

But Shirley refused her son's request to accompany her to Ryhope, and Alfie was crestfallen.

'If you see her, the girl, will you tell her I send a message of friendship?' he said.

Shirley felt her stomach turn. If the girl in the woodshed turned out to be someone James was having an affair with, a message of friendship would be the last thing she would want to deliver. She put her hand on her son's arm and kissed him lightly on the cheek.

'I'll do what I can,' she said.

It was a few days later when Shirley arrived in the great hall of Scarborough railway station with her vanity case in her hand. She walked to the ticket counter, where an elderly man waited to serve her.

'Good morning, Mrs McNally. Are you well? And how's your mother? We don't often see you in here. Off to York for the day, are you?'

Shirley hated such small talk. It was no one's business but hers where she was off to. 'Not today, John. I'd like a return ticket all the way to Ryhope East. First class. And my name, John, it's Mrs Banks-McNally. I'll be staying in York overnight and heading to Ryhope first thing in the morning.'

John gave her a look. He wondered if he should mention that he'd sold the same ticket to her husband a few days before. But Mr McNally's ticket had been a single, not a return. He glanced at her again. Her face was set, lips pursed, and she was drumming her fingers on his counter top. No, John thought, it was probably best not to mention anything, not with the bad mood she seemed to be in.

Shirley boarded the train to York. She needed to know the truth about the girl who lived in the grounds of her house. For the Uplands was as much hers as James's, given that they were married. Well, that was what her mother said, though Shirley knew the deeds belonged firmly to Angus, her father-in-law. Shirley needed to know what was going on in Ryhope. Confirmation of her suspicions about James's womanising in Scarborough was one thing. She could rise above him cavorting with the common herring girls. The girls who came and went with the tide posed no threat to her luxurious life at The Crescent. But what on earth was going on at the Uplands? Was the girl who lived in the grounds another of her husband's floozies? Was she living off James's money – money that should be going to Shirley and her son? Well, there was only one way to find out. Shirley settled herself into her seat. She was out for James's blood.

After an overnight stay at the Principal Hotel in York, with its impressive views of the Minster, her mood remained dark, although the sting of her anger had gone. She was focused now, intent on finding out the truth. And what then? she wondered. She could not risk the scandal of divorce. Gossip would spread around Scarborough and it would do her mother's nerves no good if Shirley became the object of such talk. But she could go to James's father and let him know the truth about his son, whatever she found out in Ryhope. She already had proof of her husband's nights spent with Scarborough's whores and fishwives. And now something suspicious was going on at

Ryhope, in the home James kept for his amusement. When she found out the truth, she would decide how best to use it. Perhaps she could convince Angus to set James up in his own flat in Scarborough, so he lived apart from her and their son. She'd have the house in The Crescent to herself and move her mother into the upstairs front room. That way, there would be no need for divorce and no whiff of scandal. She and Alfie could stay on at The Crescent, while James could live as he chose without bringing his errant ways into her home.

It was late in the afternoon by the time the train brought Shirley Banks-McNally to Ryhope East station. She alighted from her first-class carriage and pulled her jacket collar up to keep the autumn chill from her skin. A keen young porter appeared at her side.

'Help you with your luggage, miss?' he asked.

Shirley shook her head. All she carried was her handbag and her small overnight case. She looked up and down the platform through the steam.

'Where will I find the Uplands?' she asked.

The porter pointed to the far end of the platform and gave instructions. 'It'll take you ten or fifteen minutes to walk there,' he said.

Shirley thanked him and headed in the direction he indicated, making for the village green. Ahead of her she saw a lime-washed building, the Railway Inn. The sign above its door carried its name in ornate signage, designed to entice travellers inside. She walked straight past it. Ahead of her was another pub, the Albion Inn.

'This place has more watering holes than Scarborough!' she muttered under her breath.

She headed towards the Albion Inn, as the porter had instructed. She saw a woman sweeping the ground. She was a short woman, thin, wearing a black jacket and a green hat askew on her head, and was singing as she worked. As Shirley drew near, she caught the words of her song, something about dusky diamonds hewed from the earth. She remembered James telling her that Ryhope's fortunes were built on the business of coal, in which he was keen to invest. She thought of the deposit to the Ryhope Coal Company that he had made not long after Alfie had been born – a sum of £15 that he had taken from their accounts. Her husband was a foolish man, and Shirley couldn't recall seeing any return on that particular investment.

Ahead of her, the road split in two and she was unsure which way to turn. The woman outside the pub had caught sight of her and stopped singing. She stood with her hands clasped at the top of her broom handle, eyeing Shirley keenly.

'Which way to the Uplands?' Shirley asked.

The woman gave no response, and stared at Shirley's clothes and overnight bag. Shirley felt herself being scrutinised. This wouldn't have happened in Scarborough. There, with so many people going about their business and the number of visitors the seaside town brought in, few people had time to stop and stare.

'You a friend of Ada?' the woman asked sharply.

Shirley shook her head. 'Who's Ada?'

'So you're not a friend of Ada?'

Shirley gave an exasperated sigh. 'No. I don't know anyone by that name.'

'But you have business at the Uplands?'

'I own it,' Shirley said.

This seemed to knock the wind out of the woman's sails. 'Mrs McNally?' she asked.

'Mrs Banks-McNally.'

'We've never seen you in Ryhope before. I'd have remembered. We don't often get your sort round here.'

Shirley indicated the road with her hand. 'Which way?' she said.

'It's up there. Before you reach the corner where the village school is, turn right into Church Ward. You'll see the Uplands straight ahead.'

Shirley turned to leave, but the woman wasn't finished with her yet.

'Ada . . .'

'What about her?' Shirley said, exasperated.

'She was the housekeeper at the Uplands. Your housekeeper. She died not long since.'

Shirley set off towards the village school. After a few minutes, she heard a clatter of footsteps behind her.

'Mrs McNally?' Shirley turned to see the woman she'd just been talking to. She didn't have her sweeping brush with her this time, and a small black handbag hung over one arm.

'Thought I'd never catch you up,' the woman panted. 'I've just finished my work for the day and thought I'd walk with you, make sure you find your way there.'

Shirley was certain she could have found her own way. She felt annoyed that the odd little woman had made it her business to walk with her.

'I'm Lil Mahone, if you'd like to know,' she said.

'Nice to meet you, Mrs Mahone,' Shirley replied, being as polite as she could manage under the circumstances.

122

'I was a good friend of Ada's, you know. She told me everything that went on at the Uplands.'

Shirley stopped in her tracks. 'Everything?'

Lil nodded sagely and pursed her lips.

Shirley knew she'd have to choose her words carefully. 'My husband, Mr McNally, has given room in the grounds to a young woman . . .' she began.

'That's right, Jess Davidson.'

Shirley's heart lurched at the confirmation of what Alfie had told her. 'I wonder if she is about?' She had devised a lie in case an opportunity came to ask about the girl's whereabouts. 'I have something that belongs to her and I'd like to return it.'

'Oh, she's gone from the Uplands now. She left when Ada died; moved in to Richardson Terrace with the Atkinsons,' Lil said. 'You can't miss it; it's the house with the vegetable gardens out front.'

'Richardson Terrace? And where might I find that?'

Lil shook her head. 'It's no good going there,' she said. 'She's at Miss Gilbey's place now, on St Paul's Terrace, beside the Guide Post Inn.'

Shirley bit her tongue. This woman at her side was infuriating! 'The Guide Post Inn?' she said through gritted teeth.

'I'll walk with you. I'm heading that way.'

Shirley thought for a moment, deciding which course of action to take. She could try to find the girl and confront her, have it out with her about her affair with James and find out the truth. Or she could continue to the Uplands and let James know she was on to him. It took her just a second to decide.

'Lead on, Mrs Mahone.'

* * *

When the Grand Cinema and the Guide Post Inn came into view, Lil Mahone said goodbye and bustled away up the colliery bank. Shirley sighed with relief and carried on to the terraced house on St Paul's Terrace. She rapped at the door, and when it opened, the sight of the girl standing there almost took her breath away. Her heart turned to stone. No . . . no, this couldn't be true. Was this Jess? Was this her? Shirley stood frozen to the pavement. Her heart skipped a beat. The girl in front of her was beautiful. She was young, too. But above all she looked horribly familiar.

'Miss Davidson?' Shirley asked. 'Miss Jess Davidson?'

'Yes?' Jess said. She was confused. Why would anyone be asking for her? 'Are you here to see Miss Gilbey?'

Shirley saw the girl take in her travelling jacket and skirt and the vanity case in her hand. She was being scrutinised again, just as Lil Mahone had done earlier. She stared hard at Jess's face. It wouldn't have been obvious to a stranger. There were subtleties that others might miss, but she saw it straight away. Shirley took in Jess's features and saw the likeness there. She willed herself not to see it, she didn't want it to be true. But there was no denying what she saw with her own eyes. The girl had her husband's dark hair and features. Worse, she even looked like her son, a feminine version of Alfie. Shirley gripped the handle of her vanity case. Oh, how stupid she was not to have guessed who the girl in the woodshed was! After almost twenty years of marriage to James McNally, she knew every inch of his face. The way his chin curved, the way his dark eyes surveyed the world. This girl in front of her had the same nose, the same lips as James. Her forehead was the same, though unlike James, her face was untroubled and kind. Shirley knew. Oh, she knew. It was as if James's own eyes were staring at her.

'Can I help you?' Jess said.

'You'll never get anything from the McNallys, you hear?'

Jess was taken aback, not just at the woman's words but at the way she was dressed. She'd never seen such finery worn in Ryhope. She narrowed her eyes.

'Sorry? Who are you? What's this got to do with the McNallys?'

'Never mind who I am. I'm warning you, Miss Davidson. The Uplands is the McNallys' property. Don't you dare think for one minute that you deserve any part of it. You leave my husband and son alone. You hear me?'

Without waiting for an answer, Shirley stormed away. A tram rumbled into view coming down the bank from Silksworth. Shirley read the destination at the front of the tram and walked quickly towards the tram stop.

Jess flew out of the house after her. 'Wait! Wait! Tell me who you are!' she called.

Inside the tram, Shirley closed her eyes to block out the truth. The seat was hard and uncomfortable, but she knew she would suffer it to leave Ryhope as quickly as she could. The tram would take her to Sunderland, where she would eat and rest before beginning her return to Scarborough. There was no need to stay in Ryhope or confront James. She had seen enough. Her heart fluttered with the shock of it, and then a mischievous smile played on her lips. She'd got him. She'd caught her cheating, rotten husband at last.

She took a small notepad from her handbag and

quickly scribbled down the details Lil Mahone had freely given her: *Miss Jess Davidson, c/o Miss Gilbey, St Paul's Terrace, Ryhope*. She might need to give them to her father-in-law, or her solicitor, as proof of James's adultery. Far from being James's mistress, the truth about Jess was more threatening to Shirley than she could have known.

She would seek counsel as soon as she returned home.

Shirley knew that since Jess was James's illegitimate daughter, it would be impossible for her to inherit the Uplands. But still, far better to double-check that there was no possibility the girl could be given anything that should rightfully come to Alfie. Then she would take the news of James's secret daughter to Angus and let him deal with it as he saw fit. Finally, she'd get the lifestyle she craved in Scarborough. One without her scoundrel husband. One that was spent at her beautiful home in The Crescent, with her mother, Alfie and the McNally cash.

As the tram trundled away through the village carrying Shirley on it, Jess tried to make sense of what had just happened. Her head was spinning. Who was that woman? And what did she have to do with the Uplands? What on earth did it all mean?

Chapter Eight

Shirley returned home to The Crescent exhausted. Even with the comfort of first-class compartments, the four railway journeys tired her out. The house was empty of all but the servants when she entered. Alfie was at his studies at the maritime college, and Shirley was grateful for the peace after the noise of the trains. Ellen Roberts, the housekeeper, brought a tea tray to the drawing room. On it was a buttered scone and a pot of rhubarb jam.

'Will I unpack your vanity case and bag for you, Mrs Banks-McNally?' Ellen asked.

'Just the case,' Shirley replied. 'Please bring my bag in here.'

Ellen left the room and headed to her mistress's bedroom, where the vanity case lay on the double bed. She flicked the case open by springing the latches. What she found inside intrigued her. Almost everything appeared exactly as she had packed it for the journey to Ryhope. Hardly anything seemed to have been worn. Ellen knew this was unusual, but she also knew it wasn't her place to comment. Idle gossip had no place in The Crescent household. Ellen was a no-nonsense Yorkshirewoman, as hard-working and diligent as they came. But still, she couldn't help wondering what the trip to Ryhope had been about as her mistress hadn't stayed as long as planned or needed a change of clothes. Shirley's handbag also lay on the bed and Ellen took it down to the drawing room.

That evening when Alfie returned from his studies, he and Shirley ate together in the dining room: a feast of roast beef and Yorkshire pudding. Shirley had felt ravenous after her travels and demanded the cook prepare a large meal. Once dessert – a simple rice pudding – was served, she broached the subject of Ryhope.

'Your father will be staying at the Uplands for a while longer,' she said.

She intended to visit Angus first thing in the morning. She would make sure that word was sent to James in Ryhope letting him know her position. He was not to return to The Crescent, but would be given details of a new address in Scarborough. It would be an address she would choose for him, a bachelor apartment well away from the Sandside Inn.

Alfie took the news stoically. It didn't come as any surprise that his parents intended to spend even more time apart. In a way, he was relieved. He'd rather that than have them both at home, arguing and bitter. He wouldn't miss his father too much, for even when he was in Scarborough, James was either at work or out at meetings. His only regret was that he wanted to speak to his father on a pressing matter. It was about his studies at the maritime college, a course he was not enjoying. It had been James's idea for him to enrol; he thought a grounding in the industry would be the perfect introduction to life in the fishing business. But it was a business that Alfie had no interest in, and his days at college passed slowly. There was something else he wanted to do with his life.

'How long will he be away?' he asked.

'It is not yet decided,' Shirley replied.

Alfie bit his lip, and Shirley caught the look of indecision that skittered across his face. She looked across the table at her son. How handsome he was, with his dark hair and beautiful eyes. And, she realised with alarm, how similar he looked to the girl in Ryhope. She resolved to do everything in her power to protect what was rightfully his.

As if he had read her mind, Alfie raised his eyes shyly to meet his mother's gaze.

'Did you speak to the girl?' he said softly.

Shirley's heart skipped a beat. She picked up her spoon and attacked her rice pudding, shaking her head by way of reply.

'Alfie . . .' she said. She laid down her spoon on the table and sat back in her chair. 'I need to ask you a question and I need you to answer it honestly.'

'Of course,' he said.

'That girl . . .' she began, 'the girl at the Uplands. Did you speak to her when you were there?'

'We spoke briefly.'

'Nothing more?'

'Nothing.'

Shirley could hardly breathe, but she had to know the truth. 'You didn't . . . ?'

'What, Mother?'

'You're sure nothing else happened. You just spoke to her, that's all?'

Alfie was confused. What on earth was his mother digging for? He looked her straight in the eye.

'I was horrified, Mother, if you must know. I was disgusted with Father for allowing anyone to live in such a place. Did you see it? It's the sort of place you'd put a pig in, or a horse. Not a girl! Father should be ashamed of himself, letting someone live in conditions like that.' He took a deep breath to quell his irritation with his mother and his anger at his father. 'But in answer to your question again, I spoke to the girl and nothing more.'

Satisfied that he was telling the truth, Shirley felt a weight fall from her shoulders. The moment passed. She picked up her spoon and resumed eating.

Later that night, after dinner, Shirley and Alfie talked in the drawing room. But it wasn't long before the tiredness from four train journeys could not be put off any longer and Shirley headed to bed. Left alone, Alfie began to unpick his thoughts about his desire to leave the maritime college and enlist with the Yorkshire Regiment. He knew it would break his mother's heart when he told her his plans, but he had to do it. He would not be like his father and live a life he was unhappy with. He would not run and hide, escape to another home, to Ryhope and the Uplands, when life didn't go the way he planned. He needed to be strong. Something else niggled at him. It was the girl at the Uplands. He had seen the way his mother avoided his gaze when he asked about her at dinner. Was she hiding something from him, just as he felt his father was? So many worries whirled in Alfie's mind.

On a side table in the room was his mother's handbag, the one she had taken to Ryhope. The one that Ellen had brought down to the room earlier. Alfie stared long and hard at it. Might it contain a clue – to Ryhope? To the girl? Might it reveal something of his father, something about the Uplands? He looked away. No! He wouldn't do it. He had been brought up to be honest, respectful of other's property and belongings. But his gaze was drawn again to the bag. He stood and walked towards it, then let his hand fall to the clasp. What harm would it do to take a little look? That was all he would do, just look.

Inside were Shirley's personal effects: a phial of lily-of-the-valley parfum de Paris, her money wallet, a lipstick of pale pink. At the bottom of the bag lay two pencils and a notebook. Alfie felt a shudder run through him, but he knew he had to do it. If his mother walked into the room now, she'd be horrified to find him with his hand inside her bag. And so, he thought, he might as well reach for the notebook – may as well be hung for a sheep as a lamb.

He pulled the notebook from the bag and it fell open in his hands at a page where a name and address were written. He recognised the writing as his mother's. It was the name and address of someone in Ryhope. The address meant nothing to Alfie, but the name was sweetly familiar. The words of the girl he'd met in the grounds of the Uplands went through his mind again.

Jess Davidson. I belong to Ada, the housekeeper.

He carefully replaced the notebook and ran up to his room.

In the coming days, Miss Gilbey put Jess hard to work at the house in St Paul's Terrace. She kept a close eye on her; there was something about the girl she admired. Jess had a spirit that Miss Gilbey hadn't seen for some time. She was independent and focused, stubborn as a mule too. She worked hard and complained little and Miss Gilbey was glad she had trusted her instincts and taken her on. Her instincts were rarely wrong.

However, for Jess it seemed that no matter how hard she worked, it wasn't good enough for Miss Gilbey's exacting standards. She didn't want to stand up to the woman for fear of losing her room and board, but neither was she prepared to let Miss Gilbey's criticism go unchallenged when she knew she was doing her best.

One day after breakfast, when Amelia and Jane had left for work at the store, Miss Gilbey asked Jess to join her in her private living room. The invitation came as a shock to Jess, for none of the girls were usually allowed in there. The only areas of the house they could enter were their own rooms and the kitchen.

'Come in. Don't be shy,' Miss Gilbey said.

Jess hovered at the threshold before stepping inside. There was no linoleum on the floor as there was around the rest of the house. Instead, a mat reached almost to the walls. Three armchairs were positioned around an open fireplace, and the mantelpiece groaned under heavy brass ornaments. A large mirror hung above the mantelpiece, and on the walls around the room were framed pictures of country scenes with horses running wild.

'Please, sit,' Miss Gilbey said, indicating one of the armchairs.

Jess sat. She kept her back straight and eyed Miss Gilbey warily.

'There's to be a new girl in the house,' Miss Gilbey said. 'She'll be sharing your room. Her name's Lena Grundy. I tell you this now so that you'll know of her

132

before she arrives. She's a delicate girl, ill in the mind.' She paused. For the very first time since she had moved into Miss Gilbey's house, Jess detected a sadness about the woman. 'I am trusting you to ensure she comes to no harm.'

'Of course,' said Jess.

Miss Gilbey dismissed her with a wave of her hand. 'That is all, you may go.'

All day long Jess ran her strange encounter with Miss Gilbey through her mind. Had she imagined that vulnerable look on her face when she spoke of the new girl? Surely she must have, for she had never seen Miss Gilbey's stern expression change since the day she moved in.

Later that afternoon, Jess was on her hands and knees scrubbing the dark floor of the hallway, a metal bucket of steaming hot water beside her. A sound at the front door caught her ear. Was someone there? She waited for a knock, but none came. Instead, the door swung open of its own accord and Miss Gilbey walked in. Jess was startled; she hadn't expected her back so soon or she would never have started cleaning the hallway. Now, Miss Gilbey would get her boots wet from the floor and all of Jess's hard work would be for nothing when boots from the street brought muck in. But if Jess was surprised at the sight of Miss Gilbey, she was even more shocked by who she saw next.

A young girl followed Miss Gilbey in. Jess stood to let them walk past. As they did so, she glanced at the girl. She was very young, and wore her straight brown hair long, with a fringe that fell over the saddest pair of eyes Jess had ever seen. Her tiny mouth was downturned. She was scared, Jess could tell, her eyes darting around the hallway, from Miss Gilbey to Jess and back again.

'Jess Davidson, meet Lena Grundy,' Miss Gilbey said curtly. 'Lena, follow Jess to your room and she'll help you settle back in.' With that, she disappeared into her living room, leaving Jess and Lena alone in the hall.

Jess was struck by Miss Gilbey's words. Had Lena been at Miss Gilbey's before? She stuck her hand out in greeting, but Lena just stared as if unsure what to do and Jess dropped her hand. After a few moments the tiniest of smiles made its way to Lena's lips, and Jess breathed a sigh of relief. She remembered how nervous she had been when she'd first turned up at Miss Gilbey's house. She wondered if Lena might be feeling nervous too, even if she had been there before.

'Shall I show you your room?' she said as brightly as she could. 'It's not big and you'll be sharing with me, but . . .' She started making her way up the stairs and Lena followed slowly. When they reached the small bedroom at the back of the house, Jess pointed at the bed by the wall.

'I've made it up specially for you with clean sheets. Miss Gilbey told me you were coming, so I got it all ready.'

She watched as Lena sank on to the bed and glanced around the room.

'Don't you have any clothes with you?' she asked. She was sure she hadn't seen Miss Gilbey or Lena bring a bag into the hallway with them.

Lena shook her head. 'She sees to my things.'

Jess was puzzled by this. 'Who does? Miss Gilbey?'

Lena cast her gaze to the floor and picked at the eiderdown that Jess had smoothed out neatly. Jess noticed a vulnerability about the girl. She saw her legs twitching, saw how afraid she seemed to be. She sat on her own bed and faced Lena. The room was so small that the girls were just inches apart, their knees almost touching.

'As we're to share the same room, we can share secrets if you'd like?' she offered.

Lena shook her head.

Jess remembered Miss Gilbey's words about Lena's fragile mind. She didn't want to push the girl or upset her in any way. Instead, she took her hand and held it lightly. 'I want to be your friend, Lena,' she said.

Lena held her gaze. Then she raised Jess's hand to her face and laid it against her cheek. Jess saw tears form in the girl's eyes.

'Thank you, Jess,' Lena whispered.

One morning while Jess was preparing breakfast, she was interrupted by knocking at the front door. It was Ned Scully, the postman, and he greeted her with excited eyes.

'Special delivery,' he said, waving an envelope in front of her face. 'We don't get many of those around Ryhope.'

'For Miss Gilbey?' she asked.

'No, lass, it's for you.'

Jess took the envelope from Ned. She was startled. Who did she know who could be sending her letters, never mind by special delivery? Who on earth even knew where she lived?

'For me?'

Her heart skipped when she read her name on the front of the envelope. It had been written in a hand she didn't recognise. But there at the bottom was something she had seen before, when she'd lived at the Uplands with Ada. It was a small boat, a herring boat, Ada had told her. There were words under the boat, *Silver Darlings of the Sea*, and sure enough, a Scarborough postmark. It was a letter from the McNally family, but why on earth would they be writing to her? And how had they found her address?

Jess knew she had time to read the letter, there were five or ten minutes before Miss Gilbey and the girls expected breakfast. She ran from the house into the yard and hid around the side of the netty. She turned the envelope in her hands and ripped it open, gasping when she saw the sender's name at the bottom of the page. Her head spun. She was confused. Why this? Why now? What on earth was going on? She knew she had to make sense of it. There was only one person she could trust with the contents of the letter. She needed to speak to Mal.

Amelia arrived for breakfast first. She was always first down at mealtimes. When Jess saw her, she stiffened and pasted a smile on her face.

'Tea, Amelia?' she asked.

'Yes,' came the reply. There was never any please or thank you from Amelia, although Jane was a little more polite.

Jess set the tea pot in the middle of the table, next to the small milk jug.

'Still no sugar?' Amelia huffed.

Jess ignored the comment. Miss Gilbey did the shopping for the household and if she couldn't afford sugar, it was not for the girls to pass comment. There was something about Amelia, something sly, that Jess didn't like. She tried to get along with everyone in the house, but soon realised that trying to please everyone was nigh on impossible. Still, Miss Gilbey was less frosty towards her than she had been at the start. Being invited into her living room was proof of that. And being given the responsibility of keeping an eye on Lena, too. Miss Gilbey must trust her, and that made Jess happy.

As she went through the motions of preparing breakfast, she thought of Ada, as she did every day. Would Ada have sliced the bread thicker? Would she have been more sparing with the margarine? What would she have done if she'd met a character like Amelia? And each time Jess's thoughts turned to Ada, she heard the words Ada had spoken the day before she died. Jess had turned those words over many times, wondering what it all meant. Was there anyone she could talk to about it? She decided that when she spoke to Mal about the letter she'd received, she would bring it up with him and ask for his help.

'Hurry up, girl!' Amelia barked. 'You're going to make me late for work. You're always so slow with our breakfast. I don't know why Miss Gilbey took you on. You never get anything right.'

Jess felt anger rise in her, heat spreading up her neck. It was bad enough that she was skivvying for the girls in the house. She didn't need harsh words thrown at her too, not when she was doing her best. Miss Gilbey wasn't even paying her for the work she was doing. Her payment, as she often reminded Jess, was by way of board and lodgings.

'Just be thankful you've got a roof over your head and food in your belly,' she would say if Jess dared to complain.

Jess turned towards Amelia, who was drumming her fingers on the table. The sound cut through Jess like a knife and increased the fury inside her. She lifted the butter knife and pointed it at Amelia.

'I'm going as fast as I can,' she said.

At that moment, Miss Gilbey walked into the room and Jess dropped her hand.

'Morning, Miss Gilbey,' Amelia said. Her words rang out in a sing-song voice.

'Morning, girls,' Miss Gilbey replied. 'Everything all right, Jess?'

Jess wondered why she had asked. Was her face still flushed from her words with Amelia? She dropped her gaze to the floor. 'Yes, Miss Gilbey,' she said. She returned to the work in hand and felt her anger subside.

She took the knife and began scraping margarine on to toast, just like Ada used to do. Jane came down next, followed by Lena, who sat next to Miss Gilbey. When everyone had been served tea and toast, Jess took her own seat. Being last at the table meant she was left to drink the dregs from the teapot. And her toast was always the smallest piece left from the stottie, or the one with burnt edges that no one else wanted.

Miss Gilbey encouraged conversation at the table, but only Amelia and Jane joined in, offering details of their work at the store. Lena sat in silence, looking overwhelmed and out of place, as if she wanted to scuttle back to the safety of her bed. Jess watched them all as she ate. Not one of them said thank you for the work she'd done and the food she'd prepared, not even Miss Gilbey.

When breakfast was over and the kitchen was empty, Jess set to clearing plates and mugs. She heard Jane and

Amelia in the hallway, and wished she too had somewhere to go. She filled her metal bucket with water and placed it on the kitchen floor. Suddenly Amelia walked back into the kitchen.

'I've heard things about you,' she whispered in Jess's ear. 'Heard you lived like a wild animal in a cage at the Uplands.'

Jess's blood ran cold. 'That's not true,' she said.

'Don't care if it's true or not. It's what I've heard. It's what the gossips are saying around Ryhope. I don't know who I might pass it on to today. I haven't decided yet.'

As Amelia turned to leave, she kicked the bucket of water. It tipped over with an almighty clang, spilling water all over the floor. It happened quickly and took Jess by surprise. She was livid and ready to lash out, but Amelia was already out in the hall. The front door slammed just as Miss Gilbey poked her head around her living-room door.

'What on earth was that noise?' she cried. She saw the water spreading around the floor and the bucket on its side. She sighed heavily. 'Can't you do anything right?'

Jess stood with her hands on her hips, silently cursing Amelia.

Chapter Nine

A week later, Jess was allowed a rare day off from her chores at Miss Gilbey's. She'd been invited to tea with the Atkinsons and was helping Estelle prepare a family meal. Jess was cleaning soil from leeks pulled from Arthur and Estelle's garden. When they had been washed in a bucket of water, she handed them to Estelle, who was waiting with her best knife. She cut the very tops off the dark green leaves and threw them on the compost pile in the yard. Then she sliced what was left of the leaves and the pearly white base. The kitchen was filled with a mild onion scent. It was a pleasing smell, and the leeks were to be made into a pudding for a celebration tea.

'It's the first time Arthur's ever won the leek show,' Estelle beamed. 'He's over the moon. I've sent him to the Railway Inn for a few beers to celebrate. When he comes home, we'll have the best leek pudding you've ever tasted.'

Jess examined the leeks she was cleaning. They were healthy-looking, thick around the base, with a creamy whiteness to them. There was no rust on the leaves, a good sign. But they hardly looked like the size of show-winners. Estelle caught her appraising them.

'He didn't win with these, love. These are the ones he grows in the garden for food. It's the ones he was growing in the back yard in the old barrels that he won with.'

'Then why aren't we eating the prize-winners?' Jess asked.

Estelle didn't stop cutting and slicing as she gave her reply. 'There's no taste to them,' she said. 'They're big and they're beautiful and that's what wins the prize. It's all the food and water he gives them, and the horse manure he digs in around them.'

Jess wrinkled her nose. 'Horse manure?'

'He buys it from Meg Sutcliffe, the girl who runs the rag-and-bone round with her old horse, Stella.'

'I think I've seen her around the village,' Jess said.

'Well, Arthur wouldn't win any prizes with these garden leeks. But they taste better than any show leeks, I can tell you that now.'

Jess thought back to when she used to work with Ada, preparing vegetables at the Uplands. Her eyes pricked with tears as they did each time she brought Ada to mind. There was not a day went by when she didn't miss Ada or think about the cryptic words spoken the day before she died. She wiped the back of her hand across her eyes and pulled herself together, concentrating on the job in hand.

'Is Mal with his dad at the pub?' she asked. 'I've barely seen him and Arthur since I moved into Miss Gilbey's.'

Estelle wiped her hands on a tea towel. 'Well then. All the more reason to enjoy our celebration tea tonight.' She glanced at Jess. 'You're a good lass, Jess. Ada always spoke highly of you, and she was right to do so. How are things at Miss Gilbey's? I bet she keeps you on your toes, doesn't she?'

'Oh, it's fine. It's . . .' Jess shook her head. She'd been left hurt and confused after her run-in with the well-dressed lady who had called at Miss Gilbey's some time ago. She'd kept the encounter to herself, held it in her heart, but it gnawed at her every day. Then there was Amelia's behaviour to deal with. And as if that wasn't bad enough, she was worried about Lena. There was a sadness about the girl, a frailty, that Jess didn't understand. She was further confused as to where Lena and Miss Gilbey spent their days. They always left the house together by eleven each morning and came home at three in the afternoon, after which Miss Gilbey would head to her living room, leaving Lena watching Jess as she worked. But she didn't want to worry Estelle. 'It's all fine,' she said softly.

When Arthur and Mal came home from the pub, their faces were flushed and their spirits high. They each carried two bottles of beer.

Estelle set out four glasses and filled them with ale. 'One for you, Jess.' She winked. 'As it's a special day.' Then she carried the leek pudding to the table, holding it as if she was presenting royalty with the best meal they'd ever seen.

Jess's stomach rumbled with hunger. She'd eaten nothing since a thin slice of toast at breakfast. The pudding was spooned out and steam rose from each plate. She lifted her fork to her mouth, blew on it and gently placed it in her mouth. It was hot, too hot to chew, but she was starving for the taste. And when it finally cooled on her tongue, the taste was as delicious as the smell. Every single minute of the afternoon's work she and Estelle had put into making the pudding had been worth it. They'd chopped suet, pulled and sliced leeks, mixed flour and water. And then they'd spent hours waiting while the pudding steamed. The pudding melted on Jess's tongue. The taste was divine. The four of them around the table fell into silence. Jess saw Arthur cover Estelle's hand with his own.

'It's lovely, pet,' he said softly.

'Well done, lad,' she replied.

After dinner, when Estelle and Jess had finished clearing the kitchen and washing pots and pans, the family sat in the living room. Jess curled up at one end of the sofa. Estelle sat at the other and lifted her knitting bag from the floor. Arthur was in his armchair. Mal sat on the floor at his mother's side. They heard the sound of rain outside as it began pattering at the window. The coal fire crackled and spat in the hearth. The clock ticked on the mantelpiece. These were the only sounds in the room, until Arthur began to sing, hesitantly at first. It was a hymn that Jess recognised from school. The Atkinsons, like Ada and Jess, were not religious people, but hymns were the songs that everyone knew. Encouraged by Estelle, Arthur carried on into a second verse. Estelle hummed along, tapping her foot and nodding her head. Mal began drumming his fingers on the wooden floor in time to his dad's words. And then Jess joined in, her voice wrapping around Arthur's, sweet against his deep notes.

When they were finished, Estelle gave a round of applause. 'You've got a beautiful voice, lass,' she said.

'You have, Mam's right,' said Mal. He beamed at Jess. Jess felt his gaze and returned it, enjoying it.

Estelle picked up her knitting, and her needles started clicking and clacking. Arthur began humming, a tune Jess didn't know. And there in the room with these people she knew better than anyone else in the world, she felt at home. She felt safe and welcome, content. She looked again at Mal where he sat on the floor, and saw he'd laid his head against the sofa. His eyes were closed. The beer and the leek pudding had done their work. All four of them were sleepy and happy. Outside, the rain turned heavier, belting hard at the window. Estelle glanced at Arthur and he gave a slight nod of his head.

'You'd best stay overnight, Jess,' she said. 'You can have the armchair to sleep in. I'm not sending you out walking the streets back to Miss Gilbey's in this weather. You'll catch your death if you do.'

'Miss Gilbey won't mind, will she?' Arthur said. 'We wouldn't want to get you into any trouble with her.'

Miss Gilbey wasn't Jess's first thought. She was worried about Lena. She knew the girl would be scared, sleeping in the room on her own.

'When I wake tomorrow, I'll run straight to the house before they get up out of bed.'

'She won't be too happy to have you waking up her household. You leave her to me,' Estelle said. 'I'll go with you, but only after you've been fed here. The state of you, Jess, you're so thin. Is she feeding you properly?'

Jess dropped her gaze to the mat on the floor. She was allowed to eat with the girls at Miss Gilbey's, but had to take the last of the food from the pan. It was one of many of Miss Gilbey's rules. She was often left hungry after dinner and fell asleep with her stomach aching for food.

'Don't you worry about Miss Gilbey,' Estelle told her.

'If she's got any complaints about you staying out all night, she can complain to me.' Jess accepted Estelle's kind offer. Once it was decided that she was to stay overnight, Estelle poked her knitting needles through the ball of blue wool and tidied everything away. 'Right, Arthur,' she said. 'That's me done. I'm off to bed. You coming?'

Mal opened his eyes and watched as his mam and dad prepared to leave the room.

Arthur shot him a look. 'Don't stay up late, lad. We've got work in the morning at the vicarage garden, as long as the rain holds off.'

'Leave him be, Arthur,' Estelle said. 'The lad knows what he's doing. Night, Jess.'

'Night, Estelle. Night, Arthur,' Jess said.

Jess and Mal were left alone. The only sounds were the creaking of the floorboards above as Estelle and Arthur made their way to bed. Mal moved from his spot on the floor to sit beside Jess on the sofa.

'That was a smashing leek pudding you and Mam made,' he said. As he laid his hand on the sofa cushion next to where Jess was sitting, his fingertips brushed her skirt. His touch was light; had it been a mistake? Jess wondered. Well, there was only one way to find out. She laid her hand on the cushion too, touching Mal's. He didn't move his hand away. In silence, they worked their fingers together, slowly, hesitantly. And then they were holding hands. It was as simple and yet as thrilling as that.

Mal shifted on the sofa. 'Jess?'

Jess looked into his deep brown eyes. They were searching hers. She lifted their joined hands to her mouth and kissed his fingers, one by one. It was a sign of her trust in him, one Mal accepted with a joyful heart. With his free hand he stroked Jess's face, following the curve of her chin to her neck. He leaned towards her and Jess laid her head back against the sofa, ready to accept his lips. But a noise from above stopped them going any further.

'Mal!' It was Arthur, yelling from the bedroom upstairs. 'Get yourself up to bed, lad, or you'll never be up in the morning!'

Mal and Jess froze with their lips inches apart, then broke into giggles the way they had always done when they were children. But when their laughter died down, they continued to hold hands, not wanting to break apart.

'I'd better go,' Mal said at last. 'I don't want Dad on the warpath.' He kissed her then, his warm lips caressing hers for the briefest of moments.

'I'll see you in the morning,' Jess said.

Mal stood, still holding tight to her hand. 'Night, then,' he said.

'Night,' she replied.

Still neither of them wanted to let go of the other. It was Jess who gently pulled her hand away. 'Go on up,' she said. 'I don't want you upsetting your dad.'

Once Mal had disappeared from the room, she readied herself for bed. The dogs, Pebble and Stone, lay sleeping, curled up together in front of the fire. Jess watched as the embers burned low and darkness enveloped the room. She thought of Mal and of what had just happened. It had seemed right to want to kiss him, natural, as if it was always meant to be. But there were feelings of confusion there too. Mal was almost like a brother to her. They'd known each other since they were little. Did she really want their close friendship to change? But people did change, they grew older, grew up. She and Mal had grown and changed just as everyone around them had. And why wouldn't she want to kiss him, even dream of a future with him? He was kind and strong, honest and decent. He worked hard and had the muck ingrained in his hands to prove it. He treated his parents well and had always been kind to her, always a friend. Jess wondered if he was lying in bed thinking of her, just as she was thinking of him.

She thought of Jane, the eldest of the girls at Miss Gilbey's. Maybe she'd ask Jane what she should do next; she might know the ways of men. But where Amelia had taunted her with cruel words, Jane had simply ignored her, acted as if she didn't exist. She couldn't confide in either of those girls, and Lena, of course, was too young. Then she thought of Estelle. Under her blanket, Jess crossed her fingers and hoped for Estelle's blessing when she found out that she and Mal had feelings for each other. For a small house like the Atkinsons' was no place for secrets.

The next morning, Jess was up first. She had slept badly because of the noise from the storm that had raged all night. The rain battered the windows. Once she'd tidied away her blanket, she washed and dressed. It was only then that she remembered the letter she'd stuffed in her skirt pocket. In all the excitement of Arthur winning the show, the feast of leek pudding and the beer, the letter had been pushed from her mind.

She set to making the fire so that it was burning by the time Arthur and Estelle came downstairs. She laid the table with plates and mugs, and put the teapot to warm on the hearth. She cut thick slices of bread to toast on the fire and opened a pot of blackcurrant jam made from Arthur's summer fruit. By the time Arthur and Estelle came in yawning and stretching, ready to face the day, the room was cosy and warm. It was the least she could do for them after Estelle had let her stay. Jess loved preparing the house for the Atkinsons that morning. It made her feel part of their family, loved and safe, the first time she'd felt that way since Ada died. And she was in a home too, a family home. Living in the woodshed, she'd been cut off from Ada's loving embraces. It felt cosy and right to be in the Atkinsons' house where they talked, laughed and enjoyed each other's company. It was something she had never experienced before. She wondered if she'd feel it again. The thought brought a sadness as she waited for the kettle to boil. For she knew she'd have to leave and return to Miss Gilbey's as soon as the storm eased.

Mal came downstairs last. Jess was looking forward to seeing him, and when he came into the room they exchanged a shy smile.

'You all right?' he mouthed.

Jess nodded.

They gave no inkling to Arthur and Estelle that anything had changed between them. Jess knew that before they could tell anyone else what was happening, they had to make sense of it themselves.

As they ate breakfast and drank tea, the wind lashed outside and threw rain at the windows. In the back yard, Arthur's evergreen shrubs shook against the wind and his climbing plants were pulled from their trellises. A storm had been forecast, the village had been full of talk of it for days and now it seemed as if the gossip was true.

Arthur glanced from the window and shook his head

at the destruction of his beloved plants. His eyes turned to the leaden sky and he sucked air through his teeth. Then he turned to Estelle and gave a cheeky smile. 'Winter drawers on!' he said.

Estelle nudged him playfully in the ribs. 'Oh Arthur,' she said. 'You and your jokes. But seriously, love. You'll not get any work done in this weather at the vicarage, will you?'

'What about the pit gaffer's glasshouse up at Tunstall Terrace, Dad?' Mal suggested. 'We've been promising we'll go and sort it out. Today looks like a perfect day for being indoors.'

Arthur rubbed his chin and gave this some thought. 'That's what we'll do, lad. The summer season's pots and trays need changing now that winter's coming. We can do all the work to prepare for the spring. Probably not enough to last us all day but we'll not be idle, despite the rotten weather.'

'A glasshouse?' Estelle said in between bites of warm buttered toast. 'I'll be surprised if there's any of it left in this wind.'

Jess slid her hand into her pocket and pulled out the envelope. She glanced towards Mal. 'I wanted to tell you something,' she said. 'All of you. I received a letter at Miss Gilbey's. It came by special delivery and I wanted to let you know what it said.'

All eyes turned to the envelope in her hand, and she pulled out a single sheet of heavy paper. It had the McNally crest embossed at the head. The storm outside added to the unease that Jess felt as she held the letter with trembling hands.

'What is it, lass?' Arthur said.

'Give her a chance to read it,' Estelle scolded.

Jess looked up into Arthur's kind face. 'It's from Scarborough,' she said.

Mal kept quiet, but he was watching her, concerned.

'The McNallys?' Arthur asked. 'But James is back at the Uplands. I saw him when I was working in the grounds last week.' He stopped himself from saying that he'd been taking down the woodshed that had been Jess's home.

'It's not from James,' Jess said. 'It's from his son.'

A bolt of lightning shot through the dark sky and thunder cracked the air.

'Alfie?' Mal said. He flung his uneaten toast on to his plate. 'Why on earth is he writing to you?'

Chapter Ten

Mal picked up his toast again, took a bite and stood from the table. His chair scraped along the floor.

Jess looked up at him. She couldn't understand why he was behaving this way. Hadn't they kissed the night before? Why was he acting strangely now? Had it really been the mention of Alfie McNally's name and the letter in her hands that upset him? She straightened in her seat and glared at him. 'Sit down,' she said. She felt Estelle and Arthur looking at her and her face burned. Mal didn't move. The only sounds were the coal fire crackling and the rain clattering at the window. 'Mal, sit down. You've asked why Alfie McNally is writing to me and I'd like to read you his words.'

Mal slowly pulled his chair back towards him and sank into it. He took up his toast again and started eating as if nothing had happened.

Jess saw Estelle watching her. 'I've got nothing to keep from any of you,' she said.

'Then why's he writing letters and sending them special delivery?' Mal demanded.

'I hope you're not trying to suggest he and I have

151

secrets, Mal. I thought you knew me better than that.'

She missed the look that passed between Estelle and Arthur. But she noted the sulky tone of Mal's voice and that was when she understood that he was feeling hurt. Was he jealous of Alfie, of all people? Why, they'd only met that one time at the Uplands. She had no feelings for Alfie like the ones she had for Mal. But she had to admit there had been something, a sense of belonging, of safety, when she'd met Alfie. Still, she was as surprised as any of them that he had written to her. She held the letter tight with both hands.

Around the table, the Atkinsons listened in silence as she read. Alfie's words were of friendship, an offer of support to her from Scarborough. He explained how sorry he was when his father had told him that she had lost her home at the Uplands. He admitted to being confused about his father's actions. He also passed on his condolences to her at Ada's death. They were words that gladdened Jess's heart but also confused her. Why was he sending words of condolence when he didn't know her or Ada? And why weren't those words coming from James, the person who had employed Ada all these years? In the final sentence of the letter, Alfie asked Jess not to write in return for he was going away. He was joining the Yorkshire Regiment to do his bit after the devastation brought to Scarborough by the war.

Jess laid the letter on the table and looked at Mal. 'That's what he was writing to me about, nothing more,' she said.

'How did he know how to find you?' Mal asked. He was still suspicious, Jess knew.

She shook her head. 'I have no idea.'

'Those McNallys, they'll have ways and means of finding things out,' Arthur said. 'The likes of them with all their money will know folk who'll tell them things.'

'Well, it was a nice letter,' Estelle said with approval. 'He was offering a hand of friendship. Says a lot about the character of the man.'

'Friendship,' Jess said. She put the letter back into the envelope, then locked eyes with Mal. 'And nothing more.'

Mal opened his mouth to reply. He was ready to apologise, to say how foolish he'd been for getting angry and jealous at the mention of Alfie's name.

Estelle and Arthur waited, wanting an explanation for his outburst. Estelle was proud of her son; he was a good lad, polite and kind. And he and Jess had been friends since they were bairns. But she'd seen Mal change in ways only a mother would know. She'd noticed the way he and Jess were with each other. Once they'd been friends, running around as children on the lawn at the Uplands or helping Arthur in the yard with his plants. But now Mal had a shyness about him when he was with the girl, as if he was careful about what he said in front of her, as if her opinion of him mattered. She'd seen the way he looked at her. And what a beauty Jess had turned out. Estelle remembered when she and Arthur were that age, sixteen years old with not a care in the world and no thought for the consequences of giving in to their feelings. She wondered if she should tell Arthur to have a word with the boy. Perhaps it was time for that father-to-son talk Arthur knew he'd have to give one day.

But before any of them could say another word, there was an urgent banging at the front door. The two dogs leapt up and began barking. Jess, Mal and Estelle stayed at the breakfast table while Arthur went to answer the door. Before he even got halfway along the hall, the banging started again.

'Arthur! Arthur! We need you at the beach!' a man's voice shouted.

Estelle jumped from her seat and went to see what the fuss was. There at the front door was their neighbour, Jimmy Brown, soaked to the skin from the pelting rain. He could hardly get his words out from the shock of what he'd just seen.

'Bring Mal, bring more men,' he cried, gasping for breath. 'Bring as many as you can. We need all the help we can get.' And with that, he was gone to bang on the next door, waking as many men as he could, calling for help. Estelle had caught snippets of conversation, the odd word from Jimmy's lips but she understood enough and a chill ran through her.

When Estelle returned to the kitchen, Mal was already on his feet.

'What is it, Mam? Is it something at the pit? An accident? What?'

Estelle shook her head. 'No, it's . . . There's a ship in trouble. You've got to go. You and your dad. Go and help, do as much as you can.'

'Your mam's right,' Arthur said. 'We've got to go and help. Jimmy Brown is rounding up men from the village. The vicar's opened the church to bring people in, that's if there's any . . .' he glanced at Estelle, 'anyone we can save. We've got to get down there as fast as we can, lad. We could be the difference between whether people live or die.'

Estelle leapt into action, gathering caps, scarves and

gloves for her husband and son. When they were ready to leave, she kissed them both on the cheek. 'Promise me you'll keep each other safe,' she said. 'Be brave, both of you. Be strong. But by God, be careful.'

She and Jess stood at the front door to see them off. Before the men walked into the storm, Arthur kissed Estelle on the lips. Mal reached for Jess's hand and squeezed it tightly.

'Be careful,' Jess whispered.

And with that, the men were gone, running as fast as they could towards the beach. Other men were running too, some pushing carts or riding horses. The furious rain lashed at them, soaking them to the skin, as the Ryhope men answered the call.

One of those running to the beach was James McNally. He had been woken that morning by a furious banging at the Uplands front door. His anger and frustration at having been forced to leave his bed had not yet dissipated. For it had also meant leaving a barmaid called Dinah he'd met in the Albion Inn the night before.

'Keep the bed warm, I'll be back,' he'd told her. And now here he was, running with a pack of men in the rain on what might turn out to be a wild goose chase. But he couldn't refuse to join in, not when his reputation around Ryhope was at stake. If he'd refused, he knew word would spread and he wouldn't be welcome in any Ryhope pub again.

He wondered which ship it was that had been caught by the storm, and whether the gales had hit Scarborough. His selfish thoughts turned to the McNally fleet. He knew it wouldn't be one of his own boats caught in

Ryhope's storm, for the McNally family business was local to the Yorkshire coast. But if the storm was lashing Scarborough as badly as Ryhope was being hit, there might be damage to the harbour and the fishing boats.

As he ran, a call went up behind him.

'More men needed!'

'More hands!'

'Send them all to the beach!'

James ran on into the angry storm. At each house he passed, front doors were flung open with women standing there calling out to their men.

'Be careful!'

'God help them!'

A crowd of men and boys were streaming down to the beach in the rain. Ahead of him, the Albion Inn came into view, its doors open wide. He saw the pub landlady, Hetty Burdon, still in her nightgown with a shawl around her shoulders. She was handing bottles of spirits to a tall, thin man he recognised as her husband, Jack. And then Jack too was running, with the bottles in his hands.

At the sight of the bottles, James felt a yearning in his gut. He had not eaten breakfast, and yet his appetite already ran to rum. His whole being pulled with the need for it. His new housekeeper at the Uplands, a sturdy woman called Bella Scott, had bought him a half-bottle just the day before and he'd drunk it within hours. He'd needed more, but the housekeeper had raised her eyes when he'd asked her. In desperation, he'd gone to the store himself. Him! James McNally, shopping for himself! He bought two bottles and kept a third under a loose floorboard in his study.

The rain pelted his face and soaked his trousers,

thunder cracked overhead and lightning threatened to split the sky. But all James could think of, all that he craved, was rum. He ran towards the open door of the Albion, where Hetty stood watching the men running by.

'Give me two bottles,' he called as he neared the pub. 'I'll take them to the survivors for the shock.'

Hetty had no reason to think he had anything other than good deeds on his mind. She handed over a bottle of brandy and one of whisky to James's greedy hands. A quick glance at the labels told him they were not the spirit he hoped for, but his craving was so strong that they would have to do.

He ran on with the throng heading to the beach. Old men with walking sticks were joining in too; everyone wanted to help. Everyone, that is, apart from James McNally. He wanted to be somewhere else. And when he saw his chance, he took it. On the road to the beach as the rest of the men streamed to the sea, James veered off to the left. There was no pathway, just a hillock, wet and muddy from the rain. His feet sank into the soil as he climbed. Everyone else was intent on reaching the stricken ship as quickly as they could. The morning was dark with the clouds of the storm and no one saw him leave.

When James felt he was a safe distance from those running to the beach, he lay down behind a bush. A lightning strike lit the sky and thunder cracked. But he didn't care. His heart was going nineteen to the dozen with the exertion of his run. He heard shouting, yelling, men calling as they ran past, unaware of where he was and what he was doing. He opened the brandy and filled his throat. It was too sweet – he craved an aged rum – but it would have to do for now. Still lying down, keeping out of sight, he took another swig, and another, until a third of the bottle was gone. He lay there as the lightning splintered the sky and he raised the bottle to the heavens above. A smile played around his lips and he thought of Dinah, delicious Dinah, lying in his bed. He would wait in the grass, wait until the last man had run through, and then head back to the Uplands. His reputation would be saved. He'd answered the call, hadn't he? He'd done his duty. He'd been seen on the way to the beach. What more did he need to do?

He closed his eyes and felt the rain hit his face, his legs, his arms. He licked his lips and tipped the bottle to his mouth again. This was what he wanted, what he craved. This was what his blasted new housekeeper had refused him. He sat up and looked ahead. The last of the men had disappeared and he felt safe to leave. He stood slowly, taking it easy, knowing full well the spirit was knocking him off balance. It also made him feel brave, too brave, and he walked down the hillock, fully intent on heading home. But there were more men coming towards him – just two or three, but they had seen him.

'Come on, man! Get down there! What are you doing standing about?'

'Don't waste time, lad! There are lives that need saving!'

Before James knew what was happening, he was caught up in the small group. He was turning, spinning, didn't know if he was coming or going. But with the drink inside him he didn't care about the rain lashing at him. He was wild and free, running with a bottle of whisky in one hand and brandy in the other.

But nothing could have prepared him for what he saw

when he reached the beach. The tide was in, the waves crashing, the noise deafening. The rain lashed sideways on the wind, the thunder was rolling now, moving out over the sea. There were men all around him on the small spit of beach left untouched by the rolling tide; fifty, maybe sixty men of all ages, some in rowing boats heading out to the stricken ship.

James stood still and tried to take everything in. In all his years working with the fishing fleet in Scarborough, he'd never seen anything as hopeless as this. But then his life had been comfortable, safe, his a land-based job rather than facing any danger. Men all around him were calling, shouting, forming themselves into lines, passing boxes from the stricken ship to the shore. But it wasn't just boxes, he realised. Even in his drunken stupor, he knew there were bodies being passed from man to man. Limp bodies with limbs hanging, mouths open, heads gashed. A woman crying, a small girl, another wooden box, another dead child. He gulped.

'Don't just stand there, man! Do something!' a man bellowed into his ear. But James couldn't move. The brandy inside him had done its worst, and he bent and vomited on the rocks. When he lifted his head, he caught words on the wind.

'She was steaming north in thick fog, caught the rocks off Hendon.'

'*Percheron Blue*,' another man said, confirming the name of the ship.

James put his hand over his mouth. It was the steamer he had taken from Scarborough to Sunderland South Dock some time ago.

A shout went up.

'A lifeboat! By the cliffs!'

A group of men ran to where the lifeboat had been spotted. The tiny craft was being lifted on waves one minute, then brought crashing down the next. James couldn't watch; he didn't want to see, wanted no part of this. Why had he ever left Scarborough? He had people there to deal with this kind of thing. He was a McNally; he didn't need to get his hands dirty when tragedy struck. He employed men to do that for him. He employed men to do all manner of unseemly work. One of those men included the McNally family doctor, who had been paid handsomely to ensure he was invalided from service in the war.

James leaned against the cliff, watching, trying to focus and regain his balance, aware that the alcohol was burning him inside. In his drunken state, it seemed ludicrous to him that any attempt was being made to save those in the lifeboat. If the storm had washed the steamer ashore, then what chance did the tiny vessel have? But the men of Ryhope gave all they could. They waded out as far as they dared, dragged women and children out of the ship and carried them back to the shore. There, those with breath in their body were met by Jack Burdon, who lifted a bottle of spirits to their lips to help ease the shock and the pain. And those without breath were dragged over the pebbles to a cave in the cliffs, out of sight.

As the storm raged on, the thunder turned into a distant rumble and the lightning flickered out. The winds still blew strong and the rain lashed down too, but as the tide receded, so did the huge waves that threatened to smash the *Percheron Blue* into driftwood. The men of the Ryhope fire brigade were issuing orders, taking charge and gaining control. Reverend Daye arrived too, running down to the beach with his Bible in his hand. The sight of him was a comfort to many. Those who had survived were sitting on rocks, some crying, some in shock, silent and unbelieving at what had happened. And there were children, boys and girls of all ages, calling for their parents who'd been swallowed by the sea. It would be days before their bloated bodies would wash ashore at Nose's Point.

In all the turmoil, amid all the death, no one noticed James McNally slip away.

'Take the survivors to the church,' the vicar called to the fire brigade chief.

'We need somewhere closer,' the chief replied. 'Many of them may not make it that far.'

Arthur overheard the conversation. 'The Uplands, sir. That's closer, and it's big enough to take them all in.'

'Good idea,' the chief said. 'We can use it as a temporary hospital base for as long as it's needed. You know the man who owns the place?'

'McNally, sir,' Arthur said. He scanned the beach looking for James, hoping to point him out to the chief. But he couldn't see any sign of him among the crowd. 'There's a housekeeper there, and I'll send my son to bring the village women to help. My wife Estelle will be one of them, sir. She's a competent woman. She'll do all she can before the nurses arrive from the hospital.'

The fire brigade were in control of the situation on the beach now, the worst of it over. It became apparent to all that the *Percheron Blue* was stuck deep in sand as the tide receded. The ship was in a bad way, and would likely never sail again.

'I'll call for a boat from Sunderland South Dock to tow it away at high tide,' the chief announced.

Only when Arthur was certain that there was nothing more he could do at the beach did he decide to head home. Many of the men had started walking back already, their heads hanging low. Some of them were in tears at what they'd witnessed. A group of survivors huddled together under blankets the firemen had handed out. They were waiting for the brigade horse and cart to take them to the Uplands. The beach was littered with cargo and personal effects belonging to those on the ship. Hats, handbags and suitcases had been washed up on to the rocks. And in a cave in the cliffs, out of view, lay the bodies of those who had died.

Arthur walked slowly, exhausted, in shock and pain from his exertions. None of it seemed real. One minute he'd been sitting at the breakfast table with his family and Jess, and now he'd been caught in a nightmare. As he walked, the wind and rain eased. An older man was walking alongside him with a blanket around his shoulders. He put his hand on Arthur's arm.

'Thank you,' he said.

'What happened?' Arthur asked.

'We were coming into Hendon in the storm and the ship started grating on something. Rocks, someone said. The noise was like nothing on earth. And then we saw it, the hole in the side, and before we knew what was happening, the ship started listing. It happened slowly; the captain thought we might still make it to Hendon, but it soon became clear that we wouldn't. He said we'd head for Ryhope instead – no dock there, of course, no lifeboat crew either, but he knew there was a beach and there was a chance we might wash up safely. We were thrown about for hours. The captain did what he could, but . . .' The man shook his head. 'Two lifeboats were lowered from the ship. The second boat included ladies, but it began to fill up with water and—'

'Two lifeboats?' Arthur said. He felt sick to his stomach. Only one had been washed ashore.

At the Uplands, Bella Scott was in a right old panic. Nothing she had experienced before had equipped her to deal with the tragic souls who walked through her door. And they were using the good front door too. Oh heavens! she thought. Whatever will Mr McNally make of this?

But Mr McNally was nowhere to be seen.

Estelle was the first to arrive at the Uplands, with Jess in tow. She unpinned her hat and rolled her sleeves up.

'Jess!' she yelled. 'Jess!'

Jess was still outside, waiting by the gate. Her heart in her mouth, she hadn't dared cross the threshold. What if she came face to face with James McNally? The last time they had met, on the night Ada died, he had thrown her out of her home. But today was an exceptional day. She forced her feet towards the front door, ready to walk in and help. She felt sure Ada would understand.

Once inside, she was put to use immediately making mugs of tea. She knew the layout of the kitchen like the back of her hand. It hadn't changed since Ada had worked there. Her thoughts flew to Miss Gilbey and Lena. She'd be missed at St Paul's Terrace; they'd be wondering where she was. Despite the hard work there, meagre food rations and Amelia's bad grace, it was all Jess had to call home.

* * *

Women from the village came running to help, and as they streamed into the house to tend to the sick, Estelle commanded Bella to boil as much water as she could. She opened the larder and offered food and drink to those who needed it, and dispatched several women to collect any pillows and blankets they could find.

'This way, come on in,' Bella said as she beckoned the survivors indoors. She had nowhere to put them. She could hardly take them to her tiny room at the back of the house. There was nothing else for it. She had to put them in the drawing room at the front. It was big enough to seat a dozen, maybe more if children sat on the floor. Those who needed to lie down or those who were injured and old, she would put in the hallway. There was no point in taking any of them upstairs to the bedrooms; the poor things looked as if they couldn't walk another step by the time they reached the Uplands.

A short, stout woman bustled into the kitchen as Jess worked. She looked flustered and her hands were fluttering around her face.

'Oh my word. Oh my gosh,' she muttered.

Jess paid the woman no mind. Almost everyone was in a state of some kind or another that morning, herself included. And she had the added worry in case she came face to face with James McNally. She dreaded to think what he would do if he caught her after he'd told her never to return.

'I'm Jess,' she said. 'Estelle's asked me to make tea for everyone.'

The woman looked at her. 'I'm Bella Scott, the

housekeeper. I haven't worked here long.'

Under normal circumstances, Jess would have shot out her hand in greeting. It was what Ada had taught her to do. But she was so wrapped up in getting the water boiled and tea made that she just nodded. The new housekeeper was a lot younger than Ada had been. In fact it seemed to Jess that she wasn't much older than herself. Her light brown hair was escaping from a knot at the back of her head.

'Thank you for your help,' Bella said. 'I don't know whether I'm coming or going. What a to-do it all is. They tell me the hospital have been alerted, the nurses are on their way. Oh dearie me, I'm not sure I can cope. And now with him out there in the garden, I don't know what I'm to do.'

Jess paused with the tea scoop in her hand. 'Who? Who's out in the garden?'

'No. No, I can't say. I shouldn't have said anything. Just ignore me, dear, please. I'm imagining things. It's the worry of it all. I'm seeing things that aren't there.'

Jess put the scoop down and laid her hands on the woman's shoulders to keep her still, for it seemed as if she was wound up by clockwork. 'Is someone in the garden?'

Bella nodded.

'Who is it?'

'It's him, miss. It's Mr McNally.'

Jess felt a chill go down her spine. 'And why is he in the garden?' she asked.

Bella shook her head. 'I shouldn't say, miss.'

'You should.'

Bella hesitated for a second. 'Come with me. You'll see.'

And so, as Estelle and the village women tended to survivors in the grandest house in Ryhope, Bella and Jess headed outdoors. Sure enough, lying under the hazel trees in the corner of the grounds was James McNally himself. He was soaked to the skin from the rain, but there could be no denying who he was. At his side lay an empty brandy bottle.

'He was as drunk as a lord when I spotted him rolling in,' Bella said. 'I've warned him, you know. Told him several times. But he puts away the bottles faster than I can buy them.'

'Is he asleep?' Jess asked. She kept her distance, not daring to step forward in case James's eyes shot open.

'He's snoring like a train,' Bella said.

'Then leave him be.'

'But miss—'

'What use will he be if he wakes?' Jess said. 'He'll only get in the way when there are people who need help. Leave him until the survivors have been treated and taken away.'

'You sure, miss?' Bella asked.

Jess nodded. 'Certain. And you can stop calling me miss. My name's Jess.'

'Yes, miss.'

'Did you see if he returned home on his own or with men from the village?'

'On his own, miss, before the others. Staggered around like a fool in the storm before he fell. I saw him with my own eyes. I tried to wake him, but he was sleeping like the dead.' Bella's hand flew to her mouth. 'Oh miss, I am sorry. I didn't mean it to come out like that. All those people inside, I hear some of them have lost loved ones in the storm.'

'It's all right, Bella,' Jess said. 'Go back in and finish making the tea. I'll come and help.'

As Bella walked back to the house, Jess took a tentative step towards James McNally's drunken body. She kept her eyes on his face, making sure his eyes were tight shut. He was still sleeping. She took another step. His black hair was plastered against his head and his mouth hung open. She took another step.

'You coward!' she spat.

Then she turned and followed Bella inside.

By now, a small group of nurses had arrived from Ryhope hospital and were tending to those who needed care. The drawing room was full of chaos and crying as bandages were applied and names taken. It was important to know who had survived and who had not. In a corner of the room, a young boy was sucking his thumb. He was wrapped in a blanket and his knees were pulled up to his chest. No one seemed to have noticed him because he wasn't making a noise.

Jess put a mug of tea in front of him and rubbed his arm. 'You okay, little 'un?' she asked. But the boy just stared ahead.

Estelle put herself at the nurses' disposal and helped as much as she could. There were too many women in the room – too many had volunteered to help – and it was left to Estelle to send home those who weren't needed. She was efficient in her work and the nursing staff were appreciative.

Jess and Bella made more tea, the pots and kettles constantly boiling in the kitchen. All the while, Jess kept looking out of the window to see if James McNally was still in the garden. While he was out there, she felt safe. She would tell Arthur and Estelle what Bella had said. For if James had returned to the Uplands before every other man in Ryhope, that could mean only one thing. He had not helped in any way. He had come back with the brandy bottle in his hands and had shirked his responsibility for saving lives.

Stretcher bearers were taking those unable to walk to the hospital on Stockton Road. The young boy from the corner of the room who'd been sucking his thumb walked out holding hands with a nurse. He still wore the same blank expression on his face. When the last of the survivors had left, the fire brigade chief slumped down on the stone step at the Uplands front door. Estelle stood behind him as the village women began making their way home. She thanked every single one of them with a hug and a kiss on the cheek.

The chief watched her with admiration. 'It was a good job you did in there, Mrs . . . ?'

'Atkinson,' Estelle replied. 'My husband Arthur and son Mal were helping at the beach.'

'Brave men, the lot of them. Community! That's what it's all about,' the chief said. 'And a word of thanks must go to Mr McNally for allowing us to use his home when it was needed most. Don't know what we'd have done without his kindness. He's the hero of the hour and I'd like to shake his hand. Anyone know where he is?'

Chapter Eleven

After dinner later that week, Miss Gilbey brought the *Sunderland Echo* to the table to read. It contained news of the shipwreck of the *Percheron Blue*, news that had made its way to the front page. The report confirmed twelve deaths and many casualties. It praised the women of Ryhope for their hard work at the Uplands and the men for their bravery on the beach. But Jess felt her blood run cold when Miss Gilbey read out the final paragraph.

"'Special thanks are to be given to Mr James Henry McNally of Scarborough who resides in the Uplands, Cliff Road, Ryhope. Mr McNally was praised for his quick-thinking actions and generosity of spirit after he opened his home to survivors. He was described as 'the hero of the hour', without whom many more lives might have been lost.'"

Jess felt her stomach turn as Miss Gilbey carried on.

"'A memorial service will be held in the new year for those who perished in the wreck. Mr McNally will be honoured with an award at the service.'"

Jess was overcome with a rush of anger. She and Bella Scott were the only ones who knew the truth about what

James McNally had done on the day of the wreck. She knew that the story printed in black and white was a lie. But the local newspaper was trusted by all who read it. They would believe James was the hero the paper made him out to be. She shook her head sharply.

'No!'

Miss Gilbey looked at her. 'What's the matter, girl?'

Jess looked around the table. Everyone was staring at her. Amelia laughed out loud.

'She's going mad. That's what's wrong with her.'

'Miss Jones!'

All eyes turned from Jess to Miss Gilbey. She never used the girls' surnames like that. Never.

'I'll ask you to remember that we do not speak of madness in this house.'

Jess noticed the look that Lena gave Miss Gilbey; she saw the weak smile that appeared on the girl's lips. Then she saw the way Miss Gilbey's face coloured and noticed how she folded the *Sunderland Echo* in front of her with brisk movements. She wondered yet again if there was more to Miss Gilbey than she knew.

Over the following weeks, news of the shipwreck spread wide. Rumour was rife about treasure washing up on the beach, and some of the village lads were fool enough to believe it. They even went hunting in the caves, though their searches turned up nothing other than smashed wood strewn on the rocks. Further down the coast at Seaham, past Nose's Point, more grisly remains from the *Percheron Blue*'s second lifeboat washed ashore. Ryhope police were called to remove the dead bodies.

The shipwreck left its mark on the village in many

unseen ways. Men who had helped on the beach began to wake in the dead of night, some of them screaming, unable to forget what they'd seen. They had held dead bodies in their arms on the day the *Percheron Blue* washed ashore; passed dead children from man to man, carried injured and sick women from the ship to the sands.

At the Atkinson house on Richardson Terrace, Arthur was as stricken as any of the men with his memories of the tragedy. Estelle tended to him when he woke in the night in a sweat. She calmed him and helped ease his mind. Mal had been spared the worst of it, having been sent back to the village by Arthur to alert the women to help at the Uplands. As Arthur suffered, news reached him and Estelle that James McNally was being lauded for opening his house to the survivors. They were puzzled by this news because try as they might, neither of them could recall seeing McNally that day.

While Arthur struggled with his nightmares and Estelle fretted about his state of mind, a letter arrived from his younger sister Gloria, a spinster living in Grangetown. It explained that she'd been taken ill and had no way of paying her doctor's bill. She hated to impose on her brother and his family, but begged them to do anything they could. Estelle wanted to help immediately but Arthur was more restrained. They sat at the kitchen table with the dogs lying at their feet as they talked.

'We can't afford it, love,' he told her. 'We've got winter ahead of us with no money to spare. You know there's no gardening work going over the next few months; it's the worst time of year for men like me.'

'Then let me go out to work,' Estelle begged. 'There must be something I can do. I'll go to all the pubs and ask if they need an extra pair of hands.'

Arthur shook his head. 'No, lass. I'm not having any wife of mine serving in a pub.'

But Estelle was determined. 'Then I'll just have to take more work in. Sewing, mending, washing and ironing. Come on, Arthur. Are you really going to let Gloria suffer? She's your sister, for heaven's sake!'

Arthur sighed heavily. 'There's more to it, Estelle,' he said. 'You'd better sit down. I don't think you're going to like what you hear.'

Estelle remained standing and put her hands on her hips. 'What's going on? What have you been keeping from me?'

Arthur looked her straight in the eye. 'Have you seen our coal shed?' he asked.

'Course I have. It's half full. What's up with it?'

'When it's empty, there's no money to buy more.'

'What do you mean, there's no money? Haven't we been saving over the summer? All that work you've been doing at the Uplands this year – McNally's paid you for it, hasn't he?'

'Oh, he's paid me,' Arthur said. 'But plenty haven't. They've not been able to. You know how difficult work has been to come by for me and Mal.'

Estelle looked hard at her husband. 'You knew we were running low on money and you didn't tell me? I thought we told each other everything. We're a partnership, remember? Your stupid pride got the better of you, did it?'

'I didn't know how to start explaining it to you, love,' he said. 'I kept thinking things would improve. I thought I could turn things around by late summer. But here we are now with little prospect of work before the start of next year.'

The horrible truth of Arthur's words rocked Estelle. She sank into a chair. 'We can't afford any more coal,' she said.

Arthur shook his head. 'No, lass. No more coal. When the shed's empty, that's it. So you see, as much as I want to help my sister, I can't.'

'Then we'll have to find other work, all three of us,' Estelle said.

'Doing what?' Arthur said.

Estelle jumped from her chair and began pacing the kitchen floor. 'The store might be taking on extra staff for Christmas. There could be work going at the East End market. I'll send Mal up to the pit, see what he can find there.'

'Estelle, please!' Arthur cried. 'We made a pact, love, remember? We said we'd never send Mal underground. We said we'd never make him work at the pit.'

Estelle bit her lip. 'Oh, love. Then what are we going to do?'

Arthur held up his callused hands. 'I'm a gardener, love. It's all I can do. It's everything I am. It's what Mal is too.'

'So you'll let us freeze and starve to death?' Estelle said.

Arthur couldn't fail to notice his wife's sarcastic tone. 'Course not,' he said. He took her hands in his. 'There might be odd jobs I can do for the people whose gardens I tend. I can work indoors, offer my services as a handyman. I'll go knocking on doors all the way around Ryhope, from the colliery to the village.'

'And I'll do the same,' Estelle said. 'I'll take in as much work as I can.'

Arthur patted her hand. 'We'll get through this, lass, you'll see.'

Estelle smiled through gritted teeth. 'We've got no other choice.'

As the weeks turned from autumn to winter, the November wind and rain did little to lighten the mood at Richardson Terrace. A melancholy had set in up at Miss Gilbey's house, too. The dark rooms gave the place an oppressive air, and Jess used every excuse she could to escape outdoors. She persuaded Miss Gilbey to let her do the shopping, and welcomed the walk up the colliery bank each morning. By the time she returned, Miss Gilbey and Lena were leaving together. Lena's whereabouts during the day were the least of Jess's concerns. She was on her guard more than ever against Amelia, only too aware of how sly the girl could be. When Amelia thought no one could see her, she taunted Jess to her face, calling her a wild animal, asking her what it had been like living in her cage. It wasn't easy for Jess and she had to learn to toughen up and ignore taunts that stung like barbs.

At dinner one evening, Miss Gilbey took a deep breath and straightened in her seat.

'Girls,' she said brightly. 'You probably don't need reminding that we're coming up to Christmas. It'll be here before we know it. In order to help Jess prepare the shopping and cooking . . .'

Jess felt a sharp pain in her shin as Amelia kicked her under the table. She glared at the girl, whose face remained the image of innocence.

'Oh yes, Miss Gilbey,' Amelia cooed. 'We do enjoy Jess's cooking.'

It was a comment Miss Gilbey chose to ignore. Jess pushed her feet as far back under her chair as she could, away from Amelia's reach.

'. . . I would like to know who will be staying for Christmas dinner this year and who will not.' Miss Gilbey glanced at Lena. 'You'll be staying, Lena.' It wasn't a question.

Lena nodded, and her sad eyes flashed towards Jess.

'Amelia? Jane?' Miss Gilbey asked.

'I'd like to visit my mam, if she'll have me. I need to ask her first, see how things are back at home,' Amelia replied.

'My aunt Doris has offered to feed me,' Jane said.

Amelia looked at Jess and Lena with malice in her eyes. 'It's those with nowhere to go that I feel sorry for.'

'Then that's settled,' Miss Gilbey said, completely ignoring the spiteful comment. She turned to Jess. 'You, me and Lena. Just the three of us on Christmas Day.'

Jess thought for a moment. 'Since it's not a full house for dinner, Miss Gilbey, and if I promise to wash the pots and tidy and clean afterwards, could I take the evening off?'

'I don't see why not,' Miss Gilbey replied.

'Going somewhere special, are you? Back to the Uplands?' Amelia asked. 'Going to see your boyfriend, the Atkinson boy?'

'I don't know what's got into you today, Amelia,' Miss Gilbey rebuked, 'but I'll tell you this now. I don't appreciate your tone. Any more of it and I will have words with you later.'

Amelia held her gaze defiantly.

'And he's not my boyfriend,' Jess hissed.

Amelia stood from the table, pushed her chair back and left the room.

Over the coming weeks, Amelia kept herself to herself, chastised by Miss Gilbey's outburst, though when she knew Miss Gilbey was in her room and out of sight, she continued to taunt Jess. Jess, however, began to turn a blind eye, aware now that Miss Gilbey was on to Amelia and would not stand for more of her nastiness. But Jess wasn't a sneak, she wouldn't run to Miss Gilbey telling her what Amelia had been saying to her or about kicking her under the table or spilling her bucket of water. Instead, she was learning to ignore the other girl, to turn her back when she came into the kitchen. She was also navigating her way through the beginnings of a friendship with Lena, while Jane was at least polite to her and Miss Gilbey seemed pleased with her work. That would have to be enough. But she still felt unsettled and desperately alone.

She missed Ada every day. Ada had been all she'd known. She'd brought her up and the two of them had been inseparable. She also missed her independence, and although she'd never thought she'd admit it, she even missed her woodshed. Not the spiders and the damp, but the peace and quiet of her own space. She missed the sound of the wind rustling the leaves of the hazel trees and the chirp of the birdsong each dawn.

Lena wasn't a difficult girl to share a room with: she kept quiet and read a lot of books, she respected Jess's privacy and she sometimes made her laugh with jokes. But there was something about her that made Jess anxious and worried for her. Lena seemed not of this world, as if she was just passing through. She was delicate, tiny and thin, with a pale face and big eyes. Physically there was hardly anything to her. And she always seemed on the verge of tears, as if life was overwhelming her. She had a haunted look about her, and combined with her tiny frame, it made her look as if she was ready to fade into nothing. Jess didn't want to burden Lena with her worries when the girl appeared to have plenty of her own.

During the winter, the coal fire at Miss Gilbey's burned constantly and Jess spent much of her time in the kitchen, warming her bones at the fireside. Miss Gilbey and Lena continued to leave the house together each morning, wrapped in coats and hats. They returned by mid-afternoon and neither of them said a word about where they had been. If Jess had felt more comfortable with Lena, she would have asked. But as Lena hadn't offered any information about where she went, Jess didn't think it her place to pry. Still, she was curious.

December arrived, and the shops in Ryhope began to offer seasonal treats, putting them on display in their windows. Miss Gilbey instructed Jess to buy marmalade and jam from Bradnum's factory, along with bottled fruits and sweet mincemeat for their Christmas Day dinner. She added fresh fruit to the shopping list – apples and oranges – and even chocolate if Jess could find it on sale at the store. No festive decorations went up; no Christmas tree was bought. The house was as dark and gloomy as ever. And yet talk of Christmas seemed to put a sparkle in Miss Gilbey's eyes. Jess had never seen her so animated before, and she found herself swept up in the excitement of planning. Knowing that Amelia would be away from the house lifted her spirits even more. She would have one day of respite without the girl's wicked words.

On Christmas morning, Jess was busy in the kitchen chopping carrots, peeling potatoes and wondering how long a roast chicken should be in the oven for. She was lost in her tasks, happy to be given responsibility to cook such an important meal. As she worked, she began to sing. It was a Christmas carol she'd learned at school, a song of angels and glory, one that Ada used to enjoy. She sang it twice through without stopping, and when the song ended she heard a noise and swung around. Miss Gilbey was standing in the kitchen doorway.

'You sing well,' she said.

It was a compliment Jess had heard many times over the years; everyone told her she had a lovely voice. And yet it wasn't something she cultivated or practised; it came as naturally to her as breathing.

'When the dinner is cooking in the oven and you have time to spare, will you join me in the living room, Jess?'

Jess was stunned. She had only ever been invited into the living room once before. But then it was Christmas Day, the most special day of the year. Perhaps Miss Gilbey's normal rules didn't apply.

'Yes, of course,' she said.

When a chance came for her to leave the kitchen, she took off Ada's blue pinny and walked along the hallway. She felt her heart skip as she walked. What could Miss Gilbey want to see her for in the privacy of her room? She stood at the closed door and straightened her shoulders before knocking. At the sound of Miss Gilbey's invitation to enter, she pushed open the door. Lena was sitting in one of the chairs by the fire. Jess hadn't seen her all morning and had thought the girl was still sleeping.

'Please, take a seat,' Miss Gilbey said. She indicated the chair next to Lena. There was a pinkness in Lena's cheeks that Jess thought must've been brought on by her closeness to the fire. It was warm and cosy in the room.

As Jess sat by the fire with Lena, Miss Gilbey bustled about in a corner. Jess didn't want to appear rude and stare, but she was curious about what she was doing. She caught the sound of the tinkle of glass, and then Miss Gilbey turned around. She was carrying a tray in her hands, and on it were three tiny glasses filled with dark liquid.

'A small drink in celebration of the day,' she said. 'You'll both have one, I hope?'

Lena and Jess exchanged a look. Neither of them wanted to seem too keen to take the first glass, but this was a rare treat indeed. Alcohol! And it wasn't even dinner time. To Jess's surprise, it was Lena who indicated that Jess was to take her glass first.

'After you,' Lena said.

Jess lifted one of the tiny glasses from the tray. It felt like nothing in her hand, weightless, and yet she knew that the liquid within, whatever it was, would pack a punch. It would be little more than a mouthful, but what a treat it was. Lena took a glass too, and then Miss Gilbey laid the tray on a side table and sat in the remaining chair.

'Jess, I have something to announce,' she said sternly. 'Your guardianship has been granted. I have this week received confirmation from the town hall.'

'Thank you,' Jess said.

She glanced from Miss Gilbey to Lena and realised that she felt happy there, warm and toasty by the fire.

Finally she belonged to someone else, someone who was at least kind to her, if not loving and warm.

Miss Gilbey raised her glass. 'Merry Christmas.'

Jess and Lena waited for her to take a sip before they did the same. Jess brought the glass to her nose. Was it brandy? she wondered. Or whisky?

'Finest port wine,' Miss Gilbey said when she saw her hesitate.

Jess took the tiniest sip. It was very sweet and she didn't know if she liked it. But she had to swallow it; she couldn't refuse the gift that Miss Gilbey had given. She felt a burn in her throat as the spirit made its way down.

The three women sat in silence, the only sound in the room the crackling of the fire.

'Will we go to church today?' Lena asked.

Jess pressed her feet to the floor. She hadn't been told about any visit to church. Surely Miss Gilbey wouldn't force her to go without prior warning? The last time she'd been inside St Paul's had been the day of Ada's funeral.

'We'll go this evening,' Miss Gilbey said softly.

Jess took another sip, trying to make the tiny glassful of port wine last as long as she could. She felt a heat rise in her face and wasn't sure if it was from the drink, the flames of the fire or the surprise at being asked to attend church. She'd never known Miss Gilbey attend church before, but then, there was a lot about Miss Gilbey that she didn't know.

'After Jess has left to visit her friends.'

Jess breathed a sigh of relief, and raised her glass slightly towards the coal fire.

'To Ada,' she whispered. Then she threw the rest of the port wine down her throat.

Just then, a sound at the front door caused them all to start.

'What on earth . . . ?' Miss Gilbey cried. She ran to the hallway and Jess followed. Lena remained in her chair. As the front door flung open, Jess recoiled in horror when she caught sight of who was there, and what state she was in. It was Amelia, her face bloodied and torn.

'Help me get her inside,' Miss Gilbey said.

Jess didn't ask questions. She did as instructed. With Miss Gilbey on one side and Jess on the other, they half walked, half carried Amelia into the living room. Lena went to the kitchen and fetched a glass of water. Miss Gilbey shook her head.

'No, Lena. Pour a glass of port. She'll need it for the shock. Jess? Bring boiled water and cotton for the cuts on her face.'

Jess headed to the kitchen, leaving Miss Gilbey tending to Amelia. Her mind raced with the horror of what she'd just seen. She was full of questions, confused. And yet Miss Gilbey was taking it all in her stride, Lena too. Jess wondered if this sort of thing had happened before, if that was the reason Miss Gilbey hadn't seemed too shocked by Amelia turning up in the state she was in. She returned to the living room with cotton and water, then stood to one side and watched as Miss Gilbey tended to Amelia.

'Your dad?'

Amelia nodded.

'He didn't . . . touch you again?'

Amelia shook her head. 'Not this time. I ran out as soon as he hit me,' she said.

She winced when Miss Gilbey applied the cotton pad to her face and wiped the blood away. Miss Gilbey stood back to inspect her work. Amelia was crying now, tears running down her face.

Miss Gilbey laid a hand on her shoulder. 'Have you eaten?' she asked.

Amelia shook her head, and Miss Gilbey turned to Jess. 'Jess, lay another place for dinner. There'll be four of us eating now.'

Jess was proud of the meal she'd made, her first Christmas dinner. Miss Gilbey had been generous with the amount of money she'd given her to spend. Plates were piled with vegetables and smothered with gravy, and there were several slices of chicken each. Jess had never eaten so well. She thought back to the Christmas dinners Ada had cooked, but they weren't a patch on this feast. Even with Amelia there, an extra mouth to feed, there was plenty of food for them all. But there was tension at the table; the atmosphere in the house had changed since Amelia had turned up in her bloodied state.

Jess had heard snatches of conversation between Miss Gilbey and Amelia as she prepared dinner. And although she didn't want to pry, she was curious to know what had happened. She was scared, too. Was there a madman roaming the streets? She kept quiet and busy in the kitchen. If Miss Gilbey or Amelia wanted her to know what had happened, they would tell her. But while she ate her Christmas dinner, she kept sneaking glances across the table. Amelia's face was swollen and red, there was a cut under her eye and her hair was matted to her head. She was in a sorry state, and despite everything, Jess's heart went out to her, for no one deserved such a beating.

After dinner had been eaten, a dessert of fruit pudding

was served, then Miss Gilbey retired to her room. As Jess began to clear away the plates and dishes and start on her chores, Lena headed upstairs, leaving Amelia alone at the table. Jess was busy filling a bowl with hot water boiled on the fire and had her back turned. She didn't know that Amelia had left her seat until she felt a touch on her arm.

'Thank you for dinner,' Amelia said. That was it, just those words, nothing more. And with that, Amelia left the kitchen and headed to her room. Jess was stunned. They were the kindest words Amelia had ever spoken to her.

After the kitchen had been cleared and the pots and pans cleaned, Jess went up to her room. She needed to fetch her jacket to wear on the short walk to the Atkinsons' house. Lena was sleeping on top of her covers and Jess didn't wake her. She threw on her jacket and pushed her arms into the sleeves. As she lifted her long hair from inside the coat, the waves cascaded down her back. It was then that she had an idea. She went to her pile of clothes, Ada's blouses and skirts, and rummaged around, searching for the scarlet ribbons. She'd never worn them before. She'd always kept them hidden, a memory of Ada, but today was Christmas Day after all. She searched for the ribbons, her fingers scrabbling in the clothes. She couldn't find them. Had someone moved them? She lifted each item of clothing and shook it out, expecting the ribbons to fall to the floor. She went through her clothes twice. But they weren't there. They had gone.

Her heart going like the clappers, she looked under her bed to see if the ribbons were there, knowing full well how unlikely that was. She looked under Lena's bed too.

She was desperate to find them. Losing the ribbons was losing her last link to Ada. She scrabbled around the floor on her hands and knees, pulled at her bedsheet and eiderdown, but it was a fruitless search. She sank back against the wall and pulled her knees to her chest. She felt the hot sting of tears in her eyes, but she wouldn't cry, she didn't want to wake Lena.

Her heart stopped. Had Lena taken the ribbons? No! No! She pushed the thought away. Lena was the closest thing she had to a friend at Miss Gilbey's house. She wouldn't have gone through Jess's belongings, would she? But if not Lena, then who? Her thoughts turned to Amelia and Jane, for she felt certain that Miss Gilbey would never have stolen from any of her girls. In all the time Jess had lived in the house, she'd never once known Miss Gilbey to even make her way up the stairs, never mind into the girls' rooms. But Amelia . . . she had it in her to be wicked, Jess had suffered her cruelty first hand.

She pushed herself off the floor. Her shock had hardened to anger, and she was determined to tackle the girl. She walked across the landing to the room Amelia shared with Jane, but she was stopped in her tracks by the sound of Amelia crying in her room. The mystery of the missing ribbons could wait another day, Jess decided. Amelia had suffered enough.

At Richardson Terrace, Mal opened the door to greet Jess. The dogs rushed at her, and she made a fuss of them both.

'Merry Christmas!' Mal beamed. 'Come on in.'

She was greeted with hugs from Estelle and Arthur. Mal stood awkwardly to one side while his parents welcomed her, then he too moved forward and wrapped his arms around her, giving her a brief hug. When he stepped back, Jess was both surprised and pleased to see a blush rise on his face.

'We've got some of Arthur's marmalade for tea,' Estelle said. 'And fresh bread made this morning. Hope you're hungry, Jess.'

Jess was still full from the feast of a dinner she'd eaten, but she knew she'd never refuse Estelle's hospitality and Arthur's marmalade. She felt at home with the Atkinsons, happy there. Being with the family helped ease the pain she felt about the lost ribbons. She'd wanted to tie them in her long hair, scarlet strips in her black curls. She'd wanted Mal to admire them too.

Estelle brought a large brown teapot wrapped in a blue knitted cosy to the table. Bread was sliced, margarine and marmalade spread and a contentment settled over them all. The fire crackled and the clock on the mantelpiece ticked. Conversation turned to Miss Gilbey's house and Jess told Estelle about cooking her first Christmas meal.

'Ada would have been proud of you, love,' Arthur said. 'Been back to the Uplands at all?'

Jess shook her head.

'I don't need to go back,' she said. She felt her stomach tighten. She wondered if she should share what she knew about the day of the shipwreck. She didn't want to come across as a gossip, but if she couldn't trust the Atkinsons, then who could she trust?

'There's something I need to tell you, Arthur. And you, Estelle. It's about James McNally.'

Arthur was intrigued. James McNally wasn't high on the list of people he currently held in respect. He'd been reading things in the local paper about him taking credit for work that Arthur and some of the other Ryhope men had done when the *Percheron Blue* washed ashore.

'What is it, lass?' he asked.

Jess told them everything she knew, about James arriving at the Uplands drunk, with a bottle in his hand, and about Bella Scott finding him asleep in the grounds. And she told them how Bella had left James there after she couldn't bring him indoors. 'I saw him with my own eyes,' she finished. 'So you see, he couldn't have helped in the way everyone says he did. He returned to the Uplands long before the first survivors were brought up there.'

Arthur banged his fist on the table. 'I bloody knew it! I was the one who suggested we should use the Uplands, and Estelle alerted the housekeeper. McNally's a bastard and no mistake! Ryhope lads risked their lives at the beach when that boat washed ashore. And he's taking credit for it. By God, he even got a mention on the front page of the *Echo*!'

'Arthur, please,' Estelle said.

'Arthur's right,' Jess said softly. 'McNally is not a good man.' Falteringly she began to tell them how he had thrown her out when Ada died. She described her life with Ada and explained how she wasn't allowed to live inside the Uplands while James was in Ryhope. Her words left her hesitantly. It was the first time she had spoken of how scared she had been as a child and how alone she felt now. She spoke of Alfie and reached for Mal's hand, to assure him Alfie was simply a friend. And then she took a deep breath. 'And there's more . . .' she said.

'Are you sure you want to carry on?' Estelle asked, concerned.

Mal squeezed Jess's hand and she looked him in the eyes.

'I want you to know everything,' she said. And that's when she shared with them Ada's words spoken the day before she died.

After she had finished, Arthur rocked back in his seat. Estelle's hand flew to her heart. Mal's mouth hung open. Everyone was trying to make sense of what Ada had said about Jess deserving more than she knew from the McNallys. What could it all mean?

Chapter Twelve

After tea, Mal insisted on walking Jess back to Miss Gilbey's. She was touched by his offer and glad of the opportunity to be able to spend time alone with him. Since they'd shared their tender moment the night before the shipwreck, they'd hardly seen each other. But Mal hadn't been far from Jess's mind. She thought of him often as she worked at Miss Gilbey's, and it was only when she was with him again that she realised how much she missed him when they were apart.

They headed out into the cold Christmas night with their collars up and scarves pulled tight. The dogs, Pebble and Stone, ran ahead as they walked close together, so close that Jess felt Mal's arm brush against hers. She looked at him and smiled. Then she felt his hand on hers. Their fingers entwined and Mal squeezed Jess's hand.

'You don't mind, do you?' he asked.

'No, I like it,' she said.

They walked on in silence, past the high stone wall in Station Road that ran along the back of Ryhope Hall. The night was silent with not a soul about. Still holding hands, they headed across the road towards their old school. As they walked past it, Cliff Road came into view.

'Remember when you showed Betty Thraxter the Uplands?' Mal asked.

Jess laughed. 'How could I forget? She wouldn't believe the truth about where I lived. I had no choice but to show her. Wonder what she's doing now?'

'I heard she married and moved to Hendon,' Mal said.

'Married? But she's just the same age as us!'

Mal stopped in his tracks, took hold of Jess's free hand and pulled her towards him. 'Maybe she met someone who means the world to her,' he said. 'It can happen, can't it?'

Jess took a tiny step towards him. 'What are you saying, Mal Atkinson?' she teased.

Mal kissed her lightly on the lips. 'Oh, I think you know what I mean.'

'And what if you or I were to meet someone who means the world to us?' Jess asked.

She felt Mal's lips on hers again, and this time they didn't flutter away. The two of them stood a few minutes holding each other, kissing and whispering. But then Jess quickly pulled away.

'I don't believe it,' she said. 'Look!'

Mal turned to see what had caught her attention. On the corner of Cliff Road, a light was glowing in a front window at the Uplands.

'McNally's at home,' Jess said.

'Are you sure? It might be the housekeeper.'

'She'd never keep a light burning in one of the front rooms,' Jess said. 'It's him. It must be. He's in there. I know it.' She dropped Mal's hands and marched towards the Uplands front door.

'Where are you going?' Mal cried. 'Jess! What on earth are you doing?'

Jess felt her heart pound. She was furious, intent on having it out with the man who had thrown her out of her home without a word of explanation. The man who was falsely taking credit for a heroic act. The man who had driven Ada to an early grave. Before Mal could stop her, she banged hard at the door with her fist.

It took a few moments for the door to be opened. James McNally stood there. He was holding tight to the door handle. In his other hand he held a glass filled with dark liquid. Jess noticed his body swaying. There was no doubt he was drunk.

'You!' he spat. He tried to close the door, but Jess was already pushing herself into the hallway.

'Jess, please,' Mal pleaded. But Jess was intent on finally giving James McNally a piece of her mind. There were words she'd wanted to say ever since Ada had died and she'd never had the chance. Well, she was taking her chance now, and no one could stop her. She had nothing to lose now and was determined to tell James McNally exactly what she thought of him.

'Help me with the door,' she called to Mal.

Reluctantly he did as she asked. With both of them pushing against it, James didn't have enough fight in him to keep them out. The door swung wide and Jess stepped inside. An oil lamp in the hall cast shadows around the walls. Mal waited hesitantly by the open door, not daring to close it, afraid there might be someone else inside more capable than James of throwing them out. He didn't feel comfortable being inside the grand house. He didn't want to upset James McNally, not when he and his dad depended on the Uplands for work.

But in Jess's rage, she didn't consider anyone but herself. She felt bile rise in her throat. 'Drunk and alone, on Christmas night of all nights,' she said. 'If I didn't feel so much hate towards you, I'd almost feel sorry.'

'What do you want?' James asked.

'The truth.' Jess walked towards him; she knew he posed no threat in his sorry, drunken state. She poked him hard in the chest. 'Front-page news, you were.'

James gave up his struggle to remain standing and slowly slid down the wall to the floor. He sat staring up at Jess. 'Is it money you want?'

Jess laughed. 'Money? Why would I want money? It's the truth I'm after.'

'Jess, come on,' Mal urged.

But Jess ignored him. She knew she had to take her chance, for it might never come again.

'I'll pay—' James began.

'Be quiet and listen,' Jess said. 'I want the truth about the shipwreck to be told. The stories of your heroic acts are all lies. You weren't here to bring in survivors.'

'What is this?' James slurred.

'I saw you, McNally. I saw you drunk and asleep that morning. I know you didn't do what the newspaper says you did. It was the people of Ryhope who saved lives. People like Arthur Atkinson and his wife, Estelle. I'm going to expose you, James McNally. I'm going to—'

James kicked out from his spot on the floor, but he was slow and Jess moved easily out of his reach.

'Jess!' Mal cried.

She turned to face him. 'I'm not done here,' she said. 'You can go home if you want to. Leave me, I'll be fine.'

Mal shook his head. 'I'm not leaving you, Jess.'

James lifted his head. 'Atkinson?'

Mal turned his face away. He wanted the truth about James McNally exposed just as much as Jess. He wanted his mam and dad rightfully credited with saving lives and opening up the Uplands. But if he jeopardised any work that Mr McNally might give to his dad in the spring, he'd never forgive himself. He felt uncomfortable being there, but he knew what Jess was doing was right. As she stood over James, waging war with the man who'd made her homeless, who Jess blamed for sending Ada to an early grave, Mal felt a flutter of pride. If his dad said anything to him when he found out what had happened, he'd defend her all the way.

When Jess had said everything that she'd wanted to rid herself of, Mal took her arm and led her to the door. But she wasn't finished just yet. She watched as James struggled to rise from the floor. He was on all fours when she walked back to him. She went down on her haunches in front of him and lifted his chin with her fingers so that he was staring right at her. She saw his face fully then, saw his red-ringed eyes, how tired and haggard he was.

'You've not seen the last of me, James McNally,' she said.

Then she stood and walked away.

Mal and Jess walked from the Uplands in silence. Jess was on the verge of tears, wondering if she'd gone too far. She'd been afraid of what had come over her, but she knew that if she hadn't told James exactly what she thought of him, it would have eaten away at her and made her bitter for a long time.

Mal was in awe of Jess's determination and strength.

He took her hand again as they walked, and Jess received his touch gratefully. It helped calm her racing mind. When they arrived at the end of St Paul's Terrace, she stopped on the pavement.

'I'll walk alone to Miss Gilbey's from here,' she said. 'I don't want anyone to see me and pass comment tomorrow about me being out with a boy. You know how people gossip and it's none of their business where I go and what I do.'

Mal nodded. 'Jess, I . . .'

'You want to kiss me?' she said.

Mal laughed. 'No, that wasn't what I was going to say. Although a kiss would be nice.'

'Then what?'

He looked deep into her eyes. 'I want to say that what you did just now with McNally, I admire you for it. And I want to help you. We'll bring him down together.'

Jess sighed. 'I just wish I knew how to do it.'

She took hold of Mal's hand and gently pulled him towards her, mirroring what he had done earlier that night outside the village school. It took him by surprise but also made him laugh.

'It can happen, you know,' he said.

'What can?'

'What I said before, about meeting someone who means the world.'

'And do you think it's happened already?' Jess teased.

Their noses touched, their breath mingled in the dark night.

'Do you?' Mal asked.

'It might have,' Jess said. 'Now, how about that kiss you promised?'

* * *

Jess let herself in to Miss Gilbey's house as quietly as she could. Inside was silent and dark. At the bottom of the stairs she untied her boots and carried them in her hand. She didn't want to wake anyone. When she reached the room she shared with Lena, she turned the doorknob and tiptoed inside. But she needn't have worried about waking Lena. As soon as she closed the door, she heard a whisper.

'Did you see your boyfriend?'

In the darkness, she inched her way along the wall past Lena's bed towards her own. She undressed and slipped on her nightgown.

'Well, did you?' Lena whispered.

'He's not my boyfriend,' Jess said as she snuggled under the heavy blankets.

In all the excitement of the evening, she hadn't given much thought to what had happened earlier. But it came back to her now.

'Lena, have you found any ribbons in the house?'

There was silence for a moment.

'Lena?'

'What colour are they?' Lena asked.

'Scarlet.'

'No. Haven't seen them,' she replied quickly. 'Tell me about tonight, Jess. Tell me about the Atkinsons and what you had to eat.'

Jess was glad to talk with Lena in the dark. She felt too upset, too churned up by emotion to sleep. She was angry with James McNally and scared of how she'd behaved earlier. Had she gone too far? Would her actions come back to haunt her? While she wrestled with her thoughts, Lena threw questions at her. What did the marmalade taste like? How old was Mal? Was Estelle pretty and Arthur handsome? What furniture did the Atkinsons have in their house?

'No more questions,' she said at last. 'I'm sleepy.'

'Jess? Why do you go to the Atkinsons? Don't you have your own family?'

Jess lay still for a moment with her eyes open, staring into the blackness. She was wondering how to answer Lena, or even if she could.

'Jess? What happened to your mam?' Lena begged. 'If you tell me about your mam, I'll tell you about mine.'

Jess turned on to her side, facing Lena. 'My mam?' she said. 'I don't know who she is, or who my dad is. All I knew was Ada. She brought me up and looked after me. She was my world.'

'Did she not tell you about your mam?'

'I used to ask her when I was little. I was confused when I started school and all my friends had mams and dads and brothers and sisters and I had none of those things. I just had Ada, but she was enough. She was everything. In the end, I realised I didn't need to know where I came from. All that mattered was where I was, safe with Ada.'

'She must have loved you very much,' Lena said.

Jess felt a lump in her throat. 'She did,' she replied. 'And you? What happened to your mam and dad?'

'Dad died,' Lena whispered. 'He was a miner, killed at the pit. Mam had to go to Ryhope hospital to see if he was there but she didn't find him, not for hours. He wasn't at the hospital. His dead body was still at the pit. He'd been dragged into the lamp cabin. Mam saw his boots first. She knew it was him from his boots. She fell to her knees when she realised it was him. She wouldn't let him go. She clung on to him and they had to come in and prise her hands off him.'

'Oh Lena, I'm sorry,' Jess said. 'It must've been horrible for her. And for you. How old were you when it happened?'

'Six,' Lena replied. 'Mam was expecting another bairn. A brother or sister for me. I'd been excited about it, I remember. But it died from the shock of Dad's death.'

Jess swallowed hard and heard Lena sniffing back tears.

'And your mam, what happened then? Did she die too?'

'No, she's not dead,' Lena said in a tiny voice.

There was a silence so pure Jess felt she could hear Lena's heartbeat.

'Mam lives downstairs.'

Jess pulled herself up to sitting in her bed. 'Miss Gilbey's your mam?'

'Shh!' Lena hissed. 'She mustn't know I've told you.'

Jess swung her legs on to Lena's bed and shifted across so that she was sitting next to her. She felt the heat from the girl's body. She put her arm around Lena's shoulders.

'So that's why you go out together every day?' Jess whispered.

'We visit Dad's grave. Sometimes we pick flowers from the beach road. Dad loved walking there. The baby doesn't have a grave, so we put pebbles in the sea and say a prayer.'

'You do this every day?' Jess asked.

She felt a movement at her side as Lena shook her head.

'Most days we walk to the hospital.'

Jess remembered Miss Gilbey's words about Lena suffering ill health of the mind. 'Do you mean the asylum?' she asked softly.

Lena nodded. 'I see my doctor there. Not every day. Most days, you know, we just walk the hospital grounds. And Mam . . . Miss Gilbey walks with me. She says the fresh air is good for me. It makes me feel better, so I think she might be right. She likes you, you know. She trusts you.'

Everything began to make sense to Jess. The way Miss Gilbey treated her, inviting her into her living room and asking her to keep an eye on Lena.

'You won't tell her I've told you, will you?' Lena asked.

'Of course I won't. But why aren't you living with her downstairs?' Jess replied.

'She's still mourning my dad and her unborn child. She couldn't cope, you see, then I started having problems. My mind, it drifts off, I can't concentrate on things. They sent me to the asylum and she came to visit me, but she was suffering too, reliving the horror of Dad's accident. She grieves for him and her child even now. It's why the house is so dark. She wants it like that, to remind her. But she fills it with young women's chatter and life, their energy. Says it keeps her going. Says she wants me treated no different from those who lodge here. I don't mind. I spend my days with her.'

'Why does she call herself Miss Gilbey if she's a widow woman?'

'It's so the girls who come to live here know the house is run by a woman on her own, not a married couple. She wants them to know it's safe for them, a place of refuge.'

'For girls like Amelia, you mean?' Jess asked.

Lena shrugged. 'And for girls like me and you.'

'Do you call her Miss Gilbey when you're alone with her? Don't you want to be with her? Don't you think it odd that you're living up here and she's down there?' Jess asked.

'Who's to say what's normal or odd?' Lena said. 'I think a bit of madness runs in us all.'

Jess pulled Lena close to her and kissed the top of her head. She thought of her own life with Ada at the Uplands, Ada in the big house while she lived in the woodshed in the grounds. Whether it was the Uplands or a dark lodging house in a brick-built street, there were secrets everywhere, she thought.

'Jess? I've got something else to tell you,' Lena said.

Jess braced herself. She didn't think she could take any more drama. She'd had plenty already that night. But what Lena said next made her heart leap.

'I know where your red ribbons are.'

The next morning after breakfast, Lena handed Jess her two scarlet ribbons. She said she'd found them on the stairs, which Jess thought unlikely. She knew Lena must have taken them. But any disappointment Jess felt with the girl for stealing them was far outweighed by the closeness between the two of them now. After they'd shared their secrets in the dark, Jess forgave Lena for taking the ribbons. That is, after she'd given her a talking-to about helping herself to other people's belongings. Lena was contrite, apologetic, and Jess had to stop herself being harsh with the girl when she saw tears fill her eyes. That was when she told Lena what the ribbons meant to her, to make her understand she should never take them again.

The weeks after Christmas and into the new year of 1920 were icy, wet and windy. There was no winter snow to make the village look as pretty as a Christmas card. There were just weeks of dark days and leaden skies, blustery winds and incessant rain. Each morning Amelia and Jane left the house to walk up the colliery bank to their jobs at the store. Jess was grateful to remain indoors at Miss Gilbey's, where the coal fires kept the house warm. She felt a little happier now that she and Lena had become close. Amelia no longer taunted her, although neither was she friendly.

Jess kept Lena's secret. But she looked at Miss Gilbey differently now. The sadness in the woman's features began to make sense to her, along with the heaviness in the way she moved. The house with its dark walls still felt oppressive, but at least now she understood the reason for its mournful air. She didn't judge Miss Gilbey for cutting herself off from Lena, with one of them living upstairs and the other down. For Jess's own upbringing had been unusual, she knew that by now. She didn't belong to a family like the Atkinsons. She didn't belong to anyone. Now that Ada had gone, she wondered if she would belong to anyone again. Could there be a future for her and Mal? Would Estelle and Arthur welcome her as one of their own? If they did, she would need to work to bring in money to the Atkinson household, for hadn't Estelle told her that the three of them were already living hand to mouth? She didn't want to be a burden to them; that was the last thing she wanted.

Her thoughts turned to the Uplands, to James McNally. She bit her lip. She had threatened the man on Christmas night, enough, she hoped, to put the fear into him that his reputation was at stake. But in truth she had no clue as to what she would do with the information she had about him. Would anyone believe her word over that of James McNally, even if she announced it from the top of Tunstall Hill? She shook her head to dismiss the thought and carried on with her work.

It was the middle of January when Jess found a note pushed through the letter box at Miss Gilbey's. She was surprised to see it there. She was even more shocked when she saw her name written in black ink on the front. She unfolded the small piece of lined notepaper. It was from Mal, inviting her to tea at Richardson Terrace that weekend. Jess's heart leapt. She wanted to see Mal very much and she loved spending time with the Atkinsons. She especially enjoyed seeing Pebble and Stone and delighted in the way the dogs were at ease with each other. With arrangements made, Miss Gilbey allowed Jess to take a whole Saturday afternoon off work.

The sun had not shone all day and the pavements were still slippery with frost when Jess ventured outdoors on that January afternoon. She had to pick her way carefully along the pavements and roads, holding on to iron railings as she walked. She knew she'd have to pass the Uplands on her way to Richardson Terrace, and dared herself to peer into the windows as she passed. She saw nothing within: no housekeeper bustling about, no James McNally sitting at his desk looking out to the street. She carried on past the village school, then around to Station Road and down to where the Atkinsons lived.

Estelle greeted her with a hug and wished her a happy new year. Jess took off her jacket and scarf and sat by the fire to warm herself. It was a small fire, she noticed, almost ready to burn itself out. If she'd set such a fire at Miss Gilbey's, she'd be putting on more coal to keep it alive. She wondered why Estelle wasn't doing the same. Arthur was sitting on the small sofa, reading the local paper. Was Jess imagining things, or did he seem distant somehow? She'd greeted him warmly but he didn't seem his usual self.

Her heart leapt as she heard a clatter of footsteps in the hall. It could only be Mal. Sure enough, he walked into the room with a huge smile on his face. Tea was poured and conversation began. But still Arthur didn't join in.

'I've been looking for work,' Mal said. 'Mam won't let me go up to the pit, so I've been trying – well, me and Dad have been trying – to find something to tide us over till we start gardening again in the spring.'

Jess was saddened to hear this. 'You've no work at all?' It made sense to her now why Arthur seemed so sullen.

'I've been taking in washing,' Estelle said. 'But it won't pay the rent for much longer. And as for the coal, I daren't think what we'll do when it runs out.' She nodded her head towards the dogs. 'Then there's those two. There'll come a point when we can't afford to feed ourselves, never mind a couple of animals.'

Jess put her hand on Pebble's neck and stroked him.

'Me and Dad, we've got work some days, but it's not regular,' Mal said. 'And it doesn't pay much. I've told Mam I'll work underground. It'll earn us good money.'

'No, son,' Estelle said. Her face was stern. 'Your

father's put his foot down on this. And I agree with him. We won't allow it. Neither will we hear any more on the subject.'

Mal sighed heavily. On the sofa, Arthur rattled his newspaper. 'It's bloody ridiculous!' he cried. Then he stood, flung the newspaper down and walked out of the room.

'Arthur!' Estelle called. 'Get yourself back here.'

Jess and Mal exchanged a look. There was a moment of silence, then Arthur slowly returned to the room.

'Sit down, love,' Estelle said.

Arthur pulled a chair to the fire and the four of them sat together, huddled around the dying coals. Jess could hear Arthur's breath leaving him in short, angry bursts.

'Dad's had an offer of some money,' Mal said. He shot Estelle a look. 'Is it all right if we tell Jess, Mam?'

Estelle looked at Arthur. 'Arthur?'

'Aye, you can tell her. What a bloody mess it all is.'

Mal began speaking hesitantly, telling Jess how, the day after she'd confronted James McNally on Christmas night, he'd come to Richardson Terrace.

'The fella had a hangover,' Estelle said, shaking her head. 'He was in a state, needed a shave too. He looked a right mess.'

'Anyway, he came in,' Mal continued. 'We didn't know what to do with him. Didn't have a clue what he wanted.'

'But we soon found out.' Arthur took up the story, and what Jess heard chilled her to the bone.

James had offered to buy Arthur's silence about what had happened on the day of the shipwreck. It was a substantial amount of money by all accounts, although

Arthur didn't specify how much. Jess could tell it was an amount that made him nervous. She'd never seen him looking so on edge before.

'Bribery, that's what it is,' Estelle said.

'A small fortune for my silence,' Arthur added.

Jess looked from Estelle to Arthur. 'You haven't taken it?'

'God, no!' Estelle cried. 'I might not have much, but I've got my pride.'

'But—' Arthur said.

'No.' Estelle was firm. 'We've been through this, Arthur. We've talked about it until we're blue in the face. We haven't slept properly since the night James McNally came here.'

'There's my sister to think about. The money could clear her doctor's bills. Not to mention put coal on the fire and food in our bellies. How are we to manage till spring on the pittance you bring in with the washing?'

'I'll beg and borrow from the neighbours,' Estelle said. 'They've come to us plenty of times in the past asking for help and I've never denied them. Jimmy Brown and his wife were on their knees one winter and who helped them get through it? We did. Now it's our turn to go cap in hand. And as for your sister, you know I want to help her if and when we can, but charity begins at home, Arthur. We have to put ourselves first.'

'Mam. Dad. Please,' Mal said. 'I've heard nothing but your arguments and fighting since the night McNally called.'

Arthur gazed into the embers of the fire. Estelle lifted her mug of tea and took a long sip. Silence hung over them all. It was Jess who spoke at last.

'We always knew what evil McNally was capable of. But this is a new low, stooping to bribery to keep his reputation intact.'

'We'll never take his money,' Estelle said firmly. 'Never. It's blood money. There's no place for that in our home.'

When Jess returned to St Paul's Terrace, she was surprised to see Miss Gilbey and Lena sitting at the kitchen table deep in conversation. She didn't want to intrude, but she needed to get into the kitchen to start cooking dinner. She stopped at the door and Miss Gilbey looked up. Was Jess imagining things, or did Miss Gilbey actually smile?

'Lena tells me you've been a great help to her these past few weeks,' she said. 'Did your afternoon go as planned?'

'Yes, Miss Gilbey,' Jess said. 'I visited my friends the Atkinsons again.'

'You see them a lot, don't you?'

'They're all I have. They're as close to me as family.'

Miss Gilbey sat back in her chair and brought her hands together at her chest. 'Family. Yes. It's important to us all.' Then she straightened in her chair. 'I've been speaking to Lena, and she feels ready to help with some work around the house. Would you show her your ways of cooking and cleaning?'

Jess glanced at Lena, who was staring at Miss Gilbey. 'Yes, of course, Miss Gilbey,' she said.

'She has . . . Lena has offered to cover your work each Saturday afternoon so you may take a break from your chores. I have given this much consideration, and if you are amenable, I think we could come to a new arrangement, if it would suit you.'

'Oh, it'd suit me,' Jess said. 'It'd suit me very well.'

The following Saturday afternoon, Jess stepped out of Miss Gilbey's house into the cold afternoon. Sleet was coming down on the wind and lashed at her face and arms. She pulled her thin jacket close, but it offered little protection, so she began to run. She prayed that there would be enough coal on the fire when she reached the Atkinsons' house.

With her Saturday afternoons now free, thanks to Lena's kindness, Jess was ready to offer her services to Estelle to help bring money in. She was bristling with excitement and hoped Estelle would be happy with her news. She longed to see Mal again and wished there was privacy at Richardson Terrace for them to be alone. But the house was small and conversations easily overheard. Even when Estelle and Arthur were upstairs in their room, their voices carried to the kitchen below. It was not a house conducive to courting. In her heart she longed to move things along with Mal, but in her head she knew better. Having Mal as her friend and confidante, having Estelle and Arthur to protect and support her, would be enough for now.

When she reached Richardson Terrace, there was no reply to her knock at the door, but she heard the dogs barking inside. She pushed the door; it was unlocked and she walked in. She called out for Estelle, for Mal and Arthur, but there was no reply. Pebble and Stone came to greet her with their tails wagging. Jess walked into the kitchen and through the window saw Estelle in the back yard. She was washing clothes in the big metal tub out there. Jess washed clothes and bed sheets in the same way at Miss Gilbey's but would never have done so in such horrible weather. Despite the sleet and wind, Estelle wore a thin blouse with the sleeves rolled up.

'Where are you hoping to hang them to dry?' Jess called.

Estelle lifted her hands from the water and wiped her forehead. 'I know it's madness on a day like this,' she sighed. 'But it's the only money we've got coming in. I'll dry them indoors, in front of the fire.'

'Can I help?' Jess offered.

Estelle shook her head. 'I'm almost done, pet. I'll tell you what you can do, though. Stick the kettle on, would you? I'm parched.'

Jess did as Estelle asked. Then she headed back into the yard to help Estelle put the washing through the mangle. They hung the clothes on the wooden clothes-horse in front of the fire. The small room filled with steam that misted the windows.

'Arthur and Mal are out looking for work,' Estelle said. 'Molly Teasdale at the Railway Inn has promised them something; there's some repairs she wants doing on the old stables behind the pub. It won't pay much, but it'll keep the fire going and feed us through the week.'

Jess thought of the pantry at Miss Gilbey's, full of jars and tins of food. She thought of the fresh meat she bought at the store, the fruit and vegetables from Watson's Grocers. A thought passed through her mind and she wondered if she could smuggle some of it out. But if Miss Gilbey discovered she was stealing from her, she wouldn't be happy at all. Jess didn't want to risk losing her home.

'Are things really that bad?' she asked.

'Oh, we'll get through it. A couple more months and spring will be here, then there'll be plenty of gardening work again. I'll have to keep a tighter hold on the money this time and save more for the lean months of winter. And there's the party at the Uplands, that should bring in some cash.'

Jess's mouth hung open with shock. 'There's going to be a party at the Uplands?'

Estelle set her mug of tea on the hearth. 'Bella Scott called in to see me this week. She needs to bring in more help. She's got girls from the village to serve the food, but she needs someone in the kitchen to cook and clean. I said I'd do it, of course; I can't turn down the money, although I wish to high heaven I wasn't taking it from James McNally. I've got enough pride to refuse his blood money, but payment for hard work is different. And it will be hard work. There are dignitaries and officials coming all the way from Sunderland. They're bringing their wives too. Invitations have been sent, blue card with gilt edges, Bella said. It's going to be a big do by all accounts. And we can guess who'll be the star of the show, can't we? James flaming McNally, lording it over all and sundry, no doubt.'

'Does Bella still need help?' Jess asked.

'I expect so. Will I tell her you'll be there?'

Jess thought of Lena. A night away from the house, from Miss Gilbey, might do her the world of good. She felt certain that if she put her case to Miss Gilbey and promised to look after Lena, she'd be allowed the night off.

'Tell Bella there'll be two of us,' she said.

* * *

Meanwhile, in a fine three-storey house overlooking the sea at Seaburn, north of Ryhope, Tom Wallace collected the post from the doormat. There was a square hard-backed envelope that piqued his interest, and he opened it first. He read the contents and allowed himself a smile. He enjoyed a good party, and he felt sure his wife would too. He heard the cry of his baby son and turned to see his wife walking along the hallway with their child in her arms. She looked a little tired, he thought. But even after yet another night of disrupted sleep as she tended the baby, she still retained her beauty. Her long black hair fell to her shoulders and her dark eyes flashed at Tom.

'Anything interesting?' she asked when she saw the small pile of letters and journals in her husband's hands.

Tom held out the blue card with the gilt edge.

'You know Ryhope, don't you? Wasn't it where your family came from? We've been invited to a party there, somewhere called the Uplands. Can't say I know it myself.'

His wife took the card from his hand and stared at it in silence. Her stomach turned. Her heart thumped. She couldn't believe what she read on the card.

'Mary?' Tom cried. 'Mary, what is it? You look as if you've seen a ghost!'

Chapter Thirteen

'Mary?'

Tom grabbed baby Henry from Mary's arms as his wife leaned against the wall. The blue card with the gilt edge slipped from her hand to the floor.

'Mary? What is it, dear? Are you all right?'

Mary forced a smile. 'I'm fine,' she said weakly. 'It's been another sleepless night with the baby. I think I must be over-tired.'

'Then let's get you into the parlour. I really think it's time for you to consider taking someone on in the house. You've been stubborn on the issue for years, ever since Sarah was born. But surely you must see you need help now, with three children to look after?'

'No, Tom,' Mary said. 'This is my house, my home. I won't have another woman running around after us. It's not right.'

'But we can afford it.'

'It's not the money and you know it. Now, please, let the subject drop.'

Mary was tired of having the same conversation with her husband. Tom's position as one of the River Wear commissioners meant that they could easily afford to have staff. All of Tom's colleagues employed at least a housemaid to carry out domestic work. But ever since Mary had married Tom and moved into their seafront home at Seaburn, she was determined to do things her own way.

Tom had just about resigned himself to his wife not accepting the help he offered to pay for, even if he didn't understand. But then he didn't know everything about her past. He knew she had worked in domestic service, but had no clue that she had once been a lowly housemaid in Ryhope. Mary knew of the rigours and demands that a mistress or master could place on such girls. She knew of the long hours and pittance of pay they received. No matter how much Tom pleaded for her to employ help, she stubbornly refused. She felt ill at ease at the thought of having a girl work for her in the way she'd worked at the Uplands. It was her pride that stopped her from giving in to Tom's request to take on staff to help in the house. Mary wanted to manage her own household in her own way. She was wilful and strong and no matter how much Tom offered to pay for the best staff he could afford, Mary put her foot down, stubborn to the end.

Besides, she enjoyed caring for her three children: ten-year-old Sarah, four-year-old Rosie and baby Henry. She would never give them to another woman to look after. It was not how she'd been brought up. She thought of her mam, God rest her soul, who'd raised her and her sisters Gracie and Miriam and brother George in a tiny box of a house while their dad drank every spare penny the family earned. If her mam could bring children up, keep them fed and watered, keep them healthy and happy, then so could she. And her mam had much worse to contend with than Mary did. Mary's life was luxury compared to that.

She wished her mam had lived long enough to see what she had made of herself. How she wished she could have told her about her grandbairns and shown her where she lived. She felt sure she would've been happy and proud. But Eva had passed away not long after Mary left Ryhope. Many said she died of a broken heart at the loss of her daughter who slipped away in the night and was never seen again. Eva's spirit was broken when she woke to find her eldest girl gone. She had prayed daily for the safe return of Mary and her newborn child, but she never saw either again.

The night Mary had left her baby at the Uplands was a night she would never forget. She thought of the child often at first, thought of little else as she struggled to cope with the rigours of a new life in London, working for Mrs Guthrie's domestic agency. But the more time she spent in the city, getting used to its strange sights and sounds, the easier it became to push thoughts of her bairn to the back of her mind, though she never left her heart completely. On what would have been her baby's first birthday, 26 September 1904, Mary headed to a haberdashery store beside the mews house in Belgravia where she worked. She bought a length of red ribbon, then she headed to a quiet park she liked to walk in on her free afternoon. There were iron railings around the park, decorative and pretty, worked into a flower motif at the top. She tied the scarlet ribbon around one of the posts and fastened it in a bow. She left it blowing on the breeze.

Mary had kept in touch with her sister Gracie and wrote to her from London once she was settled in. By then, it was too late for their mam to know how she was faring. Gracie's first letter told her that Eva had passed on, and that she'd called for Mary right up to the end. Gracie asked about Mary's baby, wondering what had become of the child. The letter broke Mary's heart and she vowed then that if she ever had more bairns in the future, she would love them and keep them close. She would never run from anything again. She told Gracie that the baby had died. It was better for her sister not to know she had given her child away. And she never once mentioned James McNally. Her letters to Gracie were all about the people she worked for in London, the sights she saw on her free afternoons and how different it all was to Ryhope. In return, Gracie's letters brought Mary all the Ryhope gossip about who was getting married or in the family way.

And then Mary met Tom Wallace, a Sunderland man in London on business.

Tom had been invited to the Belgravia mews house for dinner. As Mary served the food and bustled in and out of the room with platters and dishes, she paid no mind to the guests. She was well trained in her work and kept her eyes on the table, not the men. But she couldn't help noticing Tom Wallace. He seemed to be making a point of staring at her each time she entered the room. She felt his eyes following her as she worked. Her long dark hair was tied up under her maid's cap, and she wore a black dress with a white apron on top. She didn't feel anything special to look at and was uncomfortable under his gaze. When she entered the room to clear away the dinner plates before dessert was brought in, she determined to give him a hard stare. She didn't care if she earned a reprimand from the housekeeper. She knew she couldn't say anything to the man; she wasn't allowed to speak to the guests. But she could let him know how rude she thought him with just a flash of her dark eyes. And so when she walked back into the room with a tray in her hands, she deliberately locked eyes with Tom Wallace. And that was when he smiled, disarming her completely. The grimace she'd set her face into softened. Despite herself, she returned his smile, and even felt herself blush.

From that moment on, Tom Wallace was as smitten with Mary as she was with him. He courted her in secret on her afternoons off work while he was in London. And when he returned to Sunderland, he wrote her letters of devotion, longing and love. With each letter, their relationship blossomed. Status and class were no barriers, he told her. He wanted her more than he'd ever wanted any woman. Tom paid for Mary's return to Sunderland, by train this time. No overnight coach journey like before when Mary had made her way to London with Mrs Guthrie's girls. It was first-class train travel that Tom Wallace paid for. Tom wanted to bring Mary back to Sunderland in style, for he had decided that she was the woman he wanted to wed. It was a small wedding, for many of Tom's family and friends felt he was marrying beneath him.

After Mary married Tom, she continued to write to her sister, but Gracie clearly felt Mary was living in a world in which her siblings didn't belong, and she stopped replying. And then one day in 1914, a letter arrived from her with news that their dad had died after days drinking beer in Ryhope's pubs when war had been declared. Tom had wanted to attend the funeral with Mary, but she refused his request. She knew her new life with its riches was at odds with the one she'd left behind in Ryhope. She didn't want to make her sisters uncomfortable by bringing her husband with her. It would just be the four siblings together, saying a final farewell to their dad.

But there was another reason why Mary didn't want Tom with her. She was ashamed of the way her dad had died, ashamed of the drunken addiction that had taken him. His was to be a pauper's funeral, carried out early in the morning at St Paul's Church. Mary decided to hold her head high and pay her respects to the few good memories of him that she had before his drinking took hold. But she would not, she told herself, go anywhere near the Uplands. That part of her life was over and done with. Wherever her daughter was, it was all in the past. But as she dressed for the funeral, she felt a stirring in her heart and tears pricked her eyes. She shook her head. She was turning sentimental and that would never do. It was the thought of going back to Ryhope, going back to the place she had run from years ago. That was what was causing her stomach to turn and anxiety to set in.

She swallowed hard and looked at herself in the mirror, then straightened the collar of her jacket and settled her black hat on her head. She was ready. Tom's mother had been called to look after Sarah while Tom was at work. Outside the house a car was waiting to take Mary to Ryhope. Just before she left her bedroom, she paused. She picked up her black handbag, then went to her wardrobe and opened it wide. Inside were two slim glass drawers. She pulled one towards her and picked out a length of red ribbon, then slipped it into her bag.

* * *

Mary had a husband who loved her and a family she adored. To all who saw them, she and Tom seemed an ideal family, happy with their girls and new baby boy. Mary knew she was living a charmed life. It was a life she had always craved, away from Ryhope's mucky coal and dusty farms. She'd had to put herself first, become even more stubborn and selfish to get where she wanted to be. She had suffered the rigours of living in London. Worse, she had suffered leaving her baby just days after it was born. But it had all been worth it, she kept telling herself. Her life with Tom and the children was one she adored, and she wouldn't have it any other way.

Tom was kept busy with his work at his office in central Sunderland and Mary was happy to look after their children and home. But there was a secret she kept from her husband. Tom knew nothing about the child she had left at the Uplands, or who its father was. And now an invitation had arrived to attend a party there, a party hosted by James McNally. What on earth was she to do?

She could refuse to go. She could put her foot down and tell Tom she didn't want to attend. She wouldn't be able to tell him the reason why; she'd have to invent an excuse. Perhaps she'd feign illness. If she said she was suffering from women's troubles, it would stop him from asking too many questions. But Tom was desperate to attend.

'It's an honour to be asked,' he told her. 'And by a man like James McNally! Why, he's a local hero after what he did the day of the wreck of the *Percheron Blue*. His name was all over the *Sunderland Echo*. He saved lives and deserves a medal.'

'But do we really need to go?' Mary asked urgently.

'What about the children? Who will we bring in to mind them?'

'My mother, of course,' Tom said. He was pacing the parlour floor, waving the invitation in his hand as Mary sat in an armchair with Henry in her lap. 'It'll do my position at work a great deal of good to attend, Mary. It could mean a lot, promotion perhaps, if I'm seen talking to the right men. The great and the good of the town's businessmen will be there. Men who run the shipyards, breweries, paper mills, coal mines and steelworks.'

Mary loved her husband dearly and could see the excitement in his eyes. If the party had been anywhere other than the Uplands, if it had been hosted by anyone other than James McNally, she would have jumped at the chance to go.

'Must I really come with you, dear?' she asked. 'Wouldn't it be a bore to have me there if you're intent on talking business all night?'

She saw the look on his face change. Her words had clearly upset him.

'But it says wives are invited,' he said. 'You know I want you there. To have you by my side at an event such as this would mean the world to me, Mary. Please come.'

Mary sighed heavily. She rarely refused her husband's invitations to social events; she enjoyed them as much as he did. She liked meeting new people, the wives especially, and seeing the dresses they wore, finding out where they had their hair curled and where they bought their children's clothes. She learned a great deal that way about those who lived in the affluent parts of town.

'Please say you'll come,' Tom said.

Mary looked away from her husband. All manner of

thoughts were racing through her mind. Could she go to the party and keep out of sight of James McNally? She doubted that very much. She would be expected to shake his hand at least. But it had been over sixteen years since they'd last met. She'd been a girl then, and now she was a woman, a mother and wife. Would James recognise her? Would she recognise him? If she wore her hair up, would that disguise her a little? It was silly to even think it, and she knew it. But what was the worst that could happen if she went and they recognised each other? It was hardly likely he would make a fuss; he'd wanted her pregnancy kept secret all those years ago and had thrown her out of his life.

'Please come,' Tom begged. 'Won't it be interesting for you to see Ryhope again?'

'I was there for Dad's funeral just a few years ago,' Mary said. 'I saw enough of it then.'

Tom laid his hand on her arm. 'If you won't come because of Ryhope, then come because of me. I need you there, Mary. Please.'

Mary gazed into Tom's face and he smiled the smile that had won her heart the first time they'd met. She felt baby Henry wriggle in her arms. At times like this, she thought she would burst with happiness. She had a loving, attentive husband, healthy children and the most glorious home life. Their house even had an indoor bathroom, a luxury few could afford. Tom had given her everything, and she adored him with all her heart. Could she really refuse him her company for a few hours at the Uplands? If she did, what did that say about her – that she was afraid? Would her younger self have been scared? No, the young Mary Liddle would never have shied away; she'd have been the first to arrive at the party, the first to stare down James McNally and make him quake in his boots. Mary Liddle wouldn't have been afraid. And neither would Mary Wallace.

'I'll come,' she said. She tilted her head up to her husband and kissed him full on the lips.

At the Uplands, preparations for the party continued apace. Now all Bella needed from James McNally was a list of those who had replied to the invitations, a number she could cater for. But when she knocked on James's study door, and he called out for her to enter, her heart sank. His words were slurred, again. His drinking had worsened since the turn of the year, and despite her best efforts to hide the rum, he had managed to bring more into the house. She'd even heard he'd been seen in the store buying his own. She didn't enjoy hearing gossip like that, for what did it say about her? That she couldn't manage the household? Well, she wasn't having that! But try as she might, Bella hadn't been able to keep James apart from his beloved rum.

She pushed the study door open. James was sitting at his desk, gazing through the window to the street. Bella immediately noticed the empty glass in front of him. Her eyes flickered around the room looking for the rum bottle.

'Mr McNally,' she said sternly. 'We need to firm up the numbers for the party. I can't be expected to produce food and drink if I don't know how many I'm cooking and baking for.'

James kept his back to her as she carried on.

'I've arranged for girls from the village to come in to

help with the serving. More have offered to help in the kitchen and I'll pay them what they're due. Estelle Atkinson will be in charge in the kitchen; she's a capable woman. I'll oversee them all.'

'Atkinson,' James hissed. 'That family's more trouble than they're worth.'

Bella ignored his words and strode towards his desk, intent on getting him to acknowledge her presence. She'd worked for him for several months now, ever since the former housekeeper had died. And if there was one thing she had learned about him, it was that he was an odd kind of man. There had been a flurry of female visitors after he had been lauded a hero for his work when the *Percheron Blue* washed ashore. One in particular – a young woman called Dinah, who wore heavy make-up – often stayed the night. At first Bella was shocked, what with James being a married man, but she soon learned to turn a blind eye. More recently, though, few people had been to the Uplands to visit, and he seldom left the place.

Bella knew full well that he had taken no part in saving lives on the day of the shipwreck. She was glad to have told the truth to Jess, relieved that she was not the only one who knew what a cad James was. But since then, she had kept quiet about it. She needed the money James paid her and the roof over her head. To say anything would be to risk her livelihood, and Bella was not that daft. Besides, she quite liked having the run of the Uplands. She'd worked in much worse places.

Letters from Scarborough carrying the McNally crest had arrived regularly when Bella first started work at the Uplands. But they came less frequently now. More official-looking letters with the Scarborough postmark, from solicitors and lawyers, were delivered instead. Bella knew the content of the letters, as James left them scattered around his study. And, well, if they were left lying about when she went in to clean, it wasn't really prying when she read them, was it? She had seen him alone at the Uplands over Christmas and New Year, a time when most folk had family and friends around them. Even Bella had gone to her sister's home on Christmas night. But James remained alone. He took comfort in his rum and depended on it now more than ever. And so it had come as something of a shock to her when he announced he'd decided to hold a party. She thought the idea repellent at first, and didn't hide her feelings.

'So soon after the war, sir?' she said. 'People are still mourning, still grieving. The country's not back on its feet yet, not properly.'

'Then a party will help mend a divide,' James said.

He'd asked her to make all the arrangements for the party, and she'd done her best. The blue invitations with the gilt edge had been her idea, and she'd had them printed at Thompsons in town. But the RSVPs that had come to the Uplands had been collected by James, and she had little idea where he'd put them.

'Sir, if I could take the replies to the invitations, I'll know how many to cater for.'

James opened a drawer in his desk. 'There are some here.' He pointed to the mantelpiece. 'Some behind the clock. And you'll find a few on my dressing table upstairs. They're almost all acceptances.'

'Thank you, sir,' Bella said.

She eyed the empty glass on James's desk.

'Sir?'

'What is it now, woman?'

She picked up the glass and tucked it out of sight behind her back. 'Would you like me to bring in some coffee for you?'

James was staring hard at the bare branches of an oak tree and didn't reply.

'I'll bring it straight through then. There are buttered crumpets too. I dare say you haven't touched breakfast yet.'

'Miss Scott?'

Bella stopped by the study door with her hand on the doorknob. James turned in his chair to face her.

'You say you're bringing in girls from the village to help with the party?'

'Yes, sir,' Bella said.

James nodded. 'Make sure they're respectable. I don't want any troublemakers. Girls from the village have caused enough trouble here. I never want it to happen again.'

'Of course, sir,' Bella said, and she bustled away.

At Miss Gilbey's, Jess told Lena about her idea of taking her to work at the Uplands on the night of the party.

'What if Mam . . . I mean Miss Gilbey won't allow it?' Lena said.

'Then we'll have to convince her,' Jess said. 'You want to come, don't you?'

'Oh, more than anything, yes.' Lena looked shyly up at Jess. 'Will there be boys there? Miss Gilbey doesn't allow me to meet boys, or anyone my own age. Apart from Dr Anderson at the asylum, I only know the people who live in this house.'

'No, there won't be boys. But if it's a party, there might be ladies in gowns. We can spy on them from the kitchen and see their finest feathers and lace.'

'Will your boyfriend be there?' Lena asked.

Jess laughed. 'I've told you, he's not my boyfriend.'

Lena smirked. 'You should see the way your face lights up when you talk about him.'

Jess put a hand to her cheek and felt herself blush. She thought of Mal, of their kisses in the street under the gas lamp. She thought of their whispers and the secrets they shared when he walked her back to Miss Gilbey's on Saturdays after tea with his mam and dad. She'd never had a boyfriend before, didn't know what it felt like to have one. She listened to Amelia and Jane as they talked over dinner about girls they knew, older girls who were courting. What those girls got up to sounded no different from what she and Mal did, snatching time alone when they could, sharing secrets and kisses.

'All right, I admit it. He might be my boyfriend,' she said at last.

'I knew it,' Lena giggled.

'Come on, let's go and ask Miss Gilbey. And remember, let me do the talking.'

Jess knocked at Miss Gilbey's door. But as she waited, Lena pushed past her, opened the door and walked straight in.

'Lena!' Jess cried.

Lena shrugged and beckoned Jess inside. Jess gingerly poked her head around the door, expecting to find Miss Gilbey angry at the intrusion. But instead she saw the woman's face brighten at the sight of Lena.

'Hello, dear,' she said to Lena. Then she caught sight

of Jess by the door and her face hardened. It was clear to Jess that Miss Gilbey had a softer way with Lena than with the rest of the girls.

Jess watched as Lena plonked herself down in one of the armchairs around the fire. Her tiny frame made it look as if the chair had swallowed her up. Her feet only just reached the floor.

'Jess has got something to ask you,' she said.

'Then you'd better close the door,' Miss Gilbey said.

Jess did as she was told, then walked into the room and stood next to Lena's chair. Miss Gilbey waited for her to speak, looking with bemusement from Jess to Lena and back again. 'Come on, what's going on?' she said. Jess caught a twitch of a smile playing around her mouth. It gave her the courage to speak.

'Miss Gilbey, I've been offered some paid work. It's evening work, and I'll gladly exchange my free Saturday afternoon if it might suit your arrangements here.'

'I don't see any problem there,' Miss Gilbey said. 'Where is the work, in Ryhope?'

'It's at the Uplands,' Lena chipped in. 'There's a party and I want to go too.'

'What Lena means,' said Jess hurriedly, 'is that I've been asked to work in the kitchen on the night of the party.'

'And I want to go with her,' Lena said.

Miss Gilbey glared at Lena. 'You? You want to go to a party?'

'To work in the kitchen, with Jess,' Lena said.

'It was my idea, Miss Gilbey. I thought it might do Lena good, make her happy. I promise to take care of her. And I—'

Miss Gilbey raised her hand to silence Jess. 'Are you sure, Lena?'

Lena nodded eagerly. 'I want to go and I want to help Jess.'

'And you really think you'll manage all right? You know what Dr Anderson said, we mustn't rush these things. You're still under his care.'

'I want to go,' Lena repeated.

Miss Gilbey thought for a moment. 'Very well. But only if Jess swears she will supervise you at all times.'

'I won't let her out of my sight,' Jess said. 'Thank you, Miss Gilbey.'

'Thank you, Mam,' Lena said.

Miss Gilbey's eyes darted in horror towards Jess.

'It's all right, she knows. I told her,' Lena said.

Jess didn't know what to say. Other than the whispers she and Lena shared in their room, this was the first acknowledgement of Miss Gilbey and Lena's relationship. She watched as Miss Gilbey pulled her cardigan about her as if to protect herself against a slight chill.

'Very well,' she said sternly. 'There must be work you should be getting on with. The bed sheets need airing now the rain has eased outside.'

'Yes, Miss Gilbey,' Jess said, and excused herself from the room.

The party at the Uplands was held on the second Thursday in February. It was a cold night, icy and dark. Winter hadn't yet loosened its grip. The pavement outside the house was clear of ice after Bella Scott sprinkled salt there before the first guests arrived. Inside, the place was a hive of activity. Three girls from the village stood in a line in

224

the hallway. Their proud mothers had scrubbed them clean and brushed their hair before sending them out. They were excited and more than a little nervous as Bella instructed them how to behave.

'Don't speak unless you are spoken to,' she ordered. 'And even then, say little. Be polite. Be like ghosts. Move through the guests as if they can't see or hear you. Top up their glasses, keep their plates filled with food, and above all, don't stare.'

In the kitchen, Jess was chopping carrots and Lena was peeling potatoes. Jess had dressed specially for the evening's work, wearing Ada's blue pinny over her dress. Lena too wore a pinny, one of Jess's old ones. It was too big for her but it would have to do. And there was something else that Jess wore, in memory of Ada, who had spent most of her working life at the Uplands. She had plaited her long dark hair and tied the end with a scarlet ribbon.

She felt no fear of running into James McNally, not now she knew he held no power over her. He had been cruel to her in the past, throwing her out of her home on the night Ada died. She would never forgive him for that. She knew he was a liar and a drunk. There was nothing he could say to her, even if she came face to face with him, that could make her feel threatened now. She knew about him trying to bribe Arthur. She knew too much about him for him to make a scene if he saw her in his home. But still, it would be easier for everyone if she kept away from the drawing room and out of his sight. All she had to do was pocket her wages at the end of the night and leave. She'd already decided to offer the money to Estelle to help the Atkinsons buy coal for their fire.

She and Lena worked in silence, enjoying each other's company and the change of scene. The kitchen at the Uplands was much larger than Miss Gilbey's domestic arrangement. It was dominated by an enormous coal fire, and on the hearth were cast-iron plates for cooking and warming food. Estelle bustled around the room, barking orders to the girls who were working there with her.

'Bring more water. Stoke the fire. Keep the coal burning. How is the bread? Has anyone opened the wine? Fill three jugs with water and ice.'

'Ice?' Lena whispered. Her eyes were wide with excitement. 'I've never seen ice before.'

'It's a different world in here,' Jess said.

'But you must be used to it,' Lena said. 'You lived here, didn't you?'

'Not exactly,' Jess said. She looked around the kitchen. 'This was where Ada worked. She lived in a tiny room along the hallway.'

'Didn't you live with her?'

Jess paused with the chopping knife mid-air. 'I did, for a few years. But then I had to move out. I had my own home in the grounds; I called it Hazel Cottage.'

'Your own home? Weren't you lonely and scared?'

'Sometimes,' Jess said. 'I had a puppy, a little dog called Pebble. He kept me company at night. He lives with Mal now.'

'Your boyfriend,' Lena giggled. Then she put her hand on Jess's arm and gazed into her eyes. 'I get lonely and sad too. But we've got each other now. I'll look after you, Jess.'

* * *

In the drawing room and hallway at the Uplands, oil lamps flickered merrily and shadows danced around. It was a pretty scene, warm and welcoming. Bella was relieved to find James McNally if not entirely sober, then not entirely drunk. She had seen him a lot worse of late. At least he'd had a shave and combed his hair.

She watched as he greeted his guests, shaking the hands of the gentlemen and gazing into the ladies' eyes. She heard how charmed he was to meet them, how pleased he was they'd come. She directed her staff to take the guests' outdoor clothes. One girl ran along the corridor carrying coats and hats, gloves and scarves, while another offered drinks from a tray. A third girl showed the guests into the drawing room, where everyone was gathered, a room filled with excited chatter.

Another gentleman and lady stepped into the hallway. The man thrust his hand towards James.

'Tom Wallace,' he said. 'River Wear commissioners' office. I must say, this is a splendid place you've got here, McNally. And this is my wife, Mary.'

Bella looked at Mary Wallace and found herself staring into the face of one of the most beautiful women she had ever seen. She took in Mary's silver and white floor-length gown. She admired the dark hair that fell around her shoulders. There was a determination about the woman, she thought, something tough within her that shone out through her dark eyes. Eyes that were fixed on James as if she was gazing into his soul.

It was then that Bella noticed the decoration in Mrs Wallace's hair. It was discreet and tasteful, just like the woman herself. As it caught the light from the oil lamp in the hall, Bella saw that it was a scarlet ribbon.

Chapter Fourteen

James McNally took Tom Wallace's hand and gave it a hearty shake. As he did so, he wondered how he could use the man's expertise at the River Wear commissioners' office to advance the McNally business. He glanced at the woman by Tom's side and a flicker of recognition ran through him. He tried to place her, but the memory escaped him. He was somewhat surprised when she thrust her hand towards him. A woman, expecting a handshake? How unusual the times were, he thought. The wives of other men arriving at the Uplands that night had been content to defer to their husbands. James wondered if Mary Wallace was one of those progressive types he'd heard so much about. The ones who even dared to demand the blasted vote!

He shook her hand briefly and then let it drop. The last thing he wanted in front of the businessmen gathered at the Uplands was to appear rude. He needed to be on his best behaviour. They believed him to be a hero, and he had to live up to their expectations. He planned to speak privately that evening to Mr Marshall of the Ryhope Coal Company about his offer of investment. He was hopeful that the front-page news about the shipwreck had done enough to convince Marshall that he was a man worth doing business with.

He looked again at the woman's face and long dark hair. She was a beauty and no mistake, but where did he know her from? He shook his head to clear his mind and ushered Tom and Mary Wallace towards one of the serving girls, who waited with drinks on a tray.

When Mary had decided to attend the Uplands party for the sake of her husband, she knew there could be no half measures. She would go as Mrs Mary Wallace, proud wife and mother, or she would not go at all. She raised her chin and held James's gaze for as long as she dared. She'd recognised him immediately. But then she had the advantage. She was expecting to see him and was ready to face him. Whereas James was on the back foot. Her name would have meant nothing to him if he'd seen it written on the invitation list. She searched his eyes. Had a flicker of recognition crossed his face? If it had, she hadn't seen it. But then James McNally was a man who enjoyed the company of many women. Why would he have remembered her when he'd had so many others in his bed? Mary had never let herself believe she'd been anything special to him. And he'd never meant anything more to her than an enjoyable romp. It was what had happened after their intimacy that had made Mary aware of his cruel power. He had thrown her out of her job when she'd told him she was expecting his child. And that was the last time she had seen him, more than sixteen years ago.

She had changed much in that time. Her clothes were of the finest fabric she could buy from the best Sunderland shops. Her shoes were designed and made to fit her delicate feet. Her home in Seaburn was just six miles from Ryhope, but it may as well have been a million miles away, such were the differences between the two places. Ryhope was a village of industry, of mining and farming, where thick black clouds of coal dust drifted from the pit down the colliery bank. Seaburn was a walk on the sands, genteel parks to stroll in, a breath of fresh air and houses that looked out to the sea.

But in other ways, she was still the same headstrong, wayward girl she had always been. She still wore her dark hair long. She was still a beauty. And she still had a mischievous streak in her. She knew she was taking a gamble returning to the Uplands after all that had happened. But she felt certain that James McNally would want to keep the past buried. He had much more to lose than she did if their secret was revealed.

In the kitchen, the girls continued to work under Estelle's command. Estelle issued clear orders and kept them all calm. Despite the cold February night, the room was steamy and hot. The coal fire roared and crackled. Food was taken from pans and skillets and laid on platters and in dishes. These were then given to Bella's serving girls, and Bella instructed where the food should be placed and laid out.

It was to be a different style of eating for this party, not a seated affair. Bella had thought it odd when James had suggested it. She'd never heard of such a thing, although he assured her that such events took place in Scarborough. The idea was that each guest took a plate and could choose from the table the food they wished to take. It was an informal way of dining, so that people could mingle and talk rather than being forced to sit next to someone they might not know or whose company they might not enjoy.

Bella watched as the platters were laid out on a table covered with the best tablecloth. It was the first time she'd catered for such a do at the Uplands, and she wanted to ensure it went well. She was pleased with the village girls for their hard work and diligence. Of the three she'd chosen, two were hard workers. If she had to cater another bash at the Uplands, she'd certainly ask them to return. The other, a stout lass from Smith Street, was less enthusiastic. Bella had to keep pushing her to do her fair share.

In the drawing room and parlour, all was going well. Guests were mingling, laughing and talking. The food was being enjoyed, drinks were taken and glasses refilled. In one corner of the room sat a man with a missing arm. The sleeve of his jacket was pinned against his chest. He was a casualty of war, a reminder to all who saw him that the party was at odds with the horror still fresh in everyone's minds. For many who had returned from war injured, with missing limbs or broken minds, no amount of parties would ever help them heal.

Jess and Lena worked together in the kitchen. They were cutting a slab of cheese into bite-size chunks and arranging them in a pattern on a plate. Jess noticed Lena having trouble holding her knife.

'Are you happy you came?' she asked.

Lena nodded emphatically. Jess watched as she stabbed the cheese.

'No, not like that,' she said. She placed her hand over

Lena's and gently pushed the knife forward, showing her the right way to do it. 'Got it?'

She waited for a response, but instead she saw Lena glancing around. The kitchen was bustling with girls coming and going. Jess felt happy in the middle of such activity. She loved working in Ada's role and in her kitchen. But Lena looked much less comfortable. Her eyes were wide and her breathing shallow.

'Do you need some fresh air?' Jess asked her, concerned.

Lena nodded.

'Estelle!' Jess called. 'We're taking five minutes' break.'

'Must you both go?' Estelle replied. 'We need all the hands we can get.'

'Five minutes, please,' Jess said. 'I wouldn't ask if it wasn't important.'

She ushered Lena into the grounds through the back of the house. It was silent there, cold and dark too. Lena gulped the night air as if her life depended on it.

'Breathe slowly,' Jess said. 'We have all the time in the world.'

'I get panicked sometimes,' Lena said. 'It comes on me all of a sudden and I felt it there, in the kitchen, as if the ceiling was falling in, as if the knife would slip from my hand. I had to get out, Jess. I had to . . .'

Jess took hold of Lena's hand. She'd never seen her so agitated before. 'It's all right,' she said as gently as she could. 'Everything's going to be all right.'

Lena was silent a moment, then she pointed into the darkness of the grounds. 'Did you really live out there?' she asked.

'Just there by the trees,' Jess replied. 'In a little shed with a coal fire, a bed and my puppy.'

She felt Lena's hand squeeze hers.

'It's cold standing here. Shall we go back inside?'

Lena shook her head. 'I'm not ready. You go in, I'll follow.'

Jess looked at Lena's tiny face and big eyes. 'I'm not going anywhere without you. We'll wait until you feel better.'

From inside the Uplands, she heard Estelle calling.

'She wants you back in the kitchen,' Lena said.

'I promised Miss Gilbey I'd look after you tonight. You're my priority here.'

'We should go,' Lena said. 'I don't want to upset Estelle.'

'Are you sure you're ready?' Jess said.

Lena nodded. 'I'm sure.'

She headed to the kitchen door. Just as Jess was about to follow, a movement in the grounds caught her eye. Was it a fox, lured by the noise and light from the house? She peered towards the corner of the grounds where the hazel trees grew. In the moonlight, she saw a woman in a silvery dress. She wore no coat or shawl. Her neck and arms were exposed. Jess wanted to call out, to offer to escort the woman back inside. But she knew it wasn't her place to do so.

As she watched, a shiver ran down her back. Was it the cold of the night or something else? The woman had long dark hair and she had her back to Jess. There was something about her, as if she knew what she was doing, as if she was familiar with the layout of the grounds. Jess was transfixed. Who in their right mind would stroll outside on such a cold night? Why would anyone leave the warmth of the party, and without a jacket too?

She heard Estelle call her name, more urgently this time. She wanted to respond, but found she couldn't move. And then the woman turned. Jess stepped back. She didn't want to be seen. If the woman returned to the party and told Bella she'd been slacking, she'd be disciplined. Worse, she might never be asked to help at the Uplands again. She couldn't bear the thought of losing her connection to Ada.

'Jess! For heaven's sake! Come back to work. What on earth are you doing out there? Lena needs your guidance and I need your help!'

Estelle was standing right behind Jess with her hands on her hips and a furious look on her face.

'Sorry,' Jess said. She turned and followed her back inside.

In the drawing room, James McNally was standing with four men. They were all wearing dark suits, waistcoats and ties. One had a pocket watch that he kept glancing at, as if there was somewhere else he would much rather be. The others lapped up James's words. A short, fat man with a red face called Harry Brunskill even slapped him on the back in hearty congratulations.

'Front-page news! You can't buy publicity like that. Must have done your fishing business in Scarborough a lot of good, eh? And there's been a concert arranged. Didn't you read about it in the *Echo*?'

James shook his head. He'd read little of the local paper in the weeks since Christmas, since the rum took hold of him. His only source of news now was the gossip he overheard on his nights spent drinking at the Albion Inn.

'You haven't heard of the concert?' Brunskill said,

surprised. 'It's a memorial to those who lost their lives in the shipwreck. The town orphanage is behind it; we're working with them. They took in many of the children orphaned in the wreck.'

'Did they?' James said.

'Could have been worse without your quick thinking,' Brunskill said. 'You'll be honoured, of course, at the concert. I intend to get up and give you a vote of thanks myself at the end of the night.'

'There's no need, really,' James said. He felt his throat tighten. Where on earth had his housekeeper hidden the rum? The sherry and brandy were too sweet by half.

'There's every need, man,' Brunskill said. 'We've got a fine programme of events planned for the night. The daughters of some of the men in this room will entertain the audience with a musical recital. There's a splendid soprano signed up, wife of a shipbuilder.'

He noticed that James was staring across the room and paying him little attention. He leaned in close.

'You, er, will be there, won't you?'

'Yes, yes,' James said distractedly. He was searching the room for one of the serving girls. He craved a drink, any drink. The sickly sherry would have to do if all else failed. But where were the blasted girls?

'Very good,' Brunskill said. 'Not intending to head back to Scarborough any time soon, then?'

'What?' James said. He caught sight of one of the girls with a tray of drinks in her hand and the rest of Brunskill's words were lost as he pushed through his guests to reach her.

'Scarborough?' Brunskill continued when James returned to his side.

James shook his head. He thought of his father and the last letter that had arrived from him. Angus's tone had softened since James had sent him the cutting from the *Sunderland Echo* about the shipwreck. In the letter, he had encouraged James to reconcile with Shirley, even if just for appearances' sake. He'd also told him about Alfie joining the army and about James's brother Albert rising up the ranks in the Scarborough fishing industry. James had written back to say he was busy working with Mr Marshall of the Ryhope Coal Company, though in truth, before tonight, he'd not seen the man since the night the housekeeper died.

He ran Brunskill's question through his mind. No, he was not intending to head back to Scarborough any time soon. It suited him to stay away from his family for now. He did not think his return to the Yorkshire coast would please any of them, and certainly not his wife. His son had left home and his father and brother, it seemed to James, were in cahoots. Living at the Uplands alone was fine, or so he kept telling himself. And the more he drank, the more he believed his own words.

'No, I have no plans to return,' he said.

'Then your family must come here! Invite them to Sunderland to attend the concert. I insist. Front-row seats for you all.'

'No, I don't think so,' James said.

'Now, now. I won't take any argument on this,' Brunskill said.

The last thing James wanted to do was to invite his father, wife and brother to a concert where he would be honoured for something he hadn't done. He'd never been sure how the story had started about him helping on the day of the shipwreck. The first he knew of it was when he was greeted with a free drink at the Albion Inn from landlady Hetty Burdon.

'To our local hero,' she said. 'You're welcome in here any time.'

He hadn't argued. If there was one thing he liked more than being served a drink by a handsome woman like Hetty Burdon, it was that the drink was free. He took it and didn't ask questions. But then a keen young reporter from the *Sunderland Echo* arrived, wanting to interview him. It was a story the editor wanted for the front page. On the day the reporter knocked on the front door at the Uplands, James was already deep in drink. And so he invited the reporter in, poured them both a glass of rum and gave the young man what he wanted: a strong story with a lot of appeal. Except it was all lies, and James knew it.

The story spread. Women sidled up to him in the Albion Inn, wanting to sit next to him, hoping to be asked back to the Uplands for a nightcap, or more. James did not disappoint them. The false story had brought him free drinks and free women. It was more than he could have imagined in his wildest dreams. He was happy to spin the lie in return for such riches. However, there was no certainty that the truth of his actions – or lack of them – on the day of the wreck would lie undisturbed. The girl from the woodshed, his own daughter, knew what had really happened. Would she stay quiet? And he'd been unable to guarantee the silence of the Atkinsons even with his offer of cash. They had taken the moral high ground and James felt that ground shaking, unsteady beneath him.

He bit his lip. He was to be honoured at an official ceremony, and that was news indeed. He had the decency to feel a little uncomfortable. He ran a finger around his collar. 'It's warm in here, isn't it?' he said.

Brunskill took a drink and eyed him carefully. 'So it's all set. Your family will attend with you.'

'No,' James said firmly.

Brunskill cleared his throat, then delivered his ultimatum. 'I think you'll find it's expected, Mr McNally. If we're to honour you at the concert, that is. And I'm sure that a man in your position, with business on his mind, will appreciate how important this is.'

James lifted his glass to his lips and threw the contents into his mouth. He swallowed hard and forced himself to think of his father. He wanted nothing more than to make the old man proud. He'd tried time after time in Scarborough. He'd worked harder than his brother ever did, and yet Albert was the one on whom Angus bestowed his love and affection. Could an invitation to the concert to witness the vote of thanks be a way to gain his father's approval at last?

A plan began to form in James's mind. His new housekeeper seemed a decent sort, and he felt he could trust her to make the Uplands comfortable for his father if he came to Ryhope. It had been decades since his father last saw the place. He'd insist he stay a few days at least. He'd introduce him to Marshall at the pit. He'd also speak to that man he'd just met . . . what was his name, the one with the beauty of a wife. Wallace. Tom Wallace. Didn't he say he worked for the River Wear commissioners? There must be men he could introduce his father to there. He'd invite Albert to Ryhope too, although it would be no loss if his brother wasn't able to leave Scarborough. And to further endear himself to his father, he'd even invite Shirley. It wasn't what he wanted, of course, and he doubted very much if Shirley would want to see him. But she wouldn't want to disappoint her father-in-law; James knew how close they were.

He turned to Brunskill and forced a smile. 'Front-row seats, you say?'

'Good man,' Brunskill said. 'Just tell me how many you need.'

Out in the grounds, a frantic Tom had gone in search of his wife.

'Mary! What on earth are you doing? I've been looking for you everywhere. It's freezing out here. What's got into you?'

Mary turned at the sound of Tom's voice. She hadn't realised she'd been away from the party for so long. She'd been wandering in nothing but her party gown. The ground underfoot was solid, and she'd been able to pick her way along the edge of the lawn without her shoes sinking into the soil. She'd been lost in thoughts and memories of working there as a girl. She remembered the housekeeper, Ada Davidson. Everything about domestic service that Mary knew, she'd learned from Ada. The woman's wisdom and advice had stood her in good stead when she'd applied for her job with Mrs Guthrie's agency.

She'd only returned once since she'd left her baby on the doorstep over sixteen years ago. It had been the day of her dad's funeral; the day she'd tied the red ribbon to the gate. She'd been overtaken by emotion and had fallen victim to a rush of sentimentality. Leaving the ribbon there had been foolish; she'd regretted it the minute she returned home to Seaburn and Tom. Tonight, though, when she'd entered the Uplands with Tom by her side, she was surprised to feel nothing. She'd expected a lump in her throat or tears in her eyes, but none came. Too many years had passed in which too much had happened. She felt as if she was looking at a scene from a book she'd read years ago. She was a mother to three wonderful, happy children now. She would not change that for the world. But there'd been nights when she'd wondered what had happened to her baby. Had Ada taken her in? Had James sold her on? Was she now living in Scarborough, perhaps? Was she even alive?

'Mary, love. You'll catch your death. Come inside,' Tom said. He laid his jacket around her shoulders and Mary felt warmth spread across her back.

'I was taking some air,' she said.

'Let's get you in front of the fire to warm up,' Tom said. 'You said you were over-tired the other week, love. I really do think it's time we hired some help for you at home. You can't go wandering off in the cold.'

Mary didn't argue. She would put her foot down again with Tom in the morning on his idea of hiring help.

She let Tom take her hand as they headed back towards the house. But as they passed the kitchen, Mary paused. The windows were wide open to let out the steam.

'Listen,' she said.

Tom shook his head. 'I can't hear anything.'

But Mary could. Inside the kitchen, someone was singing. Mary caught the faint notes on the breeze. It was a pretty voice, clear and true. She recognised the song, though it took her a moment to remember it fully. And when she did, memories flooded back to her of Ada singing the same song as they worked together in the kitchen. She hummed along, singing the words where she could recall them.

'Can't you hear it?' she asked Tom.

Tom nodded. 'I can hear it now, yes. It's someone singing. Most likely one of the kitchen staff. Mary, we need to get you back inside. You're frozen to the bone.'

Mary squeezed his hand and let him escort her back indoors.

In the drawing room, he settled her into an armchair by the fireplace. He brought her a plate of roast ham with freshly baked bread and a glass of brandy to ward off the cold. Mary let him fuss around her as she ate the food and sipped from her glass. She glanced round the drawing room. She recognised many of the guests from previous soirées she and Tom had attended. But it wasn't the people she was interested in. It was the room. The heavy round mirror over the fireplace was still the same, but the colours in the room had changed: new furnishings, new curtains, a new carpet even. She remembered Ada complaining about brushing the carpet, moaning about her bad back. '*My bad back-itis*,' she used to say. Ada. Mary wondered if the old housekeeper might still be alive. Might she be working in the kitchen right at that moment? Oh, what if she was? Wouldn't it be something to go in there and see her, say hello and give her a hug? Would she be proud of how Mary had turned out?

But then Mary's heart sank. If Ada Davidson was still working at the Uplands, she might ask questions. Questions about the baby left on the doorstep all those years ago. Was it better to let the past stay buried?

She looked around again. This was the room where she and James McNally had lain together on the sofa. And now here she was socialising with the cream of Sunderland's businessmen and their wives, and none of them knew her secret. She knew she had nothing to be ashamed of. She had wanted James as much as he'd wanted her. She had encouraged his advances towards her. But she was young and naïve. No one had told her about taking care of herself with a man. Her mam and Aunt Peg had never talked to her about how seeds were sown and babies born. And so an hour in James's company had turned her life around. Within weeks, James had sacked her. As her belly grew, her friends shunned her and her dad threatened to throw her out. Gossip started up around Ryhope and it shamed her mam to hear it.

Mary gazed into the flames of the fire. No, she didn't regret what had happened. If she'd never run away to London she'd never have seen the sights there, and oh, what sights they had been. She'd never have met Tom, and she wouldn't change that for the world. But her secret about her baby and about James McNally would be one she kept close. It was a part of her life that Tom didn't need to know about. She would not do anything to put her marriage in jeopardy; she loved her husband with all her heart. But there were still some things about her past that it was to Mary's advantage for him not to know. She trusted and loved Tom; he was her confidant and soulmate, her lover and friend. She was the mother of his children, the keeper of his house; she knew all there was to know about Tom Wallace. Could she ever tell him all there was to know about her? Perhaps one day, she thought.

'Penny for them?' Tom said gently.

Mary shook her head. 'Just thinking about the children,' she said.

Tom leaned over and kissed her on the cheek. 'Our three wonderful children.'

Mary stood and excused herself, saying she needed to ask one of the serving girls where the facility was. As she threaded through the crowded drawing room, Tom watched her with love in his heart. He saw the way men's eyes turned towards her. She had a beauty that men lusted after and women admired.

But it wasn't the netty that Mary was heading towards. She'd made her decision and there was something she needed to do. She was compelled to know if Ada still worked in the kitchen. If she was there, and she asked awkward questions, Mary would take her to one side and speak to her in confidence. And if she wasn't there, then Mary had to know who'd been singing Ada's song.

In the hallway, she glanced behind her. She thought she'd heard something, but there was nothing to be seen. She walked on. She remembered her way; the layout of the rooms hadn't changed. She walked down the hallway, past the pantry and the storeroom. The kitchen was right in front of her. Mary raised her hand and pushed the door open.

Chapter Fifteen

'Mrs Wallace? There's no problem, I trust?'

Mary swung round and found herself looking up into the dark eyes of James McNally. She let her hand drop from the kitchen door. Her heart thumped under her silver gown. She had no place being away from the public areas of the Uplands. She'd been caught. She lifted her chin and gave him a hard stare. She was daring him to look at her, to drink in her features. She was trying to unsettle him, searching his face for a flicker of recognition. But if he recognised her, then he was doing a fine job of hiding it.

'There's no problem at all,' she said lightly. 'I have been upstairs and appear to have lost my bearings on my way back to the drawing room.'

She locked eyes with James for what felt like a long time. She watched as his gaze fell to her bosom, then rose to her neckline. Then he did something she didn't expect. He held out his arm.

'Let me escort you back to your husband, Mrs Wallace,' he said.

Mary hesitated a second. She heard the slur of his words, knew he was drunk.

'Please,' he said, firmer this time.

It wasn't an invitation. It was a command. And Mary Wallace would not be commanded.

'Does Mrs Davidson still work at the Uplands?' she asked.

James dropped his arm with the shock of her words. 'You knew my housekeeper?'

'Knew? Does that mean she is no longer here?'

'She passed away in September last year.'

The pain of it hit her harder than she'd expected. All the while, she felt James's gaze on her face; he couldn't stop looking at her. She decided to press on with her questions, for there might not be another chance. His eyes were red-rimmed from too much alcohol, and he might not be capable of thinking straight for much longer, Mary thought, and she knew she had nothing to lose by baiting James a little more. Her husband would not chance upon them by the kitchen door, he would be deep in conversation with other businessmen.

'Her poor family. They must miss her,' she said. She raised her eyes in a challenge.

'I know nothing of her family,' he said dismissively. 'Now, please. Mrs Wallace, your husband will be wondering where you are. Let me take you back to the party.'

A wicked smile made its way to Mary's lips. 'And away from the kitchen where Ada used to work?'

'You seem to be familiar with the Uplands.'

Mary nodded slowly. 'I know all its secrets,' she said.

James offered his arm to Mary again and this time she took it. They walked together along the hallway to the drawing room. There, Mary left James's side and helped herself to another plate of food from the table.

* * *

James picked up a glass from a tray held by a serving girl, not caring what was in it this time. He threw the amber liquid down his throat, then glanced at Mary Wallace, now standing at her husband's side, talking and laughing. Who was the damned woman? Her face was familiar; who could forget a beauty like her? Who could forget such a determined soul? He watched her closely. The light from the oil lamps flickered against her gown, caught the smile on her face and the shine on her long, luscious hair. And in that second, in that very moment, he remembered.

She was the housemaid he'd lusted after when he'd been a much younger man. The one he'd made pregnant. The one who'd left her baby on the doorstep. He felt his heart quicken. It all came back to him now. How long ago was it? he wondered. He remembered escaping from Scarborough to the Uplands after Shirley had given birth to Alfie. Had it really been more than sixteen years ago? He felt his legs turn weak.

'Are you all right, Mr McNally?' Mr Marshall of the Ryhope Coal Company had appeared next to him. 'You look a little peaky.' He tapped the side of his nose. 'Too much of the old rum, I'll bet.'

'Yes . . .' James said. 'Yes. That's it. Too much rum.'

He turned and walked from the room, sinking into a chair in the hall. He knew who the woman was. Oh, he knew only too well. He sat with his head in his hands. She hadn't been Mary Wallace back then, of course. She was Mary Liddle. And oh, what trouble she'd caused. He thought of the baby left on the doorstep, the child that Ada had taken in. He remembered the money he'd paid the housekeeper for her silence – a hefty sum of fifteen pounds as well as an increase in her wages. He thought of the girl who'd lived in his woodshed, the girl he'd turfed out the night Ada died. The girl he wanted nothing to do with, who had turned his son's head. He had no idea where she was now and nor did he care.

Mary Wallace had told him that she knew the Uplands and all its secrets. James knew she was wrong. There were still secrets she didn't know.

He took himself away from the noise of the party and headed upstairs. He needed to clear his head. He was in shock. He couldn't go back to the drawing room and mingle with businessmen he wanted to impress while in this sorry state. He shouldn't have drunk so much of the dreadful sherry his housekeeper insisted on serving. What was the woman thinking? He needed time to compose himself.

He walked to his bedroom and lay down on his bed. Five minutes, he told himself, that was all he needed. Five minutes to pull himself together, to push thoughts of Mary Liddle – Mary Wallace – to the back of his mind. Five minutes and then he'd be back downstairs, ready to take Mr Marshall to one side for a confidential chat. He had to arrange an official meeting with the coal company. If he was to invite his father to the Uplands for the concert Brunskill expected him to attend, he needed to act fast with Marshall. He had to have business in hand to show his father by the time he travelled from Scarborough. Five minutes' rest. That was all. He sighed, closed his eyes and was soon snoring, fast asleep.

Downstairs in the drawing room, Mary had been drawn into conversation with Mr Brunskill's wife. Her name was Ruth, which she pronounced with an affected roll of the *R*. She obviously thought this made her appear more refined than she was, but Mary wasn't fooled. As she listened to Ruth Brunskill talk of the charity work she did for the town orphanage, she noticed the common way she pronounced some of her words. She didn't judge the woman, although she knew many would.

When she could take no more of Ruth droning on about herself, she made her excuses and headed to the hall. She paused at the foot of the stairs, glancing around to be certain the coast was clear this time. There were no footsteps walking along the landing, no one coming down the stairs. She knew she had to take her chance. She walked quickly along the hallway as she'd done earlier that night. This time there was no one behind her. This time James McNally would not reach her. She didn't know, or care, where he was. Mary reached the kitchen and stopped outside the door. Ada was dead and her passing had come as a shock. Mary thought of the song she'd heard earlier that evening as she walked in the grounds. The song had escaped through the kitchen window, sung by someone with a honey-like voice. Had the singer been taught the words by Ada herself? Curiosity ate at her. She had to know who it was. She pushed the door open and stepped boldly inside.

'Miss? You shouldn't be in here,' Estelle said when she caught sight of the woman in the silver dress. 'Is there something you need?'

Mary didn't hear her words. She was taking in the kitchen; it had hardly changed at all. Still the same roaring fire, still the same pots and pans. But it looked more careworn than it had done before, and the floor was in need of repair.

Estelle put her hands on her hips and flipped a cloth on to her shoulder. 'Miss? Can we help you?' she asked again. She didn't much like having one of the ladies from the party wandering into her domain. It wasn't right. She didn't want word getting back to Bella Scott that she couldn't control the kitchen.

'I knew the housekeeper, Ada Davidson, and I've just learned she passed on,' Mary said. 'I would like to take one last look at her kitchen, if I may.'

At the mention of Ada's name, Jess looked up from her work. Lena's eyes followed her gaze. She too wanted to know who the strange woman was who had left the luxury of the party to look at an old kitchen. How odd it all was.

'Who is she?' she whispered.

Jess recognised the silvery dress the woman was wearing. It was the woman she'd seen walking the grounds. But she couldn't reply to Lena. She couldn't speak. She couldn't move. In the garden, it had been too dark to make out the woman's features. But in the kitchen, by the light of the fire and the oil lamps around, she could see her face clearly. And what a face it was. She gasped in shock. It was like looking into a mirror.

Estelle too had seen the resemblance; she couldn't miss it. She'd known Jess since she was a small girl, had seen the way she'd blossomed over the years. She glanced from the lady in the beautiful gown to Jess in her pinny with her sleeves rolled up. The woman's long dark hair and dark eyes were identical to Jess's, though her frame was slimmer, and she was shorter where Jess was tall.

At the same time, Mary's gaze settled on Jess, and the two of them locked eyes across Ada's kitchen.

'Who is it?' Lena whispered again.

Mary walked slowly towards Jess. Jess wiped her hands on a tea cloth. There was silence. The two women faced each other, each of them wearing a scarlet ribbon in their hair. Neither of them knew what to say.

It was Estelle who broke the spell. She clapped her hands together. 'Back to work, Lena,' she barked.

'It was you, wasn't it? Singing Ada's song earlier,' Mary said.

Jess gave a tiny nod of her head.

Beside Jess, Lena was still trying to make sense of what was going on. 'She looks just like you,' she whispered.

Her words were intended for Jess, but they fluttered down around Mary too.

Jess could barely catch her breath; she was stunned. Who was this woman who looked so like her, and what did she want?

Mary turned to Estelle. 'Could she be excused a short while?'

'Of course, miss,' Estelle said.

'Let's head upstairs. I think we should talk,' Mary said as they left the kitchen. Jess followed her in silence. 'This way.' Mary pointed along the landing. 'Do they still use the box room at the back?'

Jess shook her head. She was confused. How did the woman know about the box room? It hadn't been touched in years. What on earth was going on?

The door to the box room was stiff; it hadn't been opened in a long time. Inside, the furniture was covered in dust sheets, making ghostly outlines of a dresser, a small bed and a chair. Mary closed the door and sank on to the bed, patting the space by her side.

'Please, sit with me,' she said.

Jess shook her head. She paced the floor, eyeing the woman warily. She couldn't make sense of anything. All she could focus on was the scarlet ribbon in her hair.

'I saw you earlier . . . in the grounds. You were walking by the hazel trees,' she said. 'What were you doing out there?'

Mary smoothed the skirt of her gown with both hands and raised her gaze towards Jess. 'I was looking for something. A ghost from the past.'

'Who are you?' Jess demanded.

Mary answered with a question of her own. 'How old are you, girl?'

Jess straightened her shoulders. 'Sixteen, miss,' she said. 'I'll be seventeen in September.'

Mary nodded slowly, taking this in. 'And have you always lived in Ryhope?'

'Yes, miss,' Jess said.

'Please, don't call me miss. My name's Mary. I'm Mary Wallace now, but I was Mary Liddle.'

Jess remained quiet. The names meant nothing to her.

'And what is your name?'

'Jess Davidson.'

'Davidson, eh? So you took Ada's name,' Mary said gently. 'Ada never mentioned me to you?'

Jess shook her head.

'And what of your family, your parents?' Mary asked.

'Ada was all I knew. I have no family. I have my friends the Atkinsons, and I have Miss Gilbey and Lena. They are my family now.'

'I see,' said Mary. Everything was leading to the conclusion she had known from the minute she'd set eyes on Jess.

'Did you know Ada well?' Jess asked.

Mary smiled widely. 'Oh, I knew her very well. I worked with her here.'

Jess's eyes grew wide. 'You, miss? You worked here?'

Mary rose to her feet. 'I worked as a housemaid . . .' she paused and locked eyes with Jess, 'sixteen years ago.'

Jess furrowed her brow. What did this mean? What was the woman trying to tell her? 'Sixteen?'

Mary nodded slowly. 'I was forced to leave when I found out I was pregnant . . .' She swallowed a lump in her throat. 'Pregnant with you.' She reached out her hand towards Jess, but Jess took a step back.

'No! Miss! This isn't right. What is it you want?' she cried.

'Can't you see, Jess?' Mary said softly. 'The scarlet ribbon in your hair. The scarlet ribbon in mine. Look at us. Our eyes. Our hair. Our faces. Don't you see what this means?'

Jess felt her stomach turn. She wanted to run from the room. She wanted to cry. She wanted to yell. She didn't know if she wanted to lash out at or hug the woman standing in front of her. It was too confusing, too noisy in her head, her whole mind screaming, her thoughts tumbling over each other.

'No . . . no!' she cried. 'This can't be . . . You can't be my mam.'

'Jess . . . please,' Mary whispered.

'No! Ada brought me up. I'm Ada's child. Ada's! She loved me. She was the one who cared for me.'

Mary reached out and placed her hands on Jess's shoulders, hoping to calm her. But Jess wasn't finished.

'If I'm your child, then why did you leave me? Was I so horrid that you couldn't love me?'

Mary pulled Jess towards her and wrapped her arms around her daughter for the very first time. Both of them were crying now, tears streaming down Jess's face.

'No, you weren't the horrid one. That was me. I was young and pregnant with no husband and no money. I had the shame of Ryhope upon me. My dad threatened to throw me out, my friends turned against me. I had no choice but to leave.'

'You had a choice; you could have kept me,' Jess wept.

'No, Jess. For girls like me there was no choice at all. I left you here at the Uplands, on the doorstep in a basket. It was the only thing I could do. I prayed someone would take you in, and it seems my prayers were answered. You've turned into a beautiful girl. Ada deserves all the credit.'

Jess shook her head. 'No!' she cried again. 'This isn't right. It can't be true. Look at you! Your fancy gown. No Ryhope girl could afford a dress like that. You're not from Ryhope and you're not my mam!' She pushed herself away from Mary's embrace and ran towards the door.

'Jess, wait,' Mary called.

Jess froze. 'What?' she sobbed.

'I wouldn't lie to you. Please, listen. I grew up in Ryhope, not five minutes' walk from here. My sisters Gracie and Miriam still live here, but they have nothing to do with me now. My life is different to theirs, to how my own was when I lived here.'

Jess turned slightly towards Mary, ready to hear what else she had to say.

'It's true I can afford the best gowns now, but I had no money for anything back then. I married well. I even lived in London for a while.'

'London?'

'I worked in service, Jess. I worked hard, saved what money I could. I went to London the morning after I left you on the doorstep here. That's where I met Tom, my husband.'

Jess's shoulders slumped. All the fight had left her, but her mind continued to whirl with questions. Why would this woman lie? What could she hope to gain? Could it be possible that she was telling the truth? Was she really her mam? She turned to face Mary and wiped the back of her hand across her eyes.

'The ribbons could be a coincidence,' she sniffed.

'And what if they're not?' Mary said gently.

'We can't be linked by a coincidence,' Jess said firmly. 'Just because . . . because you have dark hair and I have dark hair and—'

'You got your red ribbon from Ada, didn't you?' Mary said.

Jess's gaze dropped to the floor. She nodded. 'I found it after she died. I found two ribbons; they were in Ada's drawer with her clothes.'

'She must have kept them all these years,' Mary said gently.

Jess was puzzled. 'What do you mean?'

Mary sank back down on to the bed and patted the space by her side again. This time Jess sat close to her and listened as Mary told her how she'd tied a scarlet ribbon to the handle of the basket she'd left on the doorstep of the Uplands that night in September 1903. But Mary kept quiet about where the ribbon had come from, that it had been a gift from James. Jess sat in silence, taking it all in.

'Do you depend on the Uplands for your livelihood?' Mary asked cautiously. She was worried in case Jess might be asked to leave her job if news of her relationship with Mary became public knowledge.

'No,' Jess replied. 'I work in service at Miss Gilbey's house. She pays me in bed and board. The money I'm earning here will go to Estelle, Mrs Atkinson. She's the woman in charge of the kitchen.'

'Why on earth would you give your earnings away? Are you in debt to her?'

'No, but the Atkinsons are my friends and I want to help them.'

'You must like them very much.'

'I do. They were offered some money by . . .' Jess paused.

'By whom, Jess?'

'Mr McNally,' Jess said quietly.

'He offered them cash? To help pay their debts?'

'To keep them silent,' Jess said.

She stared into Mary's face. Had she said too much? Had she gone too far? But Mary wanted to know more. And so, in the silence of the dusty room, Jess told her everything she knew about James McNally. She told her about the day of the shipwreck, about him taking credit for saving lives when he had actually been lying in a drunken stupor in the grounds of the Uplands. When she reached the part about the night Ada died after James had run her ragged at the drunken dinner party, Mary was raging.

'The man's a bastard!' she exploded.

Jess shot her a look. She'd never heard a woman use that word before. 'He's a coward,' she said.

Mary thumped the mattress with her fist, sending motes of dust spinning in the air. 'He's a bastard!' she cried. *Thump*. 'A coward!' *Thump*. 'A flaming cheat and a liar!' Her chest heaved and her face turned red and angry.

Jess didn't get a chance to respond, for at that moment, the door opened and James McNally walked into the room. Mary jumped to her feet and flew towards him.

'Get out,' she hissed.

Jess watched the expression on James's face as he took in the sight of her with Mary. He didn't know where to look first. She could tell he was shocked. He'd had no idea she was working in the Uplands that night; she'd done her best to keep out of his sight. But now he'd seen her, and with Mary too. It took him a moment to speak.

'Well, well. You're like two peas from the same rotten pod,' he growled. 'I heard you, the pair of you. Think I don't know what you're up to in here?'

'Get out!' Mary yelled.

Jess was still sitting on the bed. Her head was spinning; there was too much to take in. She thought she was going to pass out, and she pressed her feet to the floor to steady herself. She watched as Mary took another step towards James.

'You can't tell me what to do,' James said.

'Oh, I think I can,' Mary replied. 'Because if you don't do what I say, I'll go straight downstairs and tell my husband and all of those businessmen you're hoping to impress a few secrets about you. Let's see . . .' She began counting on her fingers. 'One – lying about the shipwreck. Two – trying to bribe the Atkinsons. Three – adultery, on a very grand scale. Four – mistreatment of Mrs Davidson that led to her early death. Five – sacking your housemaid after you got her pregnant . . .'

Despite Jess's heart going nineteen to the dozen, a flutter of admiration ran through her at the way Mary was confronting James. But at the mention of her pregnancy, she stiffened. It didn't seem real. It couldn't be possible, could it? And yet the truth of her birth, of who she belonged to, was unfolding right in front of her eyes. It seemed that anything was possible now.

'Stop it!' James cried. He pointed at Jess. 'Not another word in front of her!'

Jess stood up. 'I'm number six, aren't I?' she said calmly.

'What are you on about, girl?' James hissed.

'Six – I'm your daughter. The daughter you forced to live like a dog in a shed in the garden.'

Mary glared at James. 'You did that to your own child?'

'And seven – I'm the daughter you made homeless the night Ada died.'

'Get out!' This time Mary screamed the words at the top of her voice.

James glared at Jess, and then walked out of the room without another word.

Jess was stunned into silence. Mary walked to her and Jess let herself be hugged. Enclosed in Mary's arms, she struggled to comprehend all she had learned. It was too much to take in, and she felt her head spin. Tears found their way down her face and Mary gently wiped them away.

'Is he really my dad?' she asked. She already knew the answer in her heart, but she needed to hear it from Mary.

Mary nodded. 'He is, Jess. I'm sorry.'

'I won't have it,' Jess sobbed. 'I won't come here again. I won't see him. I'll stay at Miss Gilbey's and never return. I don't want any part of him.'

Mary took a step back. 'Now listen to me. Don't say or do anything. He's your father, which makes you a McNally.'

Jess shook her head. 'No, I'll always be Ada's.'

'And Ada would want you to get what you deserve, right?'

Jess blinked hard. It was the very word Ada had used. 'She told me something, you know, on the night before she died. She said it was something involving the McNallys, that I deserved more than I knew.'

'She didn't tell you what?'

'No. She was going to tell me the next day, when I turned sixteen, but she passed away before she could. I've thought many times about what she could have meant.'

'And now you know,' Mary said firmly. 'You're a McNally girl, and there's McNally money to be had.'

'No,' Jess said, shaking her head. 'I can't take on the McNallys. I'm not entitled to anything of theirs.'

'You can take them on, but it won't be easy,' Mary said. 'James will fight you every step of the way.'

They stood a while together, both of them crying. Mary whispered to Jess that she would do what she could for her – but there was a condition attached.

'My husband must never find out what happened here all those years ago,' she said. 'My past is a different world that Tom doesn't understand. I never forgot about you, Jess, never. A part of my heart always loved you. But I had to get away, I felt smothered in Ryhope, gossiped about, taunted by everyone, and all because I wanted a life for myself, something better. And now I've got it. I worked hard for it and I never want to lose it. Tom and I have children of our own now. It wouldn't do for him to find out more than he needs to know.' She looked Jess deep in the eyes. 'You understand, don't you?'

Jess couldn't reply. She didn't understand at all. It seemed that as one secret was revealed, another was being hidden. She didn't like it one little bit. 'Ada told me never to keep secrets. She said it was wrong.'

Mary sighed deeply. 'I remember she told me that too.'

They were interrupted by a knock at the door. Jess stepped out of Mary's arms.

'Come in,' Mary said.

It was Bella. She was red in the face and wringing her hands. 'Sorry to bother you, miss, but I was hoping to find Miss Davidson. We need help downstairs, you see. Her friend Lena's in a bit of a—' She stopped dead and looked from Mary to Jess and back again, gawping like a fish.

'I must go to Lena,' Jess said, and she pushed past Mary and Bella in her haste to leave the room.

'Breathe deeply,' Jess instructed. She was walking Lena around the grounds. 'It's all right, I'm here to take care of you. I'm sorry I left you.'

Lena walked in silence and Jess felt the weight of her responsibility. She wanted nothing more than for Lena to be calm. But her absence from the girl's side in the kitchen had taken its toll. It had brought on another panic attack.

'I'm starting to feel better,' Lena said softly.

'Keep breathing,' Jess said.

'Will you sing for me, Jess?' Lena asked.

Jess was surprised by the request, but felt she couldn't refuse. She hesitated a moment.

'It'll help me feel better,' Lena said.

And so, softly and slowly, Jess began to sing the song Ada had taught her. It was a song of leaves on a springtime breeze. It began as a whisper, but once the words left her lips, she sang louder. The singing helped to calm Jess as much as it calmed Lena. Walking in the night air, feeling the breeze on her face, stilled her racing mind. She couldn't tell Lena what had happened, not while the other girl was in such a state. Perhaps she might talk to her about it when they were tucked up in their beds at Miss Gilbey's. But even then, would Lena be the right person to share such a burden with? What had happened that night would change Jess's life in ways she was scared of. She needed to tell someone she could trust, someone who wouldn't judge. She needed someone who could advise her what to do, how to handle what she'd learned. She needed to talk to Mal.

Jess and Lena walked to the corner of the grounds where the hazel trees grew. Bare branches forked this way and that in the night. Jess carried on singing, and when she reached the end of her song, she began it again. Lena joined in where she could. That was a good sign, Jess thought; Lena's panic must have passed. She decided to take her back to the kitchen, and they walked hand in hand, singing with each step they took.

* * *

At the Uplands front door, a small group of guests were saying goodbye to James McNally. Ruth and Harry Brunskill were there with Tom and Mary Wallace. James shook the hands of the two men and said good evening to Ruth but ignored Mary completely. He was still furious and reeling from the events of the night. He wanted nothing more than to get rid of his guests and lose himself in a bottle.

Brunskill pulled the collar of his coat up to keep out the chill, then stopped and listened.

'Who is that singing?' he asked.

The others looked at each other. None of them had heard it.

'Listen,' Brunskill said. 'It's beautiful.'

They all strained their ears to catch the sounds in the night. Sure enough, they heard the pure notes of a woman's voice.

'Why, she's pitch perfect, whoever she is,' Brunskill said. He set off at a pace, leaving his wife standing in the company of James McNally.

'Harry!' she called, rolling the letter *R* for maximum effect in front of the other guests. 'Where on earth are you going?'

'I've got to see who such a voice belongs to,' he called over his shoulder.

As he headed on to the lawn and around to the back of the house, the others followed. All of them were eager to see what he might find. Only Mary knew who it would be. She felt sure the girl would keep her secret and not give Tom any cause for concern. What would happen in the future between her and Jess would need careful

261

thinking about. It was a complicated relationship; they were strangers to each other, yet there was a pull on Mary's heart, bringing a mix of emotions fraught with difficulty for her. Whatever happened, she wouldn't rush into anything that might compromise her marriage. That would always be her priority.

As the small group rounded the corner of the house, they saw Brunskill stop dead in his tracks. In front of him, Jess and Lena were walking away. Jess was still singing, unaware that anyone was behind her.

'You! Miss!' Brunskill called.

Jess gripped Lena's hand tight and swung round. She saw Mary first, then James, and then noticed the others in the small group. She looked at Brunskill's hand extended towards her, unsure what to do with it. What did the man want?

Brunskill sensed Jess's unease and let his hand drop.

'You have a most extraordinary singing voice,' he said. 'It's very appealing.'

'Thank you, sir,' Jess said.

James McNally walked towards Brunskill and stood just behind him. Jess felt the weight of his gaze on her. She wondered if she would be thrown out and told never to return. She knew what James was capable of and wouldn't put it past him. But the other man was smiling kindly. What on earth was going on? Jess worried for herself, but also for Lena, for if this unusual situation was making her feel anxious, then Lena must be feeling it worse. The man was saying something about a concert. She heard the words *shipwreck* and *orphans*, *charity*, *soprano*. There was talk of daughters of businessmen giving a recital, and then an invitation to Jess to sing too.

'Me, sir?' she said.

'Why not? You'd be perfect,' Brunskill said.

James coughed loudly. 'Brunskill, I'm not entirely sure this is a good idea . . .'

'Of course it is, man! What's wrong with you?'

'She's just a kitchen girl,' James said, staring hard at Jess. 'Nothing more.'

'But that's what makes it so wonderful, don't you see?' Brunskill said. 'A serving girl from the Uplands, the very place that opened its doors as you opened your heart to take in survivors.'

'Please, Brunskill . . .' James insisted.

Brunskill spoke over him. 'No, I've made up my mind. We must have this girl singing on stage. A voice like hers is too good to waste.' He turned to Jess. 'What about it, girl? Will you sing at the concert?'

Jess looked beyond him towards Mary, illuminated in the moonlight. Mary gave a subtle nod noticed by no one but Jess. 'Will you sing?' Brunskill asked again.

Jess looked from Brunskill to James. She held James's gaze for what seemed a long time. From behind Brunskill, James silently mouthed the word *no* to Jess.

'Say you'll do it, lass. Don't be scared,' Brunskill urged.

'Do it, Jess. Sing,' Lena whispered.

'It's for a charity, you say?' Jess said.

'Think of the orphans,' Ruth Brunskill cried.

Jess pushed back her shoulders. She gave a last scathing glance towards James. Then she looked Brunskill straight in the eye.

'I'll do it.'

Chapter Sixteen

When Jess woke the next morning, she lay peacefully for a second before the previous night's events came back to her. She looked across to Lena's bed; it was empty. She wondered where Lena had gone. The day's chores lay ahead of her, and she tried to run through in her mind all she needed to do. But she didn't get very far. She couldn't think straight after what had happened at the party.

She had met her mam and dad. Not only had she learned that her parents were alive, they really existed, she even knew who they were. She should feel happy, she thought. She was a child with two parents; she should feel as if she belonged. Yet there was a darkness inside her that kept growing. Her mam was a lady who wore the finest gowns but who wanted Jess kept a secret. And her dad . . . She sighed heavily, still struggling to take it in. Her dad was James McNally. Of all the men in the world, why did it have to be him? The previous night, Mary Wallace had called her a McNally, but Jess wouldn't allow herself to be called that. She was Ada's girl, a Davidson.

Her head was spinning. She crept out of bed, shivering in the cold room, dressed quickly and went downstairs to light the coal fire. But when she headed into the kitchen, she was surprised to see the fire already burning and Lena sitting alone.

'I lit the fire like you showed me,' Lena said.

Jess sank into the seat next to her. 'How are you this morning?' she asked.

Lena turned her big soulful eyes towards Jess but she didn't reply. She just shrugged.

Jess busied herself making breakfast. Lost in her chores, she managed to push thoughts of Mary and James and Ada's red ribbons away, but only just. Tears kept threatening, and she had to swallow hard to keep her emotions in check.

When Miss Gilbey came into the kitchen, she noticed straight away that something was wrong. She asked Jess if she was feeling well. Jess kept her head down and her hands busy to stop her asking again. But each time she glanced at Lena, she saw the girl watching her, as if she wanted to ask about the night before. She guessed Lena would be curious about the woman who had walked into the kitchen at the Uplands, the woman who looked so like her. She felt her friend deserved an explanation, but she wasn't yet ready to talk. She had to make sense of it herself. And she knew that when she was ready to open her heart about all that happened, all she had learned, she wanted to share it first with Mal. He wouldn't judge, he would listen. But whether he could advise her on what to do next, she wasn't sure. She wondered if she should talk to Estelle. She would know what to do. Or, now that she knew who her parents were, perhaps she should speak to Miss Gilbey, who was her guardian after all. Oh, it was all such a mess.

For now, she thought, while she worked through it all in her mind, the fewer people who knew anything of the party at the Uplands, the better.

After an agonising day with her thoughts turning in her mind, she was desperate to speak to Mal as soon as she could. She took her chance when Miss Gilbey retired to her room that evening. She knocked on the door and asked permission to head to the Atkinsons' house.

'I'll be an hour, no more,' she promised. All she needed was time to tell Mal what she knew. If she didn't talk it out, she felt like her head might explode.

Miss Gilbey eyed her keenly. 'You seemed quiet today, Jess,' she said. 'Are you sure you're quite well?'

'Yes, Miss Gilbey.'

'I see. Well, Lena tells me she worked hard last night. But she is in good spirits. She seemed to enjoy herself. She looks up to you, Jess.'

Jess nodded. 'I enjoy her company too. But I'm afraid she panicked last night, twice.'

'But you calmed her, she told me,' Miss Gilbey said. 'I admire that about you, Jess.'

Jess felt her heart hammer. She wanted nothing more than to run out of the door and down to the Atkinsons' house. She thought Miss Gilbey was never going to give her permission. When at last she did, Jess flew from the house with her jacket in her hand. She forced her arms into the sleeves as she ran, and tied her scarf around her neck to ward off the chill of the February night. When she reached Richardson Terrace, she banged on the door with her fist. There was no time to waste. She had less than an hour.

It was Arthur who answered the door, and his face lit

up when he saw her on the doorstep. He invited her in from the cold, but Jess shook her head. She explained she only had a short time and needed to see Mal on a matter of urgency. She raised her eyes shyly. 'Alone,' she said.

'Oh,' Arthur said stiffly, 'I see,' although he wasn't really sure that he did.

Within minutes, Mal, Jess and the dogs were heading towards the village green. As they walked, Jess tried a few times to broach the subject. She'd gone over in her head many times that day all the things she would say. She'd whispered words under her breath, rehearsed them and even anticipated Mal's response. But now here they were, walking hand in hand with all the privacy they could desire, and the words wouldn't leave her lips.

Mal pointed to a wooden bench at the edge of the green under a gas lamp. They walked towards it and sat close together. He laid his arm around Jess's shoulders and she snuggled against him. The dogs ran rings around each other, chasing and playing on the grass.

'Jess?' Mal whispered. 'I've got something to tell you.'

Jess pulled away from his arm. 'I've got something to tell you too.'

'You first,' he said.

Jess shook her head. 'No, you.'

He put his arm back around her shoulders and squeezed her tight. 'You know when we were talking about Betty Thraxter?' he asked.

'I remember,' she said.

'And you know how we said that when you know someone is right for you, you just know? What I mean is, if you feel it in your heart, then it's right, isn't it?' He tipped Jess's face up to his and kissed her on the lips.

'What are you saying, Mal?' she asked.

'What I'm saying is . . .' He paused. 'What I'm saying . . . what I'm asking is . . .'

Jess felt her heart skip.

'I want to marry you, Jess.'

No! He couldn't be asking this of her! Not now. There was silence between them for a few moments.

'Will you marry me?' he asked, more urgent this time.

Jess wriggled free from his arm and sat up straight on the bench. She took his hands in hers. 'I'd love to marry you, Mal. I want to,' she said.

He threw his arms around her and hugged her to within an inch of her life. She drew away gently.

'But . . .'

His face dropped. 'What is it?'

Jess shifted in her seat.

'Jess? What's wrong?'

She began hesitantly, but as she told him about meeting Mary and her shock on discovering that James was her dad, it all came rushing out. She thought she'd never stop, thought her words would never end. Mal was astonished by it all. He let out a long, low whistle through his teeth.

'I don't know what to do, Mal,' Jess said. 'I don't know where to begin.'

Mal sat in silence, letting her words sink in. 'We should ask Mam for advice,' he said at last.

'There's someone else I was thinking of asking,' Jess said.

Mal looked at her, waiting to hear who she had in mind. But when she spoke, his face clouded over.

'Alfie McNally?' he said sullenly. 'What's he got to do with anything?'

'He's my brother! Don't you see?'

'I don't know, Jess,' he said, shaking his head.

'Do you think he knew we shared the same dad when I met him at the Uplands? Do you think that's why he wrote to me?'

'I wish I knew,' Mal sighed. He hugged Jess close. 'I wish I had the answers to your questions.' He cast his gaze to the ground. 'The day the letter came from Alfie, do you remember?' he said quietly.

'How could I forget?' Jess said. 'You were angry with me, and I still don't understand why.'

'I want to apologise,' he said. 'I was jealous of him. I thought he was after you.'

Jess laughed out loud. 'After me?' She nudged Mal in the side with her elbow. 'The only boy I want after me is you.'

'The only one?' he teased.

Jess nodded.

Just then the bells of St Paul's chimed the hour.

'I'm sorry, Mal. I've gone on about myself all night and now I've got to get back to Miss Gilbey's. She only gave me an hour away. But . . . well, your question. The one you asked me earlier. I do want to marry you, Mal. Once everything's settled, then yes. I know people will say we're too young, but why wait? Why not make the most of our happiness now that we've found it?'

She locked eyes with Mal and kissed him softly. Their breath and lips entwined. Reluctantly she pulled away.

'I've got to get back. Miss Gilbey will have my guts for garters.'

'I'll walk with you,' Mal said. He called for the dogs and together they headed from the green.

* * *

At Miss Gilbey's house, Jess kept the secret about her parents for as long as she could. It ate away at her for days until she broke down. Miss Gilbey found her weeping, and insisted that she join her in her living room, and Jess allowed herself to be led there.

Lena was there too, sitting in an armchair by the fire. Miss Gilbey sat opposite her and invited Jess to sit in the middle chair. Jess did as she was told, weary and exhausted. And there in front of the fire, as the wind whistled and the rain fell outside, she told Miss Gilbey and Lena everything she knew. She worried that it was too much for Lena to take. But still she felt the weight lift from her shoulders with each word that left her.

'You have a mam?' Lena whispered when she had finished. 'And a dad?'

'A mam who keeps secrets. And a dad who is not a good man. He's a liar, a cheat and a fraud.'

'But it's wrong,' Lena said quickly. 'It's all wrong. They can't do this to you, Jess. It's not right.' Jess heard the girl's breath quicken; she recognised the signs. Lena was being overcome by panic.

'Lena?' Miss Gilbey said sternly. She stood from her chair and walked towards her daughter. Jess watched as she took Lena's hands. 'Lena? Look at me and breathe. Breathe deeply. In. Out. Like Dr Anderson told you to, remember?' She swung around towards Jess. 'Might be best if you leave us to it,' she said.

Jess walked from the room with a heavy heart. The last thing she wanted to do was upset Lena, yet her news had sent the girl into another panic. She would need to be careful about what she told Lena; she didn't want to be responsible for causing her any more distress.

* * *

Winter began to lose its grip on Ryhope and March was ushered in on lighter, warmer days. Jess felt her spirits rise a little with the lighter mornings, but she still had much on her mind. Not least was the upcoming concert at which she'd been invited to sing. She'd said yes to Brunskill's invitation just to spite James. She wondered how wise that was now that the concert was just days away. She'd never been on stage before, apart from singing in the school assembly, and her school years seemed a long time ago. She was nervous, not just about singing in front of a hall full of people, but about seeing Mary again. For she had no doubt that Mary would be attending the concert, with her husband who didn't know about Jess. James would be there too.

The whole lot of them who had attended the party at the Uplands would be in the audience. Each time Jess thought of the concert night, a tremble of excitement ran through her. She was scared, yes. But it was a challenge she wouldn't shy away from. She would invite Mal to go with her, Estelle and Arthur too. And if Miss Gilbey was amenable, she would ask her to attend and bring Lena. She felt sure they would both enjoy a night of entertainment. When Jess thought of Lena, a smile spread on her face. If she had a sister, she would want her to be just like Lena, someone to care for and help.

Jess would have the eyes and ears of Sunderland's businessmen, their wives and families on her as she sang. It was then that a thought came to her. What if . . . what if she used that to her advantage? What if she announced to everyone there the truth about James McNally? No! No! She couldn't! She would never be so cruel. She'd heard that James was to be honoured with a medal for his bravery on the day of the shipwreck. But it was Arthur and Estelle, and the other ordinary men and women of Ryhope, who deserved the praise. Dare she say this in front of everyone on stage at the concert? She asked herself what Ada would tell her to do and knew in an instant she could never go through with it. No! She shook her head to dismiss the thought completely. She would never make a public spectacle of herself. Oh, how she needed Mal.

Mal. Just the very thought of him calmed Jess's mind. She had given his words a great deal of thought over the weeks. A proposal of marriage, no less. But her feet were firmly planted on the ground and few romantic notions passed through her mind. The only married couple she knew were Mal's parents, Arthur and Estelle. She admired them both. The Atkinsons were the closest thing she had to a family, the very thing she had wanted since Ada died. She saw how they worked together, each of them giving the other love and support, respect and friendship. That was what she wanted for her and Mal.

A delicious shiver ran through her whenever she thought of Mal. But the two of them were still young. He would need the consent of his parents, which she hoped would not prove a problem. And as for herself, she would need to have consent too, but from whom? Miss Gilbey was her guardian, and rightfully the permission to marry should come from her. But now that Mary and James had been revealed as her parents, the issue was not so clear-cut. Jess decided to ask Miss Gilbey for advice when the time was right. Until then, she threw herself into her work to earn her bed and board, pushing thoughts of

James and Mary to the back of her mind, allowing herself to dream of her future with Mal.

As the day of the concert drew close, the Uplands was a hive of activity. Bella Scott called in help from the two village girls who'd impressed her at the party. The three of them were airing bedrooms that hadn't been used in years, dusting and cleaning and preparing the place for visitors. James's father Angus, his brother Albert and his son Alfie were all en route from Scarborough. Their plan was to stay at the Uplands for two nights and take in the concert.

It was a visit that Angus, as head of the family, had been looking forward to since the telegram arrived from James. To see his wayward son presented with a medal in front of Sunderland's great and good would be an honour indeed. Albert had been surprised to hear James's news and had insisted on accompanying their father to Ryhope. It had been years since he had last set foot inside the Uplands, and he was curious to see the old place. The last time he'd visited, their mother, Florence, had still been alive.

Alfie too was looking forward to seeing the Uplands again, and he wondered if he would set eyes on the girl who had lived in the grounds. He thought of her often, of the strange connection he'd felt to her in the brief moments they'd talked. What was it about her that had kept her in his thoughts all this time? He had finished his army training and was now awaiting details of his first placement. In the meantime, he had been allowed a week's leave. He would have been perfectly happy to spend his time in Scarborough, catching up with his friends from the maritime college. But when he found out about the family trip to Ryhope, he was more than keen to join in.

The trains carrying the McNally men in their first-class carriages steamed their way from Scarborough to York, from York to Durham, from Durham to Sunderland and on to Ryhope East.

Following on in the afternoon train from Scarborough were James's wife Shirley and her mother Eleanor Banks. They had taken the later train because Shirley had business to attend to at the imposing three-storey offices of the family solicitor on Westborough in the centre of Scarborough. Eleanor had accompanied her to witness with her own eyes the documents that her daughter was signing.

'What did I tell you, Shirley?' she gloated as they left the solicitor's office. 'I always told you Angus McNally would never stand for his son's wayward behaviour. He's a decent man, proper.'

Shirley allowed herself a satisfied smile.

When Shirley had gone to Angus on her return from Ryhope with all she knew about James's secret daughter, the elder Mr McNally had remained stoical. Well, in front of Shirley at least. In private, he was furious with his son for bringing shame on the family. If news got out about James's adultery and secret daughter, what would it do to their business? The girl was a waif living in a mucky pit village, in a house for girls in trouble too. Angus was fond of Shirley; he admired her gumption and the way she'd tried to get the best from James. For heaven knows, Angus had tried and failed often enough with his son. When Shirley and Angus had talked of James's daughter, Angus warned her that he would never sanction a divorce. The whiff of scandal would damage the McNally fishing empire. And so Shirley had outlined her plan. And now that she had signed the legal papers, she was filled with a deep sense of satisfaction. Deeper perhaps, than any divorce could bring. For she was still part of the McNally family, still entitled to live in the luxury of her home on The Crescent. And she had done all she could to secure a future for Alfie, her only and beloved child.

'I feel like a celebration is in order, Mother,' she said, as they stepped from the Westborough offices. She glanced at her watch. 'We have two hours before the train leaves.'

Eleanor patted her hand. 'Shall we head to Huntriss Row and take lunch at Bonnet's café?' she said.

Shirley slipped her arm through her mother's. 'Mother, you read my mind.'

When Shirley and her mother arrived at the Uplands that evening, dinner was about to be served. Conversation was bright at the table; everyone was excited and looking forward to the concert the following night. Eleanor and Angus sat together, huddled in conversation about people they both knew in Scarborough. Albert was in good spirits, holding forth on the fishing industry to Alfie while Shirley pretended to take an interest. James sat in a petulant silence, drinking rum.

The following evening, two cars were sent to the Uplands to collect the McNally family and take them to the concert. It was being held at the Victoria Hall and Temperance Institute, on the edge of Sunderland town centre. Victoria Hall was a large, Gothic-style building that faced Sunderland's Mowbray Park, with its ponds and pleasant tree-lined walks.

'I read that the venue has a rather sad history,' Shirley whispered to her mother as they waited for the cars. 'There was a disaster back in 1883 when a large number of children were crushed. They were running to the stage to collect free gifts. Can you imagine their excitement, Mother? The noise? But as they rushed down the stairs, they were trapped by a bolted door that opened inwards to a staircase. Apparently almost two hundred children died in the crush.'

Eleanor sighed deeply. 'Oh, those poor children.'

'The disaster led to the law of the land being changed. Ever since it happened, doors in public places must open both ways. It made the news as far away as the *London Gazette*.'

'Oh my word, their grieving mothers,' Eleanor said. 'And Sunderland still allows the concert hall to be used?'

'The authorities honoured the children with a memorial, but they insisted the building must continue in use.'

'It doesn't seem right somehow,' Eleanor said.

'Sunderland Philharmonic Society performed there in 1910,' Shirley continued. 'They held a Great Jubilee Concert to celebrate their fiftieth anniversary. The singers were accompanied by the Hallé Orchestra, conducted by none other than Sir Edward Elgar.'

Eleanor's eyebrows shot up. 'Really?'

'And Mrs Pankhurst spoke there too, a few years before the war. The Sunderland branch of the Women's Social and Political Union invited her.'

Shirley had hoped this news might find favour with her mother, but one look at Eleanor's face showed that she was still reeling from the shock of the tragedy of the dead children. The women were shaken from their reverie by Angus calling to them.

'Shirley? Eleanor? You two take the first car. We men will travel in the second.'

The McNally family clambered into the luxury of the cars called into service by Brunskill for their use.

Meanwhile, in Seaburn, a car owned by Tom Wallace waited outside his three-storey home on the seafront. Inside the house, in her bedroom, Mary took one last look in the mirror before she descended the stairs. She wore a black velvet gown and white gloves. Her long dark hair had been piled up on her head in a most becoming style. Wisps fell delicately around her face.

'Ready?' Tom asked her.

'As I'll ever be,' Mary said.

And in a tram trundling its way into Sunderland town centre, Jess and Mal sat close together, holding hands. Jess wore her long dark hair in a plait, tied with one of Ada's scarlet ribbons. Mal was wearing a shirt and tie borrowed from his dad. Behind them sat Estelle, in her best blue hat, and Arthur, dressed in his only suit, the one he wore for weddings and funerals and, now, his first concert. In the row of seats behind the Atkinsons sat Miss Gilbey and Lena. Lena gazed out of the window at the world rushing by. She had an over-excited look about her and kept whispering the same three words.

'It's not right. It's not right.'

There was an excitement in the tram car, a real sense of adventure as the small group made their way to Victoria Hall. Lena had her heard turned from Miss Gilbey, who didn't hear the whispers. She didn't realise how panicked Lena was.

Inside the hall, the murmur of conversation reverberated around the walls. The McNallys took their seats in the front row and were warmly greeted by Harry Brunskill. James had so far paid little attention to his wife since she'd arrived in Ryhope. He was suspicious of what she'd been up to in the offices of the family solicitor the day before. His father had told him of her appointment there, but not what her business had been. However, even though the atmosphere between them was strained, he would not show any weakness in his marriage in front of Brunskill. He introduced his wife to the man.

'Mrs Banks-McNally!' Brunskill beamed. 'How lovely to meet you. And thank you for coming all the way from Scarborough.'

Shirley shot her husband a look and gritted her teeth. 'I wouldn't have missed it for the world,' she said.

'And you, Mrs Banks.' Brunskill smiled at Eleanor. 'What a pleasure it is to meet you. My wife Ruth is looking forward to speaking to you after the concert tonight. We trust you might be able to join us for a drink?'

'How nice,' Eleanor replied.

Seven rows behind the McNallys, Mary and Tom Wallace took their seats. As Mary headed along the row, men turned to look at her, taken by her beauty and style, while women admired her black velvet gown. And right at the back of the hall, on hard wooden benches, sat the three Atkinsons.

'Where's Jess gone?' Estelle whispered to Mal.

'She's outside, talking to Lena,' he replied. He glanced

around the vast interior of the hall. 'Says she needed calming down. I think the poor girl's overcome with anxiety being here, after what happened to the children.'

Estelle made the sign of the cross. 'Bless their souls,' she murmured.

Outside the hall, Jess was with Miss Gilbey and Lena, who was in a bad way.

'Breathe, dear. Breathe,' Miss Gilbey instructed.

Lena gulped air and stared wildly at Jess. 'It's not fair, it's not right,' she kept repeating.

Jess held her hand tight. 'Listen to me, Lena. Everything's going to be all right. You'd like to hear me sing, wouldn't you?'

Lena nodded eagerly.

'Well then. What if we go inside and find our seats?'

'Are you ready, Lena?' asked Miss Gilbey.

Lena shook her head.

Jess and Miss Gilbey exchanged a look.

'Leave her with me,' Jess said. 'I'll calm her down and bring her inside.'

A look of uncertainty crossed Miss Gilbey's face, but only for a second. She trusted Jess and knew the girl would do all she could. She headed into the hall, leaving Jess and Lena outside.

'It's not right, Jess,' Lena said again. 'You can't let him take the medal, you can't let them give him the honour. He didn't do it, you said. You told Miss Gilbey. He didn't do anything. The Atkinsons did. You said James was drunk.'

'It's all right, Lena.'

'But the shipwreck, Jess. Think of the orphans. James

McNally had nothing to do with any of it, nothing! You need to tell everyone the truth, Jess. Get up on that stage and tell them the truth.'

Jess didn't dare tell Lena that the thought had crossed her mind. She felt Lena's hands grip hers.

'Lena, please,' she urged. Lena turned her big eyes towards Jess.

'This is a secret you must keep,' Jess said. 'People like James McNally, they're different to us. The man is a liar and a fraud, we all know that now. I was there, I know the truth about what happened on the day of the shipwreck, but we can't just go in there and cause a scene. We'll get him for what he's done . . .'

'But he's your dad, Jess. Your dad!'

'We'll get him, Lena. I'll get him. Estelle and Arthur will have their reward, you'll see.'

'Miss Gilbey can help, can't she? She knows the secret too.'

'Breathe, Lena. You need to calm down. Then we'll go back inside and find Miss Gilbey.'

In the shadows of a doorway behind them, Harry Brunskill threw his cigar to the ground and stubbed it out with the toe of his shoe. He recognised the name Gilbey. It could only be Veronica Gilbey, the woman who ran a home for destitute girls in Ryhope. He'd dealt with her in the past and knew she was trustworthy. He had a list of all those attending the concert and where they were seated. It shouldn't prove too difficult to find her.

By the time Jess led Lena by the hand into Victoria Hall, an excited chatter had built up. As they made their way to the back, Jess scanned the rows looking for Mary but could find no sign of her. She saw ladies wearing hats seated next to gentlemen in suits. Children were sitting quietly, swinging their legs, under strict instruction to be quiet and on their best behaviour. At the front of the hall was a small orchestra, a harp and two violins. Jess felt a nervous excitement about singing on stage, but uppermost in her thoughts was Lena's well-being. She saw that the girl was calmer now, but still over-bright, like a firecracker ready to burn. She caught sight of Mal sitting with his parents and headed towards him, holding Lena's hand. Mal shuffled along the bench to make space for them.

'I thought you had to go backstage with the rest of the performers?' he said.

'I'm not leaving Lena,' Jess replied. She glanced around her, confused. 'Where's Miss Gilbey gone?'

Mal shrugged. 'A man came and said he needed to speak to her urgently.'

Jess thought this most peculiar and wondered what was going on. Just then, a ripple of applause began, which spread throughout the hall. She looked up to see a short red-faced man standing on the stage. She recognised him straight away as Mr Brunskill, the man who had invited her to sing.

'That's him,' Mal said. 'That's the man who asked to speak to Miss Gilbey.'

Brunskill seemed less self-important up on the stage than he'd been the night of the party at the Uplands. He seemed flustered too, and not completely in control of proceedings. He kept tripping over his words, and Jess wondered if he'd been at the ale. She saw the way his hands fluttered at his sides as he spoke. She listened as he introduced the harpist and violinists, and she joined in with the applause in appreciation of them. But still she felt something wasn't right. And where had Miss Gilbey gone?

She felt Lena shaking beside her, and when she turned towards her, the girl was mouthing and whispering words Jess couldn't hear. She put her arm around her shoulders and felt her relax at her touch.

Jess had been sent a programme of events in the post and knew she was last to sing. And so for the next hour, she sat with Lena on one side of her and Mal on the other, listening to the concert on stage. A shipbuilder's wife sang beautifully, with a voice as sweet and high as Jess had heard. More women sang, a madrigal group, and then the harpist played a solo. The hour was soon over and it was time for Jess to take the stage.

'Look after Lena,' she whispered to Mal.

A hush descended as she made her way from her seat at the back of the hall to the stage. She climbed the stairs at the side, aware that all eyes were on her. The audience would be confused, wondering who she was, which important family she belonged to. She felt her heart quicken as she walked to the centre of the stage, but there could be no going back. She was determined to stand up in front of James and Mary. She would show them she wasn't afraid. She'd been given away at birth. She'd been made to live like a dog in the grounds of the grandest Ryhope home, but she was not afraid. She glanced to the violinists and gave a sharp nod. The first notes floated out into the audience and Jess began to sing.

In the audience, Shirley gasped. She recognised Jess immediately. What on earth was going on? What was the girl thinking of, singing at such a prestigious event?

Shirley felt the blood drain from her face and a wave of nausea came over her. Her hand fluttered to her forehead.

'Are you all right, dear?' Eleanor whispered.

But Shirley couldn't reply. She was confused, upset and angry. However, she knew she couldn't cause a scene. She simply nodded towards her mother before returning her attention to Jess, unable to believe her eyes.

Behind the McNally family, Tom Wallace held tight to Mary's hand.

'That's the girl from the Uplands,' Tom whispered to Mary.

'Why, so it is,' Mary said. She did her best to keep her voice steady, but her heart fluttered with a mixture of excitement and pride under her black velvet gown. She wondered again what would happen if she invited Jess into her life. But to do that, she'd need to reveal her past to Tom, for she couldn't countenance meeting Jess without his knowledge.

She had kept her past a secret from her husband, afraid of what he might say, how he might judge her, not just for bringing an illegitimate daughter into the world but for abandoning her too. That part of her life she had kept hidden, pushing memories of it to the back of her mind. It belonged in the past, in Ryhope. She'd been a different person then, a girl with no option but to do as she'd done. A girl who didn't know any better. Now she was a woman, with a wonderful husband who adored her and who would do anything for her. She glanced at Tom, who was watching Jess on the stage. Could she tell him about Jess now that she knew the girl was alive and well? *Should* she tell him? Could he handle learning the truth?

She took his hand, and he leaned towards her and kissed her lightly on the cheek.

'I love you, Mrs Wallace,' he whispered.

Mary squeezed his hand. 'I love you too,' she replied.

She gazed at her husband and wondered again about revealing the truth. She would need to pick her moment carefully, at home one night when Tom was relaxed after a nightcap of a brandy or two. It wouldn't be easy, but if there was to be a future for Mary and Jess then there could be no more secrets from Tom. The days and weeks ahead were going to be tricky as Mary manoeuvred Jess into her conversations with Tom, but she was sure she could manage it somehow. She'd been strong-willed enough to come this far in life, after all. She patted Tom's hand and turned her gaze towards her daughter on the stage.

Jess raised her head as she sang, projecting her voice to the back of the hall, all the way to Mal, Miss Gilbey and Lena. She sang for them and for Arthur and Estelle. Most of all she sang for Ada, for the love she had been given by the woman she missed every day. The hall was silent as her voice soared, clear and true. And when her song ended, there was a beat of dead, empty air before the audience erupted into the loudest round of applause of the night.

As Jess looked out into the audience, she saw James McNally in the front row. She saw Brunskill standing next to him, whispering something into his ear. She saw James's face cloud over, then he stood and left the hall. Brunskill made his way on to the stage as Jess walked back to her seat.

'Ladies and gentlemen,' he announced. 'It has been a

truly memorable night and I would like to express my thanks to all who performed. We have made a considerable sum of money in donations this evening, which we will pass on to the Sunderland orphanage.'

There was an extended round of applause, and when it died down, Brunskill pulled uncomfortably at the collar of his shirt.

'Now, we, er . . . we were due to end the concert tonight by honouring Mr James McNally of Scarborough with an award for bravery.'

A murmur rippled through the audience.

'Hear, hear!' a man's voice shouted.

'Hero of the shipwreck!' called another.

'It was on the front page of the *Sunderland Echo*,' said a third.

Brunskill held up his hands. 'However, I am afraid I have some rather bad news.'

A few women in the audience gasped. Men shuffled in their seats. Bored children swung their legs. In the front row, Angus McNally furrowed his brow, puzzled as to what the man on stage was about to announce. Beside him, Albert sighed with impatience. Shirley and Eleanor shared a look, wondering what was going on.

'It appears we have been taken in by a false tale about the true heroes of the shipwreck.'

Brunskill cast his gaze around the expanse of the hall. He cleared his throat before he continued.

'Mr McNally is not the man we thought he was.'

Chapter Seventeen

'My own son,' Angus said, shaking his head. 'My own flesh and blood. How could he do such a thing?'

Angus was travelling back to Ryhope with Shirley and Eleanor, rather than face being in the same car as James. The shame was too much for him; he couldn't bear to be next to his son.

'He's stooped low before,' he continued, looking meaningfully at Shirley. Only Angus and Shirley knew about James's illegitimate daughter. It was their secret alone. 'But this . . . this is too much.'

Eleanor turned her head away and gazed out of the window. She felt Angus's pain and embarrassment acutely. She admired him and liked him as a friend, and it hurt her to see him like this. Shirley, sitting next to her, simply felt numb. She had always known James was a wrong 'un. And if she was honest, his roguish charm was part of his appeal. When they had wed, she had thought she might be able to change him and calm his ways. She'd taken instruction on this from her mother who was only too willing to give her opinion. In her heart, she had finished with him many times over the years. She knew about his philandering, about him spending time with the herring girls. She could just about turn a blind eye to that kind of behaviour if it meant keeping her home at The Crescent. She'd thought the final blow was finding out about the daughter he kept in Ryhope. But tonight had been too much. Angus might not want the scandal of divorce, but how could she stay married to James now that everyone knew what he'd done? It would reflect badly on her. She would take advice from her mother when they returned to Scarborough.

She couldn't wait to get away from Ryhope, from the Uplands and from the secrets the place seemed to hide. She wanted nothing more than to be back in polite society with her lady friends. It had been an upsetting night. Shirley had hoped Brunskill's announcement had been some kind of mistake, or a badly played joke. But when she'd glanced along the row, seen James's empty seat, she'd known that something was wrong. Oh, the shame and the rage she had felt as Brunskill's words had echoed around the Victoria Hall. She balled her fists in her lap. Well, there was one consolation in this sorry mess. Whatever happened between her and James in the future, she had ensured Alfie would inherit what was rightfully his.

James, Albert and Alfie were travelling in the second car. Albert glowered at his brother, shaking his head every now and then. His silence spoke of his disapproval more than any words ever could. As the elder of the McNally brothers, he could have staked his claim to the Uplands, but he had no interest in the place; it meant nothing to him. He'd had no desire to visit Ryhope over the years in the way James had done. But still he'd been uncertain about his father's plans for the future of the house. He'd privately expressed his concern to Angus over his decision to turn the place over to Alfie. But after tonight, he knew that giving the Uplands to Alfie was exactly the right thing to do. James was in no fit state to continue running the place. What a mess he'd made of it all.

'You'll be back in Scarborough tomorrow,' Albert said at last.

Both Alfie and James turned to look at him. James gave a brief nod when he realised the comment was directed at him.

'We need to talk when we return home,' Albert said.

'About what?' James asked sullenly.

'About everything. The family business. Your behaviour. About moving you out of The Crescent. The McNally fortune might stink of fish, but I will not allow our family name to be tainted by the stench of your lies.'

James turned his face from his brother.

'There's something else we need to talk about too,' Albert continued.

'What?' James muttered.

'The Uplands.' Albert turned to Alfie. 'You need to hear this too. Your grandfather will speak to you as soon as we return there tonight. After what's just happened, it's more important than ever to hear what he has to say.'

Alfie was trying to make sense of the events of the night. He'd seen the girl again, the girl from the grounds at the Uplands; she had been singing up on stage. She was as beautiful as he remembered, and the same feeling had come over him again, that sense of connection and belonging when he looked at her. What on earth was going on in his head? And then Harry Brunskill had got up on the stage, and his words about his father had made Alfie's stomach turn.

He shook his head, trying to dismiss the thoughts that ran through his mind. He wanted nothing more than to return to his regiment and take up his posting. Life in the army was organised; he knew what he was doing there, knew what was expected. There were people in the army he could rely on and trust, which was more than he could say about his own father.

In all the commotion after the concert, Alfie had gone in search of Brunskill. He wanted to know who had told him the truth about the shipwreck. Brunskill had revealed that a Miss Veronica Gilbey of Ryhope was his trusted source. The name was familiar to Alfie. Gilbey. Wasn't that the woman who ran the house where the girl from the Uplands lived? It was the house where he'd sent his letter of friendship. But try as he might, he could not recall the name of the street. He was determined to find Miss Gilbey, to speak to her and discover what she knew. Didn't his mother complain that Ryhope was a small place where everyone knew each other's business; a place where gossip spread fast? Miss Gilbey couldn't be that hard to track down.

Meanwhile, in their house on Seaburn seafront, Mary and Tom Wallace were enjoying a nightcap in their lounge. Mary lay on the sofa with her shapely legs stretched across the cushions and Tom sat in an armchair opposite. Both of them had a glass in their hand with a dash of whisky inside.

'What a peculiar evening,' Tom said. 'Most odd. I can't believe the nerve of the McNally man.'

Oh I can, Mary thought. I can believe it only too well.

* * *

And as Mary and Tom ran through the events of the evening, a tram made its way from Sunderland town centre towards Ryhope. Lena sat in the seat next to Jess, with her head on the older girl's shoulder. Jess herself felt a contentment she'd not felt for a very long time. McNally had been exposed for the liar and fraud that he was. Was it wrong that she felt satisfied to see her own flesh and blood named and shamed in front of everyone? Of course, it had crossed her mind to do the same thing, to call out James for falsely taking credit for saving lives. But she knew Ada would never have approved if she'd done that so publicly.

She wondered how Brunskill had found out the truth about James, and whether Miss Gilbey's disappearance from her seat at the concert had anything to do with it. If the two things were connected, if Miss Gilbey had passed on what Jess had told her about the shipwreck, then Jess had brought James down after all. She didn't take any comfort from destroying his reputation; he had done that himself. But she did feel relieved that the secret was out and the truth exposed. Now it was time for Arthur and Estelle to take the credit they deserved.

The following morning at the Uplands, cases were packed and a breakfast of eggs and bacon from High Farm was eaten. As Albert, Shirley and Eleanor remained at the table, James retreated to the room that had been his study over the years. But it was no longer his. Angus had shared the news when they'd returned after the concert that the Uplands now belonged to Alfie. It would no longer be a bolthole for James. He would need to find somewhere else, a home of his own, for he knew Shirley would not welcome him back at The Crescent. His wife's disdain he could take, and his father's disapproval he was used to. It was the shame he felt when he looked into his son's eyes that hurt James the most. And he had no one to blame but himself.

'Stop wallowing in self-pity, boy.'

A voice behind him made him start. He swung around and saw his father standing at the study door. Angus was a big man, tall and broad, and he filled the doorway.

'Not packed yet? Take what you need, leave what you don't. The train leaves in an hour from Ryhope East. Brunskill is sending cars to take us to the station.'

Brunskill's name cut James like a knife.

'I'm as ready as I'll ever be,' he said quietly.

'Leave the rum,' Angus ordered. 'Seems to me if you'd left the bottle alone in the past, you wouldn't be in this mess now.'

Just then, Alfie appeared behind Angus.

'Grandfather? Could I speak to you and Father, please?'

'Come in, boy,' Angus said, stepping into the room.

Alfie strode in after him, keeping his head high and his back straight. Angus closed the door and took a seat, waiting to hear what his grandson had to say. Alfie looked from James to Angus and cleared his throat.

'I'd like to stay on here for another day.'

'Are you sure?' Angus said. 'Don't you have to join your regiment?'

'Not yet. There's something I need to do before I leave.'

'Very well,' Angus said. 'You can ask the housekeeper to attend to you.'

He stood and walked towards Alfie. Putting his hands on his grandson's shoulders, he looked deep into his eyes.

'This is yours now, boy. All yours. Do what you will with it. Sell it if you must.'

James winced. But he was powerless to say anything. The Uplands was no longer his.

'Yes, Grandfather,' Alfie said. 'But I don't want to rush into anything. My priority is the regiment now.'

'Of course, lad,' Angus said proudly. 'Of course.'

With that, Alfie and Angus walked from the room, and James was left alone, staring at a half-empty bottle of rum.

Later that morning, Alfie stood at the gate that opened on to Cliff Road. He accepted a hearty handshake from his grandfather and thanked him again. Being given the Uplands was beyond anything he could have imagined, and he was not sure what he would do. He couldn't live there, not when he was expected to join his regiment within days. But neither would he sell it. It was a family home, a McNally home, and he would need to give its future serious thought.

'Now remember, lad. As soon as you return to Scarborough after whatever business you're doing in Ryhope today, you need to head to our solicitor's office. They require your signature on the deeds to the Uplands. I have already signed them, and your mother's signature is there as your parent and guardian, but they need yours too. Once you've done that, the place is yours.'

'I'll do it the moment I return,' Alfie said.

Angus took one last look at the Uplands before he turned away. Memories of happy holidays with Florence and their two boys went through his mind, but he wasn't sad to see the back of the place. As he got into the car, Eleanor and Shirley came bustling out with their travelling bags in hand. Shirley hugged Alfie.

'I'll see you back at home, son,' she said. 'Although I don't understand why you're staying in Ryhope.'

Alfie thought it best not to tell her the truth, for she would only worry. 'I want to get the feel of the place while I can. If I return to Scarborough, I'll just end up drinking in the Scarborough Arms with the boys from the maritime college.'

'Oh, leave him be,' Eleanor said. 'He's old enough to know what he's doing. He's not your little boy any more.'

Shirley stood on tiptoes to reach Alfie's cheek. Then Eleanor too kissed her grandson. Shirley noticed the two lipstick marks, one pink and one plum, and dug in her handbag for her handkerchief, rubbing at Alfie's face with the linen square.

'Mother!' Alfie said, laughing and embarrassed.

Albert was next out of the gate. 'Bye, Alfie,' he said as he passed. 'Watch what you're doing with the old place. Take care of it.'

'I will, Uncle Albert.'

Finally James walked slowly from the house. He carried nothing with him, no travelling bag or suitcase. He locked eyes with his son. Alfie held out his hand.

'I'll see you in Scarborough,' he said. 'You'll let me know where you're staying?'

'Of course,' James said. He let go of Alfie's hand and turned to leave, then paused and turned back. 'Alfie?'

'Yes, Dad?'

'I just want to say . . . What I mean is . . . I'm sorry. For everything. The truth is, I'm not sure what happened, how it all started. A rumour, you know, gossip. It spread. The next thing I knew I was on the front page of the local paper, hailed as a hero. It wasn't my fault, son. You know that, don't you?'

'You didn't put a stop to it, though, did you? You didn't once put the record straight.' James hung his head in shame, then turned and headed to the car.

The car engine roared into life and Alfie stood at the Uplands gate, waving goodbye to his family. Then he turned and headed inside his new home.

'Mrs Scott, where would I find a Miss Gilbey in Ryhope?'

Bella swung around from her work.

'Gilbey?'

'She runs a house for girls, I understand,' Alfie said.

'Ah! Miss Gilbey. It's on St Paul's Terrace, at the end. It's a smart-looking house, tidy and a bit severe,' Bella said. 'Much like Miss Gilbey herself.'

Ten minutes later, Alfie was standing outside Miss Gilbey's house. He knocked smartly on the door, but there was no reply. He waited and knocked again, louder. This time he heard noises from within, and then the sound of a bolt sliding back. The door opened, and there in front of him stood the girl from the Uplands. It was hard to say who got the bigger shock.

Jess gripped the door handle. 'Alfie? What are you doing here?'

'Can I come in?' he said. 'I'd like to speak to Miss Gilbey, on business.'

'She's not in,' Jess said quickly. Miss Gilbey had taken Lena for her scheduled visit with Dr Anderson at the asylum. 'She'll be back this afternoon. But I don't understand. What do you want from her?'

'I was hoping for the truth about my father.' He sighed. 'Mr Brunskill told me that Miss Gilbey was the source for his announcement last night.'

Jess stood to one side and held the door open. 'Come in,' she said. 'I'll tell you everything you need to know.'

'You?'

'I was the source, Alfie. I was the one who told Miss Gilbey everything she passed on to Brunskill.'

Jess watched as Alfie took a hesitant step forward, and then another. She felt him brush past her as he headed into the hall.

'Go on through,' she said, indicating the kitchen at the end of the corridor. She felt anxious about what Miss Gilbey would say if she found out that a gentleman caller had been invited into the house. But Alfie was her half-brother. How could Miss Gilbey possibly complain about that?

'Would you like tea?' she offered as they sat at the kitchen table.

Alfie shook his head. 'No. Just the truth.'

'All of it?' she asked.

'All of it,' he replied.

Jess felt her heart skip. 'I'm not sure where to start.'

'Start at the beginning,' Alfie said kindly. 'Tell me why you were living in the grounds of the Uplands.'

And so, in the silence of the kitchen, Jess told Alfie everything he wanted to know.

She kept her voice as calm as she could, watching his face as she described the hardship she had suffered, the freezing cold nights in the woodshed, the hours she had spent there alone.

'I can't believe my father was so cruel as to banish the housekeeper's child to the grounds,' Alfie said. He shook his head, puzzled.

Jess held his gaze. It was time to tell him a truth he might not want to hear.

'I wasn't the housekeeper's child.'

It took a moment for this to sink in.

'But you've just told me that Ada brought you up.'

'She did. She brought me up as her own. She gave me her name, I'm Jess Davidson and always will be. But she wasn't my mother.'

'Then who was?'

Jess paused for a moment. She straightened her back in her chair. 'A housemaid at the Uplands. She was sacked when she fell pregnant.'

'And what was her name?' Alfie asked.

Jess shook her head. She had managed without a mother for almost seventeen years. If Mary didn't want her secret to be revealed, then so be it.

'It doesn't matter who she was.'

'And your father, what of him?'

Jess stared straight at Alfie. She let his words hang between them for a few moments. Her silence told him all he needed to know.

He shook his head. 'No . . . no! This can't be right.' He rose from his chair and paced the kitchen floor. Jess saw a fury in his eyes.

'It's why he didn't want me living at the Uplands,' she said. 'He didn't want anyone to know I was his. He paid Ada to bring me up as long as I wasn't allowed inside the house.'

'No!'

Jess ran a hand through her long, dark hair. 'I'm your sister, Alfie. Look! It's McNally hair. You can't deny what you see in front of you.'

Alfie slumped back into his chair and turned his face towards Jess. There were tears in his eyes.

'That day . . .' he said, 'when I met you in the wood-shed. I think I knew something then. In the way you looked, I recognised something, myself perhaps. I didn't know what it was, of course, but there was a connection.' He put his hand to his heart. 'I felt it in here.'

Jess dropped her gaze. She had felt something too and had been unable to tell anyone. 'Is that why you wrote to me?' she asked.

Alfie nodded. 'I wanted to offer my friendship.'

'And it was received gratefully. Look, Alfie, I've had time to get used to this news about James. But I know how shocked you must be. It's not an easy truth to live with.'

A silence hung between them. Jess glanced at Alfie, waiting for him to speak, and when he did, his words left him with anger and force.

'You must despise him for what he's done, making you live like an animal in that shed!'

'I despise him more for taking credit from my friends the Atkinsons. They were the ones who helped save lives on the day of the wreck. They were the ones whose names should have been front-page news.'

'We'll make it happen. Both of us, together. We'll put right my father's wrongs.' He dropped his gaze to the floor. 'All of them,' he said quietly.

'All?' Jess asked, puzzled.

Alfie cleared his throat and sat back in his chair. He

pulled a blue linen handkerchief from his pocket and pressed it to his eyes. Jess saw the flash of the McNally crest embroidered in a corner of the blue cloth.

'I will be leaving for Scarborough on the morning train from Ryhope East,' he said. 'And I want you to come with me.'

'Me? What on earth for?' Jess cried. 'I can't leave Miss Gilbey's. This is my home, my job. I can't go running off. Why should I?'

'Because I have to sign a document tomorrow. A legal document that turns the Uplands over to me.'

Jess's mouth dropped open.

'Once I sign it, the house is mine to do with as I please. I could sell it, of course. And if I needed the money, I would.'

'Then what will you do?' Jess asked. 'Will you move to Ryhope to live?'

Alfie shook his head. 'No. My regiment is expecting me to join them this week. Wherever the army places me will become my home. Come with me to Scarborough tomorrow, Jess, and the Uplands will be yours.'

Jess shook her head. It was too much to take in.

'We'll share it. The deeds will carry both of our names. For me it will be a way of keeping my inheritance. And for you . . . well, it could be your home.'

'The Uplands? No, Alfie! No! I don't want it. I can't live somewhere like that. It's too big. I don't have any money to run it.'

'It's yours, Jess, don't you see? It's yours as much as mine. You're my half-sister. At least think about my offer. I'll help with the upkeep. Please . . . let me make amends for all my father has done.'

Jess's head was spinning. None of what Alfie was saying seemed real. But if it was . . . Oh, if it was, then the joy of living where Ada once had came to her in a flash.

'But . . . it really is too big, Alfie. Just a room, that's all I'd need. Ada's old room, that'd do me to live in. I'd come and go through the side gate, as I always did.'

'Jess, listen to me. I'm offering you the home that you should have lived in all your life.'

Jess felt the sting of tears.

'And the gate you will use is the front gate, not the side. You'll be the lady of the house, not the maid.'

'No, Alfie. No. You need to listen to me. This is wrong, it's too much. If I live in the Uplands, I would just need one room.'

'Then come with me to Scarborough tomorrow. If, by the time we arrive, you decide you don't want to sign the deeds, then what have you lost? You'll have had a perfectly nice time by the seaside. Stay overnight.'

Jess was having trouble taking all this in.

'I'll book you into a good hotel on the front and deliver you safely back to the railway station the following morning. What do you say, Jess? Please?'

'I don't know . . .'

'We are not our father,' he said sternly. 'We might be his children, his flesh and blood. But we are better than he will ever be. We are honest and loyal and true. We are everything he is not.'

Jess gripped Alfie's hand tightly. 'You're really offering me a home at the Uplands?'

'All of it. Or as much as you want. If you just want one room, that's fine. We'll speak to Bella Scott, arrange for her to stay on.'

Jess gave a wry smile at the thought of Bella cooking and cleaning for her. 'I think I can manage on my own.' She bit her lip. 'If I come to Scarborough tomorrow . . . if I take up your offer, could I bring someone with me?'

'A friend?'

'My guardian, Miss Gilbey. I'll have to let her know what is planned. Won't her signature be needed too? I'll ask her as soon as she returns.'

'You never said where she was. Is she out at work?' Alfie asked.

Jess shook her head. It was not for her to say where Miss Gilbey took Lena. Although she felt a connection to Alfie and was grateful beyond words for his generous spirit, she would hold that secret close. Alfie McNally might be her half-brother, but Lena was her sister in all but name.

After Alfie left, Jess glanced at the clock. If she was quick, if she ran, she might be able to make it to Richardson Terrace to tell Mal what had happened. She flung on her jacket and ran like the clappers, but there was no one at home. She banged at the door, called through the letter box and knocked on the windows, but she couldn't hear either of the dogs barking inside, and no one answered her call.

The next morning, Jess rose early. It was still dark outside, but she was excited and leapt from her bed.

'Lena, wake up,' she whispered. She gently rocked Lena's shoulder under her eiderdown. Lena yawned and opened her eyes. As soon as she saw Jess, she smiled widely.

'It's today!' she cried excitedly. 'We're going to Scarborough today!'

'Come downstairs for oat pudding before we leave,' Jess said.

When Jess walked into the kitchen, Miss Gilbey was already there. The fire was burning and there was a pot of tea on the table.

'There was no need for you to do all this, Miss Gilbey. I was going to do it.'

'There was every need,' Miss Gilbey said. 'There's a lot to do before we head to the railway station. There's breakfast for Amelia and Jane to prepare. And I dare say I'll have to leave a list of instructions for those girls if we're to be away overnight.'

'I've left out cooked ham and cold potatoes for their dinner. They won't starve,' Jess said.

Miss Gilbey took a step towards her. 'Jess. Before Lena comes downstairs, can I have a word with you, dear?'

Jess stopped what she was doing. She had never once heard Miss Gilbey use a term of affection towards her before. But then nothing seemed normal any more. With the news from Alfie about the Uplands, it was as if everything had been turned on its head.

'What is it?' she asked.

'Lena isn't a well-travelled girl. She has only ever known Ryhope. What I'm saying is, she may become somewhat excited today. You saw how agitated she was on the tram into Sunderland on the night of the concert. And staying overnight in a strange place, it might not be good for her mood.'

'If you're asking me to keep a close eye on her, Miss Gilbey, of course I will.'

'Thank you, Jess. I couldn't have left her behind, you realise that? I'll pay her way.'

'Of course. I'm pleased she's coming with us. And I'm grateful to you for your guidance and for taking time to come at such short notice too.'

If Jess had been surprised by Miss Gilbey's endearment earlier, then she was stunned by what she did next. She put her hand on Jess's arm and patted it, twice.

Well, Jess thought. What a peculiar start to a most unusual day.

Later that morning, at Ryhope East railway station, Alfie was waiting on the platform when Jess, Miss Gilbey and Lena arrived. He waved at Jess the minute he saw her and Jess led the others over and introduced him.

'This is Alfie, my half-brother,' she said.

'Pleased to meet you, Mr McNally,' Miss Gilbey said. 'I've heard a lot about you.'

'All good, I hope?' Alfie said.

'Which is more than can be said for your father,' Miss Gilbey sniffed.

Alfie gave Jess a wry smile, then held out his hand towards Lena. 'And who might you be?' he said.

There was a silence. Lena looked like a startled rabbit.

'Lena's a little shy,' Jess whispered.

Alfie nodded. 'Well, it's nice to meet you, Lena.'

When the train arrived, Alfie joined the women in the second-class carriage. He didn't mention that he already had a first-class return ticket, paid for by his grandfather. He'd offered to buy everyone's tickets, and Miss Gilbey had been glad to accept, although she had been prepared to pay for herself and Lena. During the journey, she quizzed him on his family, his background and his army training. As Jess's guardian, she wanted to know every last detail. As they talked, Jess listened and watched Lena, who was staring from the window, watching the north-east coast speed by. She thought of Mal and the Atkinsons. In all the excitement about the Uplands, about Scarborough, about taking a trip with Miss Gilbey and Lena, she felt a sadness too. If only she could have shared the adventure with Mal. What with everything that had happened, and so quickly too, she hadn't been able to tell him the news. How she would've loved for him to be by her side on the train. She resolved to speak to him the minute she returned.

The small party changed trains at Sunderland and then again at Durham and York. It was late afternoon by the time they reached Scarborough's railway terminus. Jess felt tired but excited when she stepped from the train. Lena was sleepy too, and Miss Gilbey had even started dozing on the York train. Alfie led the way from the station to the main street.

'The hotel I suggest you stay in is just a short walk from here,' he said.

Jess looked up at the sky. Spring clouds were scudding past, but they were white, not grey, and there was little threat of rain.

'Lead the way,' she said.

Jess walked at Alfie's side. Miss Gilbey and Lena followed behind, holding hands.

'Not much further,' Alfie said as they turned right on to Bar Street. It was a narrow thoroughfare, cobbled, with tiny bow-windowed shops. All manner of smells reached Jess's nose: freshly ground coffee from the tea shops, bread from the bakeries, and – oh! She reeled in horror as the stench of fresh fish hit her hard. It wasn't a smell she was used to. As they reached the end of Bar Street, the sea sparkled ahead.

'That's South Bay,' Alfie explained. 'Scarborough's got two bays, North and South. They're separated in the middle by the castle.'

Jess's eyes grew wide. 'There's a castle?'

'If we have time, I'll show you. But we need to get to the hotel. We'll take refreshments, then head to the solicitor. We should get there before they close for the evening, rather than leave this business till morning. After that, I'll be happy to show you around Scarborough, once I've let Mother know I've arrived.' Alfie didn't much relish telling his mother what he was going to do with the Uplands.

Jess had seen nothing like Scarborough before. It was very different to Sunderland. She'd seen the beach at Ryhope, of course, but there, the coal black sands were hidden by cliffs. In Scarborough, the bay was open. To her right was an iron bridge leading across a valley, with a toll-house taking payment from those who wanted to cross. Ahead of her was a hotel, twelve storeys high.

'That's the Grand Hotel, the biggest in Europe,' Alfie said.

'Is that where we're staying?' Jess said.

Alfie cleared his throat. 'No. It's also one of the most expensive in Europe. Not even McNally money can stretch that far.' He swung around and pointed to a large white building that wrapped itself around a corner at the top of a hill overlooking the bay. Jess counted five, six storeys to it. 'This is the one, the Royal,' he said.

'The Royal,' Miss Gilbey repeated. She was impressed

by Alfie's choice. She'd never stayed anywhere so grand before. 'Well I never.'

Inside, the hotel was as luxurious as its exterior promised. Jess and Lena were shown to their room by a bellboy wearing a blue suit with gold stripes running down the trouser legs. Miss Gilbey had the neighbouring room, the two connected by an adjoining door. Jess and Lena's room was decorated in pastel shades of green and pink. Two beds lay close together, with pink eiderdowns and the fluffiest pillows Jess had ever seen. She could never have imagined such splendour, and Lena too was lost for words. The two of them ran to the window to take in the view.

'The castle!' Jess cried. 'And look, Lena, the beach.'

'What's that?' Lena asked, pointing to what looked like a wooden crate on wheels moving down the hill in front of the hotel. As it descended, another cart on wheels travelled up. Jess strained to read a sign at the top of the hill.

'It says it's a tram lift to the beach. A funicular.'

'Can we try it, Jess? Can we?'

Jess put her arm around Lena's shoulders.

'We'll see it all, Lena. Just as soon as we've been to this solicitor's office.'

Chapter Eighteen

'What was your favourite part of Scarborough, Jess?'
Lena asked. 'My favourite was Peasholm Park, with the
ducks and the swans. Can we go again, Miss Gilbey, can
we?'

'Now, now, Lena,' Miss Gilbey chided. 'Don't get
excited. We've got a long journey ahead of us. We need to
settle down, don't we?'

The train slowly puffed its way from Scarborough
railway station and the platform filled with steam.

'What did you enjoy most, Miss Gilbey?' Jess asked.

Miss Gilbey gazed from the window. 'Oh,' she said.
'The sea air, the space of it all. The seafront and the fishing
boats. Even amongst all the war damage, there was a
determined sense that life must go on. Fish still have to be
brought in and sold.'

'But we've got sea air in Ryhope,' Lena said, confused.

'With mucky coal dust mixed in. And in Ryhope the
sea lies beyond the cliffs. In Scarborough it's there right
in front of you, as far as the eye can see.' Miss Gilbey
turned to Jess. 'Will you ever return to Scarborough?'

Jess shrugged. 'I have no reason to. All I want to do

now is get home and make sense of what's happened.'

'Wouldn't you like to come back for a holiday?' Lena asked.

'Holidays are just a dream for someone like me,' Jess said.

'I dare say you'll have your hands full taking care of the Uplands when you move in. You will be moving in, I expect? One isn't given a property like the Uplands without making the most of it,' Miss Gilbey said.

Lena bit her lip and looked at Jess. 'Does that mean you're moving away from St Paul's Terrace?'

'I haven't decided what to do yet,' Jess said. 'I need time for it all to sink in. It's happened in such a hurry. My head's spinning.'

'I'll need to replace you, of course, if you leave. And notice will be needed, as I'm sure you can appreciate. But take as much time as you need,' Miss Gilbey said.

Then she pulled a paper packet of mint rocks from her handbag and offered it round.

The train journey back to Ryhope was long, with several changes. When they finally arrived, Jess had reached a decision on what to do next. She was bursting to speak to Mal and tell him what had happened. She knew that if she headed straight back to Miss Gilbey's house, she'd be on pins, itching to break her news.

'Would you mind if I didn't come back to the house with you right away?' she asked.

'Of course not,' Miss Gilbey said. 'But remember, for now, you're still in my employ, and dinner will be expected.'

'I'll be there in time to make dinner,' Jess said.

She crossed her fingers as she spoke, to protect her against her white lie. She had no idea how long it would take her to find Mal. What if the Atkinsons' house was empty, as it had been the last time she'd gone looking for him? Crossing her fingers brought Ada to mind. She had always told Jess never to tell an untruth. Jess felt a pang of guilt in her stomach, but her news was too exciting, too overwhelming. She hoped Ada would understand. If she was a little late with dinner at Miss Gilbey's house, then she would have to deal with the sulks she knew would be forthcoming from Amelia and Jane, along with Miss Gilbey's complaints. For she had to see Mal straight away.

She left Miss Gilbey and Lena at the railway station, and ran as fast as her legs could carry her all the way to Richardson Terrace. This time she was in luck. The door opened and Estelle greeted her warmly.

'Hello, love! To what do we owe the pleasure? Come in.'

Jess stepped into the warmth of the Atkinson house, pulling at her scarf to loosen it.

'We haven't seen you since the concert. My word, what a shocker of a night that was. Lil Mahone told me that she saw James McNally leaving the Uplands with his family the day before yesterday. He should be ashamed of himself if you ask me, and—'

'Estelle? Is Mal in?' Jess asked urgently.

Estelle looked at her. 'Is everything all right?' she asked.

'Yes, yes, it's fine. I need to speak to him. Something's happened.'

Estelle's eyebrows shot up, and a disapproving look crossed her face. She eyed Jess all the way up from her boots to the dark hair that fell around her shoulders in waves. Jess could have sworn her gaze lingered on her stomach.

'Something bad or something good?' Estelle demanded.

A flicker of fear ran through her. Was the girl in the family way with Mal's child? She'd begged Arthur many times to have a serious talk with Mal on such matters.

'Something good. Very good.'

Estelle seemed to breathe a sigh of relief.

'I'll tell you, Estelle, I promise. I'll tell Arthur too, but I need to see Mal first.'

'Well, he's still out at work with his dad,' Estelle said. 'But I daresay they'll be making their way back home by now. They've been working in the gardens at Ryhope Hall.'

'I'll go there right now.' Jess turned to leave, then turned back. 'Estelle?'

'What, love?'

'Can I . . . can I come for my tea tomorrow?'

'You know you're welcome here any time, pet,' Estelle said.

Jess ran from the house all the way to the village green. Inside the small house at Richardson Terrace, Estelle shook her head and wondered what on earth was going on.

Jess found Mal and Arthur opposite the village school. The men looked tired, their clothes dirty with soil. Arthur pushed a wheelbarrow that was full of clay pots while Mal carried a garden spade. Jess couldn't get her words out quickly enough. She explained to Arthur that Estelle knew she was looking for Mal and that Mal might be late for his tea.

'You go, I'll see you back at home,' Arthur said as he walked away with the rusty old barrow. Then it was just Jess and Mal. Finally.

Jess thought her heart would burst. She looked into Mal's mucky face, smeared with dirt from an honest day's work.

'What is it?' he said.

'Come with me,' Jess said.

'Where? Miss Gilbey's?'

Jess shook her head. 'Just come.'

Mal followed her across the road and around the corner into Cliff Road.

'We're going to the Uplands?' he asked, confused. 'Why?'

Jess put a finger to her lips. She wasn't ready yet to reveal her surprise.

'The front gate? You're going in the front gate?' Mal cried when he saw which way Jess was heading. She held the gate open and he followed her inside.

'Leave your spade by the wall,' she said.

Mal shook his head. 'McNally will be out for blood if he finds us here.'

'He's not here any more. He's gone. Leave it, you'll see.'

Mal narrowed his eyes but did as he was told.

Jess reached for his hand. She pushed at the front door and heard him protest behind her.

'It's all right, we're allowed,' she said.

'Who gave you permission?' Mal whispered.

Jess didn't answer. She and Mal stepped into the hall of the Uplands. It was silent and warm from the spring sunshine that flooded in through the bay windows.

'Jess . . . we can't do this,' Mal said.

Jess turned to him and looked deep into his eyes. 'We can, Mal. It's mine.'

Mal laughed. 'Don't be daft.'

'It's mine,' she said softly.

Just then, there was the sound of a door opening along a corridor and footsteps coming towards them. Mal let go of Jess's hand and stepped away from her. Bella Scott appeared.

'Anything you need, miss?' she asked.

'Nothing, thank you,' Jess said. 'But please don't call me miss. I don't think I could ever get used to it.'

'Of course . . .' Bella paused and smiled, 'Jess.'

Mal's mouth had dropped open. 'What's going on? Is this some sort of joke?'

Bella turned to Jess. 'Will you tell him what Alfie McNally's gone and done, or will I?'

'What's Alfie got to do with this?' Mal asked.

Jess took hold of his hands, took a step towards him and kissed him full on the lips. 'I'll tell you everything,' she whispered.

She led him into the room that James McNally had once used as his study. Jess sat on the small leather sofa and Mal sat beside her. And there, in the room that had seen and heard secrets, Jess told Mal about Alfie and his offer. She told him about Scarborough and their stay in the Royal. She told him about the meeting in the solicitor's office, the deeds to the Uplands and Alfie's promise to help with the upkeep.

Mal sat in silence, letting her words sink in. 'I don't believe it,' he said. A bubble of laughter began to make its way from his lips. 'I don't believe it,' he said again. He was laughing now, unable to contain himself.

Jess felt laughter build inside her too. 'Believe it,' she said. 'This is my home, and yours.'

'Me? Live here?'

'Pebble and Stone can have the run of the grounds and . . .' Jess stopped herself from saying more.

'And what?' Mal asked.

She looked deep into his eyes.

'And there's plenty of room for your mam and dad, that's if you think they'd want to leave Richardson Terrace.'

'Oh, I'm not sure, Jess. I'm not sure about any of this. It's going to take some getting used to.'

'I know. For me too. None of it seems real. I keep pinching myself, wanting to wake up from a dream. But it's as real as my signature on the deeds in the solicitor's office in Scarborough. It's real, Mal. It's as real as the nose on my face.'

'We need to think and to plan,' Mal said.

'We should talk to your mam and dad. I don't even know where to begin.'

'Did you ever dream, Jess, when you lived in the garden, when Ada looked after you, that one day you'd end up living inside?'

Jess looked around the walls of the study. 'Never,' she said. 'Not once. I felt no connection with the bricks and mortar of the place. It's out there in the grounds, by the hazel trees, that's the place I call home.'

'Will McNally ever return?'

'James? No, but Alfie might. It's his home too, he's entitled to come any time he wants.'

'And what about Mary Wallace? Will you ever see her again?'

Jess felt her stomach flip at the mention of Mary's name. She thought back to the night of the concert. Might it be possible she'd meet Mary again?

'She has her own life, away from Ryhope, away from me,' she said. 'She moved on in the world, moved up. She wants me kept a secret from her husband. How can I be a part of her life when she doesn't want anyone to know who I am?'

'You could write to her, let her know where to find you, now that you'll have your own home.'

'I could,' Jess said. 'We'll see. It won't be easy, though.'

'Wouldn't you like to see her again? She is your real mam, after all.'

Jess laid her hand on her heart. 'In here, Ada's my mam. She always will be. Mary's more . . .' She paused a moment, searching for the right word. 'It's complicated,' she said at last. She glanced out of the window, lost in her thoughts. 'Ada once told me she wanted a garden of her own in the grounds. She never got one, of course. But we could make one for her now, couldn't we?'

Mal nodded.

'She always wanted more flowers. "Just a little patch of flowers, that's all I'd have," she used to say. Spring flowers like snowdrops and daffodils, and in summer, sweet lavender and geraniums.'

'I could grow some from seed,' Mal said.

Jess stood. 'Would you like to see the whole place?'

She grabbed Mal's hand and the two of them ran up the stairs. They peeked into each of the rooms, pushing doors open, looking at the views through every bay window. They walked hand in hand along the landing and into a room with a big double bed. They stopped and stood still. Neither dared speak. Jess felt her heart quicken. She heard Mal's breath turn heavy.

'Ada always said I should be married before . . .' she finally said.

Mal wanted Jess. He wanted to kiss her and hold her, hug her and lie on the bed with her. But he was also relieved that her words halted anything that might have happened between them right then. The truth was that he didn't actually know what to do. So many times when his dad had tried to have a father-to-son chat with him about the birds and the bees, he'd made his excuses and left. He'd been embarrassed to hear those kind of words. But now he knew he had to find out what went on. He would speak to his dad the minute his mam's back was turned.

'Then we'll wait until we're wed,' he said.

Jess pulled Mal into her arms and they kissed for a moment that turned into for ever.

The following evening, Jess was at the Atkinsons' house for her tea. Estelle had laid the table fit for a celebration. 'Well, it's not every day your only son tells you he's marrying his childhood sweetheart,' she said.

'I was worried, you know.' Jess locked eyes with her.

'Worried, pet? What on earth for?' Estelle said.

'I wasn't sure what you'd think, after everything that's happened. You know, about discovering James was my dad and that Mary had abandoned me . . .' Jess faltered. It felt wrong to talk badly of Mary, especially when there was a chance they might meet again and make something of their relationship.

'Well, pity the poor mother who leaves her bairn on a doorstep,' Estelle sniffed. 'All I can say is that she must have been going through hell at the time. No mother would leave her bairn like that if she didn't have reason to think it would be better off without her.'

Arthur rattled his newspaper. 'Estelle,' he said softly. It was a gentle rebuke that Estelle acknowledged and she quickly changed the subject.

'There's no need to be worried, Jess. Arthur and I have always been glad to have you in our lives, and we couldn't be happier now that you're going to be part of our family too.'

Jess sat on the floor in front of the coal fire with Mal by her side. Estelle and Arthur had given a great deal of thought to her offer of moving into the Uplands once she and Mal were married. There were so many rooms there, Jess didn't know what to do with them all, though one large bedroom would be kept just for Alfie, for him to use any time he visited. It was his house too, after all.

Pebble was stretched across Jess's legs, and she tickled the dog's belly. Arthur was in his armchair reading the *Sunderland Echo*. Estelle sat on the sofa darning socks.

'I see James McNally's made front-page news for a different reason this time,' Estelle said.

Arthur lowered his newspaper. 'The *Echo* have given him a rough ride.'

'And rightly so,' Estelle said.

'Did you get a mention?' Jess asked. 'When the *Echo* corrected their story about James being the hero on the day of the shipwreck?'

Estelle burst out laughing. 'You think the likes of us will get our names in the paper? Not a chance.'

Arthur rattled the pages in consternation. 'It says that local residents were first on the scene.'

'That's it?' Jess asked. 'Local residents? You don't get mentioned by name?'

'We know what we did was the proper thing to do, that's the main thing,' Arthur said. He laid the newspaper carefully in his lap. 'And while we're all sitting here, I've got news of my own I'd like to announce.'

Estelle looked up from her darning.

'I've been speaking to Mr Marshall at Ryhope Hall,' he said. 'And I've managed to get me and Mal a proper contract for looking after the grounds. It guarantees us work for the next year.'

'Oh Arthur, that's good news,' Estelle said.

'So I was thinking that if we had a bit spare coming into the house, we might send Gloria a little to cover her doctor's bills.'

Estelle paused with her darning needle mid-air and gave this some thought. They'd received another letter from Arthur's sister, and she was still poorly.

'I'll see to it,' she said.

Jess nudged Mal with her elbow.

'Now,' she whispered.

Mal cleared his throat. 'Mam? Dad? Jess and I, we've got something to say.'

Estelle looked up. 'More surprises? I'm still reeling from the news about the Uplands.'

'It's more news about the Uplands,' Jess said. 'It's about me moving in. I'm not sure when to go. It's ready whenever I am, but I need to leave Miss Gilbey with a replacement maid, someone who can live in. It might take some time to find the right girl. Once she's found, I'll move out of St Paul's Terrace and into the Uplands with Bella. And I need to find a job. My work at Miss Gilbey's will stand me in good stead for domestic work elsewhere in Ryhope.'

'And once we get married, I'll move into the Uplands too,' Mal said quickly.

Jess took his hand. 'That's what we really want to talk about now,' she said.

'The wedding, like,' Mal said.

Estelle and Arthur exchanged a smile. 'Are you telling us you want to set the date?' Arthur said.

Jess nodded. 'September the twenty-sixth. We've talked about it already. It's my birthday.'

'A birthday where you turn seventeen, Jess,' Estelle warned. 'That's still too young to get married without permission from your guardian, you know.'

Jess was resolute; she'd thought it all through. 'I'll speak to Miss Gilbey tonight. I'm certain she'll give her consent.'

'I'll come with you,' Mal said. 'If anyone is asking for permission for your hand in marriage, then it really ought to be me.'

Arthur eyed his son keenly and felt a lump form in his throat. He rummaged in his pocket and brought out a handful of coins.

'Son, do your old dad a favour and run down to the Railway Inn to pick up four bottles of ale. I think tonight calls for a celebration, don't you?' He glanced at Jess. 'You've got time to have a drink before you head back to St Paul's Terrace, haven't you?'

Jess felt a warm glow inside her. She looked at Mal, her loving, sweet Mal who she couldn't wait to start her new life with. She glanced at Estelle, a woman of common sense and decency who had shown her nothing but love and support since Ada died. And at Arthur, who was the most solid, trustworthy man she knew. In that moment, with the dogs at her feet, Mal by her side and her whole future ahead of her, Jess felt happier than she'd done in her life.

Miss Gilbey consented readily and happily to Mal's proposition. Her only sadness was that she would be losing Jess from her household. After Mal left that evening, Jess sat with her in her living room. A thought had struck her in Scarborough, and it was time to let Miss Gilbey know what had been on her mind.

'I may have found someone to take my place as your housemaid,' she said.

'Oh? Who is she?' Miss Gilbey said. 'I hope she comes with a character reference.'

'She comes with the best character reference you could wish for,' Jess said. 'It's Lena.'

Miss Gilbey sank into her armchair and her face clouded over. 'No,' she said. 'The girl is too frail. She couldn't possibly do it.'

'Yes, she can,' Jess said. 'You've got to give her a chance. You've seen with your own eyes how she's learned from me while I've worked here. She lights the coal fire each morning, she helps with the cleaning. I can show her how to cook dinner for the others who lodge here.'

Miss Gilbey let Jess's words sink in and she gave a deep sigh. 'I will give it some thought,' she said. 'And what of you? When will you leave here to move to the Uplands?'

'September the twenty-fifth, the day before my birthday.'

'The day before your wedding, too,' Miss Gilbey said.

'I want to stay here until then, if I may.'

'You're in no hurry to live at the Uplands?'

Jess bit her lip. 'I'm in no hurry to be on my own. And besides, I'll be able to train Lena up if I stay here.'

'What will you do for a wedding gown, Jess?' Miss Gilbey asked.

Jess's heart sank. In all the excitement about the Uplands and her visit to Scarborough, the only thought she'd given to her wedding was choosing the date.

'And you'll need to speak to Reverend Daye at St Paul's. There's a lot to arrange in such a short time. September is just a few months away.'

'Will you help me, Miss Gilbey? I know Mal's mam will help too, but it would mean a lot to me . . . If you wanted to, that is. I have no one else to ask.'

'I'd be honoured,' Miss Gilbey said.

Jess smiled. 'I'll miss you, Miss Gilbey,' she said softly. 'You and Lena, you've been my family since the day I moved in here. It wasn't always easy . . .'

Miss Gilbey bristled in her chair.

'. . . but I've settled in and I've grown up. I'll never forget how safe I felt here in your home.'

Miss Gilbey cleared her throat and straightened her back. 'There's one more thing, Jess. There's something I need to tell you, as your guardian.'

Jess was confused. 'There isn't a problem, I hope? Is it about the wedding?'

'No, child. There's no problem.'

Miss Gilbey walked to the mantelpiece. Jess watched as she pulled out a large brown envelope from behind the clock, then took her seat again. She raised her eyes to Jess.

'As your guardian, one of the duties I carry out is overseeing your finances.'

Jess laughed. 'I don't have any,' she said.

Miss Gilbey ran her fingers along the brown paper in her hands. 'Oh, but it appears you do. A sum of fifteen pounds was deposited in an account in the name of Mrs Ada Davidson back at the end of 1903. And the bank were given a note when the deposit was made. It's your money, Jess. Ada's note gave instructions that it was to come to you as soon as you turn eighteen.'

'Ada did that, for me?'

Miss Gilbey nodded and handed the envelope to Jess. 'Read it for yourself, make sense of what you can, and anything that requires more explanation, let me know. But it's yours, Jess, and it'll be a substantial sum with many years' worth of interest.'

Jess stared at the papers in her hand. She recognised Ada's handwriting on the bank note and she ran her fingers across the slanted letters written in black ink. She had no idea that Ada had kept savings; that she'd had any spare money at all.

Miss Gilbey coughed politely. 'Now, if you'll excuse me . . . You may go up to bed.'

'Yes, Miss Gilbey.'

As Jess rose and headed to the door, Miss Gilbey spoke again.

'Thank you,' she said gruffly. 'For everything you have done here. Thank you for your kindness with Lena.'

Jess bowed her head slightly, then headed up to her room.

* * *

On the night of 25 September 1920, Jess Davidson stood in the hallway of Miss Gilbey's house. In her hand was a small bag containing her belongings. Miss Gilbey and Lena followed her to the front door.

'We'll see you tomorrow at St Paul's,' Miss Gilbey said.

'I'm really excited about it. I've never been to a wedding before,' Lena said.

Jess looked from Lena to Miss Gilbey. She couldn't make the move through the front door and out of the house. It was as if her feet were stuck to the floor.

'I'll come and visit, every week,' she said.

'Please do,' Lena said.

Jess heard the crack in Lena's voice. How could she just walk out and leave her? Oh, but she had to, she had to begin her new life. Miss Gilbey pulled the front door open. Jess forced herself to take a step forward.

'Bye, Miss Gilbey,' she said.

'Oh, no need for that any more. I think you can call me Veronica now.'

'Can I call you Veronica too?' Lena piped up.

Jess watched in amazement as Miss Gilbey took Lena's hand and looked deep into her daughter's eyes.

'From now on,' she said, 'you can call me Mam.'

Jess walked from St Paul's Terrace to the Uplands with a lump in her throat. She had to fight back the tears. It was silly and she knew it. She should be happy. She was marrying Mal the next morning. She had the grandest house in all of Ryhope to live in. But in that moment, walking the streets on her own, carrying a small bag with her belongings, she felt more alone than ever. She hoped

Bella might have the fire lit, for the autumn day was turning cold.

'I've made your room up, Jess,' Bella said when she arrived. 'And your gown was delivered this afternoon; it's upstairs on your bed. Estelle's done a fine job. It's a beauty. You'll look a treat and you'll do Mal proud.'

Jess sipped her hot tea that Bella had made for her. She wasn't used to being waited on hand and foot and felt uncomfortable with it.

'Arthur's grown white roses, you know,' she said. 'He grew them specially this summer, just for tomorrow. Estelle's making my bouquet.'

'It'll be a grand day,' Bella said.

'You will come, Bella, won't you? There'll only be you, Mal's mam and dad and his auntie Gloria, Miss Gilbey and Lena.'

'I wouldn't miss it for the world,' Bella said.

The next morning, Jess woke in a bed that was too big, too wide and too soft. The room was too silent without Lena's bed beside her own. She yawned and stretched and a smile spread across her face when she heard the bells of St Paul's peal. Reverend Daye would be expecting her and Mal at the church at noon.

She looked at the gown that Estelle had made for her from bedding sheets Jess had found at the Uplands, stored away and forgotten about. The material was a delicate cream with a scalloped lace edge, and Estelle had fashioned it into a simple, straight, full-length dress. That way it would hide Jess's worn boots, which she couldn't afford to replace with new shoes.

She bathed at her ease that morning in the luxury of

her own indoor bathroom. When she was ready, she called Bella to her bedroom to help tie her hair up. Dark, wavy wisps fell around her delicate face. After Bella had fastened the last pin, she stood back to admire the bride-to-be.

'Beautiful.' She sniffed back a tear. 'Absolutely beautiful.'

There was a knock at the front door and Bella bustled downstairs.

'It's Arthur with the flowers,' she called.

Jess walked down the stairs, taking care not to move her head too much for fear her carefully pinned updo would fall. Arthur let out a long, low whistle through his teeth when he saw his future daughter-in-law coming towards him.

'Our Mal's a lucky lad and no mistake,' he said. He handed Jess the bouquet of white roses.

'They're gorgeous, Arthur,' she said.

'Grown them with my own hands. Mal wanted to help, but I told him I wanted to do something of my own, something special for you today.'

Jess brought the bouquet to her nose. The scent was so sweet and intoxicating, she thought she might float away on it.

'Well, I'll leave you to it. I'm heading to the church now. Mal and Estelle are on their way too. We'll all be waiting for you, Jess,' Arthur said.

'Thank you,' she whispered.

Bella closed the door as Arthur walked away.

'You should be thinking of setting off to the church soon yourself,' she said. 'I'll walk with you, Jess. Are you just about ready?'

Jess shook her head. 'No. There's something I need to do first.'

She laid her bouquet on the table in the hallway. It was the same table where seventeen years ago a willow basket had been placed when Ada took a baby in from the front step. Jess walked slowly back upstairs to her room, the room she would share with Mal as his wife from that day forward. She pulled open the top drawer in the chest that stood by the window. In it were her stockings and underwear and Ada's blouses and skirts. And underneath Ada's clothes were two ribbons. She took them both out and headed downstairs. There she picked up the bouquet of white roses and slowly, carefully wound the scarlet ribbons around the stems, then tied them in a bow.

She straightened her back and lifted her chin.

'Now I'm ready,' she said.

Reverend Daye had conducted many weddings, christenings and funerals in his time as vicar of St Paul's. But he'd rarely seen so few people at what should be one of the happiest occasions in a young couple's life. He didn't comment, for it was not his place to do so, but he did include in the wedding service words of comfort for those who found themselves alone in the world. Miss Gilbey, Lena and Bella sat on the bride's side of the church with Amelia and Jane behind them. On the groom's side sat Estelle, Arthur and his sister Gloria. At the back, unseen by Jess or Mal, sat Ryhope gossip Lil Mahone, for she never missed a wedding.

A hymn was sung – Ada's favourite, 'All Things Bright and Beautiful' – then Jess and Mal exchanged their vows. And within half an hour, the small group that had walked into the church to celebrate Jess and Mal's marriage were walking out again. Everyone knew where they were headed, for Bella had put on a spread at the Uplands, in the room that had once been James McNally's study but was now going to be a living room for the Atkinson family, all four of them. Or in the future, possibly more.

When they reached the Uplands, Jess and Mal stood at the front gate, waiting to greet their guests.

'You look gorgeous, my darling,' Estelle told her new daughter-in-law.

'Well done, the pair of you,' Arthur said.

'What a beautiful couple you make,' Mal's aunt Gloria added, dabbing at her eyes with a hankie.

Miss Gilbey and Lena were next.

'All went as well as expected,' Miss Gilbey said.

'Thank you, Miss . . . Veronica,' Jess said.

'You look so pretty,' Lena beamed.

Amelia and Jane followed Miss Gilbey and Lena. Both girls stopped briefly to kiss Jess on her cheek.

Once everyone was indoors, Mal turned to Jess and slipped his arm around her waist.

'Mrs Atkinson? May I escort you into your new home?'

'Our home,' Jess said.

She glanced at the black iron gate and then at Mal.

'Well then? Are you going to carry me over the threshold?' she teased.

Mal picked her up in his arms and carried her in through the Uplands front door.

Epilogue

Two years later

Ada Rose Atkinson ran around the grounds of the Uplands. She was heading to the lavender patch under the hazel trees. Behind her walked the two elderly dogs, Pebble and Stone. They were followed by a stray puppy called Benson that Arthur had found on the street. As Jess and Mal watched their little girl fondly, Jess laid a hand on her pregnant stomach. She was hoping for a boy this time.

In the living room of the Uplands, Ada Rose's grandparents, Arthur and Estelle, sat in companionable silence. Arthur was reading his copy of the day's *Sunderland Echo*, while Estelle sewed her granddaughter a new rag doll.

Ada Rose turned to wave at her parents. She wore her long dark hair in two bunches. A scarlet ribbon was tied in each one.

The Girl with the Scarlet Ribbon

Bonus Material

Why I Love Scarborough

In *The Girl with the Scarlet Ribbon*, the action is set between the village of Ryhope (where I was born and bred) and the seaside resort of Scarborough on the Yorkshire coast. You may be wondering why I chose Scarborough, of all places, when there were so many other towns, cities and villages that I could have set the story in. Well, Scarborough holds a very special place in my heart. And, if truth be told, I have always wanted to write the seaside resort into one of my books. When I was planning this novel, I knew that I wanted to include a family who were outsiders to Ryhope, who weren't entirely welcome there. This family became the McNallys. And when I began thinking about where the McNally family might belong, if not in Ryhope, the first place to spring to mind was Scarborough.

Scarborough is where we spent our family holidays when I was growing up. My mam and dad, two brothers and I came to love this seaside town and visited every summer for many years in the same two weeks in August during the 1970s. We'd stay in the same guest house and spend as much time as we could on the beach. The most vivid, happy memories of those days with my parents and brothers are of happy pub lunches in beer gardens, eating scampi and chips from a basket under a pub umbrella in the sun. I remember eating fish and chips on the wide sandy beaches of the south bay, train rides on the North Bay Railway, waffles on the prom, donkey rides on the beach, the funiculars, water slide and outdoor theatre.

Very special memories are of the tree walk in Peasholm Park. Back then it was the most magical place in the world, twinkling with fairy lights. Happy days indeed. We all loved going to Scarborough. And then my brothers and I grew up, left home and Scarborough was forgotten as holidays were spent further away.

Anyway, time passed, as it does. My parents began to take their growing grandchildren to Scarborough whenever they could. Everyone was happy. More time passed. And then our dad passed away and it rocked our family to the core.

Lost, trying to cope with our grief, one day my youngest brother said: 'You know what we should do?' We looked, we waited, we had to know what it was he was going to say. 'We should all go to Scarborough,' he said.

And so we did. We all went – ten of us – to remember with love the one person who couldn't be there. We played bingo and frisbee on the beach, sang karaoke, ate ice cream and chips, and did all the things Dad used to love, all the things we did as kids. And although he wasn't there, he was with us, in our own way. And he'll always be in Scarborough because he loved it more than any of us. His love for the place carries on in us all.

After that weekend celebrating Dad's life we now return to Scarborough at least twice a year, for a weekend or longer. We've rediscovered the joy, the childlike enthusiasm the place brings out in everyone who loves it. In fact, I love the place so much that I was married there, at the town's beautiful, iconic Stephen Joseph Theatre. One my brothers was married there too. Scarborough remains firmly in our hearts.

Researching for this book meant I spent a few days in Scarborough (it's a tough job, but someone's got to do it!) and it was fantastic to see my favourite place through different eyes. My days were spent in the library and local studies centre, talking to historians and visiting heritage centres and museums. I saw parts of Scarborough I'd never seen before, and being there with my 'writing head' on meant I experienced my happy place in a different way to ever before.

And so, to set this novel in both Ryhope where I grew up and in Scarborough where I continue to spend many happy times, has been something very special indeed. I really hope you enjoy it half as much as I loved writing it, for it's been a dream of a book to write.

Glenda Young

All About Ryhope

Ryhope is a village on the northeastern coast, south of the city of Sunderland in Tyne and Wear. The first mention of Ryhope was in 930AD when the Saxon King Athelstan gave the parish of South Wearmouth to the See of Durham. King Athelstan's name lives on in Ryhope with a street named after him – Athelstan Rigg.

The name Ryhope is an Old English name which means 'rugged valley'. Originally Ryhope is recorded as being called *Rive hope* and has also been recorded as *Refhoppa*, *Reshop* and *Riopp*.

Ryhope developed as a farming community and was popular as a sea bathing resort. However, in 1856 sinking operations reached coal seams deep beneath the magnesian limestone and Ryhope grew as a coal mining village. Ryhope had two separate railways with their own train stations, putting Ryhope within easy commuting distance of Sunderland. By 1905 electric trams also reached Ryhope from Sunderland. The coal mine closed in 1966, marking the end of an era for Ryhope.

For more on Ryhope's past, present and future, Sunderland City Council have a very interesting planning document showing historic pictures. You can find it at http://bit.ly/RyhopeHistory

And if you'd like to know more about the village of Ryhope, here are some good websites you might like to explore for historic maps, guided walks and a visit to the ever-popular Pumping Station at Ryhope Engines Museum.

A guided walk around Ryhope – From agriculture to coal
http://bit.ly/RyhopeWalks

Historic map of Ryhope
http://bit.ly/RyhopeMap

Ryhope Engines Museum
http://www.ryhopeengines.org.uk/

Historic Pictures of Ryhope
http://east-durham.co.uk/wp/ryhope/

Keep reading for an early preview of
Glenda's next compelling saga,

The
Paper
Mill Girl

Coming soon from Headline.

Chapter 1

September 1919

Ruth Hardy walked into the yard at Grange Paper Works, and the cold air nipped her face. Women streamed past her, some linking arms and chatting, all of them headed to the black iron gates that led from the mill to the road. Some of the women would return to husbands and children, to homes with coal fires in cosy, warm rooms. Some would return to a cooked meal. None of these would be waiting for Ruth.

There was a spit of rain in the air that brought a sea-salt taste to Ruth's lips. Behind her the ocean roared. She took her hat from her pocket and pulled it over her long brown hair, then scanned the gates where Bea always waited. She spotted her sister holding on to the gate, anchored in case she was cut adrift and floated out on the tide of women. Bea worked in the machine room, where her job was to keep the floor clear. It was a safe place to work and Ruth was grateful she didn't need to worry about her little sister. Well, not at work anyway.

She made her way through the crowd, raising her hand to wave. Bea was a year younger than Ruth's seventeen years, smaller too, and she looked lost in the throng of women streaming from the yard. She had Ruth's features – there was no denying they were sisters – but there was a fragility to Bea. Ruth had a more determined, no-nonsense look about her. It was there in the set of her mouth and the glint of steel that flashed in her eyes.

Ruth reached Bea and kissed her on her cheek. It was how they always greeted each other at the end of their working day. She noticed that her sister looked as drawn and tired as she felt herself.

'You all right?' she asked.

Bea nodded. 'You?'

'I'm tired,' Ruth said. 'You look it too.'

'I've told you, I'm fine,' Bea said quietly.

Ruth grabbed Bea's hand and the girls threaded their way through the crowd. Once they reached the road, they upped their pace. They were determined to get home quickly, for it was a long walk through muddy fields along clifftops overlooking bays of coal-blackened sand. In the fields, they lifted their skirts to stop them trailing along the wet soil. They walked in silence. Suddenly Bea stopped in her tracks and dropped Ruth's hand.

'Did you hear the news today?' she said.

Ruth didn't break her stride. 'Come on, we can't stop. Mam and Dad will be waiting.'

Bea ran to catch up.

'What news?' Ruth asked when her sister was back at her side.

'I heard the men talking. There's to be a new owner. Someone's bought the mill from the Blackwells.'

This was news Ruth didn't know, and it came as a shock. Old Mr Blackwell had passed away months ago. Ruth had heard that his wife had neither the experience nor the desire to run the mill on her own. Many said it was no job for a woman, but Ruth's friend Edie said she'd heard of women running paper mills elsewhere.

'Did the men say who the new owner will be?' she asked.

Bea shook her head. 'No names were mentioned. But I heard he's a stickler for discipline. There's talk of changes being made when he takes over. All our shifts might be changed. And they say jobs will go too.'

Bea's words hit Ruth hard and a chill ran through her. 'They really said that?'

'That's what the men were talking about today. They were huddled in groups around the room, so I took my brush and swept around them, listening. They ignore me, don't even see me. I'm as quiet as a mouse.'

Ruth felt unsettled. It was another problem to deal with, and she could do without it. 'Well, little mouse,' she said. 'If you hear any more, you must tell me.'

Bea nudged her. 'Did you see your boyfriend today?'

Ruth glanced at her sister. 'He is not my boyfriend,' she laughed.

'You like him, though, I can tell.'

'Rubbish,' Ruth replied

She walked on with her head down so that Bea couldn't see the smile on her lips or the flush in her cheeks. This rush of emotion happened every time she thought of Mick Carson. He worked on the railway that brought raw materials from the docks to the mill, such as esparto, a coarse grass that grew as far away as Africa. Ruth had met him a few times. The first time, they'd smiled shyly at each other when their paths crossed in the yard. The second time she caught sight of him, she'd waved and smiled a friendly good morning, and to her delight, Mick had waved back with a cheery hello. She'd found out his name from Edie, who knew a lot of the men at the mill. Since then, the two of them had talked often if they met in the yard. Oh, it was nothing serious, always light-hearted and fun, but she enjoyed chatting to him and passing the time of day. And Mick seemed to enjoy her company too. She had told Bea about him and Bea had teased her ever since.

© Les Mann

Glenda Young credits her local library in the village of Ryhope, where she grew up, for giving her a love of books. She still lives close by in Sunderland and often gets her ideas for her stories on long bike rides along the coast. A life-long fan of *Coronation Street*, she runs two hugely popular fan websites.

For updates on what Glenda is working on, visit her website **glendayoungbooks.com** and to find out more find her on **Facebook/GlendaYoungAuthor** and Twitter **@flaming_nora**.

Don't miss the other enthralling sagas from Glenda Young!

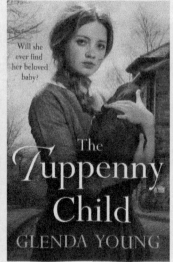

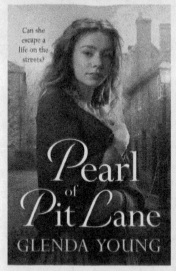

'Real sagas with female characters right at the heart'
Jane Garvey, *Woman's Hour*